RED STRING THEORY

"I devoured this! Beautifully written, DEEPLY romantic, real, funny, heartfelt." —Christina Lauren, *New York Times* bestselling author

"Jessen impresses with this surprising and sophisticated contemporary romance. It's unusually cerebral for a romance, marrying a believable love connection with a thoughtful meditation on how humans make meaning in life. The result is smart, sensitive, and striking."
—*Publishers Weekly*

"A lighthearted slow burn that's full of hope and heart. Delightful, inducing squeals and sighs in equal measure." —*Kirkus*

"There's nothing I love in romance more than fated mates, and Lauren executes it beautifully in *Red String Theory*! Her writing is as sparkling and smart as ever! Lauren delivers laughs, heart, and swoon all in one ridiculously fun story!" —Sarah Adams, *New York Times* bestselling author of *Practice Makes Perfect*

"A love story to Manhattan... Lauren Kung Jessen keeps getting better, and I can't wait to see what she delivers next!"
—Meredith Schorr, author of *Someone Just Like You*

LUNAR LOVE

"Tradition meets modern progress, and it's a delicious combination!"
  —Abby Jimenez, *New York Times* bestselling author of *Yours Truly*

"Debut author Kung Jessen does an impeccable job helping two adversarial lovers find common ground in their Chinese American heritage and creating a slow-burn romance with lots of humor, family, and food."   —*Library Journal*, starred review

"Jessen's debut rom-com hits all the beats of a tried-and-true rivals-to-lovers narrative."   —*Publishers Weekly*

"A refreshing and unexpected take on matchmaking! This will be a perfect match for any reader looking for a heartwarming romance steeped in cultural traditions."
       —Jesse Sutanto, national bestselling author of *Dial A for Aunties*

"Lauren Kung Jessen writes supremely satisfying slow burn and rivals-to-lovers. There's heat, friction, sparks—it's a lit match."
                         —Sarah Hogle, author of *Just Like Magic*

"*You've Got Mail* meets the Chinese Zodiac in Jessen's delightful ode to food, Los Angeles, family, and finding your perfect match. A delicious treat for fans of Jasmine Guillory and Helen Hoang."
                         —Georgia Clark, author of *Island Time*

"A lovingly crafted rival-to-lovers rom-com about navigating the space between traditional and modern dating! This book is a delight!"
                         —Farah Heron, author of *Jana Goes Wild*

"*Lunar Love* is a sweet romcom that shows that in the battle of tradition and modernity, love plays by its own rules."
                         —Julie Tieu, author of *The Donut Trap*

YIN YANG
LOVE
SONG

Also by Lauren Kung Jessen

Lunar Love

Red String Theory

YIN YANG LOVE SONG

LAUREN KUNG JESSEN

FOREVER

NEW YORK BOSTON

Copyright © 2025 by Lauren Kung Jessen

Reading group guide copyright © 2025 by Lauren Kung Jessen and Hachette Book Group, Inc.

Cover design and illustration by Sandra Chiu

Cover copyright © 2025 by Hachette Book Group, Inc.

Forever

Hachette Book Group

1290 Avenue of the Americas, New York, NY 10104

read-forever.com

@readforeverpub

First edition: January 2025

Forever is an imprint of Grand Central Publishing. The Forever name and logo are registered trademarks of Hachette Book Group, Inc.

The publisher is not responsible for websites (or their content) that are not owned by the publisher.

The Hachette Speakers Bureau provides a wide range of authors for speaking events. To find out more, go to hachettespeakersbureau.com or email HachetteSpeakers@hbgusa.com.

Forever books may be purchased in bulk for business, educational, or promotional use. For information, please contact your local bookseller or the Hachette Book Group Special Markets Department at special.markets@hbgusa.com.

Interior images © 2025 by Lauren Kung Jessen

Print book interior design by Marie Mundaca

Library of Congress Cataloging-in-Publication Data

Names: Jessen, Lauren Kung, author.
Title: Yin yang love song / Lauren Kung Jessen.
Description: First edition. | New York : Forever, 2025.
Identifiers: LCCN 2024026577 | ISBN 9781538741634 (trade paperback) | ISBN 9781538741658 (ebook)
Subjects: LCGFT: Romance fiction. | Novels.
Classification: LCC PS3610.E8747 Y56 2025 | DDC 813/.6—dc23/eng/20240715
LC record available at https://lccn.loc.gov/2024026577

ISBNs: 9781538741634 (trade paperback), 9781538741658 (ebook)

Printed in the United States of America

CW

10 9 8 7 6 5 4 3 2 1

To those looking for their love song

Nature does not hurry,
yet everything is accomplished.

—*Lao Tzu*

Chapter 1

CHRYSSY

It takes less than two seconds to break a person's heart.

Saying the words "I want to break up" happens in the span of a couple of heartbeats.

"We should go our separate ways."

"I don't see a future for us."

"I never want to see you again."

All statements that can be muttered, spat out, or whispered in less time than it takes to breathe in and out.

I know because, after breakup number four, I started timing it.

"We're better as friends" came from Nate. One heartbeat.

"It's not you, it's me," said Kal, who was a walking cliché from the start. Two heartbeats.

"I'm leaving town, but you should stay." Three beats. An outlier, but Leif always was.

"It's over" was from Harry. Half a heartbeat. Overachiever.

And then there was Chris, the one who there was never supposed to be a breakup with. The one who eagerly agreed to a lavender-field wedding venue and preemptively selected the type of champagne we were going to pop. The one who went through the effort of hiding an engagement ring in the lamb heart waiting to be dissected in med school to make our supposed forever a big and memorable show. The one who, I like to think, felt so badly about severing our relationship with a vague "We want different things" that he told me to keep said ring.

I know I should've seen the breakup coming, and not because "Chryssy and Chris" was a little too cute. Chris always liked a challenge, until, of course, his vision of being a power couple was the thing being challenged. And nothing threatens the dream of two high-powered doctors running the country's top hospitals like dropping out of med school.

I should've seen it coming because when you have a cursed family lineage, heartbreak is inevitable.

When you're a Hua woman, there's no escaping being broken up with or left—not then, not now, not ever. Though I do sometimes hold out for some *Everything Everywhere All at Once* alternate universe where maybe things could be different and *we're* the heartbreakers.

What baffles me is that I truly believed Chris would be different. That I would be different from my family. That I was untouchable and so in love that I actually laughed about the curse despite eight breakups in a row that should've taught me otherwise.

Then came the lamb heart and the ring and the wedding venue before minds changed and plans got canceled and everything that was to come suddenly wasn't.

I'm not laughing anymore.

Now I have guidelines in place to protect myself. I'm not special. I'm no different from any of the Hua women who came before me. The curse will always be there waiting for me, like taxes, death, and the eventual need for reading glasses.

When it comes to matters of the heart, I believe everyone has some sort of heartbreak inside of them, whether they're aware of it or not. Under typical circumstances, people can become stronger from it.

They might realize that their identities aren't tied to the breakup and that they're capable of loving again.

But heartbreak can also be sudden, and sudden changes stress our bodies. These changes throw us out of balance. With a few words and a couple of heartbeats, the entire ecosystem of a body can be disrupted. Poisoned. Thrown into chaos and sickness and pain. An entire life changes, and a dreamed-about future dissolves.

For our guests, that's where I come in.

As a Traditional Chinese Medicine chef and acupuncturist, I live and work on Whidbey Island, Washington, with my three aunties at the Wildflower Inn, a holistic retreat where we incorporate TCM practices—acupuncture, herbal medicine and nutrition, mindful movement, and immersion in nature—to help heal heartbreak. Everything we do is to help people restore balance after heartbreak throws their minds and bodies out of harmony.

And the thing with heartbreak is that it's about so much more than just the heart itself. In TCM, the heart is the king of all organs. In fact, it's so important that the other organs in our body will sacrifice energy to help maintain balance in the heart. Our Shen—our spirit—lives in the heart. We need to create a stable environment for our inner essence. To do this, we need to take care of our entire body.

Physical symptoms and ailments—digestive issues or insomnia or anxiety or chronic pain—are often the result of emotions, such as grief and heartbreak, being endured for a period of time. But in the long run, heartbreak can also balance us and give us new perspectives on love, life, and ourselves. We learn the value of love through loss. It's the yin and yang of love.

Heartbreak gives our guests an opportunity to reset. To rebalance. To heal. To start again.

This was a lesson I had to learn the hard way.

All these thoughts of heartbreak swirl around in my head as I watch snow machines being rolled into a large tent. Instead of working with clients at the inn, today I'm in the backyard of a Beverly Hills mansion owned by none other than A-list actress Rita Sharpe and her big-time movie producer husband, Brent Sharpe. As a former Wildflower Inn guest who stayed three whole months and completely revamped her lifestyle, Rita doesn't know how to do anything halfway. When she commits, she goes all in.

This $100,000-plus-budget birthday party for her four-year-old son, Charlie, is just more proof. The theme is supposedly inspired by Antonio Vivaldi's *The Four Seasons*, four violin concertos that depict spring, summer, fall, and winter.

Rita and Brent are convinced that Charlie is a violin prodigy. He was, after all, born on the exact same day as Vivaldi. There's roughly 343 years between the two, but who knows? Maybe Charlie really is Vivaldi reincarnate.

Despite this coincidence, there was leniency with the dates. Since March 4 falls on a school day and the Oscar-winning director wasn't available until now to direct the livestream that's being broadcast to Rita's millions of social media followers, we're celebrating in mid-May.

My theory? It's a manifestation party, but what do I know about prodigies? I'm here to provide herbal beverages and baked goods for a modest sum that will plump up our marketing budget. And to get some face time with Rita, the new ambassador of our flower tea line, In Full Bloom. When we launch next month, our product should get a huge boost from Rita's famous name alone, and her endorsement will help us recoup the savings my aunties and I poured into this venture. After an unsuccessful product pitch to the Hua women, we only have my dad's investment to help cover mailing out product bundles to influencers.

To celebrate, Rita and Brent have re-created the four seasons on their property. In the farthest corner of the yard is spring, which we've just come from. Hundreds of buckets of fresh flowers were artfully arranged to look like blooming meadows and new beginnings. For thirty minutes, kids made daisy garlands and learned the art of flower arranging.

Now we're in summer, where kids are building sandcastles on hauled-in sand from Santa Monica Beach. Colorful balloon garlands stretch over vendors offering face painting, artisanal ice cream, and tutorials on weaving camp lanyards. Once everyone's eaten enough hot dogs, we'll walk over to fall, where mounds of crunchy sepia-toned leaves await. The entire event is picture-perfect, as it should be. In addition to the livestream, it's being photographed for national newspapers and lifestyle magazines.

My phone vibrates against the table, drawing my attention away from the backdrop of rock music played on some kind of string instruments blasting over the speakers.

I tap into a social media post Auntie Violet has sent me. Magnolia, my second cousin, poses in a selfie on the peak of Arthur's Seat in Edinburgh. The caption below explains that she's moving on to her next adventure. One *without* her boyfriend of five years. Last I heard, this was supposed to be the trip where they got engaged.

The curse strikes again, Auntie Violet includes with the post.

I glance once more at the smiley digital memento from Magnolia's solo trip to Scotland. A signal that she's doing totally fine and that nothing's going to stop her from seeing the world.

Heartbreak be damned.

In her eyes, though, I see a tinge of sadness, and my heart aches at the sight. I email myself a note to send her a "bouquet" of In Full Bloom. When she gets back to the States, she'll have chrysanthemum, rose, and chamomile teas waiting for her.

I reach into the mini-fridge next to my table for a beverage of my own when I realize that what should be a cool fridge is now a slightly warm one. I press the button on my electric teakettle. No power there, either. The light on the power strip is off, refusing to turn on as I flip the switch back and forth.

No one's waiting for tea, so I abandon my table and follow the power strip cord to its source, stepping around photographers, vendors, and screaming children. Once I'm past the pool, I yank the cord. There's no resistance.

My suspicions are confirmed: I've been unplugged.

Through a group of parents trying to enjoy the music while also keeping one eye on their children, I spot two men playing instruments a few feet from the power station. I tilt my head, catching glimpses of the duo through the crowd. Their eyes are closed as they perform, totally immersed in a song I can't quite place. Near their feet, a tangled mass of cords surrounds them.

I duck down to stay out of sight in my search for an empty outlet.

Time to get my power back.

The musicians play what look like electric cellos, their equipment taking up a couple of outlets. I slowly crawl behind them, my movements partially hidden by their speakers, which are connected to a different power source. The only nonessential use I find is the outlet charging a laptop. I pull the charger out of its socket.

No more wilting herbs for me! But before I can plug my cord in, a voice booms over me.

"You," the deep voice says.

I peer up at the man from my position on all fours, my knees digging into the sand. He's an ominous shadowy figure with the sun flaring behind him.

He steps into full view, revealing the face of none other than Vin Chao, one-half of the rock cellist duo the Chao Brothers. I don't know much about them other than they're often making headlines, not for their relationships but for their breakups. You don't become known as the Heartbreaker Cellists of Rock without a few *It's not you, it's mes*.

I don't personally listen to their music, but Auntie Violet is a big fan. She's always playing their songs a little too loudly from her acupuncture room. The Chao Brothers have made cameos as themselves in a few star-studded movies—a heist film, an adventure, and a comedy—which is the main reason why I recognize them at all.

I try to absorb every second of this interaction, knowing that I'll need to recall this moment to Auntie Violet in a very detailed play-by-play.

I stand, rubbing my sandy hands together. I look from the man in front of me to the one behind him. The other guy must be Leo. Though they're brothers and share similarities, they're pretty distinct looking. Vin's hair is shorter and a shade darker, one strand going rogue and forming a reverse comma across his forehead. Leo has lighter, longer hair that extends past his earlobes.

Typically, the celebrities or musicians I meet or see from afar are shorter in real life, the screen and stage giving them a boost. This isn't the case with the Chao Brothers. Up close and personal, they're true to size, if not taller.

The music has stopped, even though Leo is still moving his bow over the strings. Odd. I watch on, confused at the action-sound disconnect.

When Vin sees what I'm witnessing, he places his cello in its stand and rushes over to Leo. He says something to him and then to the crowd surrounding them. The group begins to disperse, though a few people hold out invitations and cocktail napkins for him to sign.

I'm turning to leave when Vin's voice stops me again. "Did you want an autograph?"

I spin back slowly. "That's not why I came over here," I say, though getting them to sign something would be a great birthday present for Auntie Violet.

I peek over at Leo, who's no longer playing. He keeps his eyes trained on the ground and his arms crossed over a stained black T-shirt.

Vin holds his hand over his chest, the buttons of his dark gray top visible between his fingers. "I'm Vin. Vin Chao," he says in a humbling move, as though he's not a world-famous musician I recognize. "Is there something else I might be able to help you with then . . . ?"

Vin's deep voice is steeped with what sounds a lot like charm. His mouth hooks up into a grin as he rests his hand on the back of his cello. Is Vin Chao flirting with me?

"Chrysanthemum," I say. "Chryssy."

"Very nice to meet you, Chrysanthemum Chryssy," Vin says.

When my eyes lock with his, my breath catches in my chest, and I fumble with the cord, nearly dropping it. I'm momentarily distracted from my mission: Get Power Back.

I raise an eyebrow at him. "Delighted to make your acquaintance, Vin Vin Chao."

Vin's smile grows before he narrows his eyes at me, one of his lower eyelids slightly twitching as he does so. The stare-off gives me time to understand what's happening here but also to get a good look at him. Vin's face looks freshly shaven, whereas his brother's has a slight stubble, and his intense, light brown eyes pierce straight through me.

My gaze slides down his left-leaning nose that disrupts his otherwise symmetrical features. The incline is endearing, in a way. It gives his objectively handsome face an edge of personality. It's a less-than-perfect feature in a man whose innate talent has been deemed by many as "flawless."

Vin reaches for his laptop cord to reconnect it to the source, clearly unbothered by my electrical needs. Looks like the power imbalance won't be restored.

"Was there something else?" Vin asks, lingering. Given what I

YIN YANG LOVE SONG 9

know about his reputation, he's probably waiting for me to give him my number or something.

"You give love a bad name," I say with a snap of my fingers.

A temporary storm cloud passes over Vin's face, and his grin morphs into a deep frown.

I point to his cello. "The song you were playing. Bon Jovi, right?"

For a second, his face neutralizes. "Oh." Then he nods. That's it. Just nods. Not even a "yeah" or any other verbal confirmation.

My eyes dart between his instrument and the laptop. "Are you..."

"No."

"You don't know what I was going to ask," I say.

After a beat, he exhales. "Are you what?"

I twist one of my flower earrings, the silver petals digging into the pads of my fingers. I look from the laptop to the speaker to the outlet. Why did their laptop stop the music? It's then I notice that Leo's cello isn't actually plugged in. The pieces click into place: laptop, music, Leo's soundless playing.

"Oh. I see," I mumble.

"What do you see?" Vin asks, his charm-coated voice now thick with skepticism.

I stand on my toes to get closer to Vin's ear. "Your secret's safe with me," I whisper, swinging my cord around in small circles like a lasso. "You can keep my outlet."

A literal grunt escapes Vin, though it sounds more like a growl.

I sneak a longer glance at Leo. Shallow breathing, zoned-out expression, pretending to play...my mind whirs with possibilities, but all signs point to heartbreak. Vin's playing for real, but his partner is a prerecorded Leo, not the real one.

In my mind, I run through my list of ingredients. I think I brought everything I'd need for my Heartbreak Tea Blend. "I'll be back with some tea to help balance you both out," I offer.

"We're going to have to pass, as delicious as that sounds," Vin says. His tone very clearly tells me he doesn't really think so.

I blink a few times. "Okay, no problem," I say, holding my hands up. "I'll let you get back to...playing."

My tone gives me away, and Vin catches it.

"We're playing," he insists.

"And you do it well," I reassure him, fully knowing their playing is as real as the snow we're about to experience over in winter. To make matters worse, I throw a thumbs-up at him.

A few people have started to circle around us, maybe thinking I'm part of the next song. Vin watches them, clearly becoming aware of the small crowd forming.

"That's why the music stopped!" Rita says behind me, as though the three of us gathered together explains everything. It's a high seventy degrees, and she's been running around from season to season, yet there's not a bead of sweat on her. How do celebrities do it? "Chrysanthemum! I was just on my way to your table. But here you are! And I see you've met Vin and Leo Chao, our two superstars of today's event."

I glance over at the brothers. While Vin looks displeased, Leo looks like he might...cry?

"Our wires got crossed," I supply.

"What an honor to have you both here!" Rita says to Vin and Leo as her eyes nearly shape-shift into stars. "I'm— It's...wow. Seriously. Thank you. My little Charlie's going to be just like you two when he grows up."

Vin releases an irritated sigh through his nose, his chest deflating on the exhale, but throws on a smile and says, "He'll be even better."

Rita holds her hands in prayer formation, and I'm mesmerized by the sparkle of the diamond on her ring finger that's the size of a hydrated rosebud. She definitely didn't have that when she came to the inn heartbroken. Rita may have money and be incredibly famous, but without all of the styled hair and makeup, she was unrecognizable to me as *the* Rita Sharpe, the Asian American actress making waves in Hollywood.

At the time, she was going through a bad breakup and wasn't eating or sleeping. She took us up on the full program that we offer. Over time, she regained her appetite, her blood pressure stabilized, and her Qi rebalanced. Now she treats me like she's indebted to me, but she was the one who made the lifestyle changes.

Within the year, Rita met the love of her life and, shortly after, had Charlie. Now, four years later, here we are. There's nothing more fulfilling than helping someone through pain and heartbreak and seeing them come out happier and healthier on the other side.

Rita wraps her arm around my shoulders. "I'm so glad you've met Chrysanthemum. This one cleans up your messes," she tells the brothers.

The muscles running up Vin's jawline stretch. He reaches into his pocket and reveals his phone. "I need to take this," he says.

I shake my head at his classic get-out-of-a-conversation trick.

Vin places his bow on a hook before stomping toward the guesthouse with his phone pressed to his ear.

Leo does the same and trails behind as Vin pushes past the small group waiting for music, ignoring their requests for autographs. I attempt a half-hearted wave but hastily pull my hand back when they don't look my way again. Not even a *goodbye* or *nice to meet you*, which would've been an overstatement for us both.

"Come!" Rita says with a clap, turning me away from the brothers. She swishes her head toward me, and her dark brown hair lands perfectly in place under her floppy sun hat. The aroma of her spa-like scent gives me secondhand relaxation. "What'd you think of those two? Brent just worked on a movie with them and said they're wonderful."

"Brent thinks that because he wasn't broken up with by them," I retort.

Rita laughs and links her arm through mine. "They may be serial daters, but their commitment to music is admirable. I really do hope my Charlie can have a career like theirs one day," she says. "Vin played for the president when he was just five years old."

"A lot can happen in a year," I tell her encouragingly.

"You have to start them young," she says. "Vin and Leo are around your age now, I think. What are you, thirty?"

"Thirty-two."

"Leo's the oldest. Thirty-four maybe? Vin must be your age," Rita calculates. "Surely you've seen them plastered on billboards all over town. They're the new faces of that prestigious coffee company, Brew Haus. 'Barista-quality, brewed at home.'" Her voice takes on a sales-y tone.

"I don't drink coffee," I admit, still stuck on the brothers' brand. "Being heartbreakers is an interesting identity to proudly claim, don't you think?"

Rita waves to a group of parents across the saltwater pool. "It's not what I'd choose to be," she says, shuffling next to me. "Come to think of it, I should introduce him to the other Leo."

"DiCaprio?"

"I think they'd really hit it off," she says before stopping herself. "No, wait. They played at his birthday party a few years back. They're friends." We pause for her to accept a small scoop of cantaloupe with a thin shaving of prosciutto and mint. "The Chao Brothers are some of the best at what they do. Honestly iconic. Between them both they have a case full of Grammys, Emmys, and a potential Oscar nomination, thanks to Brent's movie. Fingers crossed!"

"Impressive," I mutter to myself.

Rita pulls the melon ball off the toothpick with her teeth. "Just don't date them," she says around a bite. "They'll only break your heart."

"No chance of that," I say assuredly.

Rita and I have known each other for a while, but what she doesn't know is that I can't get my heart broken. To be heartbroken means you have to care. Caring requires a certain degree of vulnerability, which means opening yourself up to love. And that is exactly what I'm *not* doing anymore.

After Chris, I'm tired. Tired of all the emotions that come with being in a relationship. Tired of being broken up with nine times in a row with no end to the tally in sight.

I've seen too many heartbreaks in clients, in my family's life, and in my own. If I'm ever in a relationship again, it needs to be casual. A middle ground with no highs or lows. I just need to be with someone I can tolerate, maybe even enjoy being around, but not someone who I'll be in shambles over when the relationship ends. Because it always, inevitably, without a doubt, ends. It has for generations.

"Though maybe you should get their number. It could be good for business if they can send all their exes your way," Rita muses.

The last thing I need is the number of yet another heartbreaker.

When we reach my table, Rita immediately grabs a flower-pressed rosemary and ginger scone and takes a big bite. "I missed these!" she mumbles around a mouthful of the baked good. "You're my best-kept secret. More people need to know about you."

I smile. "Thanks, but they don't need to know about *me*. They need to know about In Full Bloom, and with your help, they will!" I say on a relieved exhale as a cameraman circles us and snaps photos.

Rita starts chewing a little too fast. She barely swallows before taking another bite. It's obvious she's trying to avoid telling me something. Her face is serene, but the tiniest wrinkle of hesitation next to her eyebrow gives her away.

"What is it?" I ask, my voice cracking.

Rita wipes crumbs from her lips and pastes on a cheery expression, hyperaware of the cameras. "About that. I don't know how to tell you this, but I can't be your brand ambassador anymore," she says through a forced million-dollar smile, her lips hardly moving. She looks happy, but her bummed-out tone tells me otherwise.

Disappointment floods through me all at once, but I try my hardest not to let it show.

Rita leans in close, turning toward me. "This is top secret, but I'm starting a gin company. I'm not actually running it, of course, but I'll be the face. You know how Hollywood is. My looks will fade, but alcohol is forever."

"Literally," I mumble, thinking about the homemade, vodka-soaked vanilla bean extract that's been handed down through our family line like heirloom jewelry and superstitions. And, yes, even curses.

"I'm very sorry, Chrysanthemum. I feel terrible," she says earnestly. "I didn't realize I was already legally bound to the gin company before you and I shook on it."

Handshake agreements may work in Hollywood, but they're clearly pretty weak. I've gone cold, my skin sensitive to the warm afternoon, but Rita's been nothing but supportive. The least I can do is be excited about her big news.

I compose myself and clasp her sconeless hand in mine. "Congrats, Rita. That's exciting. Ryan Reynolds never saw you coming."

Rita lets out a breathy but equally disappointed sigh as she squeezes my hand. "I owe you."

"You really don't," I tell her. And it's true. What she's paying me to be here today helped cover half of our marketing budget. We'll just have to get scrappy and creative with our promo.

A woman with a headset approaches us and gives Rita a signal.

Our former brand ambassador sets the half-eaten scone down on the table. "This isn't over, but I do need to scoot. We're getting ready for the summer finale," Rita says. "The fire dancers couldn't make it, so we've upped the pyrotechnics."

"See you in the fall," I say, breaking off the end of her unfinished scone and tossing it into my mouth.

Four heartbeats this time. Another outlier.

Chapter 2

VIN

Vin and Leo here," I say into my phone.

As we round the corner behind the guesthouse, I put the call on speaker.

"Guys, it's Greg. I have Jim on the line, too. How are our heart-breakers doing today?" our tour manager asks.

"We're fine," I reply. "But we're kind of in the middle of something."

Jim, our publicist, speaks next. "I'd say. We saw the photo and wanted to hop on a quick call."

I shake my head, not following. "A photo of..."

"You and a mystery woman. You're at Rita and Brent Sharpe's party today, right?" Jim asks.

"Yeah, but the only person I'm here with is Leo," I say.

"This livestream would say otherwise," Greg jumps in. "Taylor sent us a screengrab. Who is she?"

Greg's assistant happens to see me talking to a woman and the immediate assumption is that I'm dating her. It's not the first time I've been linked to the nearest woman breathing within a five-foot range, but this is a reach.

"I guess it could be anyone. The mom of a kid here? Rita? Someone from the crew helping set up?" I offer. "You tell me. I don't even know what photo you're talking about."

"She's whispering in your ear," Jim says. "You two look pretty close."

"Look, we need to get back," I say.

"Vin, we've gotta be ahead of the news. And when an eligible bachelor hasn't been spotted with a woman in months, well, you know this makes headlines," Jim says. "I just got a couple of calls for a comment."

"Did you tell them there's nothing to comment on?" I ask.

It's quiet on the other end. "We can use this," Jim says.

"Tickets have been live for three weeks, and it didn't exactly sell out overnight," Greg informs us. "We need butts in seats. All of them, if we can help it."

"Something like a relationship would help us build hype," Jim follows up. "We've been talking to a few people. We can get someone on board."

I glance at Leo, who shrugs with disinterest. "On board with what, exactly?" I probe.

"A relationship," Jim states plainly. "It's not clear in the photo who this woman is, but we have a couple of debut singers who could use the press. We'll feed the rumors from this livestream, get a couple of photos of you with Lacy or Adriana, whoever, and then you'll end it."

My teeth squeak from grinding so hard. "I take offense to that, Jim. I don't need help finding women."

Jim laughs. "Evidenced by your history. But then how do you explain your recent...singleness?" he asks.

It's only been six months since my last relationship ended, if two weeks qualifies as an actual relationship. "Work? Preparing for the tour we're all going to make a lot of money on?" I retort.

"*If* we sell tickets," Greg unhelpfully adds. "And your tour is literally called Heartbreak on Tour."

"Let people read into whatever it is they think they saw," I say. "They can use their imaginations. In fact, let them run wild."

"We need a little more than a photo. You two haven't had public relationships in a while, and we're feeling the effect of that. Here's what we'll do. We're going to pair you both up, and you'll end the romances before tour, or during, whenever," Jim strategizes. "A failed relationship will help stoke the embers of your reputation. It needs a good fanning every now and then to remind people you exist."

I don't agree with Jim and Greg all the time, but our star rose once we signed with them ten years ago. I go along with a lot. This, though, is pushing it.

"Chaobreakers know we exist. People listen to our music," I say, pinching the bridge of my nose. "We just put out an album two months ago."

"I don't think I need to remind you, of all people, Vin, that this world tour is important. It's your biggest yet," Greg says. "We got the green light this morning for the Colosseum, a bucket-list venue. Your words." Those were actually Leo's words, but I agree with the sentiment all the same. "Not just anyone gets to play there, but they made an exception for you guys. It's going to be private. Exclusive. Expensive. We need to sell those pricey tickets, too. You know what will do that?"

"Good marketi—" I start.

"Your love lives," Jim says over me. "And ultimately, your heart-breaking."

I'll have to process the win of securing the Colosseum later. I inhale fresh air deep into my lungs. Is this what it's come to? Selling out to sell out? I know good sales help with getting better terms for our upcoming contract negotiations, but I'm not going to pretend to date someone to sell tickets. People already want to come to our concerts. The success of our tour shouldn't come down to who we're dating. No, who we're *pretending* to date. That's not what we've worked for our entire lives or what our parents sacrificed for.

But at the end of the day, we're heartbreakers. I've accepted this fact years ago. We don't get forever afters. We get the historical landmark venues, sold-out concerts, and a shit-ton of royalties.

"What about Leo then? Will he date someone?" Jim asks. "I think Lacy would be perf—"

"Leo's not interested, either," I interrupt when Leo doesn't say anything. He's fully distracted by kids whacking each other with pool noodles. He's in no state to keep up appearances with anyone for pretend, or for real.

Jim makes a clicking noise. "I can't sell you as heartbreakers if you're not out there, you know, breaking hearts. Heartbreak sells, and people want that heartbreak on the road." He adds a little laugh at the end to keep the mood light. "And certainly in your next album."

"I hear you both, I do," I say. "We, more than anyone, don't want to perform to empty venues. For now, tell people you have no comment. You know how speculation feeds the media."

"Think about—"

I hang up and exhale at the same time.

"Don't you think that was a little rude?" Leo asks, finally speaking.

I shoot a glare at him. "*Now* you know words," I mumble. "They'll get over it."

"What? No. Not that," Leo says. "With Chryssy."

I scoff. "The person who unplugged us in front of a crowd? Who almost revealed . . . you know."

Leo makes a face. "No one caught on."

"Yet. Would you rather play for real?" I ask. "Because I'd gladly welcome that."

Leo slides down to the ground against the guesthouse, the only area of the property not decorated to look like any of the seasons. "You sure you can't go on without me? I'm useless," he says, burying his face in his hands. "These kids couldn't care less about us."

I huff out an exasperated sigh and join him on the ground, leaning my head back against the wood siding.

"We're the Chao Brothers. Plural. We do this together. Besides, we're not here for *these* kids. We're here for the very large, generous donation that Brent's making to Soar for Strings," I remind Leo. "*Those* kids, the ones who actually want but can't afford instruments, are the ones we're here for."

And because this party is for the son of the producer of the movie we recently scored, but that's beside the point.

"You should be proud," Leo says. "You not only came up with the plan to prerecord my part, but you're also going along with it. That's growth."

"I could've played the chorus of 'Cryin'' better," I mumble, tossing a rock into a bush. "And my bow work was weak in the second passage."

"I thought you nailed it," Leo says. "Are you grumpy because you never got one of these parties? We should've celebrated you being a prodigy more, I'll say that."

"Yeah, right. The balloons alone must've cost twenty thousand dollars. Did you see the party favors? They're violins," I say. "Though I wouldn't have minded more cake."

In the distance, kids smash into each other as they run around with buckets over their heads.

"That's how I feel right now," Leo says, watching the same scene unfold in front of us. "Like I've been rammed into with a bucket on my head."

"When's the last time you changed that shirt? Or eaten something?" I ask.

"Why do you care what I wear?" Leo finally says.

"I care about hygiene. And your mood. And clearly, your calorie intake," I say, noticing Leo's subtle weight loss over the past week. "Clean clothing and a big lunch would help."

Leo shakes his head. "I'll live in these clothes. I'll die in these clothes. What does it matter anyway?"

"I need you properly fed. We need to work on our next album. Rehearsals for the world tour start in a couple of weeks," I say, running through a fraction of our to-do list.

"Don't forget the tour merch meeting," Leo adds, his eyes following the fireworks exploding overhead as they burst like a star into purple and red streaks. "And do we still want to do a holiday album? Maybe I can pencil in 'Get Over Heartbreak' between the cover photoshoot and the documentary interview."

I refrain from adding more, even though there is a lot, lot more on the list. "There's still some time," I reassure him. "Don't forget our contract is coming up for renewal."

It's a day we've been waiting years for. We can afford lawyers now. We can negotiate our own terms. We have the album purchases, the streaming numbers, and the ticket sales to prove that we're valuable to them. And thanks to our reputation, we're high earners. They're not going to want to mess with that. We're not going to want to mess with it.

Everything changed when we went from the Chao Brothers to the Heartbreakers. Fans even started calling themselves Chaobreakers. We're at the top of our game. We play music for a living and get paid a lot of money doing it. We can support our parents and live up to our potential. We're getting a new generation excited about string instruments. We're pretty much living the dream. Maybe not in this exact moment, but generally.

"Don't remind me," Leo says, looking over at me. His hair is disheveled, his eyes bloodshot. "Especially not after…" His eyes become glossy.

"I'm sorry about Aubrey," I say, turning to face him.

"Don't say her name," Leo grumbles, covering his ears.

"Right," I say, holding my hands up. "I'm sorry about…her."

"Two years together. Why say yes to a marriage proposal if you're just going to break it off days later? I know the proposal wasn't flashy, but you know what flashy draws? Attention," Leo says, his words one giant run-on sentence. "Oh, and she's keeping the ring since I was never around. A four-carat diamond ring that I could only afford *because* I wasn't around. I can't talk about this anymore."

While I wait for Leo to catch his breath, I watch people carry oversize, colorful plastic gumdrops into the winter tent set up on a different patch of the yard.

"It might help to play for real. Maybe it'll distract you," I offer.

"Easy for you to say," Leo says. "You've never experienced heartbreak."

I shrug. "No. I'm a heartless monster who only thrives on breaking hearts, remember?"

Apparently, always ending relationships, regardless of the why, gets you labeled as a heartbreaker by the media. A couple of my breakups coincided with Leo ending a relationship, and our reputation was solidified. A brand we couldn't outplay.

The media frenzy surrounding our simultaneous breakups benefited our careers, so it didn't take long for our new identities to take shape. Maybe there is something to what Jim and Greg are proposing.

Leo sighs. "My point is something hard can happen and you can play through it. In your sleep, with violent food poisoning, under public scrutiny. And in those moments, you're still better than me."

"The food poisoning was just the one time," I quip. "I can't guarantee that I could do it again." I pluck along the seam of my jeans to the tune of "Last Christmas" in preparation. "Look, you're here. Even if it is the autopilot version of you. Let's finish the day out strong. And if you want to cry, that's okay, too."

Leo rubs his temples. "Do we really need to play holiday music?" he asks. "It's too jolly for how I feel. I think I'm gonna be sick."

"We're playing the sad ones, remember? But sure, screw Santa," I say.

A subdued laugh escapes Leo. "Why does heartbreak have to sell so much?" he asks.

"People can't look away from a car accident," I say, burrowing the heel of my boot into the gravel. "Hey, if you can, make your playing look just a little more real. Chryssy's already onto us."

Leo huffs out a sound of disbelief. "You want me to make my fake-playing look more real? You hear yourself, right?"

"We need to have *some* standards," I say, turning toward him.

"Let's get this over with," he says somberly. "And I want to throw a snowball at you."

I groan, pushing myself off the ground. I pull Leo up and slap him on the back. "Let's go give 'em a car crash."

Like time tends to do, fall flies by, even though getting Leo through fake playing is like pulling teeth. We shuffle over to the massive tent where fans and air conditioners are set up to create realistic wintry temperatures. I pull on my leather jacket to ward off the chill. Kids are handed shiny Moncler jackets to stay warm as they build snowmen and sled down makeshift hills.

We're slated to play under the porch awning of a gingerbread house the size of a large shed, next to a miniature skating rink. My boots sink into machine-made snow as small, falling flakes melt on my shoulders. If there wasn't still sand in my shoes from the summer, I might actually believe it was winter.

As we arrive, Chryssy heads directly toward us. She's pointing at an empty patch of snow to the left of our gingerbread house. Within seconds, four kids are setting down her table next to us, and she hands them sprigs of rosemary before they run off toward a snowball fight.

Chryssy looks at us with a sneaky expression. "Eyebrows for their snowmen."

"You're back," I say, stating the obvious.

Chryssy reveals aluminum packets of s'mores from her bag. "Here. Obviously, you're both going through something. Chocolate will help," she says.

First, we steal her electricity, and then *she* brings *us* treats.

"Sorry, we have a strong no-taking-food-from-strangers policy," I say, taking the s'mores packets from her anyway.

When she laughs, the noise that escapes her is soft and musical. It's an upbeat sound that disappears before I have a chance to memorize the notes. I fight the urge to do something to make her laugh, just to hear it one more time.

"I had no visitors in fall, but winter requires warm drinks. I'm setting up next to you to draw attention to myself," she says. "And like I said, I'm here to help."

"Help who? Us?" My eyebrows pinch together. "We don't need help."

"It kind of seems like he does," she whispers to me. Leo jumps out of his seat and runs to a nearby bush. He bends over and throws up.

"See. That's why we have a strong no-taking-food-from-strangers policy," I deadpan, grabbing a travel-size tissue from my pack to have ready for Leo when he's back. I stay where I am to give him space. "He's...tired."

"I really can be useful here. I have dried herbs and flowers. These are my instruments," Chryssy says. From a bag, she pulls out a long tube filled with pink petals. "Give me a few minutes."

"Fine," I say, giving up. I have a feeling Chryssy will figure out how to help in one way or another. "I look forward to hearing your... song."

A tall, blond woman interrupts us when she taps my shoulder and hands me a crinkled receipt with a number written on the back.

"When you're done with your set, I'm over there," she says, pointing to a wreath-making station. "Text me?"

I run my finger down the paper. She gives a little wave and heads back to her table.

Chryssy watches this entire interaction with a smirk on her face. "She's pretty."

I take a step closer to her, my boots crunching over the snow. "You want to take a picture of this so you can call her?" I ask, waving the receipt. "You know, since you clean up my messes."

"I wouldn't put it that way, exactly," Chryssy says as she organizes a bouquet of mint sprigs in a jar.

"Then how would you put it, *exactly*?" I ask, narrowing my eyes at her.

Chryssy huffs out a short laugh, her breath forming a small cloud. She releases the mint and closes the gap between us until there's only a couple of feet left. "I just want to help," she says, waiting a few seconds before turning back to arrange cinnamon sticks on her table.

"If you really want to make a difference, I think those children you bribed with herbs could use another hand rolling the base of their snowman," I say, moving back to my cello. "Didn't seem like she was looking for anything serious, anyway. She probably won't need your services. Whatever it is you do."

"Don't write yourself off so fast," she says, glancing at me over her shoulder. "You seem like the type to make other women quickly fall under your spell."

"What, like I've got some kind of love potion?" I ask.

"Maybe your music is enchanting, I don't know." Chryssy nods toward the wreath-making station. "Don't look now, but she's smiling at you."

I'm too focused on Chryssy to look. "Other women," I echo, offering her a grin. "So women other than *you* fall under my spell?"

Chryssy presses her lips together, but it's not a return of my smile. "I don't do love potions. I find them to be too bitter."

She presses a button on an electric kettle. In a little cloth bag, she adds dried flowers, an assortment of herbs, and slices of fresh ginger. I realize I'm still watching her as she pours hot water over the mixture.

In this moment, Chryssy's face takes up residence in my visual memory. Her glowing skin, sweet smile, heart-shaped face, rounded nose, the small mole just above her left arched eyebrow. Three small flower studs run up each of her earlobes, while the charm on her silver necklace gleams in the light. After today, I hope it won't be hard to forget her light brown eyes or the way her nose wrinkled when she realized I wasn't giving her electricity back. If I look at her even just a few times more, I'll have fully memorized her, like a chord or a melody I didn't even have to practice to remember.

She catches me staring at her. "I'm used to people watching me in my element," she says, seemingly unaware of my documentation of her features. "Just like you are, I'm sure. And it's not every day you get a front-row seat to prodigies." She pushes a strand of her straight, shoulder-length dark-brown hair behind her ear.

"Prodigy. Singular. Just him," Leo says, startling me. I didn't realize he'd come back. Instead of resuming his position at the cello, he's lying very still in the snow, his arms spread wide in a half-assed snow angel attempt. "Though I want to take some credit. He only started playing cello because I did. I'm basically his muse."

I hand him the tissue. "You okay? You're looking pale."

Leo wipes his mouth and hands the tissue back to me. "The snow is numbing my pain," he mumbles.

As Chryssy passes me to get to Leo, I catch a light whiff of something floral and sweet. She kneels and hands him a cup, explaining that the tea will help his nausea and warm him up.

Leo leans forward to drink the tea. He looks comforted. Calm.

When Chryssy comes back to her table, her arms are covered in goose bumps. "Where's your jacket? It's the middle of winter," I say.

Chryssy pours hot water into a second cup. "It's fine. I have ginger."

"What's that supposed to do? Here." I tuck the tissue into my case and tug my jacket off.

"What's that for?" she asks, staring at my jacket like I've offered her Leo's used tissue.

I grunt. "I can see your breath. And you're shivering," I tell her.

"Sorry, I have a strong no-taking-jackets-from-strangers policy," she says, the trace of a smile on her lips. The bright white of the snow reflects in her playful eyes, making them shine.

From the ground, Leo laughs.

Chryssy hesitates but accepts my jacket, sliding an arm through one of the sleeves. The excess leather bunches up around her shoulders. "Thanks. They really should've warned us to expect snow in LA."

She blinks up at me sweetly, and a warm sensation begins pooling in my chest.

I nod curtly. Enough of this. We need to play. We have a job to do. I nudge Leo with my foot. "Ready?"

Leo's eyes are glazed over as he stares at a freshly rolled snowman couple, complete with carrot noses and rosemary sprig eyebrows.

"If you think about it," he says somberly, "love is like snow. It's sudden and beautiful, and then it turns into dirty, gray slush. Melts and disappears before you've even had a chance to enjoy it."

Chryssy looks at him compassionately. "You got that right," she agrees.

"Don't worry about him," I say. "I— We do need to play now, though."

I set myself up for "Blue Christmas." Leo watches me get ready but doesn't make a move. I let out a curse and a breath, maintaining my finger positioning over the strings.

"Leo's heartbroken, isn't he?" Chryssy says low enough for only me to hear, drawing my attention back to her. She takes a bite of a half-eaten scone with purple and yellow flowers pressed onto the top. "The nausea. Paleness. Distant gaze. Puffy red eyes. Shortness of breath. They're classic symptoms."

My hand glides down the neck of my cello. I give it a spin, the endpin crunching in the snow. "What are you, some kind of tea-and-scone detective?" I ask, placing my instrument back on its stand.

She looks around me at Leo, who's staring into his tea as though the answers to all of his problems are at the bottom of that cup. Chryssy hooks her hand into my elbow and pulls me away from my cello and over to the other side of her table. The contact makes my heart jump in its unexpectedness.

"Has he been sleeping?" Chryssy asks.

I sigh, resigned. "Based on the three a.m. text messages from him, no. It happened last week."

"Fresh heartbreak. He must still be in shock. It hasn't fully sunk in yet," she says, nodding to herself. "Okay. I'm going to give you chry-santhemum and honeysuckle tea that you can make for him three times a day, or anytime he wants something comforting to drink. There's a great lamb noodle soup with a tonifying bone broth I can send you the recipe for. Most of our body's Qi comes from food. What he eats is important."

"The chances of me making whatever it is you just said are slim to none. Let's go with none," I say.

"We won't know the extent of his pain," Chryssy continues, either not hearing me or purposely ignoring me. It's also unclear where she fits into this. "Make sure he doesn't lie in bed all day. Get him up and outside. We definitely want him moving around."

I move closer to her. "Who'd you say you were again?"

Chryssy crosses her arms and mirrors my step forward, tilting her head all the way back to look up at me. "I'm Chrysanthemum Hua Williams."

She grabs her bag, reaches in, and hands me a small, speckled piece of paper. The tips of our fingers graze in the handoff, and a spark of a current runs through my left arm. No big deal. Every now and then my arm gets irritated. Tendonitis is common for cellists. I pull back and squeeze my fist, directing my attention to the card.

"You're a Traditional Chinese Medicine chef and acupuncturist," I say, reading her title.

"My aunties and I can help your brother. We help heal heartbreak. Call me," Chryssy says, her nose scrunching. "And I don't mean like *that*."

I give her my best smile. The one many have called charming. It usually works, well, like a charm. "And what if I *want* to call you like that?" I ask, just to see how she responds. Just to test that she's not fully immune to me.

Chryssy's eyes lock with mine. "Don't," she says. "Unless it's about Leo." She nods toward the card. "Then you can toss that into the dirt and let nature work its magic. It's embedded with wildflower seeds."

I look at the card with the words *The Wildflower Inn* at the top. "So, you fix what I break?"

"That seems a little harsh. How about, I pick up where you leave off?" she says. "We have very different ways of approaching heartbreak."

"Am I being messed with? Are you about to try to sell me something?"

"I don't love that phrasing, but our services cost money, yes," she says quietly. "We can help Leo."

"Doubtful," I murmur.

I don't expect Chryssy to hold her hand out for a shake, but that's exactly what she does.

I reluctantly grab her hand in return. The current is back, zinging up my right arm now. Fine. Not the tendonitis, but likely a reaction to the dropping temperature. It's just a handshake. A simple, common gesture that I've done countless times at awards shows and ceremonies. And yet it feels completely out of the ordinary with this woman. My hand takes on a life of its own and doesn't let go right away. Instead, I end up giving her hand a light squeeze.

She smiles up at me. "Either way, nice to officially meet you."

Chryssy grabs the teakettle and walks over to Leo to refill his cup. She leans down to meet him at eye level. It's a gesture filled with such warmth. Leo doesn't resist when Chryssy sets the kettle in the snow and places two fingers on the inside of his wrist, like she's checking his pulse.

"Can you stick your tongue out for me?" she asks Leo. "I'd like to assess its color, shape, moisture, and coating."

Here, too, Leo doesn't hesitate.

"This helps me understand the health of your organs. I'll give you a tea blend to take with you, but I want to make sure I'm giving you the right one," Chryssy explains. "It's also how I learn about all your secrets." She wiggles her eyebrows at this.

"Do you need to see his, too?" is what I think Leo says. It's hard to tell with his tongue hanging out of his mouth.

Chryssy tilts her head in my direction and looks me up and down. She shakes her head and says without blinking, "Nah. I already know enough of his secrets."

Chapter 3

CHRYSSY

I'm dodging bees when Auntie Violet lets me in on her secret.

"I'm a Chaobreaker," she reveals.

I lift a frame out of the beehive and watch the bees go about their business on the honeycomb. "You're not...are you?" I ask.

Chaobreakers are Vin and Leo's fandom name, like BTS's A.R.M.Y. Taylor Swift's Swifties. Blackpink's Blinks. After the Prodigy Party, I went down a very deep rabbit hole listening to the Chao Brothers' music, watching music videos, and reading interviews they've done. They're essentially Yo-Yo Ma meets Red Hot Chili Peppers. At some point during the concert, they play while standing, walking, and lying down on the stage as lights flash around them. The Chao Brothers and the Chaobreakers all look like they're having the time of their lives. And why wouldn't they? Their shows are basically rock concerts.

Auntie Violet chuckles from behind her bee hat and veil. "Proudly but covertly."

I reverse the frame and slide it back in. "The 'breaker' part's a little much, no?" I ask, once again questioning the pride they take in breaking hearts.

"The Chao Brothers are Italian-Chinese Americans. Chao is their last name, but 'ciao' in Italian is used for 'hi' and 'goodbye.'

'Hi, girlfriends!' 'Bye, girlfriends!'" Auntie Violet explains. "Rumor has it they might play at the Colosseum. I saw them last year on my girls' trip to Copenhagen where they performed at Rosenborg Castle. Very regal." She reverses another frame. "I left with a bucket list item checked off and a pair of shimmery lilac pants I can still fit into. Now that was a good trip!"

I remember those purple pants. Auntie Violet specifically bought them to match the exterior of the Wildflower Inn. What I didn't know was that she fangirled in them over two rock cellists.

"Given that they're heartbreakers and we're trying to, you know, help the heartbroken, I'm not sure your obsession with them looks as good as you do in those pants," I tell her.

She's reversing the frames in a purple hive built to look like a mini version of the inn. Mine's a smaller yellow hive built to look like the converted shed I live in, which we call the Dandelion. Meanwhile, my aunties live in the top three rooms above the inn. The remaining six rooms are for guests who stay anywhere from a long weekend to three months.

"Remember, Chryssy, even heartbreakers can experience heartbreak," Auntie Violet says as she checks the second hive's food supply. "What were they like? They say to never meet your heroes."

"The Chao Brothers are not *my* heroes, but the experience was still somewhat disappointing. Leo was nice. Vin, though... he's a smartass. *Tried* to be charming, in his own heartbreaking way." I finish my last frame reversals and place the lid back on the hive before checking to make sure the bees have enough food.

Auntie Violet tilts her head, like she's disagreeing with my assessment of him. "He's focused. There's more to him than meets the eye."

"I can't recall you ever getting starstruck by a celebrity guest," I say.

"Starstruck? Please. I'm a professional," Auntie Violet insists. "Our guests are usually actors, though. Musicians have a different type of vulnerability." She puffs the smoker a few times toward the bees. "We're not in a spot to complain. Those photos of you two together put us on the map in a big way. Let's enjoy the effects—"

"Consequences," I correct.

"—*results*," Auntie Violet insists, "while we can. An editor from *Condé Nast Traveler* booked a stay. Maybe they'll do a write-up!"

For most of its existence, the Wildflower Inn has flown under the radar. The celebrity guests started coming only in recent years, but the inn has always relied on a word-of-mouth marketing strategy ever since Auntie Rose, Auntie Daisy, and Auntie Violet, my mom's sisters, opened it in the early 2000s.

Per tradition in my family, every Hua—which means "flower" in Chinese—woman is named after a specific flower that has relevance in TCM as an homage to my great-great-great-great-grandfather, who had his own apothecary. Beyond their names, many wildflowers symbolize strength, healing, renewal, and perseverance—everything my aunties wanted this place to represent.

Since the inn opened, not much has changed. The exterior paint is the original color. The main herb and flower gardens continue to take up most of the backyard, with the addition of a potting shed a few years back. Heartbreak is still the focus.

When people don't understand or trust what we do at the inn, especially with TCM, they think of us as a last resort until they experience it for themselves. While we treat the entire body and person as a whole, we're at the top of the recommendation list for those with heartache.

What has changed is that now I'm here. At first I wasn't supposed to be, but life doesn't care about the plans you make. When I started working at the inn, I brought not only my emotional baggage but a suitcase filled with ideas like planting a moon garden and offering medicinal cooking classes. The aunties shared their dream of starting a product line, and suddenly, we were all in on it together, as though I had been here from the very start. After years of squeezing in product brainstorming sessions between helping guests, we're on the verge of launching In Full Bloom at the end of June.

"Yeah, Auntie Rose told me that as of next weekend, the waiting list for rooms is several months long," I say, accepting the bee smoker from Auntie Violet.

A three-month waiting list because of a few photos.

There were screengrabs of the livestream of me whispering to Vin, as well as a few candid photographs of us in the winter tent. I didn't think I was laughing at anything he said, but my mouth curled just enough at the right time for the media to think I was. It's astonishing what eye contact and a solid handshake can lead to. It didn't help that I was wearing his leather jacket. In less than a week, rumors caught fire and spread across the internet.

"This is our last weekend below full capacity. We better save up our energy," Auntie Violet says. "This is the kind of publicity we need for In Full Bloom."

I puff a stream of smoke through the bee smoker funnel. "Debatable."

"At this point, we should be counting our lucky starflowers that anyone's talking about us at all. Our website has been live since March, and our only preorders are from family members and former guests," Auntie Violet says. "You know how hard it's been to grow social media and secure media placements. There's a lot of product to move."

We spent months getting the website ready, taking photos of all the flowers and writing copy, only for it to launch and collect digital cobwebs.

Auntie Violet straightens to face me. "You really must not have liked him. Did he say something to offend you?"

Before starting the inn, Auntie Violet was a dating show producer. She's asked—and answered—a lot of questions in her time, especially to vet contestants before anyone ever made it to air. She also loves drama.

I release my grip on the smoker. "We can't be associated with their brand, Auntie. Not professionally, and certainly not personally. People like us are on the receiving end of people like him."

And yet, now I am associated with the Chao Brothers without having any choice in the matter. My chest tightens at the resistance I feel against Vin, another feeling I don't seem to have a choice over. He didn't come off as a bad guy, but everything he stands for rubs me the wrong way.

"I'm sure it'll pass," I say, reassuring myself. "And he probably doesn't care, so why should I? This is just another day in the life for him."

In the distance, tires crunch on gravel before rolling to a stop. A shadowy figure exits a black car and moves toward the trunk.

"Check-in isn't until three," Auntie Violet says, setting the cover on the hive. "Ms. Conrad's early."

I follow her to the car to greet our guest. It's when I get closer that I realize I'm not waving to Ms. Conrad. Instead, I'm welcoming... Vin?

I must say his name out loud because he looks at me with a funny expression, his eyebrows arched. This man has existed only in my memory and the occasional YouTube video since the party, and now here he is, taller than I recall and with sharper features. He's in a black shirt, dark jeans, and that same leather jacket. His brown hair looks only slightly windblown from the ferry ride. He carries his intense aura in with him on the breeze.

A second door slams as another person—Leo—steps out of the car.

Vin gives me a single nod. "Chrysanthemum Chryssy."

The man throws out this inside joke like we know each other.

Clearly, he stores nuggets of information away until he can use them later to turn on the charm. To show that these small, casual details were important enough to remember. This is a heartbreaker at work, and I'm seeing clearly how the spells are cast.

At this moment, I'm grateful for my rules. They keep me immune from men like this, with their good looks and even better memories.

Suddenly, I feel a whoosh of air and an arm brush up against my side as Auntie Violet pushes past me. A loud screeching noise, reminiscent of an eagle, escapes her mouth.

"Sorry, I thought I saw a snake," Auntie Violet says, trying to gain her composure. "Mr. and Mr. Chao! It's so wonderful to meet you both!"

Leo smiles but his eyes are the opposite of happy. This isn't surprising. Heartbreak presents itself in a thousand different ways, for unquantifiable periods of time.

Still, Leo says, "It's wonderful to meet you, too."

It's only when I look at my auntie that I realize we're both still covered head to toe in our bee suits. We remove our hats and veils and slip out of our honey- and wax-splattered outfits. The strap of Auntie Violet's hat gets caught in the necklace the aunties and I each have a version of—a heart broken into four different pieces. I have the rounded curve of the heart's left side on mine.

Vin, seeing the stuck strap, steps forward to help untangle it, and Auntie Violet's knees start visibly shaking. He passes Auntie Violet the hat and accepts her gloved hand in his, giving it a firm shake.

"Just Vin is fine. And the pleasure's ours," he says, his statement accompanied by that charming grin.

Then he shifts his penetrating gaze to me, and my own knees wobble in what I hope is solidarity with Auntie Violet's.

"To who— To what do we owe the pleasure?" Auntie Violet asks, wide-eyed.

Vin is still looking at me. "I need to talk to you," he says, then turns to Auntie Violet and adds, "If you'll excuse us for a minute?"

Auntie Violet nods quickly. "Of course! Leo, have you eaten? You're here in time for the afternoon tea break."

While Auntie Violet leads Leo to the tearoom, I guide Vin to the area behind the herb garden out back. Potted plants surround us, adding a layer of privacy.

"Is everything okay? Is it Leo?" I ask. "If he needs somewhere to stay, I'm sure we can make accommodations, but—"

"Leo's just with me because he doesn't want to be alone," Vin says, pushing a hand through his hair.

The shock seems to have worn off from when I last saw Leo. This is how it goes, though. The shock comes in and out, as do the symptoms and emotions.

"Makes sense," I say, running my fingers through a rosemary bush. The earthy scent fills the air between us.

Vin looks over a lavender bush. "Are these heart-shaped seats?"

"A previous guest was a carpenter," I share. "His favorite part of being here was the Heartbreak Circle. This is where guests can talk about what they're going through as a group. He sent these chairs over as a thank-you gift afterwards."

"A Heartbreak Circle?" Vin asks. "Actually, don't tell me."

I suppress an eye roll. "What has Leo tried? Have you been getting him outside and walking? Made him any comforting foods?"

Vin frowns. "There was a denial phase once the shock wore off. That seemed promising, but then his ex came to get her stuff. The past week has been a fast descent back into darkness. Holing up in the bedroom, not eating much. We're supposed to start rehearsing in a week."

"Oh, yeah. That'll do it," I say. "Do you want to sit?"

Vin looks at the chair, his foot tapping impatiently. "No," he says. "Thanks. I've been sitting all day."

I sit in the nearest heart-shaped seat. "Is there anything he has listened to you about?"

"I told him to unfollow his ex on social media. I've heard people advise that before," Vin says, looming over me.

"That's a great start. What else?"

Vin starts to pace over the grass. "He refuses to go to the doctor. When he realized hospitals were nothing like *Grey's Anatomy*, he swore off them. Uh, I told him to drink excessively and text his ex before crying himself to sleep. You've gotta get that out of the way, right?"

I raise an eyebrow at him, catching his sarcasm. "As early as possible. Has he tried journaling? What about watching romantic comedies and eating pints of ice cream?"

"Sure, I'll get him a nice notebook, and he can try writing down... I don't know... things," Vin says. "We can check the movies off the list, though." He grunts. "If I have to watch *Notting Hill* one more time..."

I hold back a smile at this. It's clear Vin cares about Leo a lot. He just doesn't know how to help. "You've tried everything, and now you're here for real help," I say. "I'll admit I'm surprised. Pleasantly, though."

"Leo didn't want to talk to his therapist. I doubt he'll want to talk to anyone here." Vin notices a sage leaf on the ground. He picks it up and rubs the leaf between his fingers. "And that's not why I'm here."

"Oh," I say. "What made you get on a plane, a car, and a ferry to come all this way then?"

Vin swallows and takes a seat next to me. "Can I just say, this place looks really special. Quaint. I bet you make a lot of healing lamb noodle soups here. And a Heartbreak Circle? Wow."

"Cut the flattery, Vin," I say, crossing my arms. "Why are you at our inn?"

A few heartbeats pass.

"A while back, when I was still with my ex, I agreed to attend a charity event," he eventually says. "As a couple."

If my research serves me right, this was the guitarist he broke up with after a little over two weeks. She did an interview with *People* afterward, shortly followed by a stint as a musical guest on *Saturday Night Live*. Not the worst way to get over an ex.

Next to me, a bee lands on a lavender sprig. "Sounds like you'll be going solo now," I say toward it before turning back to Vin. "Why are you telling me this?"

Vin passes the sage leaf back and forth between his fingers. "There are these photos of us."

"I'm well aware," I say, nodding slowly.

Vin studies me and leans forward, resting his elbows on his thighs. "You're not mad?"

Above us, the leaves create a natural wind chime as they dance in the wind. Vin's eyes are a darker brown in the tree's shade.

"It's not my favorite photo of myself, but people are going to think what they want. Doesn't make it true, right?" I ask.

Vin doesn't agree one way or another. "The charity event has already been marketing it as this whole celebrity couple's thing. Tickets have been purchased. It's set to be one of the biggest fund-raisers for them," he explains, closing his eyes for a few seconds like he's summoning the strength to ask something difficult. "What would you say to going with me?"

I choke back a laugh. "Like, as your date? I don't play guitar," I say before registering that I've just given myself—and my online sleuthing—away.

"You wouldn't be pretending to be my ex," Vin says with a knowing smirk. "That wouldn't make any sense. You'd be you, pretending to be…"

"Your girlfriend?" I supply when Vin trails off.

"My *date*," he maintains.

"Wouldn't that just feed the headlines?" I ask. The last thing I need is to become friendly with a good-looking cellist heartbreaker. Objectively, of course. "Maybe you can be photographed with someone else. The blonde from the party? Have you tried her?"

Tall and leggy does seem to be his type. In my research, I learned a lot about Vin's past relationships. If you can call them that. They were more like flings, lasting less than a month. There was the actress who does only very serious films. The principal dancer in the New York City Ballet. Then there was the Victoria's Secret model. How one could break an angel's heart, I'll never know. When I couldn't find anything from the past six months, I turned to *Gardeners' World* for higher-quality entertainment.

"The photos have already laid the foundation," he says. Then he mumbles to himself, "I hate that I'm even asking this."

I hear it, and I feel the need to understand. "Then why are you? You're an eligible bachelor. What if you auction off a date with you to raise even more money for this event?"

Vin lifts an eyebrow at me. "Not a terrible idea, though that would take time to set up. The event's next week. I was planning on bringing Leo, but now…I would hate to ask that of him when he's feeling down."

It's a good instinct. While it's important for some people to be around others and socializing during heartbreak, for some it's too soon.

"I don't know, Vin," I say. "Me going on a date with you? It's too… unlikely. No one would believe we're together."

I realize this isn't necessarily true, if the headlines were any indication. The fact the claims aren't being outright rejected means people believe there's some percentage of truth to it. This baffles me.

The muscle in Vin's jaw flexes. "Maybe it's so unlikely, it's believable," he says.

"And then what? We just go our separate ways after? Won't people still be curious about us?" I ask.

"That's when I could...break up with you," he says so quickly that it takes me a second to process his words. "You did say you wanted to help, right?" He attempts a weak smile.

"Wow," I say, standing slowly. Now it's my turn to pace. Does this guy actually prefer to break up with people? Is that his shtick? "Let me get this straight. You traveled all this way just to ask to break up with me? You should've saved yourself the trouble and called."

Whatever the opposite of a grand gesture is, this is that.

"I figured you'd hang up on me," he says.

I don't respond. I like to think that's what I would've done, but I've never hung up on anyone before.

Vin's so straightforward with his ask that I don't know whether I should be offended or impressed.

"Well, thanks for stopping by, but this is a little strange to me," I say. "Do you always give the women you date a heads-up that you're going to end things with them?"

Vin runs a hand down his face. "Despite what you'd like to believe, never. But these are different circumstances," he says. "And honestly, this is weird for me, too."

I prop my hands on my hips. "What if I don't want to be broken up with?"

Vin exhales through his nose. "I need a breakup."

It's safe to say that this man and I have very different needs.

"What makes you think I'd be so easy to break up with?" I ask, working through my thoughts, stunning myself that I haven't said no yet.

Vin's lower eyelid twitches slightly, but his mouth is firmly set in a straight line. "I don't think anything about you is easy," he says, standing to meet me.

He towers over me, but his shoulders are slightly hunched. It's not like he came here demanding I do this. Vin really is asking. He needs this.

"We have this tour, and it'd probably be best to go our separate ways before then," he continues. "We probably just need to be seen together once more. Then I'll get out of your way. And at the event, we only need to interact when absolutely necessary. You'll hardly notice me."

This is the moment that I do, in fact, start to notice him. Like, really notice him. The way he can't ever be still, a part of him always in motion. His long fingers that are always fiddling with something. The tapping of his foot and the reshifting of positions every few minutes. He squeezes his hand into a fist while stretching out his arm.

I don't know what Vin's heartbreak is yet, but I can sense that there's something there. I see remnants of it in his tired eyes, his frown, his constant being on edge, his shallow breathing. I wonder if I'd be able to help.

"When's the tour?" I ask.

"In three months."

"You think Leo's going to be well enough for a world tour in, what, August?" I ask, counting the months under my breath. "You're more optimistic than you let on."

"He has to be. People don't know Leo was in a relationship," Vin reveals. "If they find out that he's heartbroken, well, that's just not what we do."

"Of course, you don't do heartbreak. You just do the heartbreaking,"

I mumble a little too bitterly before immediately gasping. I didn't mean to say it, not really. It just slipped out, this weird tension inside of me bursting at the seams and ripping all the way open. Something buried deep inside of me grows its way toward the surface. Something I didn't know still bothered me. "I'm sorry, I didn't mean—"

"Think what you want. You can even say what you want. It's nothing I haven't heard before," Vin says, cutting me off. He studies my face for a moment. "I get it. You hate people like me because you have to clean up my messes."

He crosses his arms, and I instinctively mirror him. We're in an accidental face-off that I didn't intend to be in, and what a beautiful face his is. As he takes another step forward, I catch a whiff of him. His scent matches his steely exterior, but there's something sweet beneath the surface. The combination of black tea, dark berries, and eucalyptus temporarily overwhelms me despite its subtlety.

I push away all the bright, shiny performances and interviews of Vin that I've watched in passing (fine, studied) in the past month. That man is not the same version of the man in front of me. He's a blank slate, a new recipe whose ingredients I've yet to determine.

There's a long, tension-filled silence. I'm both irritated and intrigued by Vin, but I don't know what to name this feeling.

I manage to get a few words out. "I don't know you well enough to hate you."

My breath hitches in my throat as I stare down Vin. I force myself to think about my ingredient lists and what the weather might be like tomorrow. I have food to prep and a product line to work on and hearts to heal. These are the things I need to be thinking about.

What should not be on my mind is Vin Chao and whatever it is my body is doing in reaction to him.

"What is this between us?" Vin asks, like he's just read my thoughts. "Have I done something to you?"

"Other than show up here unannounced asking to break up with me?" I ask, my tone revealing a low-level irritation.

"I know this is a lot," Vin says. "In hindsight, I really should've called. If I bother you this much, then I'll go." He starts to back up. "I'm sorry to waste your time."

"Wait," I say, stopping him in his tracks. "I think you—"

He shakes his head. "You what? You think you know me? Because whatever made-up image or thought you have of me, I can promise you that's not who I am."

I close my eyes for a long second. "I don't know." I feel my expression softening. "You make me nervous, I guess."

I exhale sharply, having suddenly pinpointed the annoyance this man causes me.

"Well, you make me...you make me nervous, too," Vin says quietly. He's flustered in the most annoyingly adorable way.

I relax a little at hearing this admission. It's a strange kind of comfort knowing that we both make each other feel similarly.

Vin catalogs me with his intense eyes. It's quick, but I notice his glance drop to my lips. Without even trying, all that suddenly remains in focus for me is Vin's firm mouth. I tear my eyes away too late, and in that split second, he catches me looking at his lips, too.

I resign myself to being caught, not knowing how to get out of this one. Heat swarms in my chest.

I need time. Time to think about this, time to work through every angle of it.

"Come on. Let's go get tea," I say, knowing I'll be throwing a few extra mint leaves in mine.

I really need to cool down.

Chapter 4

VIN

Chryssy guides me to a floral-wallpapered room where everything is set up for afternoon tea. The *clink, clink, clink* of ceramic mixes with...Leo's laughter?

"Chryssy, hi. Vin," Leo says, patting the empty spot next to him on the velvet bench. "I was just telling the aunties why we're here. How'd it go?"

"The *aunties*?" I ask, raising an eyebrow at his word choice.

"Well, that's what they are, aren't they?" Leo says.

"Vin, these are my other aunties, Rose and Daisy," Chryssy introduces as she sits in a chair across from me.

Everyone's seated around tables topped with ceramic teapots and three-tiered stands containing little sandwiches and scones. Through the large bay windows, sunshine casts streaks over the room, warming the space. A couple of tables are occupied on the far end by guests reading and puzzling. Tea sets and animal-shaped creamers rest on pink shelves lining the far walls.

A woman in a dress with hair swept back in a jade-claw clip introduces herself as Rose. She offers a tight-lipped smile as she does so.

Chryssy's other auntie, Daisy, greets me with a friendly smile. She removes her yellow glasses and lets them hang from a beaded chain around her neck. "Welcome to the Wildflower Inn," she says, dropping flowers into a bone china teacup that she pushes toward me. "Lotus will help calm and relax you. It'll be perfect after your long day of travel."

"Thank you for the tea and snacks," I say, eyeing the fresh-cut flowers sprouting from an eclectic assortment of bud vases.

Rose moves the kettle around the table and fills each cup with hot water.

I instinctively check my phone for messages. I swipe away notifications about missed calls from Jim but make the mistake of reading an email from him.

Vin—Got a few options lined up for a little see and be seen. Let me know when you can talk. —J

"Leo filled us in on your situation, Vin," Violet says before taking a bite of scone.

I tuck my phone into my back pocket. "Is this why you came along?" I ask Leo. "To have a gossip session with the aunties?"

Leo shrugs. "Talking to them has been the highlight of my past two weeks, so yeah," he says. "Rose used to be a divorce lawyer, and you should hear the stories she has. I couldn't imagine feeling this way while also dealing with paperwork."

Rose has definitely nailed her inscrutable expression.

"I'm sure," I say. "But don't worry about my situation. I'm handling it so you can focus on getting better."

"Are you going to do it?" Violet asks Chryssy.

"I have no idea," Chryssy says. "I haven't committed either way yet." She takes a long sip of tea.

"Not even to help Vin with all the pressures he's facing with his record label?" Daisy asks her.

Chryssy peers at me over the rim of her cup. "I only knew about the charity event," she says, setting her tea down slowly. "Vin, I can't help you if you don't tell me what's really going on. If you want to go on a fake date, it needs to be built on truth and trust."

I glare at Leo before filling in the parts I left out.

Chryssy furrows her brows at the tower of sweet treats. "This is something you're really willing to do?" she asks.

An unexpected knot forms in my stomach at her question. I don't want to act like I'm dating someone for real. Who would actually want to do that? But I can't deny there would be obvious benefits.

"I'm willing to do what it takes to succeed," I say. "Always have."

As Violet reaches for another scone, her arm brushes against the flowers in the vase and a few petals drop on the table.

"Look. It's dying in front of us," Rose tells her sister. "If you want to see flowers, Violet, look outside."

"You have to be dying to be living," Violet retorts. "I like having nature surrounding me, inside and outside."

Daisy reaches for the flower that lost its petal. "Since it's on its way out, I might as well press it," she says.

Rose looks pained by this. "I don't like it, Chryssy," she says bluntly, suddenly switching topics. "I'll support whatever you choose to do, but our family has had enough heartbreak as it is. You want to prevent later problems? Don't do this. It'll only be a distraction, and we have real things to focus on."

"Speculation led to bookings, Rose," Violet says. "Imagine what this could do for In Full Bloom."

Rose seems to consider this while examining a mini berry-topped tart. "I'm just trying to look out for the family," she states.

"People do love the start of things, especially relationships," Daisy says. "It's an escape in the form of a love story, even if it is fake."

"This is just one date, not a relationship," I clarify.

"And it's definitely not a love story," Chryssy adds.

"Sounds harmless then," Violet says. "What are you thinking, Chryssy?"

"Still working on it," Chryssy says. She pushes a strand of hair behind an ear as she thinks. While I wait for her response, I sweep my eyes over the light smattering of freckles across her nose and cheeks.

"I'm hearing that as not a no," I say, my tone a little too hopeful. "I know it would be hard for people to believe that we're together—"

"Now that, I agree with," Chryssy says.

"—but we wouldn't be the strangest pairing to ever get together," I finish.

"You have nothing to lose, Chryssy," Violet says cryptically.

Chryssy takes a long breath in, tapping her teacup with her pointer finger. "If I pretend to date you," she says, "I'm going to need something in return."

"Understandable," I say right away. "What do you need? Money?"

Chryssy laughs once. "I don't want you to pay me to go on a date," she says, shaking her head. "If I go with you to your charity event, you have to come with me to a family thing."

"And what, pretend to be your boyfriend?" I ask.

"This is too temporary for labels. It's a date for a date," she says. "My family would never forgive me if they thought I was dating you and I didn't bring you to this. And like Auntie Violet said, the more places we're seen together, the better for your reputation and our business."

"What do you get out of it?" I ask.

Chryssy flattens her hands on the table. "We're promoting our tea line at this event," she says. "We need to drive preorders and email sign-ups. You'd need to wear the swag and drink a cup of tea."

My grin flatlines. "We're highly selective with our brands, and I'm a coffee guy."

"You can't drink both coffee and tea?" she asks.

"I'm a coffee guy, too, but I'm enjoying this tea," Leo interjects.

"I've found you're usually on one team or another," I say, bumping him. "And I'm firmly on the non-tea team. What else do you want?"

Chryssy plucks a berry off her own tart and tosses it into her mouth. "There's nothing else I want. Having someone of your caliber promote our brand even for just a day would do so much more than money could."

"Me?" I ask. "A heartbreaker?"

"You're so unlikely it'd be believable," she says, throwing my words back at me.

"Come on, Vin. You can wear a hat," Leo says. "It's not like there's a conflict of interest." He turns to the group. "We were considering working with a high-end amaro brand, and Brew Haus allowed it. And even if they didn't, we've broken rules before."

I haven't thought about a backup plan, but I know I don't want Jim's options. If anything fake is going to happen, I want it to at least be on my terms.

"Okay," I say before Chryssy changes her mind. "Deal." I hold out my hand for a shake across the table, careful to avoid the flowers and towers of treats.

"You sure?" she asks, eyeing my hand. "This is what seemed to get us in trouble last time."

I keep my arm out, and Chryssy slips her hand into mine.

"And you thought I wouldn't be helpful," she says, her eyes playful.

A smile breaks free on my face, and I'm not trying to be charming. It's not forced, either. For the first time all week, I'm relieved.

Leo claps, startling me. "Great, now that that's settled, there's something else. I've decided I want to stay here."

I drop Chryssy's hand as I swivel toward Leo. As I do so, my knee bumps Chryssy's under the table. The contact is noticeable enough that she jerks away, shifting back in her seat, safely out of touching range.

"What's that?" I ask him.

"This place is amazing, Vin," Leo says. "You should hear what they do here. If I'm going to be better for tour, I need to heal. This is where I want to do that."

"Rehearsals start on the second," I remind him. "Can you heal him in that amount of time?"

The aunties take sips of their tea and glance at one another.

"It happens as fast as it happens," Rose says. "Two, maybe three, months is a safe timeline to ensure that we're not rushing through the treatment plan. Of course, this can be shorter. Some guests pop in and out. Given your fast-paced lives, there will be an adjustment period to slow down."

"Our life is fast-paced for a reason," I say, crumbling a scone between my fingers. "We can't afford to go slower than we do."

"Every heart heals on its own time," Daisy says.

"Leo's in good hands here with us," Chryssy says gently.

"I don't want to go home," Leo says while fiddling with the tail of a cat creamer.

"I'm not just going to leave you out on this island," I tell him. "And we have rehearsals. Meetings. Work. What about all that?"

"This is my last hope before the world tour, Vin," Leo says. "I know you want to plan, but right now I'm just sad. Can't I just be sad for a little bit?"

"What physical sensations have you been experiencing? Have you been feeling fluttery? Dizzy?" Violet asks.

Leo sits up in his seat. "Exactly and yes. I've had shortness of breath over the past couple of weeks," he says, holding a hand to his chest. "Sometimes it feels like my heart is skipping a beat."

Rose, Daisy, and Violet nod in sync.

"Heart palpitations," Rose says, narrowing her eyes at Leo's chest like she can see right through him. "What you're feeling are irregular heartbeats."

"You've had a serious loss," Daisy adds. "You're undoubtedly and understandably grieving and experiencing severe stress and anxiety. This can result in physical pain and cardiac symptoms. It's good you're not ignoring this."

"If I could, I would," Leo says. "Preferably in the form of sleep. Then I don't have to think about how my heart was ripped out, stomped on, and forgotten about." He takes a shallow, wobbly breath. "You go from talking every day to someone, merging your lives together, thinking about them constantly...just to one day not. There was still so much I wanted to tell her. So much I wanted to do together. How does all of that just go away after a phone call?"

"Like having kids, there's no convenient time for heartbreak," Rose says.

"You really think you'll be able to help him?" I ask, my hesitation obvious.

"It's what we do," Chryssy answers confidently. She props her elbow on the edge of the table and rests her chin against her fist. "Did you know that, in America alone, there are roughly twenty thousand wildflower species?"

Her question is apparently rhetorical. She doesn't wait for me to respond.

"The way I see it, that's how many species of heartbreak there are," Chryssy elaborates. "Heartbreak presents itself in different ways for every person. Like a wildflower or fingerprint, each experience is uniquely its own. Often, it's shock, sometimes it's rage, other times it comes in the form of physical ailments. When we leave something unattended in ourselves and don't work through it, it manifests in other ways."

Instinctively, I flex my arm. "Can you connect the dots a bit more?"

Chryssy smiles. "Happy to. Because heartbreak is unique for each person, treatment plans need to reflect what's best for individual guests. Sometimes people throw themselves into work to avoid having to think about the grief. Others numb themselves however they can. Some guests don't want to get out of bed."

"I wish," Leo mumbles next to me.

"Leo, you might spend a few days in bed before you're encouraged to get up and moving so that it's more of a gradual process," she says. "In our bodies, and in the natural world, we have Qi, or life force. Leo likely has Qi deficiency, which is what we see most commonly with heartbreak here. Digestion issues, exhaustion, shortness of breath. We can help with this."

"Walking. Fresh air. Lamb soup," I list off, recalling what she told me at the party.

Chryssy leans back against her seat, taking her teacup with her. "Partly. We get to know guests before creating their treatment plan so that we can best serve them according to their personalities and what's going on with them. Have either of you heard of Yin and Yang?"

"Of course," I say while Leo nods. "The black-and-white circle. It's iconic."

"Yin and Yang symbolize how everything is interconnected. It's all about balance," Chryssy explains as she grabs a scone. "The light side of the symbol is Yang, which is associated with qualities that are hot, dry, more active. The dark side is Yin, which has cold, passive, wet, slower qualities." She moves her cup and scone up and down like she's weighing them to help demonstrate her points. "The two are fluid, constantly flowing between each other on a sliding scale. Like moon phases."

"So that's what staying here will be about? Rebalancing Leo?" I ask. "What if he's always been a little off-balance?"

My joke lands, and Leo coughs out a tight laugh as he elbows my side. "Just me?"

I hear what Chryssy and her aunties are saying, and I don't want Leo to be in pain. I don't like it, but it wouldn't be the first time we've toured without months of practice. When we toured in our twenties, we could get by on a few weeks' worth of rehearsals. Now, though, there's too much to lose.

I'm about to say this when I see a flicker of hope in Leo's tired eyes. They're puffy and red, the typical playfulness in them dimmed by the situation. I've officially never seen him like this. I feel myself scowling at the innocent platter of scones as though they've wronged me somehow. But just like it's not these scones' fault, Leo's not to blame for what's happened, either. The love of his life just destroyed him. After all he's felt and been through these past two weeks, maybe a little balance really could help him.

"What if we push rehearsals to the end of June?" I propose. "That gives you a little over a month at the inn and a month and a half for practice."

Leo closes his eyes and nods. "That would be...yes. Please. Would that work?" he asks Chryssy's aunties.

"We can work with that," Daisy says, nodding to her sisters. "You can take the last open room. Next week, we'll have to figure out an alternative room plan." She looks between me and Chryssy. "Thanks to you two, we'll be fully booked."

"Sounds like lots of people are benefiting from those photos. That's really nice," Leo says, smirking at me. "If it's too much trouble, I can get a room somewhere nearby."

"Guests stay on property," Rose says decidedly. "Violet and I will share a room to make space."

"It'll be like summer camp," Violet says. "I feel young again!"

"I'll have our stuff and cellos shipped out," I offer.

"Our?" Leo asks.

"I'm staying," I decide. "I can do my work from here. I'll stay in a hotel in town."

"Nonsense!" Violet says. "Vin, you're just as much a guest. You'll stay here."

"He can stay with me," Leo offers. "I'll order you a blow-up bed, Vin. My treat."

Violet's eyes dart over to Rose, then to Chryssy. "Well, what about the Dandelion?" she says.

Chryssy's head swerves in Violet's direction. "You're suggesting Vin stay...with me?" she asks.

I put my hands up. "Seriously. Don't worry. I'll find a place of my own."

"It's not really *with* Chryssy," Violet says. "The Dandelion is a converted two-bedroom shed."

"Wedding season is starting," Daisy says. "And renting a place is too expensive."

"It's not a problem," I insist.

"I won't hear about it anymore," Rose says. "There's an empty room in the Dandelion. That's where you'll stay."

Chryssy's eyes widen. "We'd have to share a bathroom. We can't allow a guest to share a bathroom. Let alone a rock star. A cellist rock star? A cellstar? A rockist?" she rambles.

I surprise myself by saying, "I don't mind." I clear my throat. "I just mean I don't want to be an inconvenience. Please don't think of me as a guest here. We're grateful to have gotten a room at all. I'll sleep in the car if I have to."

"Obviously we're not going to make you sleep in the car," Rose says. "We can't handle that kind of liability. It gets cold here at night."

"Chryssy, you can stay with me if you'd like," Daisy offers.

"I wouldn't want to impose on you," Chryssy tells her before turning back to me. "I'd be happy to share the Dandelion. It's important that Leo is taken care of, and if you insist on being here, too, then we'd love for you to stay...with us." She says this as though she doesn't work at an inn. That's how she earns a living. By strangers literally staying with them.

I dip my head. "I appreciate it."

"Vin, Leo, I want to be forthright with you both that I'm a Chaobreaker," Violet says seriously. "But I will not let that influence the way I provide care for you. And rest assured that I will not ask you questions like, Can you serenade me to sleep? Or can you maybe play me a soft melody while I enjoy my breakfast? That would be wrong of me. And I will definitely not ask you to perform a rambunctious tune if I need uplifting." She thinks for a moment. "Yeah. No. I won't do that."

"And we will not ask you where the liquor cabinet is," I reply with a grin.

"Honestly, I'm your fan already," Leo tells Violet. He turns to Rose and Daisy. "All of you, really."

"Leo, we'll do the full intake form and observation tomorrow once you've rested. That way we can come up with your treatment plan," Rose says. "There will be acupuncture treatments, meals that will help balance your Qi, morning Qigong, and gardening. Optional off-site trips will also be offered."

"We allow very limited technology usage at first but aim to get that down to zero percent. Here we're connecting to life in a different way," Daisy informs us as she stands. "You must both be tired. Leo, we'll show you to your room. Chryssy, will you get Vin set up?"

Chryssy drains the rest of her tea. "Happily," she says, though she sounds anything but. She gestures toward the door. "After you."

So much for just a date.

Chapter 5

VIN

"Welcome to the Dandelion. It's probably not as luxurious as you're used to, but it's private," Chryssy says, opening the door to the yellow shed out past the inn's garden.

I follow Chryssy's lead and remove my shoes at the door. We step into a small living room with patterned rugs layered over the hardwood floor. Empty mugs sit on the side table next to a set of purple chairs covered in clothing and unfolded blankets.

"Aren't dandelions weeds?" I ask, moving past a dining table covered with water-glass-stained notebook pages and a bunch of product packaging.

"Or so they've been labeled," Chryssy says. "They're misunderstood. People view them negatively because they're pervasive and persistent. They're hard to control."

"Doesn't sound great," I say.

"Well, I like them because of those reasons. Even in the harshest of conditions, like concrete, they find a way out," she says. "They're actually herbs, though, and are great for detoxing and nourishing your liver." Chryssy grabs a few empty mugs. "I'll clean up a bit. Promise I'll be a good inn-mate." She frowns at how that sounded. "Shed-mate?"

"Inmate" is probably more accurate.

"Are you sure this is okay?" I ask. Shades are drawn over the windows on both sides of the shed while open shelving fills in the rest of the room. They're overflowing with books stacked vertically and sideways, candles, and baskets. It's so much of Chryssy all at once. Her personal space, her personal belongings.

Chryssy blinks a few times before nodding. "Honestly, I'd rather have you here with me than me stay with Auntie Daisy. She doesn't just talk in her sleep. She has full-on conversations and expects responses. She was a therapist in a past life, and I don't know what buried emotions I'll reveal when I'm not fully conscious. I don't need that kind of psychoanalyzing." She points across the room. "I should mention we have a third roommate. Watch out for Goji."

That's when I see something furry poke its head up from a crocheted blanket across the living room. It peers at me with glossy, beady eyes, one ear sticking straight up while the other flops over the side of its head.

Chryssy brings Goji over, cradling him in her arms. He lies there, just being a rabbit.

"Do you want to hold him?" she asks, scratching his flopped-down ear.

"I'm good. What's a Goji anyway?" I ask as the rabbit's nose twitches.

"Goji berries. He looks like one." She retrieves an unlabeled glass jar containing dried, oval-shaped, dark orange-red berries from the cabinet and gently presses it against the rabbit's fur. "Pretty close, right?" She sets Goji on the counter and places a few berries in front of him. He devours them. "They're called the 'red diamond' because they're so good for you. It's a very important ingredient in TCM," she says, twisting the cap back on.

"Is that what Leo will be eating?"

Chryssy casts her eyes back to me, looking me up and down. "I

use them a lot in dishes, so yes. Looks like you'll be eating them, too."
She points behind her. "Bathroom's down the hall. My bedroom's off
to the right, and yours will be across the way. There's a front door and
a side entry," she says, using her hands like she's a flight attendant
marking the exits. I take note of each one. "If you want to take a
bubble bath, the bathroom's all yours. There's a lovely lavender-mint
bath bomb you can try."

"Yeah, I'm not going to touch that," I say.

"They're heart-shaped," she tempts.

"The scent reminds me of cleaning products."

"You would." Chryssy blinks at me, nodding. "You would."

I shake my head. "I would…what, exactly?" I ask, the tension
between us back in full force.

"Nothing," she says. "Sorry, nerves. I haven't lived with a guy in…
ever. I didn't expect this day to end with a roommate."

I feel my guard come down. "Me neither. And for the record, I
fucking love bath bombs. I just can't stand lavender."

"You'll love this then," she says, guiding me through the small hall-
way. We turn left into the most purple room I've ever seen. "Surprise!
You get the lavender room!" She gestures for me to go first. "Auntie
Violet designed all the rooms at the inn, including the ones out here.
This was supposed to be for guests who required more privacy, but
when I moved out here, I needed some space."

Now I know what the inside of Barney's bowels looks like.

My eyes land on visual relief: a green chair in the corner. "Oh, hey.
There's the mint."

"You like the pillows?" she asks, noticing me looking at the pile of
them on the chair. "The aunties and I needlepoint almost every night
to wind down. Feel free to join anytime."

That won't be happening, but I nod anyway.

Lilac walls with painted sprigs of lavender shoot up from the baseboard. Dried lavender is angled above the door and bed and housed in vases on the nightstands. The mattress is missing sheets, which I assume are also purple.

Chryssy pulls open a drawer in the bureau against the far wall. "We love a theme here, clearly," she says as she removes—surprise—purple sheets.

She flaps them out and starts making the bed.

"I can do that," I say, reaching for the other side.

Chryssy stops me. "You're a guest here."

"Seriously, don't think of me as one," I insist. "I also have a preference for how my bed gets made anyway."

She looks at the sheet in her hands, like she's reluctant to let it go. "I'll leave these here then," she finally says, setting her corner down on the mattress. "Let me get you the pillowcases."

As she rummages through drawers, I open the doors of an armoire, curious to see how much space I have to work with for the foreseeable future. It's empty except for an antique lacquered mahogany writing box on the top shelf.

I lift the lid to the box, peering inside. There's a leather satchel, a couple of notebooks, and a stack of paper tied off with string. I open one of the notebooks to a random page.

"'Lion's mane,'" I read out loud, my voice hollow against the empty shelves. "'Lily bulb.'"

"What?" Chryssy asks, peeking from behind the door. She gasps. "Vin! Don't open that!"

I look up. "What?"

"That box! We don't touch it, and we definitely don't open it," she says, flinging the pillowcases onto the bed and running out of the room. She comes back seconds later with oven mitts on. She delicately takes the notebook from me. "I don't know how this got in here."

"Oh, shit. Sorry, I've never seen anything like this in person. I didn't mean to snoop," I say. "Looks like a cookbook or something."

She looks confused. "A cookbook? Well, we have enough of those in the kitchen. It's fine. We're going to be fine."

I frown. "Why wouldn't we be? Seems like a pretty harmless box. It's actually a pretty nice antique. You could probably get some good money for that."

"Last I heard, this was supposed to be destroyed, like, twenty years ago. This thing just doesn't go away," she mumbles. "I'll take care of it."

Chryssy slides the notebook back into the writing box, closing the lid with a heavy thud. I follow her out into the living room as she carefully carries the box with her mitts.

"Mind getting the door?" she asks.

I quickly pull it open and watch as Chryssy slips outside and places the box on the ground beside the shed. When she's back, she slides the mitts off and releases a short exhale.

"I've been living in here with that for who knows how long," she mumbles to herself, clearly frazzled. She recovers quickly and gestures toward the living room. Technically, the entire room is one giant entryway and kitchen, the furniture dividing up the space. "Please sit. Feel free to treat this shed as you would your own home." She clears a pile of clothing from one of the chairs.

I move a patchwork quilt before claiming the other chair. "Thanks, but this is way more of a home than my own."

"What do you mean?" she asks.

"Well, for instance, I don't own a couch," I admit.

"You don't have a couch? What do you sit on?" she asks as she starts loading cups into the dishwasher. Goji watches her from the counter.

"I have a table and chair where I eat. I practice on that chair, too,"

I explain, grabbing a cup from the coffee table and bringing it to her. "Can I help you with that?"

Chryssy waves me off. "I got it. Please sit and relax," she insists. "Where do guests sit when they visit you?"

"I don't have guests over," I say, launching into my justifications. "I haven't found the right couch yet, and I'm hardly ever home. Why spend money on something if it isn't exactly what I want?"

"How minimalist of you."

I sit back down on the chair, the bouncy cushion throwing me off balance. A muffled voice in the room startles me, and I look around to identify the source.

"Is your butt talking?" Chryssy asks, holding a fork midair.

I listen closer and realize the sound is coming from behind me. I remember what I was listening to on the way to the inn and quickly tug my phone from my pocket, fumbling with the buttons on the side to lower the volume. The voice slowly fades.

Chryssy's lips part. "That wasn't...was it?"

After the party, curiosity got the best of me, so I did some casual research. Chryssy cooks all the food at the Wildflower Inn and puts out a podcast called *Wild Flours with Chrysanthemum*. Each episode is released every Wednesday and features a flower used in Traditional Chinese Medicine paired with food. Violet honey and scones. Honeysuckle jelly and biscuits. I appreciate looking at flowers, and I appreciate eating food. It's as simple as that.

"Yeah." I shrug nonchalantly. "So?"

What Chryssy doesn't need to know is that casual googling led to tuning into every episode of *Wild Flours*. I never did get another laugh out of her at the party, but in every podcast episode, I get to hear it again. Somehow, I made it through almost every episode. I'm down to the most recent one—safflower and ginger madeleines—which is what Chryssy unfortunately heard.

Chryssy rinses one of Goji's food bowls. "I do love that pairing in baked goods," she says. "Safflower is great for improving blood circulation and reducing inflammation. But you know that already." A surprised laugh tumbles out of her. This one's higher in tone but still as musical as I remember.

"Shit," I mumble. "I . . . yeah. I may have listened to an episode or two."

She scans me up and down. "Are you the one trolling me with comments about pollen, bugs, and allergens?"

"No, I'm the one complaining about your choice of intro and outro music," I joke.

She laughs again. "I can't afford licensed music, so for now it's royalty-free chimes. Anyway, thanks for listening. Always nice to meet a fan."

"Don't think I said I was a fan," I say playfully, glancing over at her.

She smirks and snaps her fingers. "That would explain the drop-off in listening stats."

"Guilty," I lie. There was no drop-off on my end.

My eyes connect with Chryssy's as she closes the dishwasher, the gentle breeze from the movement blowing her hair back. The ends graze her shoulders, drawing my attention to a scattering of small moles dotting them. I don't mean to, but suddenly my eyes are tracing the lines of her arms down to her hands as she dries them on a towel.

I tear my eyes away, focusing instead on a red chrysanthemum sketch hanging against the wall.

"That's actually string," Chryssy says, clocking my observation. "The entire piece is made of one long piece woven around small nails. An artist made it for me after I gave her tea for her heartbreak. Don't worry, everything worked out."

"Well, that's a relief," I mutter. The longer I look at it, the more distinct each strand becomes. "It's incredible." I glance over at Chryssy, whose features are soft as she loses herself for a moment in the red web. She's even prettier than I remember from the party. I have an excellent memory, but it did not do her justice.

Chryssy smiles at the art piece and looks over at me. "It's getting late," she says. "I was going to needlepoint and listen to an audiobook. If you want to rest out here for a bit, feel free."

I shift on the seat more carefully this time. "I need to catch up on emails."

Chryssy doesn't laugh at this. Instead, she watches me with curious eyes.

"Why are you looking at me like that?" I ask.

"How am I looking at you?"

"Like you're analyzing me. Reading me."

She tilts her head. "Maybe I am."

"Can you not?"

"Read you or look at you like this?"

"Both?" I ask. "Or maybe don't let me know you're assessing me."

Chryssy starts tidying the coffee table, which is covered in stacks of paper and books on flowers and herbs. "When's the last time you had a break?" she probes.

I lean forward in the chair, taking it upon myself to fold the quilt. "How does one really define a break?"

"You don't need to clean," Chryssy says when she spots me straightening a pile of books on the floor. "You're a . . . visitor here."

"That's just another word for 'guest,' which I'm not."

"Vin. When?" Chryssy presses.

I sigh. "When I was ten, I traveled to Italy with my family."

Chryssy makes a face. "When you were ten years old?"

"It was for my grandpa's funeral."

"You're telling me you haven't had a break in twenty-two years?"

Chryssy asks, her eyes wide. "And that the last time you traveled for something other than work was for a funeral? I'm sorry for your loss."

"Thanks."

"You work like our hearts do," Chryssy says. "Nonstop."

"We're both also good at keeping beats," I reply. "Wait, why do you know how old I am?"

Chryssy pulls colorful threads and a canvas from a basket embroidered with "Needlepointing Is a State of Mind." "You listened to my podcast. I watched your interviews. And I googled you. I wanted to be ready in case you contacted us about helping Leo," she quickly justifies, turning away from me.

I smirk. "Sure, okay." I spot a bundle of purple thread on the floor and offer it to Chryssy. "I better get used to this color, huh?"

Chryssy takes the thread from me. A shock runs up my arm as her hand brushes against mine. We really need to stop handing each other things.

"What about when you're not on tour? Or when you're done with an album?" Chryssy asks. "What do you do then?"

"When we're not on tour, we're making albums. When we're not making albums, we're on tour," I reason. "Add a few more projects into the mix, and that's my life."

"If you won't give yourself permission to rest, I'll give it to you," she declares. "This time off isn't just for rebalancing Leo. We may also need to rebalance you."

"Me? I'm fine. There's no being off for me." Even if I wanted to rest, there's no room for it in this life we've created for ourselves. At least not right now. "My life is normally chaos," I continue. "A good chaos. It's what I've worked toward."

"Chaos sounds tiring," Chryssy says, her voice filled not with judgment but with kindness. Genuine curiosity.

"I've made my metaphorical bed," I say, earning a sympathetic grin from Chryssy. "I accept that. I make it and live in it every single day."

"You live in your metaphorically made bed to *not* get rest," Chryssy reasons. Her nose scrunches, little creases fanning out above her cheeks.

"Exactly," I confirm, hearing the irony. "I can't fit rest in right now. I'm already behind on everything."

"From being here half a day?"

"Leo and I work together, so a lot of what we do requires both of us, and we've lost two weeks at this point. Because, you know." I point toward the left side of my chest.

"Matters of the heart can be so derailing," she says on a sigh.

I lift my phone. "And now I get to derail other people's plans, too. I have to call my publicist and tour manager. Let them know we need to push rehearsals."

"I'm sure they'll understand. Leo's going through something big," Chryssy says, turning the thread bundle between her fingers.

"Well...they didn't know about Leo and Aubrey," I tell her. "No one did. Leo's ex wanted their relationship to be just for them and not the public. If the media found out about her, they'd invade her privacy, scrutinize her life. If they think they can get a story or a photo or the inside scoop, they'll wait her out. She might've blown up Leo's heart, but he wouldn't want that for her. Which is why I'm going to have to make up a reason for why there's going to be a delay."

"You can tell them you're working on something new," she suggests. "You needed time away to figure out your next heartbreak album?"

"At a heartbreak healing retreat?" I ask.

Chryssy considers this. "It's ironic, but the marketing angle could work. You're going straight to the source. Very Method," she says. "You could tell them you're here with me, the woman from the photos. Weren't they the ones who wanted another heartbreak out of you?"

I nod. "They might go for that," I say. "I couldn't stand the thought of being away from you, so I'm spending some time here."

"Makes perfect sense to me," Chryssy says with a smile. "And you dragged Leo with you so you could still work."

"Now that they'd definitely believe."

This morning, I got on a plane, a car, and a ferry to convince Chryssy to go on a date with me. Now we're rooming—and scheming—together.

Somehow, it worked out for both of us.

Chryssy gets exposure for her product, and I cover for Leo's whereabouts, placate our record label while staying in control of the situation, and get a breakup out of it.

The best part? I won't hurt her because she's in on it.

"Keep it vague. They don't have to know that we're just going on two dates," she says.

"Right," I agree. Maybe it's time for my team's imaginations to run wild for a bit. "My manager might be a little confused why I went rogue and am now promoting tea, but hey, love makes you do spontaneous things, right?"

"Love? So fast?" Chryssy asks.

I tilt my head in consideration. "True. They won't believe me if I bring up the L word."

Chryssy half smiles. "I'd like to try something if that's okay. It's nothing weird. I just want to look at your tongue."

I huff out a disbelieving sound. Of all the things she could've said, I didn't expect that. "I didn't fall for this at the party. I'm not falling for it now."

"For tongue diagnosis!" Chryssy says in response to my reaction. "Just a quick peek."

I stand and back away. "You mean you want to confirm how imbalanced you think I am? No thanks," I say. "You're not getting anywhere near my tongue. And you know enough of my secrets from your online sleuthing."

Chryssy doesn't push it. "There's still time. I'm going to get a look at that tongue one way or another."

I start dialing Jim's number. "Not if I can help it."

Chapter 6

CHRYSSY

Are you sleepless in Seattle?" a low voice asks outside the edge of the garden, startling both me and Goji. I spin around, holding my shovel up in front of me for protection.

I peer over the flowers to find Vin lying on his leather jacket on the grass, his arms crossed behind his head.

"You scared me!" I say, my heart hammering. "And I'm actually sleepless just outside of Seattle."

Vin stands and pulls his jacket on, his eyes narrowing when he sees the shovel. I wonder how seeing me in my Billy Joel sleepy shirt, dirt-covered leggings, and slippers, with a shovel and a bunny accomplice, changes his idea of who I am.

Now that we're set to go on two dates while also simultaneously living together, the tension between us has taken on a new shape.

"Your hair's wet," I blurt out to fill the silence.

"I figured I'd shower while you were out," he says. "I didn't want to get in your way."

"No, that's fine," I say, lowering the shovel. "It's just, Auntie Violet's always telling me not to go to bed with wet hair. You have to keep the back of your neck warm and dry to prevent wind invasions. It's a vulnerable spot."

"Uh, okay," Vin says, pushing his fingers through the damp strands. "I'll dry it. I can't take any chances. I don't have time to get sick." He directs his attention to the hole I've dug, his mouth tightening into a firmer line. "If that's for me, you've got a ways to go. Is it because of all the noise?"

"In case you weren't aware, you've been practicing all night," I say. "But no. You're safe tonight."

He nods. "I seem to always be intruding on your space. Sorry. I'll leave you be. Good night."

"Or is it good morning?" I pose.

Vin pushes back his sleeve, noting the time on his fancy-looking watch. "One a.m. It's the in-between hours, so neither?"

In the low light, I can barely make out Vin's features until he steps closer to me. The solar-powered lights faintly brighten his face from below.

"I'm going to finish...this." I redirect my attention, bending down to push the wrapped-up writing box into the dug-out space.

"Here, let me help," Vin says, entering the garden through a metal circular opening. He looks up at it and raises his eyebrows. "Moon gate?"

"You can't have a moon garden without a moon gate," I say. "I'd show you the moonflowers, but they haven't bloomed yet." I nod toward the white peonies. "Those, though, are close. I'm hoping they'll open in a few weeks."

Vin kneels beside me as Goji hops over to him. He wiggles the writing box until it fits, the lid a foot below ground level, and then shovels dirt over the top until it's fully covered.

"Thanks," I say, watching the veins in Vin's hands swell with each movement. "Glad to know you're a bury-the-box type of roommate."

He taps the top of the dirt before laying the shovel down next to it. "You want to tell me why we're burying this thing behind a bush in the middle of the night, early morning? And I don't think it's actually because you have too many cookbooks."

I sigh. "It's better you don't know."

"Chryssy, if we're going to be fake-dating each other, it needs to be based on a foundation of truth and trust," Vin says in a mock-serious tone.

"Hilarious," I say, laughing despite myself. "I don't know how else to say this, Vin, so I'm not going to sugarcoat it. I'm cursed goods."

I have no idea what compels me to reveal this to Vin so easily, but I do. I feel relief when he doesn't laugh or look at me like I'm being overly dramatic.

"What kind of curse are we talking here? Like, what's the degree of cursage?" Vin asks, his concern genuine sounding.

Where do I even start?

According to the family legend, the curse goes like this: The women of the Hua family are doomed to never find lasting love.

The origin of how this came to be varies slightly from person to person, but the common thread of the story is that my great-great-great-great-grandmother, Lily, stole an herbal blend from 4G, my great-great-great-great-grandfather, and destroyed the recipe. Deprived of the blend, the people in town cast her out, condemning her to never find long-lasting love again after what she did.

Lily left her husband and her children, and ran away with the blend to profit on her own. No one knows what happened to her after that, but her fate lived on through the children she left behind. It was from that point forward that the Hua women were cursed to being brokenhearted. Lily became known to us as Èyùn. Bad luck. Misfortune. The cause of denying us happy-ever-afters. The curse even followed my great-grandmother to America in the 1900s. So much for a clean start.

If someone had told me this about their own family, I don't know that I'd have believed them. I'd think it was the stuff of folklore and bitter family drama and gossip. But I believe in my family's curse because I haven't ever been given a reason not to. Not only have I experienced breakup after breakup, but I've seen the curse come true with my own eyes, from my parents' divorce to every single other relationship a Hua woman has ever had.

Auntie Rose and her wife's values didn't align, and one morning, she woke up in an empty bed.

Auntie Violet's husband died young.

Auntie Daisy's boyfriend just wanted a wife, but she wanted to work.

Auntie Primrose's husband was in the relationship for her money.

Auntie Marigold's husband cheated.

Great-Aunt Angelica's husband had a secret second family.

My cousin Cassia's ex couldn't handle long distance.

My second cousin Poppy was dumped for the prom queen on prom night.

As for my parents and their divorce, my mom simply blames the curse.

So on and so forth. We've seen and heard it all through the generations. As for my uncles? They all have happy, long relationships and marriages.

Every time the Hua women see each other's heartbreak, we're affirmed in our beliefs. Kind of like a collective fool-me-once mentality. Instead of trading beauty secrets, we trade tips about how to protect our hearts.

The rule I now live by? Prevention is the cure. It's a key TCM principle that I think applies perfectly to our situation.

Prevent yourself from falling in love, and you avoid the pain.

Prevent yourself from making future plans with someone, and you don't end up bitter and hurt.

"As a Hua woman, I'll never find lasting love," I share. "Every last one of us has been broken up with."

I elaborate with details about my family's herbal blend, the betrayal, and the long line of heartbreak through the generations.

"And you're trying to bury the curse?" Vin asks, eyeing the fresh burial spot.

"That's the Curse Box. Apparently, it's filled with Èyùn's belongings and reminders of why we are the way we are. We don't look at it or touch it or *open* it. Apparently, the last time someone—Auntie Chamomile, maybe?—opened it, her husband left her a week later. It was clearly a little too discoverable," I explain. "This way it won't be."

He processes what I've said. "You really believe in it? The curse?"

I scrunch my nose at the bluntness of his question. I don't mind the straightforwardness, but it's strange hearing him say those words. For him to know that such a thing exists for me, for my family. It's freeing, in a way, not having to hide it from someone outside of the Hua bloodline.

"I have no reason not to," I answer honestly. "I've never spoken about this with anyone other than family. One of my aunties loves to talk about it, but beyond a small circle of people, it's private." I peek up at Vin to analyze his reaction. "It was all my mom talked about with my dad, so I thought that if I did the opposite in the relationships I've had, maybe that would do the trick. Not that we're in a relationship. Or even a fake one." I give him a look. "But that doesn't work, either."

"Is that why you agreed to me breaking up with you?" he asks, tilting his head back. "What was it your auntie said? You have nothing to lose."

"What's one more breakup?"

Vin watches me for a second, his eyes not judging but surprisingly kind. "I don't take the responsibility of knowing lightly," he says, brushing dirt off his hands.

"You're not skeptical. Why?"

Vin looks up at the moon, and I steal those few seconds to take in his face. "In classical music, there's the Curse of the Ninth from the late Romantic period. A belief that the Ninth Symphony is the composer's last. They're destined to die writing it or right after. Beethoven. Schubert. Mahler." He shrugs. "Is it superstition? I have no clue. It was a somewhat small number of composers, just like this curse is limited to your family. Still, real people died." Vin tucks his hands into his pockets as he exhales. Finally, in a gravelly voice he says, "And I was a prodigy. That in and of itself was like a curse."

This admission surprises me. "I've never thought about it like that."

"As you know, you learn to live with it," he says. After a few long beats, he adds, "So, this garden. You created it?"

I'm thankful for the change in conversation. "I wanted it to be more of an escape," I share. "When I first came to live here, I couldn't sleep. It wasn't just a me thing. Many of the guests who come through can't sleep when they're heartbroken. I wanted to create a place where people could come at night and have something pretty to look at."

I lift my quilt off the ground and pull it around myself. We stroll between rows of low-growing candytuft flowers, their bright white petals gleaming in the sliver of moonlight. Above us, more dimly lit stars come into view as my eyes adjust to the darkness.

"It's beautiful," he says, looking around. "Those ones are practically glowing." Vin takes a few steps over to the honeysuckle and leans down to get a closer look.

"I like that this garden forces you to be more present. Where you step, what's around you, what your heightened senses are telling you. You're forced to pay closer attention," I say, looking at the surrounding plants. There's just enough moonlight to see the white flowering quince in full bloom. "How often do we spend time in the dark when we're awake?"

"I don't know. I think we try to avoid the darkness," Vin says, dropping one knee to the ground.

With his arm draped over his thigh, he looks up at me and smiles. His entire face lights up, the creases around his eyes shadowed by the garden lights. Goji hops over to Vin as he slowly reaches out and strokes the fur on Goji's nose and between his ears. Goji leans into it, closing his eyes more with each pet.

The smile on Vin's face grows, revealing a row of straight white teeth. Goji hops into his lap, and Vin lets him.

He takes Goji in his arms, then stands to face me. His typically straight posture is slightly bent, resembling the way he positions himself around his cello. For someone who doesn't rest, it almost looks like he's…relaxed? Goji looks as content as Vin does.

"Being in the moon garden helps me view things differently," I say, guiding Vin around. "The plants and flowers take on different shapes, textures, and colors if you pay close enough attention. It's active out here, yet still peacefully quiet."

"Peaceful?" Vin stops walking and closes his eyes. "This place is too quiet."

"One of the perks of being on an island," I say.

Vin opens one of his eyes and keeps the other one squinted shut. "And now you've reminded me that I'm trapped," he says with a smirk. "Thanks for that."

I smile in return. "Depends on how good of a swimmer you are. Though your cello wouldn't make the journey, I'm afraid. Guess you're stuck here with me."

Vin holds my eye contact. "If I had to be stuck on an island, I'd want it to be with you."

My heart takes on a mind of its own and skips a beat. But then Vin says, "Because you know how to cook with plants. We'd survive anywhere."

I take a deep breath to calm my elevated heart rate. "Glad I can be of practical use to you. If I were stuck with you, at least I'd know I'd die to good music."

"Everyone needs an exit song," Vin jokes.

We walk side by side through the garden, unintentionally bumping each other every few steps. To my left, white ranunculus with multilayered petals float cloudlike against a sky of dark green leaves.

"What are you trying to view differently?" Vin asks, disrupting the quiet.

I fill my lungs with cool night air before exhaling sharply. "Kind of everything? Truthfully, I can't believe I agreed to pretend to date you so quickly. In my line of work, I'm so careful about fakes," I say. "I spend a lot of time thinking about what we consume. There are a lot of fake foods out there. Honey, cheese, olive oil, meat, seafood, spices. Even tea! A lot of tea out there is stale, contains artificial additives, glue, billions of microplastics. And that's just in one tea bag. Then there are promises and plans that turn out to be fake. And, you know, a lot of people think what I do is fake."

"TCM?" Vin asks.

I nod. "Some call it a pseudoscience. And don't even get me started on acupuncture."

Vin looks up at the night sky for so long I think he's started counting the stars. "I can understand the hesitation around pretending. For your work to be undervalued and misunderstood, that's tough," he says cryptically.

"Really?" I ask, watching his expression remain serious. "People think you're amazing for being able to play the way you do. No way people can doubt your skills."

"Can they doubt yours? Last I checked, you're good at what you do."

"Yeah. There's so much skepticism around TCM. Especially in America, it doesn't fit into people's idea of what medicine is or should be," I explain as we continue our garden stroll. "That's why I love working at the inn. People come to us here. We don't have to explain ourselves as much. We can focus on helping people."

"What about your product?" Vin asks. "That'll be going out to a lot more people than the ones who visit you here."

"Yeah, I hope. Even though we're selling flower tea, I expect push-back still, given the brand, the inn, Qi," I admit.

He absentmindedly reaches under his forearm, which Goji's nestled on. He squeezes as though it might be irritated.

"You okay?" I ask before realizing I've given away that I've been watching. "I have a balm that will relax your muscles."

"I'm fine," he says, quickly moving his hand away from his arm.

It's here in the darkness, next to the snowdrops, their bell-shaped heads drooping as though they've fallen asleep standing up, that Vin comes into focus a little clearer. My heightened senses about him are slowly sharpening. The reputation, the music, the label—could these be the source of his heartbreak?

With Vin staying here and us going on dates, maybe I'll have a chance to find out.

Being in the garden activates a memory. "A couple of years ago, Auntie Daisy planted dahlias in the main garden," I say, gesturing across the field. "She wanted to surprise my great-aunt Angelica with flower garlands for her birthday. The snails were hungry that year and ate all the young dahlia leaves. It needed reviving, so we planted a bunch of rosemary next to it. Last year, there were no problems."

Vin looks lost. "Congratulations?"

"Companion planting," I say. "It's when different plant species are grown together. The idea is that they'll benefit each other and support the overall growth. Rosemary has a strong scent that repels pests from damaging the dahlias, while the dahlias are aesthetically pleasing and pop against the green herb."

"Great idea," Vin says. "And?"

"I know it's just two events, but it's kind of like we're dahlias and rosemary," I clarify.

Vin looks over at me. "Who's the arm candy and who's the one with the strong smell?"

"I think we both know the answer to that," I retort.

"What are you saying?" he asks.

I stifle a laugh. "I'm saying maybe the lavender-mint bath bomb might be a good idea."

Vin flashes me a fake smile. "I didn't realize comedy hour started at midnight."

"We're different, but maybe with these dates, we actually will help each other," I say.

Vin gently pets a sleeping Goji in his arms. A shiver runs down my spine at the sight, and I pull the quilt tighter against myself as a shield from what must be the dropping temperature.

"The charity event is in Vegas, and it's their biggest fundraiser of the year," Vin says. "We should get a lot of eyes on us."

"Same with my family event," I say. "Great-Aunt Angelica loves to talk, so word about us will spread. One of my second cousins—she's a social media influencer—will be streaming the whole thing, too."

"We just need to be seen. We'll keep it as surface level as Wikipedia," Vin says, shrugging. "You practically know everything you need to."

We've rounded back to the moonflowers. I hold the cone-shaped bud of one against the palm of my hand.

For someone whose life is so out in the open, Vin is a mystery to me. I want to know more about the man behind the prodigy persona. None of my research told me that Vin only opens up late at night, hates lavender, and doesn't own a couch. An urge flows through me to get to the heart of Vin, and maybe a small part of me wants to see if I'm right that there's a little bit of breakage there.

I stand here in my slippers next to the unbloomed moonflowers, facing a man holding my bunny, and hear myself say, "I can promise you this. Even though it won't be real, I won't phone it in. I'll be such a good date."

Vin's mouth quirks before he full-on smiles, and it nearly splits me in two. The way his eyes crinkle tells me there's nothing fake about it.

"I don't love the lying aspect of this, but for what it's worth, maybe sometimes fake can be good?" he says. "I heard somewhere that fake plants and pictures of nature can have a positive impact on our moods, so it's also a scientific fact."

Under the stars, I beam at him. "That was episode five. I thought you said you only listened to one or two episodes of my podcast."

Vin's muscle flexes down the length of his jaw. "Yeah. That was one of the two."

"Riiiight," I say, biting down a smile.

"Right," he echoes, rocking back on his heels.

Goji stirs in Vin's arms, and he lets him down on the ground. As he does, Vin's usual strand of hair flops across his forehead, altering the way the moonlight falls over it.

Seeing Vin in this way suddenly feels too intimate.

All I have to do is get through two dates with this man and endure yet another breakup.

My cursed love life has been training me for this moment.

I've *totally* got this.

Chapter 7

CHRYSSY

Five days after making a very questionable decision, I find myself strapped to Vin as we cling to each other for dear life.

Literally.

We're about to jump together off a building eight hundred feet above the ground while attached to nothing more than a thick cable and a few straps. It was explained to me as a decelerator descent, which is essentially a fast-moving, roof-to-ground chair lift in reverse. Minus the chair.

I've always imagined what it would feel like to be the seed of a dandelion floating through the air. Now I finally get my chance.

I admire the expanse of Las Vegas below us as we stand near the edge of the hotel we're about to leap from while event goers wait in anticipation. Vin and I are pressed up against each other for our tandem jump. We're buckled and clipped into the right cords that will allegedly support us both, and are being safety checked for a third time. Against my throat, Vin's chest throbs. His heartbeat is like a Ping-Pong ball bouncing off my head.

"You doing okay?" I ask after a long stretch of silence. Vin hasn't said a single word since we started this entire process.

Vin grunts. "Fine."

I tilt my head back to get a good look at his face. His eyes are closed, his pinched eyebrows creating a deeply grooved quotation mark.

He's scared.

Tandem-jumping off this building together now sounds like a terrible idea.

"We don't have to do this," I say softly, feeling my own heartbeat quickening in parallel to his. "We can turn back now."

"It's too late," he mumbles. He blinks one eye open, peering out over the ledge before squeezing it shut again. In this brief second, I notice that his pupils are dilated, the black circles dominating the light brown.

"Remind me why we're doing this again?" I ask.

"For the kids."

"Right. The kids," I echo. "What if I tell them it was me? I couldn't jump." I place my hand over my chest. "You know, I am starting to feel a little nauseous."

"That wouldn't explain me. I'd have to go solo," he says, his voice shaky. "That's worse."

Though nonexistent at first, my nerves start to mirror Vin's, increasing with every passing second. Through his turquoise bodysuit, I can feel excess heat. "Okay, we're both feeling sick?" I suggest.

"I made a promise," Vin says. "The only path down is that way."

"Would it be easier if you threw me off?" I offer in an attempt to make him laugh.

An immediate smile forms on Vin's face, but no sound accompanies it. "We're attached. I'd go right along with you," he says skeptically.

"Well, yes. Throw me, jump yourself, whatever you need to get through this. A little perspective shift might help," I say.

He groans in response.

The waiting isn't helping. It's as though being this high off the ground is making time slow down, and the longer we're up here, the more terrifying it's becoming. We're instructed to wait for the signal from below when the Take a Bow director finishes his introductions of the program and us. Once that happens, the crew will clear us to jump. Until then, all we've got is time.

I spin one of my little flower stud earrings. "Okay, uh"—thinking, thinking—"I have this flower," I say, holding up my fist like I'm really holding one in it. "Do you like the smell?"

Vin's eyes slowly open. "What?"

"Do you like the smell?" I repeat, holding my fist a little higher. "Of my flower."

He makes a face. "Is the altitude getting to you?"

"There's a good chance, but indulge me, will you?" I ask. "It's one of the best-smelling flowers there is."

Vin narrows his eyes at me but leans his head down to play pretend with me.

He sniffs the imaginary flower. "Smells like exhaust, false hope, and regret."

"My flower smells nothing like those things," I say, biting down a smile. "Try it again. For longer this time."

He seems resigned, but Vin does as I instruct. He takes a long, deep breath in through his nose.

"Nice, right?" I ask.

Vin does it once more, deeply inhaling.

He doesn't have to tell me he's calming down. I can feel it. His thumping heart has slowed a beat. Vin's contracting pupils also show me.

He smirks. "I see what you did there."

"I just wanted you to enjoy my imaginary flower," I say, grinning back. "Can you smell it once more, but this time release the breath through your mouth?"

Vin does, and his shoulders drop an inch.

I look out past him at the view that I'd typically see from an airplane: sky for miles. Until we're prompted to leap, this is our hangout spot for the foreseeable future. If I can keep Vin breathing—and talking—we can get through this.

"When you said 'nonprofit event,' I imagined something kind of glamorous like, I don't know, the Met Gala or something," I say.

"The Met Gala isn't as glamorous as it looks," he says, still pale. "But I thought this event would be, too. No wonder they wanted me to have a plus-one. Normally these things are boring, red-carpet situations. Take a Bow wanted to shake up expectations for their Soar for Strings event. The organization raises money for string instruments for children who can't afford them."

"They did a good job shaking," I say. "This is the opposite of boring."

Vin nods one too many times. "I think that was the point. This gets people's attention, which is ultimately good. Every jump raises money, so us doing this together is two times the amount. Our soar is going to buy ten children good beginner cellos."

The thought of kids playing their first chords on a violin or cello or guitar comforts me. I close my eyes and can practically hear the bow scraping against the strings. It takes me a few moments to realize that it's the clicking of a carabiner that's making the noise.

"Have they tested this thing? Maybe we should've let Yo-Yo Ma go first," I say.

I hold my hand steady against Vin's back, feeling his muscles contract under his bodysuit as he shifts his footing. Vin's hands are around me, too, his biceps bulging around my upper arms.

"Guess we're just diving headfirst into this date, huh?" I babble, making pathetic jokes. "No better place to go for a fake date than Vegas."

"Technically, we're not jumping headfirst," he adds. "It's more of a vertical zipline straight down."

"Fine. Dive in *feet*first. You sure you don't want to up the stakes and get married tonight?" I ask. "Dip our toes all the way in? Divorce is much messier than a breakup, though."

"We haven't tried that angle yet," Vin jokes.

"And with the prenup I'd need you to sign, it's better to keep things clean when you end this in a few months." I maintain a serious look. "Why do you look so shocked? You're not walking away with half of our future tea empire."

Another ghost of a smile appears on Vin's face as he shakes his head. A desire flows through me to help distract him more.

"I'm rambling, aren't I? Nerves, probably," I admit. "I have no idea what I'm doing."

"This whole…thing…is new territory for us both," Vin says.

I wrinkle my nose. "Well, yes, the fake part. But also, with dating. It's been a while for me."

Vin looks surprised. "What's a while?"

"Two—" I start, coughing out "—years. Not like it makes a difference to me, but I'm a little rusty, so you're going to need to take the lead. I'm prepared to be wooed. Do whatever it is you do."

"With all my spells and love potions?" he asks, recalling my words from the party. A quiet sound escapes his mouth.

I smile. "Oh, good. I'm glad we can laugh about that now."

Vin grunts. "That wasn't me laughing. You'll know when I laugh."

"Why? Is it a loud, barky type of laugh? Something that might shock us all?" I ask, widening my eyes for effect.

"If the rumors are true, it's throatier, I guess," he responds sarcastically.

"I'll believe it when I hear it," I say, catching him in a moment when we're both smiling. "I know it's only a couple of dates, but I wonder if it would help to have some rules."

"Rules?" Vin asks, one eyebrow raised in question.

"For…us. For this," I say, gesturing between us with my chin. "What do we say to people tonight? And fair warning, my family will absolutely have questions. Like, are we in love? In strong like? How much touching should there be? Do we have nicknames for each other? Oh my god, am I a Chaobreaker?"

Vin scoffs. "You don't strike me as one."

I raise my eyebrows in return. "And why is that?"

"Name one of our albums."

"Oh! There's the one with you and Leo on the cover," I recall, though I could've guessed that and still gotten it right. "You both have…cellos in front of you?" When my mind goes blank, I ask, "Can I phone an auntie?"

Vin's mouth curves into a smile. "You're not a superfan, and we're not in love. You like me for me and not because of my music," he says, his voice shifting into something softer.

I nod in agreement. "Great. That I can do. And we'll touch only when necessary and exclusively in public. Right now qualifies as one of those moments," I say, gesturing around us.

I look out past the crowd waiting for us down below and take in the flat surrounding area. The beige desert is dotted with trees and framed by navy mountains in the distance. It's a stark contrast from the concentration of hotel and casino lights that create an intense glow. As the seconds pass, the neon from the Vegas Strip twinkles brighter and brighter as the periwinkle sky fades into darkness. Watching the sun set from up here is beautiful. The proximity to Vin is also surprisingly not terrible, either.

I straighten my shoulders. "Just no hand-holding, okay?"

"You have a weird thing about fingers or something?" Vin asks, seemingly amused.

"It's too . . . romantic," I reveal.

"And romance is bad?"

"Romance is like wearing rose-colored glasses," I say. "It's too intimate. It creates confusion and makes relationships complicated. Better to keep things practical."

"I don't disagree," Vin says.

"Can a heartbreaker even *do* romance?" I ask.

"I guess I've always waited to see if a relationship will go anywhere before things get to that level," he says. "Romance is best left to music."

I relate to his need to remain clearheaded.

"Great. We'll agree to agree. No romance. We can link arms, or you can put your arm over my shoulders. I'm even comfortable kissing if we absolutely must," I say, tripping over my words at this offering. "Not that we'd need to kiss on our first date. Or even the second, for that matter."

"It might up the believability," Vin ponders. "And other people don't know how many dates we've been on."

Naturally, his words make me look at his lips. I can't help it. They're *right there*, just inches from my own lips.

Kissing. Something else I didn't consider when I agreed to be his date.

For some reason, I go along with him. "True. If we come out strong, we won't have to prolong this."

"Exactly," Vin says. A few seconds later, he asks, "You're okay with kissing, but not hand-holding? Isn't kissing romantic?"

"Not really. It's so showy," I reveal. "Hand-holding is way more intimate. These little extensions of you clinging to someone else, even when no one knows about it because you just have to be touching in a private moment. Hand-holding keeps you connected for longer, too, even when you're not kissing."

"I guess looking at tongues is how you do your job," Vin says, shrugging. "Works for me. I can't risk anything happening to my hands."

"And don't bring me flowers for the family thing," I add.

"Too cliché?"

"Not even," I say. "It'd be like growing a green pepper and letting it sit out to die. Flowers aren't for display. They're for healing. And it'll spark an entire debate about which flower is best among my family. You don't want to be caught in the middle of that. Trust me."

Vin grumbles in acknowledgment. "Noted."

"And, uh, we're not going to be...seeing other people, right?" I ask. "I just think it would be good for us to only be with each other until our deal is done."

"That's the only way I do relationships," Vin says.

I nod. "Cool. If you get numbers or anything, don't feel like you need to reject them on my behalf," I add. "But maybe just call once you've broken up with me? Of course, I can't tell you how to live your life—"

"Chryssy, I'm not going to be calling anyone," Vin says, his intense eyes staying on me as he says this. My awareness of his hands on my back heightens as heat floods through me. "Is there anything we *can* do? Besides linking arms and kissing."

I swallow. "Right. We could work on nicknames. I did like Vin Vin."

"I don't do nicknames," Vin says.

I flash him a sweet smile. "Whatever you say, Vinny. If you want this to look real, then we need to pay attention to the details."

Vin looks more horrified at that than he does at our current situation. "No."

"Okay, I'll stop, Vinley. Vinster?" I offer. "Needs some work-shopping."

Vin groans. "I despise all of those. No nicknames."

"Maybe the nickname *is* your name," I say, giving up. "Like, we're the couple that doesn't need nicknames, you know?"

Vin glances down at me. "Would you like a nickname?"

"Yes. Yes I would, Vinnyboy," I say.

"I could call you, I don't know, Dandelion, but that seems weird."

"Because I'm a weed or an herb?" I ask, feigning offense. "Or a shed?"

A short laugh escapes Vin, and my hands move with his body as it relaxes a little more. I snap to attention. The rumors are true. His laugh is throaty and deep, and I want to hear it again. I'll do whatever I have to do to make him laugh so I can hear it even just once more.

"I'm undecided," he says. "No, this is good. Onstage performing, you need to commit. People can hear half-assed-ness. We don't want to half-ass this."

"Then let's sell it, Vinny-poo," I tease.

"Absolutely not." Vin grimaces, but there's warmth in his voice.

Down on Planet Earth, the director's speech echoes, barely reaching us: "And now, Vin Chao and his girlfriend, Chrysanthemum Hua Williams."

"Thought that might be a nice touch," Vin says. He sounds pleased. "Really get your name out there."

I nod. "That should make it very clear. Our work here is done."

Before we can call this off and back down, a woman with a headset waves us forward and guides us to the end of the diving-board-like ledge. Our feet are inches away from air.

Our moment is here. It's time to soar.

I smush my cheek against Vin's chest. All sounds, lights, and nerves still as I grip tighter and press my body as close to his as it can go. Vin wraps his arms around me, securing me in place.

"We're really doing this?" I ask.

"Here goes nothing," Vin says.

We jump feetfirst and a swooping feeling—like when you miss the last step—swirls through my stomach. My scream turns into a laugh, wind whipping through my hair.

Forget trying to take in the view or being a dandelion seed gently blowing on a breeze. This is an aggressive gust, and everything's a blur: the city's flashing signs, the replica landmarks, the emerging stars against the dusky sky.

When we near the ground after what simultaneously feels like forever and no time at all, we brace ourselves as the cord we're attached to slows our momentum. It's maybe the most ungraceful touchdown this landing pad has ever witnessed. I topple onto Vin, sliding over him as adrenaline courses through my veins.

"So sorry for screaming in your ear the entire way down," I say, catching my breath. My stomach is unsettled from the sudden rush of falling.

"Did you? I blacked out. What just happened?" Vin says. His hair is windswept, but the color is back in his cheeks. We end up lying sideways on the mat, our bodies still strapped together. When Vin leans back, I'm pulled with him. Wherever he goes, I go, and vice versa. He lets out a whoosh of air as I collapse onto his stomach. "You okay?"

I pat down the side of my body. "Still in one piece."

My senses come back to me, and I finally hear the clapping of the large group of donors around us. They seem eager to see Vin, who gives a small wave to the crowd from the ground.

One of the people on the jump crew unbuckles us in seconds, a realization that makes me chuckle given how long it took to strap us in. I roll off of Vin, slowly separating from him like cheesy pull-apart bread. Ugh. How can I think of food at a time like this?

As we stand, our attention is drawn to the six-foot cardboard guitar cutout propped up by a microphone stand. A volunteer colors in with green marker along the neck of the guitar the amount of money we raised by soaring. The line moves from $15,000 to $35,000. More claps all around.

"Our leap raised $20,000?" I ask. "Get back up there. Let's go again!"

"Hey, Vin! Chrysanthemum! Smile!" a photographer calls out to us. "Where's Leo tonight?"

"Couldn't make it," Vin responds, keeping it vague.

"Glad to have you here," the photographer says. "Mind if I take some pictures?"

We stay close together, posing in our bodysuits, unkempt hair and all.

Tentatively, I reach up and push Vin's rogue strand of hair off his forehead.

I feel a light tingle in my other hand as Vin's hand grazes mine.

"Shit. Sorry," he says, pulling his hand back. "Totally accidental."

A smile breaks across my face. I have too much adrenaline after all that to hold any emotions back. Flashes from the camera remind me of where we are and why we're here.

"Give us a kiss!" the photographer shouts.

Vin looks at me, his eyes intensely dark. "I'll follow your lead."

I nod, and the next thing I know, I'm swept up into Vin's arms, his hands cradling my lower back as he lifts me against his chest. I wrap my arms over his shoulders, latching onto his bodysuit to stabilize myself.

Our faces are now centimeters apart as Vin slides his fingers along the back of my neck while mine run through his tousled hair. He gently presses his thumb on my chin, his fingertip grazing the edge of my bottom lip.

In less than two heartbeats, our lips meet. My stomach flips and flops, but this time for a very different reason.

We pull away from each other. My eyes don't move from Vin's.

This man is potentially dangerous.

I need to make sure.

I tug him toward me, our lips meeting again.

Yep. He's a dangerous one.

More flashes, more clicking.

Moment captured. Message sent.

Chapter 8

VIN

As Chryssy and I walk down the winding hallways in our Vegas hotel, I distract myself by thinking about stage lighting, the color of our merchandise, and what song to open each show with. I push to the front of my mind anything related to work, so I don't think about the kiss.

Sure, I've kissed my fair share of women, but the kisses weren't like that.

Hats. We should sell hats on tour.

I press my tongue against the back of my teeth to numb the sensation of how it felt in Chryssy's mouth and how her rosebud lips blossomed with the lightest pressure. How is it possible that the woman tastes like lavender, too? Oh god. Am I starting to enjoy the taste of lavender?

Shit. One kiss and this is what it's done to me. Am I really that rusty? The whole thing lasted no more than three seconds. Then again, it's been a while since my last girlfriend. This is a natural physical response.

We make another turn, and a long stretch of yet another hallway greets us. I roll both of our suitcases beside me on the thick carpeting.

Vinyl. We'll have a special run made exclusively for this tour.

I shake it off, chalking up these feelings to adrenaline and leaping off a building, something I'm pretty sure insurance would not have covered.

Dammit. Does this hallway never end?

A few more turns later and we finally reach the room. I tap the key card against the black box on the door until it beeps, gaining us entry.

I rethink why I was so eager to get here. For the first time since the kiss, Chryssy and I will be alone.

I glance over at Chryssy, and she's frowning, our earlier moment together hopefully not on her mind.

"Eight-oh-two? We're not staying in a penthouse?" she asks.

I push our suitcases into the room's entrance. "We leave tomorrow," I say. "Why pay for all that space when this has everything we need? There's a bed. Shower. Sink. Toilet."

Chryssy explores the standard hotel room, opening every dresser and desk drawer, flipping open binders with menus and spa services. When she sees one bed, she frowns.

"Don't worry, you're in the next room." I hand her a plastic key card and point to a door in the wall. "You can open it on the other side, though there's probably no reason for that."

"Connecting rooms?"

"Optics."

"Right. If we were really dating, we wouldn't be in separate rooms," she says, slapping the key card against her palm. "Probably could've prevented this on the top floor. Isn't that for VIPs only?"

"You didn't strike me as a penthouse kind of person," I say.

Chryssy tucks a loose strand of hair behind her ear. "This discovery surprises me, too," she says, half-serious. "I'm coming across the wrong way, probably. This hotel is really nice. I'll admit I wanted a peek into the lifestyles of the rich and famous. I just imagined, with you being as famous as you are, you'd be in a hotel room with the works."

"The works?"

"Yeah, like those ones with hot tubs in the middle of the living room. Or a pool table off the kitchen. Or five rooms, one to match whatever mood you're in. Your entire life is about entertaining people and making them feel things. I guess I thought, when you're not onstage, you'd want to stay in hotel rooms that, I don't know, entertain you?"

"And you think a hot tub in the living room would entertain me?" I ask, amused.

Chryssy smiles. "Well, not *you*, but yes, regular people."

"Like you."

My sarcasm lands.

"Exactly," she says with a laugh. "A hot tub for all of my bath bombs."

"You want lifestyles of the rich and famous? How's this?" I walk over to the window and fling the curtain back dramatically. "Et voilà! We have a view of the Eiffel Tower." The half-size replica glows a coppery orange. "It comes with a light show. It doesn't have the same effect as the sparkle on the real one, but there you go."

"Well, I've never seen the real one, so I'll take it!" she says, snapping a photo with her phone. She swipes into something else on the screen.

"Pictures from tonight are online." She turns her phone toward me. "We must've been pretty convincing. My family texted."

I'm face-to-face with a photo of us midkiss. It's so crisp that I'm practically back on the landing pad. Right there, in high-res, is a permanent reminder that the moment really happened. Chryssy's left hand grips my bodysuit while her other hand wraps around my neck. I'm holding her by the waist, her body arched against mine. A vertical tie connecting two notes.

In the picture, my eyebrows are slightly furrowed, like I'm taking the kiss very seriously. Have I always looked like an angry kisser?

Chryssy looks out the window once more at the Eiffel Tower before grabbing her suitcase and heading toward her door. "Well, it's late. I'll just be…on the other side of the wall. Good night, Vin," she says.

"Good morning, Chryssy."

Thirty minutes later, I'm tossing and turning trying to fall asleep when my phone lights up in the dark. I ignore it, but the screen appears again a few minutes later.

Chryssy (1:16 a.m.): Vinilus.

Chryssy (1:16 a.m.): Vinny bear.

Chryssy (1:16 a.m.): Vin-Vin!

Vin (1:20 a.m.): I refuse to respond to any of those.

Chryssy (1:20 a.m.): What about just V? That's kind of badass.

Vin (1:22 a.m.): I'm sleeping.

Chryssy (1:22 a.m.): Do you always sleep with the light on? I can see a lamp on under your door.

Vin (1:23 a.m.): Fine. I WAS sleeping. What is it?

Chryssy (1:23 a.m.): I'm hungry. Do you want anything from room service? It's twenty-four hours.

At the mention of room service, my stomach grumbles. Now that it's settled after an eight-hundred-foot fall, I could eat.

Vin (1:24 a.m.): Anything good on the menu?

Chryssy (1:24 a.m.): I was thinking the classic room service meal. Caesar salad and fries.

Vin (1:25 a.m.): Sounds good. I'll call.

Chryssy (1:25 a.m.): Wow. You're a great fake date. Extra dressing and a side of ranch, please. Oh! And hot water.

I call room service and ask for everything Chryssy wants, along with a carafe of coffee.

Chryssy (1:29 a.m.): Do you have extra toothpaste?

Vin (1:30 a.m.): You forgot toothpaste?

Chryssy (1:30 a.m.): I didn't forget. I also need floss.

Vin (1:31 a.m.): Tell me you at least have a toothbrush.

Chryssy (1:31 a.m.): Okay…I have a toothbrush…

Vin (1:31 a.m.): You didn't bring a toothbrush, did you?

Chryssy (1:32 a.m.): My toiletry bag may have fallen into the toilet. These non-penthouse bathrooms don't have much counter space.

Vin (1:32 a.m.): Meet me at our connecting doors in a minute.

I put together the equivalent of a dentist to-go bag and meet Chryssy at the doors. Her hair is half up in a little bun, and she's wearing spandex shorts that reach midthigh, an oversize Billy Joel concert tee, and fuzzy socks.

"If you wanted to get in my bed, there's an easier way to do it," I joke. I immediately regret it.

Chryssy arches an eyebrow at me. "Thanks, but no thanks. This, however, *hello*! Ooh, fancy. The whitening kind," she says, reading the toothpaste tube. Her brows crease together. "Do you always carry around extra toothbrushes?"

"Do you always wear shirts with the Piano Man on them?" I ask.

She laughs and stretches out the T-shirt from the bottom. "Tour shirts become sleepy shirts," she says. "I got to see him at Madison Square Garden when I was in New York for an acupuncture conference a couple of years ago." She waves the toothbrush around, still expecting an answer.

"I have extra toothbrushes exclusively for instances like this one," I say before realizing how it sounds.

"Oh?" she says.

I feel the need to clarify. "*Not* for unexpected night guests. When Leo and I were younger, before all of this—actual hotels—we traveled around Europe touring on our own playing little pubs and clubs. We stayed in hostels. My toothbrush fell on the shower floor once. Obviously, I couldn't use it, and it was too late to get a new one. Best to have backups."

Chryssy props her foot against her inner thigh, processing this. "Interesting."

"You asked," I say, moving to shut my door. "I'll let you know when the food's here."

"You're not staying? Are you working on something?" she asks, opening her door wider and gesturing for me to come in. Her room looks like mine but reversed. There's a movie playing on her TV.

My hand grips the gold doorknob. Sharing a small space with Chryssy right now doesn't feel like a smart idea. "I have work to do."

"Well, you can't practice right now. Can you do whatever work it is over here?" She sits on one side of the bed, tapping the other side. "It's my Yin Night. Want to join?"

"On the bed?"

"You're acting like our bodies weren't clinging to each other for dear life tonight," she says. "Given that this is all fake, I'd say we're safe. Or you can sit in the desk chair."

"Sure, I'll answer emails later. So. This night of yours. What have I agreed to?" I ask as I jump onto the bed.

Chryssy laughs as she's jostled side to side. "Every week, I try to have what I call a Yin Night. In med school, I got sick and had to actively force myself to rest. I get overwhelmed if I don't maintain it."

"You got sick? Are you okay?" I ask without considering my words first. "Shit. That's personal. I'm sorry."

"No, it's okay," Chryssy says. "I don't mind talking about it. I'm much better now." She tucks her knees to her chest. "I went to med school to become a cardiologist. I wanted to help fix people's hearts. The experience was stressful and anxiety-inducing, and I didn't know how to manage it. I wasn't even a year in when I started getting rashes and chronic inflammation. I was sick all the time. I wasn't exercising, was hardly sleeping, and ate food that drained me instead of sustained me. Basically, I didn't take care of myself, and I felt it."

I nod, listening intently. "That sounds…miserable."

Chryssy rests her chin on her arms. "It was. I went to a lot of doctors," she says. "They either prescribed medications or gave me shots. It was so reactive and didn't get to the source of the problem. I felt like I was getting worse. I finally caved, took a break, and went to the inn to heal, thanks to my aunties practically dragging me there." She pauses and smiles. "That's when I fell in love with what my aunties do. I left med school, went through a breakup, attended herbalism school, and have been at the inn ever since."

"I'm glad you're better now," I say, feeling relieved. "And that you still get to help people."

"Thanks," Chryssy says, her eyes meeting mine. "Me too. It felt like I was at an intersection of my life. I needed to reprioritize my health in a way I hadn't before. It was incredibly hard. Still is sometimes. Yin Nights helped me reframe the way I thought about rest at first, and it's just kind of stuck. I don't think I knew the definition of rest during that period of my life."

Her words poke at something deep inside of me, but I don't care to explore the feeling. "So Yin Night is when you rest."

"Yin Night is when I rest," she affirms with a smile. "When I'm not cooking, working on the product line, treating clients, helping my aunties at the inn, gardening, or, you know, fake-dating men I've just met, I'm needlepointing or watching movies."

She sounds as busy as I do. I find unexpected comfort in knowing that she can relate to a hectic schedule.

"I need to be better about doing it more consistently, but it doesn't always happen that way," she adds. "Are you okay with *Sleepless in Seattle*? Unfortunately, it's the only movie on right now that's not about to end."

"Never seen it," I say as I relax into the pillow propped up against the headboard.

Chryssy keeps the volume relatively low so we can still hear each other.

She looks confused. "But you made a joke about it in the moon garden."

"It felt relevant. Like if there were a movie called *Sleepless in Vegas*, I'd make a joke about that right now."

"That's hardly a joke," Chryssy says. "Prepare yourself. There are commercials."

"With actual products being sold to people?" I ask with dramatized shock.

Based on what's happening, I'd say the movie's halfway through. I'm drawn into it as fifteen or twenty minutes pass. I want to know if Tom Hanks and Meg Ryan will find their way to each other. The movie's surprisingly not terrible, and I like the soundtrack.

During a commercial break, there's a knock at my door. I sign for the food and carry the tray back to Chryssy's room. Under dulled stainless steel plate covers are our salads and the fries in parchment-lined baskets.

Chryssy snorts. "You just missed a ridiculous line," she says. "Rosie O'Donnell tells Meg Ryan, 'You don't want to be in love. You want to be in love in a movie.'" She sighs.

"What's ridiculous about that?" I ask.

Chryssy taps ketchup onto a bread plate before swirling ranch dressing in. "Who wants to be in love in a movie?" she asks with a shake of her head. "No thank you."

"I thought these were hopeful movies with happy endings," I say, chasing a bite of fry with coffee.

She laughs emptily. "Exactly. It's happy. I prefer the tragic ones. Love in movies has stood the test of time. They're as iconic as the love they portray. But I want to be able to relate to something," she says, dragging a fry through her condiment combo. "For me, happy endings aren't real. These movies may sell hope for other people, but for me, they're a lie."

I relate to the first part she said. "The same can be said for classical music. Love standing the test of time in movies," I start, shifting to face Chryssy, "that's how I feel about music. Some of the most iconic classical pieces are over three hundred years old. Music like that isn't made anymore. When I'm playing, I get lost in it. Like it's an out-of-body experience. When I was a kid playing, these complex pieces captured emotions I had never felt in real life. Even so, it was as though I had fully lived it when I played."

"Really? What kinds of emotions?"

"Optimism. Grief. Falling in love. Even heartbreak. The greatest music touches on all those feelings, sometimes in the same song. I suppose some of those I'm still only experiencing through music," I reveal.

Chryssy's eyes linger on mine. "I'd really like to hear you play live sometime," she says. "Somewhere that's not a children's birthday party."

"Yeah, that doesn't count," I say.

"Music videos and recordings don't, either," Chryssy adds. "I want to hear you with my own ears. You know, in case anyone asks for my opinion on your music."

I smirk. "I don't give private concerts."

"What if I wasn't your fake date but the faux love of your life? Would you do it then?" she asks, her expression playful.

"I'd maybe consider it," I say.

She takes a bite of salad and smiles around the fork.

I lift the linen napkin from the breadbasket, revealing warm rolls. "There's this beautiful piece by Chopin that captures what I imagine falling in love feels like," I continue, handing a roll to Chryssy. "It's the third movement, Largo, of his Cello Sonata in G Minor. There's such longing in it. It's slow and soulful, fluctuating between loud and soft. It's filled with desire. The way the cello and piano play off each other is brilliant. It's perfect. It's everything I want in a relationship."

She smiles and bites into the bread. "You don't want to be in love. You want to be in love in a song," she says. "A classic love song, nonetheless."

"You know what? You're right," I say. "And you. You just haven't found the right love song. Your tune's out there somewhere." Shouts on the street temporarily draw my attention. "There's something special about being able to bring the past to life in the present. I wish I got to do it more."

"Like blending classical with rock?" Chryssy asks. "That'd be a cool way to introduce classical music to modern ears."

I nod. "Like how you are with TCM."

Chryssy studies me. "You know, you're not like what I thought you'd be. You're more…human."

"Have been my whole life," I say playfully. "Well, really, cello's been my whole life. It's the most interesting and the most boring thing about me."

"I don't think that's true," Chryssy responds.

I grunt. "You're right. Me being a heartbreaker is probably the most interesting thing."

She smooths out the comforter under her plate. "You've really broken up with every single one of your girlfriends?"

"It's not like I do it for pleasure."

"You do it for pain, then?" Chryssy asks sincerely, holding my eye contact. "I don't say that mockingly. People will often do things because they think they deserve it, even when it hurts. Not saying that's you."

"Sometimes you have to do things that hurt to avoid greater pain," I admit. "But no, I've never wanted to hurt people."

She scrunches her nose. "I think I had the wrong idea of you. I thought you took pride in your dating history."

"And what about me made you think that?" I ask.

Chryssy pierces a crouton with her fork. "Well, your reputation, for one. And probably because I'm biased," she replies honestly. "I see heartbreak all day every day, and I know it all too well from personal experience. It's hard to never have a choice in the matter."

I drain my cup. "It's okay. You're not the first one to think I'm someone I'm not."

"No, but it doesn't mean it's right," Chryssy says, biting a fry in half.

"I'm surprised you eat this stuff," I say toward a mostly devoured room service meal. "I thought you were all about food being healing. Everything you make is relatively healthy."

"Food is medicine, but moderation is also important," she says, studying me. "We seem to have a lot of thoughts about each other, huh?"

"We do, don't we?" I say, tilting my head.

A trace of a smile plays on Chryssy's lips as we go quiet. The low volume of the movie's soundtrack continues playing in the background.

I feel myself almost begin to relax when a notification on my phone vibrates the bed. When I see the subject line, I'm too curious not to tap into the email from Jim.

SUBJECT: Tix Update

Solid jump in tickets after tonight. Colosseum's now 75% sold out. If you need more time for this relationship, no problems on our end. Glad you considered what we discussed. Just don't break her heart too badly. She looks like a nice one. —J

Frustration and relief ripple through me, but hope wins out over both emotions. This media attention should satisfy the label—and maybe even the Chaobreakers—for a while.

I must make a noise because Chryssy asks if something's wrong.

"It's my publicist, Jim. We've sold tickets already," I tell her. "Thanks again for coming with me tonight."

"I'm glad it worked," Chryssy says. "That must make your team happy. They'll have another breakup to promote next week."

"This family event of yours doesn't involve any tall buildings, does it?" I ask, realizing I have no idea what I'll be walking into in a few days.

Chryssy smiles. "There will be no jumping required."

A question I hadn't thought of before comes to me now. "Given your family's curse, are they going to hate me right away?" I ask. "You know, given my track record."

She takes a moment before responding. "I think, once they meet you, any negative preconceptions they have about you will fade." She shifts on her side of the bed to face me. "You were famous before your heartbreaker reputation, weren't you?" Her tone is careful but curious, the skepticism from days ago gone. "I watched a few videos of you playing in concert halls at seven years old. I can't imagine you were breaking hearts at that age."

"Then you underestimate me," I say, grinning.

Chryssy smiles back. "Fair. You were a cute kid."

"Your auntie Daisy was right in that people love the start of things," I say. "But they also love the end and the drama about why something didn't work out and what went wrong. After enough breakups, it became our thing, and before Leo and I knew it, we became known on a more mainstream level. We used to play concert halls. Now? We sell out stadiums and arenas."

"Always through fake dating?" Chryssy asks, blinking innocently at me.

I smirk. "Never," I share. "Not once. Guess that's what a drought of breakups will do."

"I guess, with so many musicians and products," Chryssy says, "having a memorable brand is important."

We're memorable, but is it for the right reasons?

Chryssy rests her hand on my shoulder, as though she can sense my unease, and holds it there for a few long seconds. "There's still a lot of time before tour. You'll sell out," she says.

Admittedly, Chryssy's words are nice to hear.

"Thanks," I mumble, reaching for the carafe. As I lean closer to her, I catch the scent of lilac and roses. The fact that Chryssy smells like a bouquet makes me smile.

"Can I tempt you with flowers instead of a second cup? I think coffee might be affecting your sleep," she offers.

"I'm good." I refill my cup with the still-hot coffee.

"All right, okay." Chryssy grabs a packet from her bag and rips it open, then lets the dry chamomile flowers slide into a cup. "Have you seen our product yet? This is it!"

At the bottom of the cup are a handful of golden flowers waiting to be hydrated. Chryssy pours steaming hot water over them, and the flowers spin around and around. They appear to slowly come back to life, their petals expanding.

"Chamomile is good for the heart, cools heat, and is calming for the spirit," she explains. "Perfect for Yin Night. And digestion."

"That's it? Just the flower?" I ask, adding a splash of milk into my dark roast. My coffee dominates any chamomile scent, the smell of roasted beans relaxing me.

"That's it," she says. "No blends, no added herbs. Nothing fancy, but there's so much good packed into each drink. Flowers are full of Qi, particularly when they've bloomed." She removes a little pot of honey from her bag. "You might recognize this one from my podcast." Her eyes flit up to mine. "It's Auntie Violet's wild violet honey. Cute, huh? Want to try?"

"After how much you hyped it up, of course."

She spreads a thin layer on the remains of my bread. "Honey's also great for your Qi. Yin nourishing and tonifying."

I take a bite, and the sweetness of the combination bursts on my tongue. "That's good," I tell her. "Worthy of an entire episode."

"I think so, too," she says. "It takes twelve bees their entire lives to make just one teaspoon."

I wipe the corner of my mouth with my knuckle. "Sometimes the sweetest creations require a lifetime to produce," I respond, thinking about how sometimes it took Beethoven years to write his compositions.

"If bees can give their best, don't be afraid to give me yours," she says, slowly drizzling the golden nectar into her tea. "I promise I can handle it."

"I don't have any lines," I say. "And I don't even have moves. I just, I don't know, do what comes to mind."

Chryssy stirs her tea, the metal spoon lightly clinking against the sides of her cup. "Really? No moves?" She arches her left eyebrow, lifting the small mole above it. "Come on. Woo me with your best shot."

To appease her, I prop myself up on my elbow, extending my legs out. "How's this?"

"Is that comfortable? You don't look comfortable," Chryssy says, holding back a laugh.

I chuckle. "I'll let you know when my arm goes numb."

Chryssy leans back against her pillow and smiles sleepily at me. "It's fine. Pickup lines weren't accounted for in the rules," she says, cradling the mug between her hands. "Next time you can try the tea."

Next time. With those two small words, I'm both panicked and reassured that there will be such a thing. Because of course there will be. I willingly signed up for it.

What I can't quite grasp is why I'm suddenly too warm at the thought or why my heart rate has noticeably picked up at the solidification of those unknown but certain plans.

So much for Yin Night. I store away the mental note: Next time, accept Chryssy's cooling chamomile tea.

Next time.

Chapter 9

VIN

It's like being in a garden when Chryssy talks to her family. But in this setting, they talk back.

"Auntie Marigold, you're looking very pretty today. Here's a hat for you," she says to the woman she explained is her first cousin once removed.

Marigold pulls the bucket hat over her curly dark hair. "Oh good, this will keep me shaded. I also need water, please," she says, stretching out her arms.

"Here. Let me know if you need more," Chryssy says, handing her a bottle. "You're growing so nicely."

Marigold laughs and takes a sip.

We move down the line passing out branded swag to the two dozen Hua women who showed up to the outdoor festival that's taking place on Lake Union in Seattle.

"Auntie Primrose, what a beautiful shade of magenta," Chryssy says, handing her a shirt as the woman pouts her lips.

"It really is my color," she agrees. "I want to look good in photos. This is our year. I can feel it." Primrose shakes out the pink shirt and squints at the In Full Bloom logo printed across the front. "Sorry I couldn't invest, Chryssy. I can't afford it right now. I should've had Rose as my lawyer. My ex wouldn't have gotten half."

"Is this where the money would've gone?" Chryssy's great-aunt Angelica asks, pushing up her sleeves. She's decked out in an In Full Bloom hat and shirt and applying sunscreen to her arms. "I thought you needed money for digital things."

"We did," Chryssy says. "I worked an event earlier this month, and we used that money on digital ads and to secure a table at an upcoming tea expo."

A teenage girl comes up to us, her hands occupied with a phone and a paper cup with a whole flower in it. "It's not going to rain, is it?" she says, glaring up at the cloud-speckled sky. "We live in the twenty-first century. How are phones not waterproof yet?"

"It wouldn't be Seattle without the threat of rain," Chryssy says. "You haven't met Vin yet, have you? Vin, this is my second cousin Poppy."

"I know who you are," Poppy says, eyeing me up and down. "You've been very popular online lately."

"Yeah, what's going on with you two?" Angelica asks. "Is this for real?"

"Is who real?" a woman who introduced herself as "Cami, short for Chamomile," asks.

"Chryssy and Vin," Angelica says. "They're dating, apparently. Haven't you seen the photos of them?"

"Is that who you were with, Chryssy?" Cami asks, squinting at me. "It was hard to tell with your faces pressed together."

"Yes, this is who I was with. We're really here together right now, aren't we?" Chryssy says, dodging the question. She wraps her arm around me tentatively, patting my shoulder a couple of times. "Vin's my boy—room...boy." She shakes her head. "Labels aren't important."

"Your boy-room-boy?" Poppy asks, letting out a laugh. "And people think Gen Z has confusing slang."

"What does that mean, a boy-room-boy?" Angelica asks suspiciously. "I've never heard of such a thing."

"I think Clove had one of those," Cami says.

"You two are really together?" a woman who looks a lot like Chryssy asks as she approaches. "I didn't believe the photos, but here you are in the flesh. When did this happen? Why am I always the last to know?"

"We're...new," Chryssy says. She gestures toward me. "Mom, this is Vin. Vin, meet my mom."

"I'm Peony," Chryssy's mom says, giving me a once-over.

"Pleasure to meet you, Peony. And it's true," I say without overthinking it. "I'm her new...boyfriend." I place my arm around Chryssy's waist, pulling her in closer. She doesn't resist, her body molding seamlessly against mine.

Angelica balks. "Well, if she's going to be broken up with, it might as well be by the best."

"Thank you?" I mutter.

"Speaking of breakups, did you hear about Rue's latest relationship?" Primrose whispers, glancing over her shoulder at another group of women wearing In Full Bloom shirts. "Her girlfriend pulled a ghost. Ghosting. Ghostbuster? Whatever it is when someone just, poof, goes away. Gone. Disappears. I warned her, but my daughter doesn't listen."

"Did you all see what's happening with my daughter?" Cami asks, lowering her own voice. "Clove hasn't had an official boyfriend yet— ever—because of the fear of the curse. And I'm sure you've all seen on the social media what's happened with Magnolia."

Poppy seems uninterested in the gossip and takes a sip from her cup. "The tea does taste pretty, Chryssy," she says.

Chryssy peers into Poppy's cup. "Nice pick. I'll give your followers ten percent off if you do a post."

The whole flowers in Poppy's cup continue to expand. The chamomile and rose petals unfurl like they're waking up from hibernation, tinting the water a light shade of pink.

"Chamomile calms the spirit. And rose helps with stress and anxiety," I say, recalling what Chryssy told me when she tried yet again to get me to drink tea yesterday. I might've tried it if my new shipment of Brew Haus beans hadn't arrived.

I catch Chryssy giving me a curious look. "Good memory," she mumbles.

"Too bad pretty doesn't break curses. Isn't it because of all this herbal stuff that we're cursed to begin with?" Poppy asks, looking up from her phone.

"Don't write off herbalism so fast," Chryssy says. "When 4G ran his apothecary, he helped a lot of people. That's ultimately where we'd like to be, where every product we put out will also help people. We want to counteract the bad of the curse with our future formulas."

"How does that help us? Did you find 4G's blend?" Primrose asks. "Can we take it and break the curse?"

"Well, no, we don't have the blend," Chryssy tells them. "And even if we did, I don't think the curse works like that."

Marigold reaches for Chryssy's arm. "Are you going to try to find 4G's recipe?" she asks. "Re-create it, maybe?"

"An herbal blend from the 1800s? That's long gone," Chryssy's mom says, waving her off.

"We're starting with teas," Chryssy says, taking a step back. "People will get to know us first before we add in something more complex like supplements. When we do, we'll focus on starting with the right blend."

The Hua women talk among themselves, looking skeptical. "At

any rate, we'll gladly accept your muscles for today's race," Marigold says to me.

"What race?" I ask.

"The Dragon Boat Race," Angelica replies. "The whole reason we're here. It's the Dragon Boat Festival!"

"I never celebrated this growing up," I say, casting a confused look at Chryssy and hoping for answers.

Angelica jumps in. "The festival commemorates Qu Yuan, a Chinese poet and politician who jumped into the river and drowned after learning tragic news about his state's surrender. He had been exiled and accused of being disloyal, but turns out he hadn't been," she tells me. "On this day, we offer zongzi to feed his water spirit."

"Now the sticky rice is wrapped in bamboo leaves because water dragons intercepted the food at first," Chryssy adds.

The information comes together in my mind. "That's what you've been making for the past few days," I say.

"Right," Chryssy confirms. "Dragon boat racing commemorates Qu Yuan's death. The paddles splashing in the water and the drumming scare away any evil spirits. Which brings me to why you're here." She smiles at me. "Vin won't be rowing in today's race. He's our drummer. Normally, I do it, but—"

"The girl can't keep a beat!" Angelica says, patting Chryssy's shoulder.

Chryssy gestures in my direction. "Hence my replacement."

"Vin's going to be on our boat? Wait, I need to start streaming this now!" Poppy says, tapping her phone screen and holding it up to me. "Can you say all that again?"

"Vin's only on camera when he's in a hat and shirt. Meet you down there!" Chryssy says, dragging me away from her family and behind the tent where there's more branded clothing.

"What's this about drumming?" I ask, pulling my black shirt off.

"Oh, I didn't mention it?" Chryssy asks innocently. "You said it yourself: You're good at keeping a beat." She looks at me over her shoulder and I don't miss the way her eyes widen at the sight of me shirtless. Her cheeks turn as pink as the T-shirts. She sucks in a sharp breath and turns away, holding out the shirt. "Here."

"Feel free to look if you like what you see," I joke, stifling a grin.

Chryssy's head spins back to me. "What I'm seeing is someone who knows how to stay in rhythm," she says. "*That's* what I like to see. This is a big responsibility."

I pull the shirt down over my torso. "I agreed to an event, not a race."

We cross over toward the tent where Daisy, Rose, and Violet pass out zongzi and tea.

"The race *is* the event," Chryssy says as she places sticky rice on a paper plate.

"Don't think I'm not noticing your brand printed all over," I say, looking down at the illustrated flower logo.

"In Full Bloom is sponsoring the Hua women," Chryssy says. "It's good exposure for the news coverage this event should get and with Poppy's stream. I pitched my family on investing, but it didn't go so well. Some family members are like me and don't want people outside the family to know about the curse, but for others it's their entire personalities."

"Your great-aunt Angelica seemed excited to talk to me about it," I reflect.

"Give her a stage to talk about our family's drama, and she'll whip out a top hat and a cane," Chryssy says. "It's Great-Aunt Angelica's way to get pity, empathy, or compassion, depending on her mood. She's even been comped meals at restaurants before."

"Free meals? That changes things," I joke. "Sorry they didn't invest."

Chryssy sighs. "It's their loss. Last year, the global TCM market was valued at just under twenty-nine billion dollars. In ten years, it's expected to be around fifty billion."

"Seriously? How much are you looking for?" I ask.

"I don't do business with guests," Chryssy says. "And I thought you were a coffee guy."

I grin. "Not a guest, and maybe I'm looking to diversify."

"You wearing that shirt is plenty." She removes the string and unwraps the bamboo leaves holding the rice together. "You'll need energy. Fuel up."

I accept the plate and pair of chopsticks Chryssy hands me.

Five spice and soy sauce burst on my taste buds as soon as I take a bite. It's a comforting sensation, shortly followed by the sticky texture of rice, Chinese sausage, mushrooms, peanuts, and pork belly.

"Shit," I mumble. "That's good."

Chryssy smiles. "I'm glad you like it, *boyfriend*."

"Your aunties are going to ask nonstop questions trying to understand what this is," I explain. "Better to give an easy answer. They don't seem to have a lot of faith in us."

"They know we won't last," Chryssy states nonchalantly. "They don't expect any relationship to. It wouldn't matter if we were together for two dates or two hundred." She lifts her shoulders before letting them drop dramatically. "I can just imagine what my mom is talking about with them."

"I take it she'd talk about the curse?" I guess, recalling Chryssy's mention of her in the moon garden.

Chryssy's eyes dart over to me. "Which is why I don't talk to her about the people I date. I made that mistake with my first crush in middle school. I went on and on about how cute this guy was and how maybe he'd dance with me at the eighth-grade formal." She laugh-shivers. "Mom told me that I could like him all I wanted, but he'd never like me enough to stay. I'm sure she'd say the same about you."

Unconsciously, my jaw tightens. "Damn. Weren't you like, fourteen?" I ask. "Is that how old eighth graders are?"

"I was thirteen. It's just how my mom is, especially right after the divorce. It wasn't something I needed to hear as a lovestruck, hormonal teenager, though," Chryssy says. "What would your mom say about us?"

"She'd be thrilled," I admit. "She'd be like, finally. Someone who's not after you for your fame and money. Not for real, at least." I take another bite of zongzi. "Did you dance with him anyway?"

Chryssy watches me for a moment, her face pensive. "I didn't go."

I blow out a breath. "I'm sorry to hear that," I say. "If it makes you feel any less alone, I didn't go to my eighth-grade dance either. I had to practice for tour."

"I'm sure you had a lot more fun practicing," she says. "Apparently, those dances are cringey."

I make a face. "You should've heard me practicing Bach's Cello Suite No. 1 in G Major."

This makes Chryssy laugh again. "Only you."

"I'm really good at it now, I swear," I say.

The way pink fills Chryssy's cheeks and how she squeezes her eyes shut as she laughs harder are too damn cute.

"Come on, I'll show you the boat," she says, waving me along.

We pass groups of people in company-branded clothing warming up before the big event. I didn't realize some of these spectators were my competition.

"This one's ours," she says, tapping a long purple-and-gold-patterned boat with a colorful carved dragon head on the front and an intricate tail shooting off the back. It rests next to blue, green, red, and orange boats.

"I assume this is where I'll sit?" I ask, tapping a chair behind the dragon's head. "You do realize this isn't the instrument I play, right?"

Chryssy shrugs. "Honestly, I don't trust you steering, and if you rowed, you'd be among nineteen five-foot-something Hua women. The imbalance alone would throw us off course." She runs her hand along the painted scales spanning the length of the boat. "Every year, the Hua women compete. And even though we practice and have the best intentions, and ultimately are here for the fun of it, we never place."

I look over at the group of Hua women, spanning the generations, who are decked out in matching gear, stretching out their arms and hamstrings. "Not once?" I ask. "There are only five boats in the race."

"Hey!" Chryssy laughs, gently thwacking my arm. "It's harder than it sounds."

"I'm all for winning, but why the sudden desire?" I ask. "Is that what your family wants?"

"Do you see what the boat name is?" Chryssy asks, pointing to the gold-painted letters. "It's called *Favorite Mistake*, named after a Sheryl Crow song. Love—and loss—is complex. Her song captures that. The aunties who aren't obsessed with you and Leo are her biggest fans, and the Hua women's boat name couldn't *not* be a breakup song." She sighs. "I just want them to win—to come first—for a change."

It doesn't take much for my competitive spirit to come out in full force. If Chryssy wants a win for her family, then that's what she's going to get.

I nod. "You may never have placed, but that changes today."

"You may have just become my favorite mistake," Chryssy says with a dramatic wink.

Forty-five minutes later, after a welcome greeting and a chaotic sequence of moving the dragon from land to water, I'm seated at the front of the boat containing two rows of ten women each, while Poppy steers at the very back.

The Seattle skyline sprawls out ahead of me with the Space Needle popping up from behind a building to my right. The clouds drifting overhead are reflected on the surface of the lake, and the thousands of spectators in the distance look like a cluster of musical notes.

I take a deep breath in and slowly release it, letting the act focus me. I'm bobbing side to side in a boat that looks like a dragon and facing twenty-one Hua women, and it dawns on me that this might be the most unique place I've ever played an instrument. And here, an entire family relies on me to keep us in rhythm enough to win.

I squeeze the drumsticks. If I can play all of Bach's cello suites, I can beat this damn drum.

The countdown begins over the speakers. I clear my throat and try to get everyone to focus.

Chryssy and Violet sit directly in front of me, looking up expectantly.

Suddenly, we're in single digits, and it's time to get serious. I can't let Chryssy's family down.

I yell "Attention!" and add a "Please!" because I can't boss around these women without manners.

It's showtime.

"Follow my beat," I call out so everyone can hear me. "It's time to scare away some evil spirits!"

Forty-two eyes are on me as the horn sounds and I start beating the drum with both sticks.

It's an admittedly messy start on everyone's end, mine included. A true symphony of chaos.

Water splashes everywhere as arms flail. The Hua women elbow each other, trying to get their strokes in as their paddles crash into one another.

It's a small miracle the boat isn't spinning in circles or sinking.

My steady beat isn't inspiring any synchronicity, and I lose track of the rhythm among all the screaming from the spectators and shouts from the other boats, who have easily gained several feet on us.

I need to meet my audience where they are. I only know the chorus, but it might be enough.

I take a deep breath in and scream-shout the first line of the chorus of Sheryl Crow's "Soak Up the Sun," quickening the beat. Luckily, I know the lyrics. The Grammys afterparty we went to one year had a hard-to-forget-even-if-you-tried karaoke portion. This song was the favorite of the night.

Dun, dun, dun, dun, dun.

This gets everyone's attention, though I can't be sure if it's my singing or the song they're most caught off guard by.

"Keep my beat!" I shout, then sing the next line, and then the next.

Chryssy and Violet join in, and before I know it, we're gliding through the water and gaining on the other boats. I could be flying right now as the wind rushes past the back of my head.

I hold my beat steady, watching for small cues from Chryssy's family in the same way I would watch Leo and play off him onstage. Speeding up where his momentum gained and slowing when he needed to catch up. I've missed this feeling.

Everyone I'd met earlier is focused, determined, and now singing at the top of their lungs. I can hear Chryssy's voice the loudest. It motivates me to stay the course.

The rows are in sync. The lyrics are, too. The tune's slightly off, but it hardly matters.

We've bypassed the blue dragon by a few feet and are coming up on the others.

We might actually win this thing.

It's a premature thought because, as it crosses my mind, we're interrupted by a wake.

I watch for signals from Poppy in the back, who can see what's ahead of us. She takes a break from simultaneously steering and livestreaming to reorient the direction of our boat. I slow my drumming until we're balanced back out.

The interruption allows the orange boat to recover. On my left, the team sponsored by a local dentist closes in on the gains we had made. We're dragon head to dragon head, edging back and forth.

"One more time!" I shout at the top of my lungs before joining the chorus of Huas.

We make one final sprint to the end to beat out the competition, our dragon boat powered by rowing Hua women singing "Soak Up the Sun" all the way to the finish line.

When the horn blows, I hold the drumsticks against the barrel, panting in anticipation.

A man's voice booms over the speakers. "Taking third place is... *Bright Smiles*!" he shouts.

Next to us, the orange boat erupts in applause. The sounds of their happiness are amplified on the water, their shouts so loud they might as well be coming from our boat.

It's when I look back at the women in front of me that I realize the shouts of happiness *are* coming from our boat. Everyone's... cheering?

Violet has tears streaming down her cheeks, but she looks happy. Chryssy's family screams as they high-five and hug each other, smiles dominating their faces.

"We got fourth!" Violet says, pumping her fists in the air.

I frown. "We didn't even place."

"But we didn't get last!" Chryssy says, reaching for me and shaking my shoulders. "We did it!"

We didn't do it, though. We placed four out of five, and the entire thing was streamed for everyone to see.

I tuck my head into my arms. The moment is way too jovial for how we should all feel. We lost.

Chryssy rests her hand on my forearm. There's a tingling sensation that I want to blame on the drumming.

"Vin, we placed!" she says, breathless.

I look up at her. "We aimed for gold, and we got… nothing."

A light pressure point on my forehead startles me. There's another. A single raindrop rolls down Chryssy's cheek. Drops plop over our heads and into the boat, disappearing immediately when they touch the water. The Hua women don't seem to care about any of it, as the rain blends in with their tears of joy.

"And we're rewarded with rain," I mumble, holding my palms out.

"But it was fun, right?" Chryssy asks. "This was the best race yet, and you kept such good rhythm! Honestly, cello who?" She gives me the biggest grin I've seen from her yet. "We did it!"

The sight is almost enough to shake off my thoughts. Her enthusiasm is undeniably contagious. For some reason, my stomach flips with nerves.

There's that feeling again.

Time is suspended as Chryssy and I hold each other's gaze for a few long seconds.

"Yeah," I finally admit, feeling my features relax. "It was fun."

Suddenly, the light sprinkle turns into a full-on rainstorm. Behind Chryssy, her mom squints up at the sky and frowns at the unexpected change in weather.

"Cursed," Peony mutters under her breath just loud enough for us to hear. "Every last one of us."

Chapter 10

CHRYSSY

You two looked like you were fresh out of the rain scene of *The Notebook*," Auntie Violet observes. She pinches my phone screen and zooms in. "Still cute even when drenched. What a fun day."

I can't tell if she's referencing me or Vin in the photo. By the time we rowed the boat back to shore, we were soaked through. Vin in pink was admittedly cute. Vin in *see-through* pink was...an image I shouldn't be thinking about.

"The event went well," I reflect. "Maybe too well."

It didn't take long for Vin's Flavor of the Week–type articles to make their way around the internet. Having only been an observer of famous people and their love lives, it's surreal being written about.

Between the Soar for Strings event and Poppy's livestream blowing up on social media, In Full Bloom has been getting hundreds of website hits, along with a surprise jump in preorders. It's not a slow trickle. The orders are pouring in. It was the last scenario I could've anticipated.

If orders continue at this rate, our entire inventory will be wiped out, and there won't be enough for customers to buy on Day One.

Auntie Violet and I are visiting flower farms in a quest to source another partner for our teas so we can build up our inventory as soon as possible. Because we can only grow so much in our own garden, we rely on other small farms for the bulk of our flowers.

The other two farms we've visited have already committed this year's flowers to florists and wedding planners but were open to discussions for future partnerships.

We have more roses and chamomile than chrysanthemums, which has quickly become the most popular flower of the three. And because chrysanthemums usually bloom at the end of summer or in early fall, even if we could find another partner, this year's batch won't be dried and packaged in time for June's launch. We'll only have what we've grown at the inn and from the other flower farms we currently work with.

Beth, the owner of Salty Stems, a small, family-owned farm in Bellingham, Washington, ends her call and redirects her attention to us. "Sorry, wedding season. It gets busy. What were you saying about the process, Violet?" she asks.

"When the flowers bloom, they need to be handpicked and washed and dried," Auntie Violet repeats.

So far, Beth and her farm sound promising. Sitting on just over twenty-five acres of land, Salty Stems broke ground several years ago. Rows of hundreds of nearly bloomed flowers surround us, their purple, orange, pink, and yellow buds resembling nature's kaleidoscope.

While Auntie Violet continues explaining our packaging process to Beth, I allow myself to get swept up in the sea of peachy orange and pink anemones, ranunculus, sunflowers, and peonies.

These flowers are breathtaking, but better yet, they're consistent. While each flower is uniquely its own, the growth is harmonious with one another in their color, sizing, and quantity. All things that we're looking for so we can live up to having the word "trustworthy" in our mission statement.

I imagine what the polytunnel will look like when the temperatures drop and the chrysanthemums bloom in the fall, their vibrant petals exploding in color. Ever since moving to the inn, I've been astounded by how something so visually stunning can also hold so much goodness. People have been drinking chrysanthemum tea for thousands of years, and its medicinal properties have been documented as early as the Han Dynasty. With their cooling properties, chrysanthemums clear heat, restore balance, reduce inflammation and blood pressure, and are a powerful antioxidant. And then some. It never ceases to amaze me how healing nature can be.

I turn back to Auntie Violet and Beth when I hear my name—and not the flower we've been talking about all afternoon—intentionally called.

"Beth's grabbing her notebook to take down information," Auntie Violet says, filling me in. "I like the look of these. You know what else I liked the look of?"

"The way Beth designed the greenhouse entrance? Because that was elega—"

"You and Vin. If I didn't know either of you, I'd think you were really dating," she says. "Very natural. Especially with that kiss."

Heat blooms in my cheeks at the memory of it. "He's definitely unexpected," I say.

"Unexpected? What's that mean?" Auntie Violet asks, leaning in. "I need details!"

"You know I don't kiss and tell," I reply jokingly, "but he's a lot more complex than the media gives him credit for. And more than I ever thought."

"Details!" Auntie Violet cries.

"Okay, geez. I'll say that the man has excellent oral hygiene. I'll leave it at that."

Auntie Violet looks impressed by this. "He does have a wonderful smile," she says. "That was some excellent acting from you two. I was very convinced."

I turn away from her. "Good. That was the point."

The day after the Dragon Boat Festival, I learned that my aunties—including Auntie Rose, who insisted she had to be involved to advocate for me—had decided to fully immerse themselves in our fake-dating plan.

The potting shed has been temporarily renamed the Plotting Shed, a makeshift headquarters for my aunties to document our dates. They even repurposed their treasured corkboard used for meticulously tracking flower- and herb-growing timelines.

A printed-out photo of our kiss in Vegas has been pinned up, complete with hand-drawn arrows and commentary for what we could improve to strengthen the believability.

Arrow one led to my hand on Vin's chest with the words, "Hand placement should be closer to the heart to look less strangle-y."

Arrow two pointed directly at Vin's scrunched forehead and read, "Should not look like he's mad about kissing Chryssy."

Arrow three pointed to our feet.

"Look at the way their toes are pointed toward each other," Auntie Violet had said. "Body language experts say that this means the two people are interested in each other. Good attention to detail."

I'd been surprised to see the second pinned-up photo from Vegas that lacked annotations. We're standing with the group watching other musicians make their descents, standing close together and trading grins. Still riding that adrenaline high, most likely. I hadn't realized we were being photographed, but we look genuinely happy and just the right amount of intimate. We sold that fake date more than I thought we would've.

It's officially a family affair but ultimately a useless endeavor. Our deal is done.

"So now what?" Auntie Violet asks.

"For me and Vin? Nothing," I tell her as we stroll down a new row. "Well, one more thing. He needs to break up with me."

"Right when things started taking off," Auntie Violet says. "Too bad."

"We hardly have enough flowers for the preorders we've received, let alone for the few store orders that have come in. I don't think we need more exposure."

As I say this, I'm looking at an orange tulip that's held on long past its bloom, and because my brain recalls the most random information at the most random times, I think of tulip mania. *Not* because we're going to cause an economic collapse with our product, or that we'll even charge high amounts for it, but because now there's a spike in demand for our product, which is the entire point of our dating plan, and there's not enough for customers. Worry expands in me like a dried flower bud in hot water.

"Do you think this was a mistake?" I ask Auntie Violet, who looks totally at ease among the flowers.

"Is this because of the kiss? I'll admit I was worried at first," she says.

"What? No, I'm asking if it was a mistake trying to get exposure when we clearly weren't ready for it."

"No one could've predicted how powerful your impact would be," Auntie Violet says, patting my hand.

"We need to talk about adding a fourth flower," I say.

"We are not launching with four teas," Auntie Violet says firmly. "Four is unlucky. We'll need to launch with five flowers if we do increase it."

"So now we need to find chrysanthemums and *two* more flowers? How are we going to do that?" I ask as my auntie's previous words catch up to me. "Wait, what were you worried about? The kiss?"

Auntie Violet pulls the quarter of her heart necklace between her fingers. "It just seems that it would be hard to kiss a man like that and not develop some sort of feelings. I don't want to see you hurt. For real, that is."

"Don't worry about me. It's over now," I reassure her. "It was just a kiss."

Somehow, this doesn't feel true when I say it.

I reach forward to twist the stem of a peony, the swirling pink petals creating an optical illusion. But there's a bigger illusion at play here. Any unknowing viewer would focus on the peonies' pretty pastel colors and their puffy, delicate, multilayered ring of petals. What they may not know, though, is that it's belowground where the magic happens for this flowering plant. They're known more widely as common peonies, but Chinese peony roots contain powerful healing properties: liver detoxification, anti-inflammation, improved mental and emotional clarity.

Maybe, in this case, I'm the unknowing viewer looking at this moment without the full knowledge of what it means. Is there something deeper here with a root system that will do me some good? Could the hype around Vin and me "dating" each other lead to a broader conversation about TCM and our work holistically? Or will I just find more dirt?

My phone buzzes in my bag with a text from Rita.

Rita (2:36 p.m.): I couldn't be your ambassador, but I could still help in my small way. xoxo RS

I have zero guesses as to what this could mean, so I don't attempt to entertain any. I tap into the attached link that takes me to a *Vanity Fair* article featuring Rita's son's Prodigy Party. The first image is a compilation of the four different seasons that all took place in her backyard.

I scroll past quotes from the party planner and vendors who went to extra lengths to make sure the seasons were never to be forgotten.

Tucked between classical music playlist recommendations and photos of reconstructed flower fields and custom snow sculptures are quotes from Rita revealing the effort that went into organizing a party on this scale.

She's also talking about me.

> This was so much more than a party. It was a celebration of natural musical talent, forming community, and strengthening existing bonds, both platonically and romantically. Chrysanthemum and Vin met here! In fact, I was the one to formally introduce them.

Rita reveals that she came to the Wildflower Inn to heal heartbreak, an admission guests are technically allowed to make on their own. It's a lovely shout-out.

And then I keep reading.

> Chrysanthemum healed my heartbreak. She's my Heartbreak Herbalist. That's what she and her aunties do there. Soon they'll be releasing a flower tea line, In Full Bloom, so if you're looking for a little heart-soothing tonic in your life, look no further. And who knows? Maybe Chrysanthemum will heal Vin's heartbreaking ways once and for all.

Before I can marvel at the free advertising handed to us on a silver platter from our A-list former client, I need to have a mild freak-out. Preferably with someone.

I fast-walk over to Auntie Violet, who's wandered out of the greenhouse. I apologize to a daffodil I nearly trample trying to catch up to her, and thrust my phone into Auntie Violet's hands. She squints at my phone screen, reading the highlighted section I point out.

As I wait impatiently for her to finish, my stomach flips at the feeling of people reading these articles and forming opinions about me.

About what we do. Already I can hear comments people might make. It's been a week, and I'm not sure I like the feeling of being perceived. Is this how Vin has felt his entire life?

Auntie Violet looks pleased. "Can you print that out? I'd like to put that up on the board. The Heartbreak Herbalist. That's good!"

"We don't fix heartbreakers. We help heal the symptoms of heartbreak," I say to an audience of one who is the last person who needs to hear this. "It's an oversimplification."

Auntie Violet flaps a hand at me. "It's a sound bite."

"In *Vanity Fair*!" I reread the article. We don't actively capitalize on heartbreak. We only address it when heartbreak symptoms present themselves. And we don't focus on one part of the body exclusively.

Also! This isn't about me. But I can't believe our brand is being talked about by Rita Sharpe. This placement is huge.

"This will help Vin and Leo, too," I say, my mind whirring. They officially sold out of Colosseum tickets as of this morning, but there are still a few stadiums to fill.

"It should. And the good news is that the Chaobreakers care about you two," Auntie Violet shares. "Though the majority are curious what the breakup album will sound like."

Strangely, I feel sad hearing this. They've already assumed the worst of Vin. Yes, it's his reputation, but there's so much they don't know about him.

"It's too soon to know how this will all turn out," Auntie Violet says. "But we've never had this much awareness before. Who knows? This might help us expand faster."

"Especially if we can secure these flower farms and make back the money we put in," I reason. "But what happened to keeping the business manageable?"

The aunties and I have all felt the scales of balance tip toward burnout. No one's trying to work eighty-hour weeks again.

"I know we never planned for this level of exposure, but this is new territory," Auntie Violet says. "Wildflowers are adaptable. We can be, too. Let's spread as much beauty as we can, while we can."

There's something to what Auntie Violet's saying. Chances for explosive growth like this don't come around every day. Normally, we're bound to nature's timing.

And people like Vin don't come around every day.

Auntie Violet rests her hand on my shoulder and gives it a light squeeze. "Chryssy, we have a lead for chrysanthemums, a shout-out in *Vanity Fair* from Rita Sharpe, of all people, you just got a catchy nickname, *and* your arm candy is Vin Chao."

"Temporary arm candy," I correct.

She nods slowly. "Still. I'm failing to see any reason why you should have that look on your face right now."

I relax my expression. "I didn't expect so many things to go right all at once. Even good problems are problems."

Auntie Violet raises her eyebrows at me as she pulls her long hair back into a low ponytail. "If you have to deal with it either way, it might as well be good. Sometimes, when it rains, it really does pour. That doesn't only apply to bad things."

A thought tickles the edge of my brain: Is this the peak bloom before all our petals start to wilt and fall off? I can't worry about the pending droop. If this is the moment, I need to maximize it.

"Daisy told me we have two thousand new followers on Instagram, and the wait list has grown every day. We're booked out through the rest of the year," Auntie Violet shares. "You're not going to hear me complaining."

Out of curiosity, I pull up the listening stats on my podcast. There's triple the number of subscribers, which isn't saying much considering what it's been, but it's something.

"We'll take it day by day," Auntie Violet says. "The press is hot right now, but that won't always be the case. Tomorrow, we'll be wishing we had more of it once something new takes over. If anything, enjoy being the Heartbreak Herbalist for the day."

"You're right. We could use this moment," I say, twisting my earring. "Oh! I sold the engagement ring Chris gave me. We can use that money for more packaging."

Auntie Violet hums in response. "The diamond, huh?"

"One of the few times heartbreak has helped me," I say half-heartedly.

Auntie Violet delicately runs her fingertips over the thin, long petals of a bright yellow sunflower. "After the week you've had, you and Vin deserve a break. Invite him to come clamming tomorrow," she suggests. "Leo's going. We want to get him out on the water, feel the sand between his toes. A little nature could be good for Vin, too."

I can't disagree with this. Vin could use a break.

I text Vin a clamming invite and toss my phone into my bag, then follow Auntie Violet across the field to a waving Beth.

"Sorry that took so long. Got another phone call about an order," Beth says. "We run a small operation here. A few florists expressed interest in showcasing mums for their fall weddings, but historically they haven't been too popular, so you might be in luck. Let me follow up. If they don't want 'em, they're yours."

We thank Beth for her time, and she sends us off with a bouquet of freshly cut marigolds that we'll wash, dry, and taste-test at the inn. Perhaps one day—maybe sooner than we planned—they'll join the In Full Bloom lineup.

I rub my thumb over the marigold's ruffled, golden petals. I don't know what's coming. All I know is that when a fake-dating plan works and a famous actress wants to call me a Heartbreak Herbalist, well, maybe I should take the wins where I can.

Chapter 11

VIN

I'm not only trapped on an island, but a muddy one at that.

Clamming day turns out to be overcast. The beach, water, and low-lying land in the distance look like they're covered in gray filters.

The weather is fitting for the state of my life, actually. Where it's typically very clear what my routine and purpose are, now it just feels like I'm living in one big gray zone.

I desperately want to work, want to rehearse with Leo, want to be anywhere but here. I want the comforting sounds of home, of the steady hum of New York City traffic. The crescendo of rush hour. The rattling of the subway underground. The loud, improvisational music of the city.

What I don't want is the type of stillness that comes with being here.

It's too damn quiet on this island. Squeaking brakes have been replaced by chirping birds. Winds whistling down the avenues are now light breezes blowing through tall grass. The door buzzer announcing my takeout has become Chryssy clanging pots and pans when she's cooking.

I used to love silence. Especially the kind that happens the moment before a performance when the audience falls quiet. Everyone holding

their breath, swallowing down coughs and sneezes, waiting in anticipation for the first note.

But now, in the quiet, I hear too many of my own thoughts.

I listen carefully for something, anything, that might take me out
of my own head. Waves breaking on land is a good start. Nearby,
unleashed dogs chase balls and kick up sand while kids scream back
and forth to one another while digging for edible buried treasures.
For a few seconds, thoughts of work drift away and I'm brought back
to the muddy present.

With a bucket and shovel in hand, I trudge over wet sand in my
tall rubber boots to catch up with Chryssy and the rest of the group.
She's kneeling, surrounded by Leo, her three aunties, a slender white
man in a "Remain Clam" T-shirt, and a few guests staying at the inn
who wanted to join in on a day of what many of them have been calling fun.

Chryssy explains that we should look for the dimples in the sand,
which indicate where the clam is buried. She demonstrates digging a
hole with a clam tube and pulling it up.

After her demo, the "Remain Clam" man extends his hand for
a shake. "You must be the other Chao brother," he says. "I'm Dan,
Chryssy's old man."

"Vin," I say, returning the shake. "Nice to meet you."

"You and your brother are both welcome to the restaurant anytime. Lunch is on me," Dan says.

I thank him for the invite as Leo kicks my bucket with his mud-
caked boot.

"Five bucks says I'll get more clams than you," Leo wagers.

I nod. "You're on."

A little friendly competition adds a bright spot to this day. Seeing
Chryssy again isn't so bad, either. After the Dragon Boat Festival, I
made a stop in LA to review our latest film-scoring project and to take

some meetings about the tour. I've also had to field questions from the media wanting to know Leo's whereabouts and more about me and Chryssy. How serious are we? What do we do when we're together? Is Chryssy trying to fix me, or is the Heartbreak Herbalist going to be left heartbroken? No doubt everyone's bets are on the latter.

"I'm glad you came," Leo says when we break away from the group. "I was worried you'd be holed up practicing the entire time. Glad you're socializing."

"I wouldn't say I came to socialize, but I'm here," I say. "How's everything at the inn going?"

"It's been a total one-eighty from our real life, man," Leo says. "It's a little surreal. The aunties are sticking me with needles and doing this thing called cupping? Painful but it works. I'm eating better food than all that takeout. Chryssy really knows how to cook. We talk about what we're going through, and I've even planted my own herbs. You need to join us for a sunrise Qigong one morning. It's beyond relaxing."

"Okay, that sounds…promising," I say, which it does, even if I don't fully understand what most of it means. "What about your heart?"

"There are specific acupoints Auntie Rose focuses on during my sessions," he explains. "I've been out of balance for a long time. We both have been. I'm still sad, but physically I'm starting to feel better."

"Okay," I exhale. "Good. That's good."

"It'll be a journey," he says. "This is just the beginning, but I'm glad I didn't ignore it. Thank you for bringing me here, and for staying."

"I'm here for you," I say.

"I know this puts a lot of pressure on you and our schedule," Leo adds. "They won't admit it, but I think the aunties have been fielding calls from the tabloids."

I run my hand across the back of my neck. "People are curious about where you are," I admit, leaving out the news I learned in LA about how we also secured the Acropolis after selling out the Colosseum. Our booking more venues is the last thing Leo needs to hear right now, especially when we're not slated to start practicing until the end of the month.

"I'm starting to like the idea of being a man of mystery," Leo says. "I guess you start to want that more when your life is always so exposed. But I do want to help since you've been so supportive." He hesitates for a moment. "You know that photoshoot we have next week? I'll do it."

"Is that really a good idea?" I ask. "You're making progress."

Leo keeps his focus on the sand. "It won't require playing, and if you're about to break up with Chryssy, I need to show my face somewhere. We can figure out a new excuse later."

The conversation's over when Leo suddenly remembers our bet and runs over to a dimple in the sand. He lunges for it with his tube and claims the spot. I don't fight him on the clam or the photoshoot. If he makes an appearance, it'll hopefully take some pressure off the headlines about Chryssy and me. We can get back to focusing on the music.

Chryssy yells "Clam!" and snaps me back to the moment. She hands me the clam tube, and I push it into the sand directly over the dime-size indent, twisting as quickly as I can so the clam doesn't tunnel deeper beneath the surface. I cover my thumb over the hole of the tube like she taught us and pull up. The sand around it dries out as water is suctioned away. I reach for the razor clam, whose long bronze body spans the length of my palm.

"You got it!" Chryssy says while I rinse off the clam in the swash that rushes up the sand after the wave breaks. "You're a natural."

When the water recedes, the only evidence of its existence is the foam residue on our boots.

"Think I can make a career out of this, too?" I ask.

"You can call it Cellos and Clams. A cello bar where there are live clams," she jokes. "Or a clam bar where there are live cellos."

"That sounds like an interesting retirement plan. Don't tell your dad and give him any ideas," I say, turning the clam. I admire the amber shell and count the dark rings to tell its age. ("Like the rings on a tree," Chryssy mentioned earlier, during the demonstration.) "Do these help calm the spirit, too?"

Chryssy smiles. "Clam shells help clear heat and have cooling properties. Very Yin," she says.

"Must be why this one's giving me the cold shoulder," I joke.

"Say clammy!" Violet says, getting up in our faces with her phone camera. With the surf to our backs, I hold up the clam. Chryssy lifts the bucket and tilts her head into my shoulder as she poses beside me.

Violet gives us a thumbs-up and walks back to Daisy, Rose, and Leo, who's working the clam tube into the sand. He's committed to the task, looking proud when he finds another clam. Leo radiates ease and has gained back the few pounds he'd lost. He looks like he's finally slept through the night. It's a comfort knowing that he might be starting to heal.

I set the clam in the bucket, and we continue our hunt. A little farther down the beach, I point a short distance ahead of us. "What's that over there?" I ask. "Is that a big clam?"

She squints into the distance. "Looks like trash," she says. "People can be disgusting."

"Yeah, people are, but I don't know," I say. "Looks like a clam to me. Maybe we should check it out."

"Uh, sure. Okay, let's go look," she says, walking over to the lump in the sand. "See? Trash. Not a clam."

"Can you pick it up?"

I am not good at this.

"Can I... pick up that trash? Without gloves?" Chryssy asks, giving me a look. "It's a wet bag. You pick it up."

"I'm not picking that up. Are you sure it's not a clam? Just look to be sure," I press.

"Okaaay," Chryssy says, lifting the bag with her pointer finger and thumb. "If I catch something..."

Chryssy holds up the clear bag with a rolled T-shirt inside. "What is this?"

I take the bucket from her. "Are you sure it's not a clam? Maybe you should open it up to make sure."

She narrows her eyes at me. "Is this yours?"

I squeeze my eyes shut. "I really just think you should open it up and make sure it's not a clam."

Chryssy sighs with a smile, opening the bag. "Oh, wait. You know what? You're right. I think this *is* a clam."

She removes the shirt and unrolls it to reveal me and Leo on the front holding cellos, with flames shooting up behind us.

"It's sample tour merch," I say. "In case you ever get tired of the Piano Man."

Her eyes take on a glossy sheen. "You brought me a sleepy shirt?" she asks softly before clearing her throat. "This is, um, thank you."

Oh shit.

"Is this like hand-holding or kissing?" I ask. "You don't have to wear it to sleep. You can wear it grocery shopping. Changing the oil in your car. Gardening. Whatever you want."

"No, this is nice. This is a kiss, Vin," she says, holding the shirt against her. "A good one. What's the name of the tour? The Chao Brothers, Flame-Kissed?"

I smile. "I was worried we looked a little too well-done."

We continue strolling down the beach.

"Are there any other clams we need to go find?" she asks. "Or is this a new tour promo strategy?"

"There was a tour beanie," I say, "but someone beat you to it."

There's that laugh again, the notes catching in the shell of my ear.

We pass by Chryssy's dad holding up a clam in front of Leo. "He's probably talking about adductor muscles," Chryssy says, following my line of sight.

I move around a pile of washed-up seaweed. "What was it about seafood that compelled your dad to open an oyster bar?" I ask.

"Oh, well, he's a chef and had always wanted to live abroad and work in the best restaurants around the world. He never got to do it, so he brought his dream here," she says. "He loves how interactive oyster bars are. His place gets booked out almost immediately at the beginning of every month."

"Wow. I'll have to take him up on his offer before we leave," I say.

"You should! The food is delicious," Chryssy says, swinging the bucket back and forth. "He and my mom first met when she came into the restaurant where he was the poissonnier. My mom's fish was still raw, so she sent the dish back. The restaurant manager made my dad apologize. She made a joke about how she was a cardiologist and how dare he deprive her of a heart-healthy meal. The next day, she came back and ordered the same dish, this time complaining that my dad left out a very important ingredient: his phone number."

I smirk. "Nice. I didn't realize your mom's a cardiologist. That's what you went to school for."

Chryssy nods. "She's not thrilled I didn't finish school, but I think it has less to do with me following in her footsteps than it is about stability. Funny that, in very different ways, we both work with hearts." She crouches to assess a divot that turns out to be a false lead. "To this day, my dad's favorite trip he's ever taken is the babymoon he and my mom went on before I was born. They went to Paris for New Year's. Apparently, during that time of year, there are pop-up oyster stalls on the streets. He'd have his oysters raw with a heavy squeeze of lemon and mignonette, and my mom would catch up at dinner eating them fully cooked au gratin with loads of butter and herbs and breadcrumbs. So much for heart-healthy, right?" Her smile disappears. "After their divorce, Dad opened Pearl. I haven't seen Mom eat an oyster since."

When I hear this, I think of the songs written about lost loves and ex-partners. Pearl almost sounds like Chryssy's dad's love song to her mom.

"I was a little surprised to see your dad," I admit. "I guess I thought with all the Hua women being left that your partners were the bad ones."

"There have been bad people, but they're not all villains," she says. "My dad was the one who initiated the divorce, but he was affected by their marriage ending. I was ten, and it was the first time I'd ever seen him cry. I'll never forget it." She drags her boot across the wet sand, the imprint dissolving almost immediately. "Hence why my aunties say that even heartbreakers can be heartbroken. Their empathy runs deep. Sometimes I forget that while the women are left, we're not the only ones who hurt. Yes, my dad broke my mom's heart. But he broke his own, too."

"I imagine it would be hard for him to see you get your heart broken. Does he know about...this? Us?" I ask, not sure how exactly to phrase it.

Chryssy looks back toward her dad. "I told him we're casually seeing each other but it's not serious, which is technically true," she says. "He thinks the curse has already created enough instability and drama. I think he's just happy I haven't completely given up on dating. Have you told your parents?"

"I haven't had a chance to call them back after they texted about the event photos," I say. "They also worry about me."

Chryssy glances up at me. "What's their romantic origin story?"

"It surprisingly wasn't too romantic for people who have been together for almost thirty-five years," I say. "They were both violinists, playing small gigs and working odd jobs to pay the bills. My mom's dream was to secure a seat in a touring chamber orchestra. Her family didn't have a lot, so she never got to travel. That was her ticket to seeing the world. But on the way to the audition, the subway broke down, and she missed it."

Chryssy gasps. She's stopped to face me, her head tilted in captivation like she's right there on the subway with my mom decades ago.

"The lights only flickered, but it was just enough time for someone to grab my mom's violin," I continue. "She chased him through the subway cars but lost him when she tripped over my dad's violin case. The guy was gone. So was her violin. She took it as a sign it wasn't meant to be, and violins aren't cheap. She couldn't afford another one."

Chryssy groans, her hand placed over her heart. "But to run into your dad like that!"

"Right. He offered to take her to a pastry shop nearby to buy her a comfort croissant, but she had to file a police report. He couldn't wait, though."

"But not because he didn't want to, I imagine?"

"Because he had to get to the audition—"

"No! Don't say it!" Chryssy pleads.

"—that my mom was going to. He had a later time slot." I involuntarily grin. "This is where it does get a little romantic."

Chryssy spins back to me. "Ew, no!" she says dramatically before changing her tune. "Tell me."

"They get to the symphony hall, and my dad gives my mom his time slot. She plays his violin."

Just like any good song that requires tension, I let a long silence pass.

Chryssy shakes her head. "And?"

"And she didn't get a seat."

Chryssy's mouth forms a small oval. "But the point was that they met, and that they tried, right?" she says, nailing the moral of the story.

"Within the year, they were married," I say. It's only once I reach the end of this story that I realize I've never shared it with anyone before.

"All these years later, here we are," Chryssy says, looking down at a small pile of shells.

"Yeah. They're having a big thirty-five-year anniversary in a couple of weeks," I say.

"Unbelievable. Literally," she says, her gaze lingering on me as she seems to disappear into her thoughts. "But I love that for them."

I grunt. "You're making that face again. The one where you analyze me."

Chryssy casts her eyes away from me.

"What did you learn from looking at me that time?" I ask, half-amused.

She twists her lips to the side. "I think that story tells me a lot more about you than it does about them."

I don't ask for clarification because I know what she'd say.

That I feel some sort of responsibility for honoring my parents' musical dreams, which they never got to live out.

That I work to be the best so that their sacrifices to put us through lessons and saving up for instruments and tours were worth it.

That I want my parents to have everything now that they didn't get to have then.

After our hotel room confessional, she's probably even connecting the dots that I want a love-song kind of love story. That I want a love like theirs.

And she'd be right.

But heartbreakers don't get stories like that. We get some of what we want, but we don't get everything.

Chryssy leaves it at that, letting her epiphany float away on the wind, and we continue walking side by side. Enough of the afternoon passes, and slowly, the tide rises. We splash through the ankle-deep water rushing up and down the beach.

I take a deep inhale as I look out into the distance, following the receding water all the way out to the bay and then past the horizon. I can practically feel my eyes and mind stretching after staring at screens and sheet music for what feels like my whole life.

"Can you make our breakup as memorable as your parents' love story? I want a powerful *loved* story like that to tell," Chryssy asks. She holds the tour shirt tighter against her chest.

Like my boots in the sand, my heart sinks a little at this. "You deserve the best breakup. I may need a little more time, though, to figure out something memorable. Our second date kind of snuck up on me."

Chryssy presses her lips together as she watches a bird circle above us. "What if—what if we didn't stop quite yet?" she asks.

"What do you mean?"

"Well, we've already planted the seed, and you're here with Leo anyway," she says slowly, as though she's thinking out loud. "We could just...keep going?"

My eyebrows pull together. "Like, what if we kept dating?" I ask. "Is there another race your family needs a drummer for?"

Chryssy smiles. "Trust me, if there were, you'd be the first person we'd all call." She takes a big gulp of air. "It's just that this worked really well. Us dating. Yes, we have more preorders than we know what to do with, but we're already working on solving that. And I saw on your website that you added a few more tour dates and locations. I hear Greece is lovely in September."

I kick at the sand, considering Chryssy's proposal. "It would give us an excuse for where Leo and I are."

"Right," she says.

"How long would we have to date?"

"I resent your use of *have to*," Chryssy says, mock-insulted.

I hold up my hands. "Sorry, sorry. How long would I *get* to date *you*?" I correct.

A pleased look appears on Chryssy's face. "We could date until the end of June. Then I'll focus on In Full Bloom, and you'll start rehearsals."

"We'd need to be in New York that week," I confirm, processing her proposition. "It would be double the time of my usual relationship."

"It'll look like we're more serious this way," she says. "And you still need to break up with me?"

"It's what people expect," I say, looking away from her.

Chryssy turns to me. "I can't believe I'm even saying this, but if we date for longer, it'd be an even bigger breakup for you."

"I suppose it would get more attention."

"Which makes me wonder," Chryssy says. "You'd be getting guaranteed heartbreak out of this, but more preorders for our tea isn't necessarily a sure thing, despite how things have gone so far."

"What would be a sure thing?" I ask.

Chryssy points to a small depression in the sand, and I dig up the clam.

"You being our brand ambassador," she says quickly. "You learned the flower benefits very fast, and I think it helped that you're not an obvious choice. And now we know you look good in pink. You'd need to drink our tea, talk it up. Maybe we take some pictures of you with it."

"You know I get paid millions to represent brands, right?" I inform her.

Chryssy scrunches her nose. "What's my fake love worth to you?" she asks.

I rub my chin as I pretend to think hard about it. "Probably all the fake money in the world."

She lets out a laugh and gently swings the bucket toward me.

"The preorders are one part of the equation," she says. "You bring attention to what we're doing and how we can help. But people won't just listen to me. That's where the ambassador—you—comes in. Brands wouldn't pay you so much if you didn't sell things. If people didn't trust you. It's like when one person believes something about you, more start to."

"I know it very well."

"And even heartbreakers experience heartbreak, right?" Chryssy says.

"Turns out we do." I spot Leo across the beach chatting with another guest. His healing process seems to be going in the right direction, and we're not leaving quite yet. Chryssy and I have seen tangible benefits already. What's a few more weeks? "You really want to do this?"

Chryssy glances at her aunties. "I know, with our family curse, we can't stop the women in our family from being heartbroken, but we want to at least try to help others with their own broken hearts. The more people we can help, the better, and you only get to launch once."

She's the answer to my problem, and it looks like I'm the solution to hers.

"It's settled then," I say. "We keep up appearances, and then I'll rehearse, you'll launch your product line, and Leo will hopefully be in a better place."

"That's a little grim," Chryssy says, her eyebrows pinching.

I frown. "Let me rephrase. Leo will hopefully be less heartbroken and back to playing again."

Chryssy grins. "Better. We'll squeeze in as many events as we can, but we can supplement that with photos on social media."

"Makes sense. We shouldn't only be seen together at public outings," I reason.

"I'd shake on it, but I've been burned by handshake agreements before," she says. "And something tells me I can trust you."

"We'll do a verbal agreement then," I say.

The clams rattle against the sides of the bucket as it bumps between our legs. Chryssy's eyes sparkle in the bright overcast light as they lock with mine.

I take a step back from her, giving whatever is happening between us right now some breathing room. She turns away from me and focuses intently on a dime-size indent.

I look out toward the strip of land in the distance. "I wonder if I'll ever get used to the fact that we're on an island."

Ahead of me, Chryssy nods. "I feel both connected and disconnected at the same time."

A few weeks ago, I wouldn't have understood what she meant. Now her vague comment actually makes a little bit of sense, even though I still don't love being completely surrounded by water.

"I think I'm a little stuck," I say.

"There's a bridge that connects the island to the mainland," she says, looking out at the trees across the water. "I'm surprised you haven't made your great escape yet."

"I would if I could move."

"Yeah, I feel stagnant, too, sometimes," Chryssy says, still not looking at me. "We have less than a month left. If we can just get through it, a lot will become unblocked for us."

"No," I say. "I'm literally stuck."

Chryssy turns around and notices my left foot that's sunk halfway down into the mud. "Here!" she says, springing into action and setting the bucket on the ground. "Use this to stabilize yourself."

I bend over to grip the sides of the bucket. I lift my left leg, trying to remove my shin-deep boot. Chryssy stands in front of me, holding my shoulders to help steady me.

I pull my leg up harder, in turn pushing too firmly against the bucket. It slides in the mud, and before I can exert any control over myself or the situation, I lose my balance and fall forward. Without thinking, I twist my body to try to avoid tumbling into Chryssy as I go down, but her hold on me was too tight, and she's thrown off balance, too.

Chryssy crashes onto my chest, her entire body flat against me. Next to us, clams spill out of the tipped-over bucket.

"Are you okay?" she asks, remaining very still. Her face is inches from mine.

"My foot's no longer stuck, but my entire body might be," I say, my back cool from the water seeping through my clothes. A second cooling sensation runs down the length of my spine. My body feels the curves of hers, and naturally, it's reacting. I shiver in response to all of it.

I wipe my forehead with the back of my hand, accidentally leaving a trail of mud in my fingers' wake.

I groan. "Tell me I didn't just make it worse."

Chryssy laughs. "Cleaning your pores and digging for clams. Your ambition knows no bounds, Vinny."

I flop my head back against the sand, signifying defeat. "They say multitasking can't be done, but look at me now."

"Might as well make sand angels while we're down here," Chryssy says, climbing off me and collapsing onto her own back in solidarity.

It's an out-of-body experience imagining what we must look like. The rumbling first starts in my stomach before making its way up my chest and throat. My laughter spills out of me, receding with the waves. Chryssy cracks up, too, her entire body shuddering next to mine. The sounds of our laughter overlap, creating a new melody I very much like the sound of, even though it's slightly off-key. Both this tune, along with Chryssy's bright smile against this gray day, burrow their way deeper into me.

None of this is attractive or comfortable, and I really don't love being covered in mud, but, just like the Dragon Boat Race, this is fun. And between gasps of amusement, I think I start to understand what Leo meant by us being out of balance. I can't remember the last time I laughed like this.

"Water's coming in," Chryssy says, quickly but carefully standing. She reaches her hand down to help pull me up. We're off the sand right as the water splashes against us, the thrill of the narrow escape bursting through me. We scramble to collect our scattered clams while a few of them get swept away.

There's wet sand caked in my hair and covering my entire backside. I'm as muddy as the dogs sprinting down the beach and the children chasing them. It's such a little thing, to be covered in mud. But never before have I been messy like this. I didn't spend my youth outdoors getting dirty or scratched. My mess looked like out-of-tune scales and half-memorized compositions. Poor techniques that I cleaned up with practice.

We take turns changing—me into an extra "Remain Clam" shirt that Dan brought for everyone and Chryssy in the one with my face on it—before heading back to the group.

I'm feeling both calm and like an actual clam, taking the directives of my T-shirt too literally.

This afternoon got me out of my head and my element.

And even though I've committed myself to another three weeks with Chryssy, I also begin to feel a little less stuck.

Chapter 12

CHRYSSY

Around midnight, there's a strange, muted noise coming from Vin's room that I try very hard to ignore.

"Is that my imagination or are you hearing that, too?" I whisper to Goji, who's sleeping on my bed unbothered.

I save a blog post for our website about the benefits of TCM and flowers, then make a note in my planner to review it tomorrow. I'm about to research more flower farm partners when the subsequent sound of metal clanging concerns me enough to check in on Vin.

I knock a few times, unsure if he'll hear me. "Vinnegan!"

I hear him cross the room in five steps before he opens the door just enough for me to see his face.

"What?"

His brows are furrowed, his eyes unfocused. Then his entire expression softens when he looks at me.

"Is that really what my face looks like?" he asks. "I look like an ass."

It takes me a second to realize he's talking about the shirt he gave me that I forgot I was wearing.

"But the flames are a nice demonic touch," I say.

He grunts. "I'm glad it's getting used. Did I wake you up?"

"I'm still working," I say.

Vin looks surprised.

"Did you hear that noise, too?" I ask, cupping my hand behind my ear.

He senses my sarcasm and makes a face. "I'm practicing 'This Is Tomorrow.' It's not going great."

I cross my arms. "It sounds like you're practicing it right now."

"That's the song name. Never mind. Did you need something from me?" he asks.

"Yes. Your sense of time. It's the middle of the night. Everything okay in here?" I ask. When he doesn't budge, I wave my hands in front of him. "This whole hiding-behind-the-door thing is a major mood."

Vin grunts again before opening the door wider. "Be my guest."

It's when he takes a step back that I notice that the walls and ceiling are covered in blue and black eggcrate foam, not a fleck of lavender paint to be seen.

"What's all this? Auntie Violet is not going to be happy," I mumble.

"Soundproofing," Vin states. "It won't absorb everything, but I didn't want to annoy you when I practice."

I raise an eyebrow. "You're a world-class talent. I would love to hear you play. When did you even do this?" I ask, observing how neatly every foam pad is lined up and cut to the specifications of the room.

"Yesterday when you were in your room all afternoon," he says. "It was Friday, so you must've been recording your podcast."

This makes me smile. "I was. Thanks for your comment on last week's episode. Glad someone's listening."

He bites down a grin. "Hey, if you ever want to use my room to record, go for it. I can also keep it up when Leo and I leave."

I push my fingers into the foam a little too hard when he says this, the indent popping back when I remove my hand. "Oh. Yeah. Great.

Thanks." I take in his stressed expression. "So, what's really going on? Did something happen?"

Vin pushes his hair back, a few strands sticking up. "The terms came back from the label," he says, his face telling me all I need to know. The contract must not have been what he was hoping for. "I need to talk to Leo, but his phone is off."

After a few beats, I wave him toward me. "Okay. Come with me."

He hesitates, looking back at his cello that needs playing, but finally agrees. "Fine."

"When you're feeling low, what do you like to eat?" I ask, leading Vin to the kitchenette–slash–living room.

"I don't know, whatever I have in my fridge or am craving from takeout," he says.

"Which is usually what?" I ask. "When you think about something comforting to eat, what comes to mind? My comfort food is herbal poached artichoke hearts."

"Mine's definitely not that," Vin says, running his hand down his face as he thinks. "Chryssy, I don't know. I need to go practice."

"Humor me?"

He looks up at the ceiling, thinking. "Uh, my mom used to make us risotto after lessons. I liked that. Does coffee count?"

I smile. "Vin, I know there's nothing more in the world that you'd rather do than go back into that oddly padded room and practice," I say, "but I can also tell you there's nothing more that I want in this world than for you to make me a cup of coffee."

Vin smirks. "You want coffee? Right now. At midnight. You don't even drink coffee."

"I'd prefer moon milk, but whatever it takes to get you in the kitchen cooking with me, I'll do it," I say.

He puffs out an exhale, his lone curl blowing up over his forehead. There's a glimmer of excitement in Vin's eyes as he walks over to the machine and polishes the touchscreen with his shirt. "I think I can do that for you," he says.

"How did this machine even get in here?" I ask.

"As soon as I knew we were staying, I asked the brand to send me one," Vin says as he presses a button. The coffee machine does all the work of grinding the beans. "You prefer oat milk, right?"

When I nod, he grabs milk from the fridge and pours it into a jar. The milk flies through a tube from the jar to the machine, depositing a frothy foam layer on top of the coffee.

Vin presents me with the cup like it's a delicate heirloom. "There you go. Give that a try."

I take a sip. It's surprisingly smooth, the taste not as bitter as I had anticipated.

"What is that, nutmeg? That's not bad," I admit, taking another sip. "My turn. Here." I toss him an apron. "It's risotto time."

He accepts the apron but doesn't put it on. "I...don't know how to cook."

This delights me. Watching someone learn how to cook is like watching people fall in love. It's a lovely mess at first, and then soon enough you're regretting all the meals you never made.

"The best time to learn is in the middle of the night," I say, grabbing a shallot. "Why do you look surprised?"

Vin taps out a rhythm on the counter. "This is just another thing I can't do right."

I shake my head. "It's just a song you haven't learned yet."

Vin frowns. "Usually when this becomes known in relationships, my girlfriends laugh, express disapproval, mock me. Say things like, 'You're a prodigy and yet you can't boil water?' Which is wildly inaccurate. I have definitely boiled water before."

"Lucky for you, I'm not a real girlfriend," I say. "Let me teach you how to push rice around in a pot, okay?"

He looks at me for a long moment, his expression neutral. Then he concedes and says, "Yes, Chef."

It lacks enthusiasm, but we can work on that.

For the next ten minutes or so, I walk Vin through the steps of making risotto with Qi broth, peas, herbs, chanterelle mushrooms, cheese, and parsley. I get the broth on heat and soak the dehydrated mushrooms in preparation.

Learning how to cut a shallot is lesson number one. Vin's a fast learner and easily picks up cutting the shallot both vertically and horizontally.

I peek over Vin's shoulder to see his progress. He curves his hand over the shallot like it's the neck of a cello, coming from the top with the knife and cutting downward. Little translucent rectangles, cut at a sharp angle, slide up the blade and onto the cutting board.

"What's happening to me?" he asks, squeezing his eyes shut. "It burns."

"Sorry. I need to sharpen the knives," I say while I pluck sage leaves off their stalk. "The duller it is, the more you cry. It's the shallot's chemical compounds."

I wave my hands toward his face to generate airflow.

"Let me try again," he says, blinking rapidly as he makes a smooth cut through the shallot. "I want to get it right."

It's his first obstacle, but he gets through it.

I add olive oil to the cast-iron Dutch oven, and it crackles against the heat. The shallots and sage sizzle when we slide them into the pot, every inch of the Dandelion filling with one of the Top Five Best Scents Ever.

He gives me a look when I hand him a bottle of white wine. "You've been holding out on me."

"This is *cooking* wine," I say with a smile, grabbing two small glasses for us.

He pours the gold liquid into the glasses before adding a splash into the shallots. We raise our glasses and take sips at the same time.

I pour arborio rice from the container straight into the pot, eyeballing a cup.

"Now what?" he asks.

"Now we'll add broth so it barely covers the rice, and stir until it absorbs. Then we'll add more broth. Rinse and repeat," I explain. "This is going to be good for us. There's astragalus and Chinese angelica root in the Qi broth."

Vin looks at me. "All I heard was how much stirring there is."

"We'll call it our Patience Risotto," I say. "It takes a while to make, but it forces us to slow down. We can't—and shouldn't—rush the process."

"You make this look so easy," he says.

I arch an eyebrow at him. "Like how you make playing the cello look easy."

We stand opposite each other on the same side of the stove, hovering over the pot as rice slowly soaks up the broth. In the glow of the kitchen lamps, I can practically see the tension melting away from Vin's shoulders. The sounds of simmering liquid, our slow breathing, and our conversation punctuate the quiet night.

"If Leo's unavailable and you need someone to talk to, I'm here," I offer, stirring the rice.

Vin's mouth tugs downward, but he's not quite frowning. After a long minute, he asks, "Have you ever gotten exactly what you wanted at the exact wrong time?"

He holds my gaze a heartbeat too long, and I'm suddenly too warm from the stove's heat.

"I've never gotten millions of dollars at an inconvenient time, no," I say.

Vin smirks and takes a sip of wine. "If only all the money in the world could fix or solve our problems."

"Sounds like you're looking for life to be perfect."

He shakes his head. "Not life. Maybe love. Is that too much to ask for?"

"These are really hard questions," I say. "But I get it."

"I've got another hard question for you. What are you looking for in love?" Vin asks. He clears his throat and focuses intensely on the risotto.

I don't need to think on this one. "Oh, well that one's easy. I'm looking for interesting but not too interesting, funny but not too funny, handsome—"

"But not too handsome?" he guesses as he adds a few more ladles of broth while I stir. The liquid seeps around the rice, and each grain slowly swells.

I point a rosemary sprig at him. "No. Drop-dead gorgeous."

"So... in other words, perfect," he says, half smiling at me. "You're looking for a Goldilocks relationship."

I shrug. "Sure, if you want to call it something. It needs to be just right. Because of the curse, it's safer this way. You'd think I'd be used to it by now, all the breaking up. That my scarred heart would be tough or numb. Especially with what I do. I'm literally around heartbreak in my personal and professional lives. I truly can't escape it."

"I don't think that could be true. That you could be used to it," he says.

I hand him a block of Parmesan to grate. "Oh yeah? Why not?"

"Because every relationship—or heartbreak—is different, no matter how many times you go through it," he says, moving the block back and forth as a mini cheese mountain forms. "I've played cello for so long that I've practiced and performed certain songs thousands of times. You might think that playing the exact same notes would come out sounding identical, but I could sit down right now to play that song again and it would sound different based on my energy levels and the expression I'm trying to convey. The weather, setting, and audience affect the music, too. Every performance belongs to the moment. Like relationships and heartbreak."

A small smile plays on my lips. "Like how, when my moonflowers blossom, despite being the same type of flower, each one will be different."

"Yeah. Something like that," he says, fully grinning now.

I instruct Vin to cut the hydrated mushrooms while I chop parsley and rosemary.

"Thank you. You've helped me prove my point," I say. "I'm better suited for relationships that are casual. One where there's no risk of getting hurt. Companionship. A solid friendship."

Something tells me Vin couldn't be my Just Right relationship. Without barriers and rules in place, he'd become Too Right. I allow myself to think it, though, just this once: *Wouldn't it be nice if he could be?* The thought evaporates as slowly as the broth on the stove, lingering a little too long in my mind. I stir this thought in with the rest of the ones that have been sidelined in this moment.

I redirect my focus to adding the remaining mushrooms, peas, herbs, and cheese, and mixing everything together. I scoop out a bite and hold it toward Vin to try. "This is what patience tastes like," I say.

Vin wraps his mouth around the spoon and closes his eyes. A sound of pleasure escapes his throat. "It was worth waiting for."

I grab a second spoon, and we eat straight out of the pot.

"So good," I say before throwing the question back to him. "I want to know what your version of perfect looks like."

"That one's easy for me, too," he says. "I want what my parents have. After all these years, they're still going strong."

After what Vin told me at the hotel and on our clamming day, this doesn't surprise me.

"They got exactly what they wanted at the exact right time. They just didn't know it yet," I reflect. "Sounds like it's not that you don't want to settle down. It's the opposite. You don't want to settle."

Vin takes another bite. "Yeah, I guess you're right."

"Maybe you'll feel it when you meet your perfect person," I say. "If such a thing even exists."

Vin nods just once. "I'll know exactly how it feels."

Chapter 13

VIN

We're four hours out from our flight to New York, and I've been duped. When Leo asked to meet, I thought maybe he wanted to discuss the contract. I didn't think I'd find myself sitting in the Heartbreak Circle with him, Daisy, and a few other guests.

For the past twenty minutes everyone's been sharing what brought them here and how they're feeling. For some it's been a few days, for others a few weeks. I'm too distracted about why I'm here to catch anyone's names.

"As heartbreakers, it feels wrong to be here," I whisper to Leo.

"Shhh," he says, waving me off.

"I'm not even a guest," I mumble to myself.

I've clearly said this too loudly and am now the focus of the group.

"Vin, would you care to share?" Daisy says.

"Share what exactly?" I ask.

"What your favorite game to play as a child was?" she says. "We're taking some time to lean into nostalgia. When we do this, we're brought down a path of thinking about what our past held. What we've maybe lost. We can be nostalgic for hopscotch, as Garen shared. Or capture the flag or yo-yoing, as Ruth and Marisol enjoyed."

"I liked Floor Is Lava," Leo shares, looking into the distance. "Those were happier days."

Daisy smiles. "These games may not be in our lives anymore, but they shaped us. And we still have the capacity to look back on them fondly, should we so choose."

This must be where we all share something from our past, and Daisy connects it to how this type of longing and reminiscing is relevant to what we feel with heartbreak.

No thanks. Not interested.

"So, what about you?" she asks.

I look from person to person as they patiently wait for me to share. I can feel my heart pounding in my ears, my throat suddenly dry.

I reach into the depths of my brain to conjure up something, anything. I can't even think of one. The only games circling in my brain are the ones that Daisy just listed out, but those are other people's memories. A stupid game from childhood should not be this hard to recall.

Ask me for a song name, and I'll give you twenty. "Ave Maria." *The Carnival of the Animals.* Brahms's Symphony No. 3.

"I'm not here as a participant," I croak.

"Take a minute to think about it, if you need," Daisy says kindly, moving on to the person next to me.

I don't need a minute, or two, or ten. I don't need any of this right now.

"I need to go pack," I murmur.

I stand, knocking my heart-shaped seat backward. I leave, breaking the circle. Breaking yet another heart.

New York City is at its best in the spring. The signs of life are everywhere: Daffodils blossom to let us know winter is officially behind us, trees leaf out, birds sing their songs. I notice my tension ease a little when someone on the street below leans on their car horn. The city sounds I'm used to are back in my life temporarily, plus the addition of a new one.

A faint musical laugh spills out of Chryssy. It dissipates into a rare breeze, but I can still hear it in my mind's ear. She's radiant in the sun in her yellow dress, the thin straps accentuating her shoulders.

"I'd ask how the fake dating is going, but I don't think I need to," Leo says, watching me watch Chryssy.

Chryssy joined Leo and me for our two-day photoshoot at the Metropolitan Museum of Art. The first day she was busy taking meetings with shops who want to sell In Full Bloom. Today, with the Met as our backdrop, there are more opportunities for Chryssy and me to be photographed together. When Leo and I weren't posing or walking up the Met steps with cello cases in hand for the commercial, I'd sneak away to find her and we'd allow ourselves to be caught in the act of existing together. Now, one clothing change later, we're up on the Met's rooftop for a different set of photos. Behind us, the Manhattan skyline and treetops of Central Park shine in the afternoon light.

Leo being here not only takes some of the heat off him, but it also helps my relationship with Chryssy. People can finally start focusing on us instead of where he's been. With proof that my brother's alive, this should also help ticket sales. The show must go on, after all.

And Leo loves the brand we're working with. When Lu & Co. approached us for a new watch they're debuting this summer, Leo jumped at the opportunity. We don't wear watches while performing, but any other public appearances we make will require us to wear them. The luxury jewelry company has a respectable reputation and has been around since the late 1800s, which intrigued me. I don't only want to work with new companies but also ones that have a long-standing history and tradition. Ones that have stood the test of time.

"The point of us doing this is for it to look real, so I'm making it look real," I say, clamping my mouth shut when the makeup artist comes over to sweep powder over our noses and foreheads.

Disposable garment sheets are tucked into our necklines to protect the high-end black linen sweaters we're wearing. We have our cellos with us, and to my surprise, Leo played a few chords even though we aren't contractually obligated to. It gives me hope that we'll be able to rehearse soon.

Our sleeves have been strategically rolled up to showcase the slim watch and its rectangular face, and the leather bands have been tightened comfortably around our wrists so we can move around without any shifting. The watch's theme is centered around music, which is why we were tapped to promote the product. Every hour, one of the dozen music notes on the face of the watch tilts in a different direction to signify the time.

"I should've known it was never just going to be two dates," Leo says.

"How could you possibly have known that?" I ask.

Leo shakes his head. "It was only a matter of time before you gave in to her. I saw the way you were looking at her at the party."

I grunt in disagreement. "I didn't look at anybody like anything."

"Oh, come on! You couldn't stop looking at her. You thought she was pretty the moment you saw her," Leo says. "Your eye twitched."

"Pretty" would be an understatement. Chryssy's gorgeous.

"It didn't. What does that even mean?" I ask, reaching up to feel my eye.

"When other people's eyes sparkle in excitement, yours twitch. It's a rare occurrence, but it happens when you like something you see."

A scoff comes out. "Oh yeah? Like what?"

Leo thinks for a moment. "Like when you first saw a Stradivarius cello. I think *both* of your eyes had a reaction."

I give him an exasperated look. "It was a *Strad*. Anybody with a pulse would have a reaction to that."

"It's been a while since you've been that expressive," Leo says, waiting for the makeup artist to leave before adding, "She called us out, and you liked it. No one ever calls you out."

"I'm about to call you out," I respond.

"Easy. You're acting like I've said you're gonna marry the woman," Leo says, while I maintain silence. He's entertained, and I'm glad to see it, even if it is at my expense. "Well, maybe *fake*-marry."

"That's it. You're walking back to the inn," I tell him.

Leo pulls on his blazer's lapel. "Fine! Geez. In all seriousness, how's it been when it's just you two alone?"

"Easier than I thought it would be," I say, glancing over again at Chryssy. She's lingering around the craft table, plate in hand. "Even living together has been fine. Comfortable, even."

"It seems like you two are becoming friends," Leo says, bouncing his eyebrows up and down.

I shrug. "Friends? Sure, we're that."

Leo leans in closer to my face. "Your eye twitch hasn't gone away, for the record," he says. "And this is happening after you've known her for a while. Oh man."

"'Oh man,' what?" I press.

"You like her," Leo says, his appearance earnest. "You made her breakfast before our flight yesterday, randomly bought her a toothbrush at the airport—which I thought was kind of strange, but hey, I'm not here to judge—and gave her your window seat. That was today alone."

"You can hardly call it a breakfast. It was burned toast," I say.

"Yeah, but you don't cook. And you tried. For her. What's that about?"

Leo doesn't need to know the details about how Chryssy and I have been cooking together at night.

I shrug. "I'm learning."

"Oh *man*," he says again.

"You're a pain in the ass, you know that?" I tell him. "This is just an extended deal. Nothing more, nothing less."

"I've never seen you burn toast for anyone before, is all," Leo says smugly.

I blame the quiet of the island, or the fresh air. I don't know how else to explain it. It must've been all the short but repetitive interactions. There were the dates, yes. But there's also seeing Chryssy wash her face every night, squeezing past her in the hallway every morning, being in each other's sphere day in and day out. Is fake-dating Chryssy like playing scales? What starts out slow at first turns into, with time, improved precision and speed?

"We needed to eat. I don't dislike her, so yeah, I guess logic says I like her. What's not to like?" I ask, my tone a tad too defensive for the mildness of his accusation.

Leo rubs his hands together. "Your logic is illogical."

In less than three weeks, Chryssy and I are supposed to split up and go our separate ways. I tug at my sweater, feeling extra hot in the rising temperature.

"Speaking of logic and not having any, have you been checking your emails?" I ask.

Leo shakes his head. "I still haven't turned on my phone."

"Well, the new terms came through. They're offering three times what we expected," I say, waiting for his reaction before I share the rest.

His eyes, as expected, pop. "Are you serious?"

I huff out a laugh. "We got everything we wanted. It's just not... there's a stipulation."

"What stipulation?"

Around us, the crew looks preoccupied setting up the next shot. "We need to maintain the heartbreaker brand."

Leo rubs his forehead, which the makeup artist had explicitly instructed us not to do. "We have to remain heartbreakers?" he asks. "Did we expect something different? Isn't this whole plan with Chryssy for the purposes of maintaining our brand?"

I shift in my seat. "Yeah? Yes. It is," I say, hearing how false my voice sounds.

Leo watches a pigeon walk across the set. "They should be signing us because we're good. Do we not have a say in our own careers? Our own legacy?"

"Maybe we can push back?" I say, dodging the pigeon as it flies away. "Get it struck from the contract. Can that even be in there?"

"We make them too much money. They'll never go for it," he says. "Man, we'll never escape it. We'll never be as free as that bird."

"Maybe there's no trying to escape it," I say. "It's in ink. It feels pretty permanent."

Leo stares into the distance. "Do you ever wonder what life would be like if we never picked up cellos?"

"Well, we wouldn't be modeling watches whose prices are only available upon request," I say before acknowledging what he's really getting at. "And we wouldn't be heartbreakers."

"We wouldn't be *called* heartbreakers," Leo clarifies. "Vin, I know you. I know your heart. You're not a heartbreaker in the sense everyone thinks you are. You're not out there womanizing and sleeping around. You've broken hearts, yes."

"My specialty," I say.

"There were good people you broke things off with because they weren't what you were looking for," Leo adds. "But you've also refused to settle for people who treated you poorly or took advantage of you, or women who wanted to use you for your fame, money, and decent looks, which I think we can both admit you get from me."

I smirk. "Not Mom and Dad?"

"Yeah, sure. Them too," Leo says. "But would you have broken as many hearts as you have if you weren't famous? Would you have met Chryssy if you weren't famous?"

"The truth doesn't matter if people think I'm all of those things," I say. "There's no point in playing this game, Leo. This is the life we have." I backtrack on any thoughts otherwise.

And if I want to sign the biggest deal of my life, I have to break up with Chryssy.

"Why? Do you wish we played guitars instead?" I ask.

Leo glances my way, squinting against the sun. "I...nothing. Guitars definitely would've been more portable," he jokes unenthusiastically.

"We—Chryssy and I—will stick to the plan. You and I are going to get everything we ever wanted," I say half-heartedly.

"*We?*" Leo asks, leaning back on his stool. "You two sound like a bona fide couple."

"That's where you're wrong, big brother," I say. "What Chryssy and I have is fake. Not real at all. One hundred percent fabricated."

They're all lies, and I know it.

Leo's forehead wrinkles as he makes a disbelieving face. "You're really good at lying to yourself, you know that?"

"Thank you," I say. "And you're good at avoidance. You can't escape the contract forever. This is what we've been working toward. This deal could give us and our family security for a long time."

"Whatever we do, we'll be okay," Leo says.

Chryssy approaches us, balancing a fruit plate and a few cups. "They told me to tell you it's going to be fifteen more minutes, so I come bearing snacks."

"Life- and conversation saver," Leo says, lifting a strawberry to her in a toast-like fashion.

She hands us each a paper cup. "And tea, of course. I'm giving both of you roses to drink."

Leo holds up a packet. "No need! I've got my own," he says, waving it around. "I prefer chamomile."

"Perfect for digestion," I retort.

Chryssy tosses ginger into our cups. "Because we were on an airplane."

"They have ginger over there?" Leo asks.

"I carry extra ginger around with me," Chryssy says. "For moments exactly like this. Kind of like your toothbrushes, Vin."

Leo accepts the tea, watching our interaction with a smirk on his face. "Why do I get the feeling I'm on the outside of an inside joke? Whatever it is, it's very cute. I'll leave you two be."

Leo heads over to the makeup artist to get his powder fixed again as Chryssy takes his seat.

"Question for you," she says, leaning closer to me. "Is this your typical on-set energy? Because if you're going to represent our brand, I'm going to need more charisma."

I can't tell if it's her body heat or mine warming me up. "These are always so awkward. Too much attention on us. And I'm not a model. At least not a symmetrical one," I say, turning my head to the side and pointing to my nose.

In my peripheral, I see Chryssy tracing my profile with her eyes. She takes her time doing it.

"Do you not see it? Feel this."

"Oh, I see it. It's subtle," she says, taking me up on my invite to feel the broken bridge.

She closes her eyes and gently runs the pad of her finger down the slope of my nose. When she reaches the part where it starts to veer off, her eyes blink open in surprise.

"The groove is deeper than it looks. How'd it happen?" she asks.

"I was a cello casualty. Leo and I were on tour, taking the train from Bologna to Milan. I put my cello up on the luggage rack across the aisle. The train rocked before coming to a sharp halt, and my cello came flying down. My face stopped it. I pushed my nose back in place the best I could," I say with a shrug. "We had a performance that night. Detours were out of the question."

Chryssy gives me a look of concern, her hand flying to my forearm. I unconsciously pull back as a noise escapes me.

"Sorry," she says. "Did I hurt you?"

"It's just my arm," I say.

Chryssy retrieves a gold tin from her bag. "Here. Let me see it."

"What's that?" I ask, tucking my arm back.

"It's a cooling balm. You've still got a couple more hours of showing off your wrist. I can help you make it a little less painful."

I push my sleeve up higher, tentatively extending my arm toward her. "Okay."

She gently rubs the balm around my elbow, and the light layer is both cooling and warming. Cinnamon and eucalyptus scent the air. "At the inn, we heal more than just hearts," she says.

"I think it's just from overuse. It'll get better."

"I'm guessing this isn't the first time you've had something like this?"

"Yeah, but it'll be fine," I say.

She dips her chin. "Okay, well, that's good then." When she removes her hand, the cooling sensation strengthens. I don't want her to stop touching me.

My throat tightens at this realization. I hear my response to Leo repeating itself in my mind. *I like her.* And I do. I like Chryssy. But what am I supposed to do with that?

My mind is playing tricks on me. It seems to me it would be completely natural to feel sparks or *something* for people you spend your midnight hours with. Liking people doesn't mean you're going to marry them, or even fall in love with them. Even if you are pretending to date them.

"Vin? You okay?" Chryssy asks, suspending my thoughts.

And then she has to go and smile. Chryssy carries her happiness in her eyes. Seeing her light up makes me happy in return.

"Oh. Yeah. Just thinking about the pain," I say.

"Of your nose or arm?" she asks.

"Both?" I reply, groaning at having just related breaking my nose to thinking about liking Chryssy. Both do feel like unexpected smacks in the face.

"Can I admit something to you?" she asks, twisting the lid back on the balm. "This might sound weird, but your nose was one of the first things I noticed about you. I think it's cute. I like that it's not perfect."

My chest tightens in response to hearing this. Chryssy thinks I'm cute. Wait, no. She thinks my *nose* is cute.

"Thanks" is all I can come up with before deflecting. "How's it going over there?"

"Everyone's nice. Now that I'm the Heartbreak Herbalist, people want easy answers for immediate results on health," she says before biting into an apple slice.

This designated title isn't so different from mine, but fortunately, Chryssy's label puts her in a good light.

"How have you felt about it?" I ask.

Chryssy sucks in a breath of air. "It's not something I expected, to be honest, but I want to own it," she says. "People have a lot of thoughts about what TCM is, and many times, Asian cultures are stereotyped, misrepresented, and mocked in mainstream culture. It took me some time to reconcile how we're often perceived with the work we do at the inn, but ultimately, I take pride in it. We're doing our small part and helping people when we can."

"You are," I say. "Your work is important."

Chryssy twists a strawberry around on her plate like a top toy. "Thank you. And more than ever before, I feel more connected to

YIN YANG LOVE SONG

my culture and to my ancestors, especially my great-great-great-great-grandfather. If this nickname helps get more eyes on TCM and its benefits, I view that as a good thing." She wiggles her eyebrows at me. "Hey, how do you heal heartbreak as the Heartbreak Herbalist?"

I give it five seconds to be polite. "Just tell me," I finally say. "I don't like guessing punch lines."

"You don't like *guessing punch lines*?" Chryssy asks, laughing.

"I thrive under pressure, but not that kind."

Her mouth curves into a smile. "Fine. It's only a matter of thyme." Chryssy makes a face as she holds up a sprig of thyme from her plate. "You can thank Mike in Props for that one."

I groan, shaking my head.

"I'll leave you with that gem," she says, tucking the herb behind my ear. "Oh! Auntie Violet wants a photo for socials. Our photo from clamming got ten thousand likes." Chryssy holds out her phone in front of us. "Let's hold up our cups, and we can share in the caption what we're drinking. Can you smile?"

"No one likes to be told to smile, Chrysalis," I say.

That makes her laugh as she snaps a few photos, capturing our heads pressed close together and the city skyline in the background. In the image, she looks happy. I'm smiling, too, despite myself.

"I knew, deep down, we'd eventually become the couple that gives each other nicknames," she says.

Her use of *we* makes my heart beat in double time.

"It was only a matter of *thyme*," I say, straight-faced.

Chryssy rolls her eyes before laughing again. She types into her phone when it lights up. "Okay, I need to respond to some messages. I somehow have over twenty thousand followers on Instagram now. A magazine reached out about an interview, and the evening show *Sweet Dreams, Seattle* wants me on for a cooking segment."

"Wow, that's great," I say. Chryssy's busier than I've ever seen her.

"I didn't realize there could be such a thing as too much exposure," she says. "Our plan worked a little too well for me. Salty Stems hasn't gotten back to us yet, so we need to keep looking for flower farm partners." She takes a deep breath in and smiles. It's one that doesn't carry through to her eyes.

"Is there anything I can do to help?" I ask.

"I appreciate you listening," she says. "We'll figure it out."

I absentmindedly reach for her hand. It takes us both a few seconds to realize I'm stroking her thumb with mine.

Whether she's aware of the touching or not, Chryssy allows it. "You know, I'm not friends with any of my exes, but I think I'd like to stay friends with you after all this," she says. "If that's okay with you?"

"Friends." The word rings out like a jarring note, its squeak echoing in a concert hall. The word feels worse than the pain from my tendonitis. "If we can do a secret relationship, I think we can handle a secret friendship," I say.

Chryssy nods. Then, like the hollow silence that follows the abrupt ending of a performance, she pulls her arm back and busies herself with a blueberry.

"Sorry," I say, holding my hands up where she can see them. "Did not mean to get all romantic on you."

Her cheeks turn rosy, but she waves it off. "I won't hold it against you this time. Hey, can I ask you something? When you first proposed this plan," she starts, gesturing between us, "you said you didn't think anyone would believe us being together. What did you mean by that?"

She peers up at me under her thick lashes.

"I said that because I could tell that you're this incredibly empathetic, caring woman. You deserve more than a heartbreaker like me," I admit.

Chryssy squeezes the berry between her fingers. "You know, I only agreed with you when you said that because you're this larger-than-life guy, and I'm just a cursed woman living on an island healing heartbreak. I didn't think people would truly believe us being together."

"You're not *just* anything," I tell her.

She blushes for a second time. "Here we are, getting the wrong idea about each other all over again, huh?"

"That does seem to be the trend."

Getting the wrong idea. Catching the wrong feelings. None of this was part of the plan, and sticking to the plan is what I do best. I decide in this moment that I'll get ahold of any emotions I have for Chryssy. They need to be put second to our arrangement.

It's also the moment I know Leo is right.

I'm really good at lying to myself.

Chapter 14

CHRYSSY

Late mornings at the inn are usually the sweet spot of my day. Guests are either in sessions, gardening, or resting. The breakfast rush is over, with lunch a couple of hours out. This is the window of time when I can steal moments away from cooking for guests and working on our product line to do recipe testing. I have binders filled with TCM-inspired recipes for a future cookbook I'd love to create one day.

This morning, though, I'm working on a honey, lavender, and chrysanthemum egg tart recipe for the cooking segment for *Sweet Dreams, Seattle*. It'll have a subtle flavor difference that allows me to spotlight In Full Bloom, and the egg tart molds already look like flowers. The tarts will be delicious and aesthetically pleasing, and they'll give me talking points for what we do at the inn.

I glance at the rose illustration framed on the wall with 4G's Chinese seal stamped in the corner, indicating his signature. He often drew the flowers, herbs, and roots he worked with. We keep it around us as a reminder of the long line of people we descend from who have helped others. Inspired, I sketch a chrysanthemum of my own in the margins of my recipe before getting to work.

I wrap an apron around my violet-colored dress and grab dried chrysanthemums and lavender buds from the apothecary cabinet, then move effortlessly through my recipe's steps: mix the dough, steep the flowers, add honey. The custard filling proves to be a challenge. I haven't gotten the ratio of evaporated milk and eggs quite right yet.

As I'm cracking eggs for a second batch of filling, I hear a door shut. It's a little early for sessions to be over.

A blur of a human passes by the doorway. Vin?

He doubles back and storms into the kitchen.

"Are you looking for Leo? He just went into a session," I say.

"Not Leo. Rose. Where is she?" Vin asks with an undercurrent of annoyance.

He has thin acupuncture needles sticking out of various points in his face, down his arms, and around his feet.

"Are you okay?" I ask, discarding an eggshell. "What's wrong?"

"I don't know. Rose just left me there," he says, pointing behind him.

"Once she puts the needles in, you're supposed to lie there for a while. She leaves to give you privacy. Did she explain that?" I ask.

Vin grunts. "Yes, but it's been an hour at least."

I glance at the clock. "Sessions started twenty minutes ago."

"No way that's true," Vin says, holding his arms stiffly out in front of him. "I'm supposed to lie there? And do what?"

I wash my hands as Vin walks toward me, his entire body rigid.

"Some people fall asleep. You can meditate. You could try relaxing. You shouldn't be moving around this much," I tell him.

"No," he says before adding a "thanks," like he knows I'm the only one who can help him out of his situation right now.

"Are you hungry?" I ask. "We always have scones on hand, or there's lavender shortbread." Yesterday's recipe test.

"What's that dough for?" Vin asks, distracted by my mess.

"It's for the cooking show," I say, remembering a question I had for him. It's not the best time, but he also does need something from me...

"Thoughts on going with me?" I ask casually. "I thought we could use it as another way to be seen together. Keep up appearances."

Vin's entire body loosens by a tiny percentage, as though he's forgotten his circumstances. Still, he hesitates. "Will there be cooking involved?" he asks.

"Considering it's a cooking show, that would be a safe assumption," I say, organizing the tart molds. "You can just pat the dough or something. Show off those wrists. Maybe wear that fancy watch."

This gets a laugh out of Vin. "With all my new cooking skills?" he says. "Let me at least crack an egg."

I smile. "Does that mean you'll do it?"

Vin takes a whiff of my honey-lavender-chrysanthemum concoction and raises his eyebrows in a way that tells me he likes what he smells. "I don't think so."

"What? Why not?"

"The focus should be on you, not me. Or even us. This is your moment," he says, frowning at me. "What's wrong?"

My face feels scrunched with tension. "I just...I don't want it to be all about me. What we do here is bigger than me, and it started with my aunties." I add vanilla extract to the mixture. "I don't really want to be alone on camera."

"What about your aunties? Do they want to do it?" Vin asks.

I whisk the sweet-smelling filling. "They said they'd rather have their hearts broken all over again. They're behind-the-scenes people."

Vin taps his fingers along the countertop. "Oh. Then count me in."

"Really?"

"I didn't want to get in your way," he says. "But if you'd like me to be there, then I'll come."

"Well, don't get *all* the way in my way," I joke.

"Spotlight's all yours," he says, smiling. "It'd be an honor to stand in your shadow."

A warming sensation creeps up my neck while my heart throws itself against my chest. I glance at the stove, but the burners aren't on. Nothing's cooking. This is all me.

"Can I thank you with a cup of tea?" I offer.

"You can express your gratitude by getting *these* out of me," he says, gesturing up and down his body.

He's both flustered and impatient, two states of being that soften his typically hard features. It's endearing, in a way.

"Okay, okay. Try to stay still," I say, setting my whisk down. "I'll help you remove them. Give me one second."

I go back to Vin's session room and grab a sharps container. Back in the kitchen, I approach Vin slowly as he stands stiffly in place. I guide him to the table, and we sit facing one another.

I start with his face, plucking out the needle between his eyebrows and behind one of his ears. Under his loose black T-shirt, his chest noticeably rises and falls.

"Did you do it yet?" he asks.

I show him the evidence. "It's done."

"Hmm," he says. "I didn't feel it."

I drop the needles into the sharps container.

"These are hair-thin. When they're inserted, you might feel a little zing and then tingling sensations. Some people don't feel anything, though. Or it's a dull sensation," I explain.

"Then what's the point if I can't feel it?" he asks

"Just because you can't feel it doesn't mean nothing's happening," I say. "We want to balance the flow of Qi in the body's energy meridians. Get the blood circulating. There are hundreds of points, and we target the ones that correspond with what you're experiencing. We're treating the root causes of the pain or illness."

"The pain's in my arm. What does my face have to do with that?" Vin asks.

I jump at any opportunity to share more about what we do. "Usually, one point isn't enough to do anything, so we combine points on a meridian. This is a common way to restore circulation. From the various points, I can see that Auntie Rose was targeting more than just your elbow pain. We can work on healing many health issues in each session. Auntie Rose knows there's more going on with you."

Vin laughs through his nose. "Is that why she asked me so many questions?"

I nod. "We want to understand not just what's going on with you physically, but also emotionally and psychologically. It's all about the mind-body connection. Even from just our short time together, I can tell that you likely experience anxiety and insomnia. Would you agree with that?"

On a reluctant-sounding exhale, Vin agrees.

"I'll give you an example," I say, pointing to the spot where I removed the needle between his eyebrows. He follows my finger with his eyes. "Yintang is an acupoint that can help relieve anxiety and stress, but also insomnia. There's a lot of heat in this area that we want to clear out. Imbalances in the heart can cause anxiety and insomnia, so that's what we want to regulate and help calm. And this point right here is called Large Intestine 11." I remove the needle from the point located at the crease in his elbow.

"All the points relate to something specific?" Vin asks, surveying his body. "How do you remember what's what, and where?"

"How do you play pieces without sheet music?" I ask.

One corner of his mouth pulls up into a half smile. He nods to himself, and then says to me, "I had a realization the other day." Vin's fingers tighten into fists, the muscles contracting up his forearms. "You inspire me," he says as his eyes meet mine.

I slide the sharps container closer. "Me? How?"

"You were on this path in med school, but it wasn't working for you," Vin says. "Instead of forcing yourself to continue on, you transitioned into something you really love and that you're passionate about. That was—*you are*—brave."

"I don't know if it was brave or necessary. I had to ask myself if anything was worth more than my health," I say. "All I knew was that I couldn't keep going down the path I was on. My body let me know that I had pushed myself too far, and I listened."

I move on to the rest of the points along his arm. My eyes betray me as they take in Vin's smooth skin, tracing the paths of his muscles and veins curving around his arms like ivy.

Vin watches me, like he's studying my face for signs. Of what? I'm not sure.

He sucks in a sharp breath of air.

"Did I hurt you?" I ask.

"No. Is that…my music?" he asks, turning his head to find the source: my phone propped up on the counter. From its little speaker, classical music streams out at a low volume. He's now relaxed enough to notice subtle sounds.

"You weren't supposed to be in here right now, so I thought I'd do some catching up. Just in case anyone asks what my favorite song of yours is or something," I justify.

And because when I can't be around Vin himself, I've been finding other ways to be. It's a new development that I'm not sure how to feel about. From the outside looking in, I know it looks like I'm becoming attached. Recording my podcast in his foamed-up room. Attempting to read the sheet music he leaves on the chairs as though it could bring me closer to what goes through his mind, even though I have no idea what each note sounds like. Listening to his music.

I almost burned a batch of scones last week looking at photos of us on my phone from the photoshoot. I'm acting like someone who has a crush, which I certainly do *not*. The fake relationship was—is—perfect exactly as it's stated in its name. Fake. Pretend. *Not real.*

I tell myself I'm just getting to know my roommate. It's for the betterment of everyone involved that we have a pleasant living situation while Leo heals. I talk myself into thinking that it doesn't mean anything serious when Vin makes me rubbery eggs and dry blueberry muffins. That the secrets we've been trading are all part of creating a credible illusion.

I've *almost* convinced myself.

"This one sounds like classical, though. Don't you guys do rock?" I ask. A new, way more energetic and intense song has started.

"This one's Vivaldi's *Four Seasons*. Summer, third movement." Vin closes his eyes as he listens, his head making sharp jolts as though he's performing it on a miniature scale.

"It's like we're back at the Prodigy Party all over again," I say. "You stay away from the outlets."

Vin smiles. "We rarely get to play these pieces anymore. I first heard it when I was six and immediately knew I was going to love playing it."

"That's not a sentence you hear every day," I say. "In Vegas you mentioned wishing you got to play classical music more. Why don't you?"

Vin takes a moment to respond. "We're all about rock, and at this point, it fits our brand best," he says with finality. "That's what people come to see. We do try to put our own spin on the music we play."

"Is that why you play the electric cello?"

"Yeah, that one's fun to play. I also have a cello that was built in 1763. You can really hear the difference compared to modern cellos. There's a rich depth of sound with it. It's complex." His eyes widen. "I'll stop there before I start talking about how the strings used to be made out of animal intestines."

It's too sweet how excited Vin gets when he's talking about music and old cellos.

"Anyway, we'll be playing at some incredible historic venues on tour, and this song would be surreal to perform live," he says. "One day, I'd love to play with various symphony orchestras around the world."

"Right now it's just you two?" I ask.

"Occasionally we have a drummer, but we arrange the music for just us two." He thinks for a moment. "Leo and I get our names on the billboards, but to put on the type of shows we do, it pretty much takes an orchestra, as they say," he says with a grin that quickly falls. "It's why pushing rehearsals wasn't so simple. Everyone who's a part of this tour and their families rely on us to show up and do our job so that they can do theirs."

I nod. That's a lot of pressure to have so many people relying on you. My shoulders tighten at the thought of all the stress Vin carries. While I think this unexpected detour to the inn has some benefits for him, it's also adding more weight to his already full plate.

"Anyway, with this one, I really am playing with an orchestra," he says.

I actively listen to the song, noting the fluctuation of high and deep tones and the urgency present in every note. String instruments are played one after the other before they all come back together as one. Instead of just hearing an assortment of notes, I feel something. There's a pull of excitement in my chest as my heartbeat quickens to match the rhythm.

I imagine the man in front of me playing this, and it gives me goose bumps. I've only caught glimpses of Vin playing at the Prodigy Party and then again on my laptop screen. I imagine the real thing must be spectacular.

"Whoa," Vin says as I remove a needle from his wrist. "That spot felt…hot?"

"Nerve stimulation. That's good. Gotta get that Qi moving," I tell him. The last notes of the song fade away as it ends. "Wow. That was just…it's beautiful. I'm sure it's even more incredible live." He smiles as I remove a few last needles from his ankles and do a quick check to make sure I got all of them. "You're clear."

"Thanks. My tendonitis flares up every now and then," he says. "The first time was when we were in the middle of a tour and just getting started in our careers. I played through it."

The thought of him in pain and pushing through it makes me ache.

"Physical injury can be the source of heartbreak for many people," I tell him. "If you couldn't play because of your arm pain, let's say, but making music is a big part of your identity, you might start to feel aimless. Unfocused. Not good enough. Frustrated. You wouldn't be doing something you love to the best of your ability. We've worked with ex–sports players who injured themselves to the point of no return on the field or the court. There's heartbreak in that."

Vin sighs. "Honestly, I've imagined that moment thousands of times. The moment it could all end. The potential performance anxiety. The unexplained vanishing of ability. So, yeah. That heartbreak I get."

"You can do things differently this time. I'd like to help you if you'd let me," I say. I reach for his arm, my hand landing on top of his wrist.

Vin's eyes find mine. In even just three weeks, I can already see the small differences being here has had on him. His slowed-down demeanor. The way his hair is more tousled than tamed. One of many layers of exhaustion shed like an expired petal. A new openness to even consider acupuncture to begin with. A hairline crack in the perfection he strives for, whether he realizes it or not.

His mouth forms a firm line, but he nods. "Okay. I trust you."

"We'll try again tomorrow. Your tendons are inflamed, and acupuncture will create an anti-inflammatory response," I explain. "We want to rebalance this area. Our job is to treat the cause. We want to help you prevent this, instead of always focusing on the cure."

"And what does that look like?" Vin asks, holding eye contact.

I raise one eyebrow. "Things you probably don't want to hear. More rest. More sleep. Relaxing for a change. Working on lowering your stress levels."

"So, a full-on lifestyle change. Plus acupuncture, even though I hardly felt anything."

"If you don't want to keep pushing through the pain and risking this becoming chronic, yes," I say. "You know how, when you listen to music, you can't actually see the notes? Well, maybe *you* can, but people like me can't. Acupuncture points are like music notes. Both are invisible, but they have an effect on the body. On our hearts. On our overall well-being. You may not always feel it in the moment, but they leave an impression."

"Did you just relate acupuncture to music?" he says, his voice low. He leans in closer.

Vin's lips aren't in a firm line anymore. They're curved slightly upward, and his body is relaxed.

"I figured that might really drive the point home," I say, noticing my own voice softening. "Did it work?"

In our proximity, his thighs have found mine. It's when he glances at his arm that I realize my fingers are still on his wrist. I don't have to apply too much pressure to feel the rapid beat of his pulse.

He flips his hand so that the pads of my fingers fall onto his palm. I trace the lines until they reach his calloused fingertips. My fingers fold into his grasp, like we're testing something out.

"I'd say so," he says.

With my other hand, I unconsciously brush the one strand of hair that curls in on itself away from his forehead. Instead of bringing my arm back, I shock myself by stroking his cheek. I'm at ease in the quiet hum of the kitchen with the soothing sounds of classical music playing next to the stove, a honey-sweet mixture scenting the air.

Vin grunts and reaches forward, cupping my jaw in his hand. The act draws me toward him like a flower to the sun.

We bend forward in our chairs to close what's left of the few inches between us, and our lips collide in a very different way than they did in Vegas. This kiss isn't tentative. In fact, there's no question about it. Vin glides his tongue over my bottom lip as I take his top one between my own. I run my hand down his neck to his chest, which is firm to the touch over the thin fabric of his T-shirt. His hand moves across my back, and my skin tingles at his touch.

Whatever this is isn't for show. It's just for us.

Vin kisses like a heartbreaker. When his tongue meets mine, he playfully flicks it before he pulls it back. He's clearly as passionate when he kisses as he is when he plays. It's no wonder he has a legendary status.

A thought pops into my mind that is so disruptive I can feel it all the way down in the depths of my chest. Do I like this man? My heart squeezes in response.

It's official. I've caught feelings.

I sink into the kiss. If I'm going to be crushed, it might as well be fun.

Heat blooms across my chest, spreading to and stimulating every corner of my body.

I want to experience his body pressed against mine, to know what his heartbeat feels like against my own. Before we have a chance to, I hear Vin's name being called out. Or is that me saying his name?

It's me. I'm saying his name.

But it's *also* someone else.

The voice grows louder, and we fling ourselves back against our chairs as Auntie Rose steps into the kitchen.

"There you are," she says, huffing in exasperation. "Why are you out here? And where are the needles?"

"He couldn't sit still," I say, stealing a glance at him. There's a light pink coloring his cheeks. I didn't realize Vin Chao was capable of blushing.

Auntie Rose eyes the space between us, probably noting our poor attempt to make it look like we haven't just been making out.

"Practicing?" she asks.

"She was explaining acupuncture to me," Vin says, covering for us.

Auntie Rose sighs. "I meant the other kind of practicing."

I follow her gaze to Vin's hand where my fingers are still intertwined with his.

We pull our arms back at the same time. "Oh. Yeah," I say. "We're very committed to making this plan work."

Auntie Rose just waves her hand over her head as she turns and leaves the kitchen, closing the door behind her.

Vin reaches for me again. I don't object. As my skin burns under his touch, my brain floods with oxytocin. Mind-body connection.

Then Vin stands, and I do, too. When he leads me to the back door, down the steps, and toward the Dandelion, I follow.

Chapter 15

CHRYSSY

I practically float to the Dandelion and barely make it inside before I'm in Vin's arms. He lifts me against the back of the door, his fingers gripping my thighs as my legs wrap around his waist. I slide my fingers through his hair as I pull his mouth to mine. I'm caught up in the melody of his low groans against my lips, each *mmm* introducing new depths to a song I won't be able to get out of my head. His lips travel down my jaw and throat before he spins me around. Our movements are a whirlwind.

Vin looks from the chairs to the kitchen counter to the floor covered in books. None are viable options. I nod toward my bedroom, and even though the hallway's only three steps long, it feels like ages to get there.

He lowers me gently onto my bed, taking a long pause to lock eyes with me. Vin's dilated pupils are mesmerizing as they catalog my face, taking me in. I glide my palm up his chest and around the back of his neck, tugging him closer to me. I'm desperate for more of him, to taste him, to feel him.

Vin traces his fingers along my chin, and the roughness sends chills down my spine. My pulse transfers its energy into his hand, and for a second we're connected by a single beat.

I peel Vin's shirt off first, spreading my fingertips over his broad shoulders. He kneels over me and swiftly undoes each button on my dress, his nimble fingers never once catching.

I scoot backward until my head finds a pillow, my eyes never once leaving Vin's. He lowers himself until there's just enough of his weight on me. A Vin-shaped weighted blanket. At once I'm comforted and calm, wanting him in so many ways. Vin's skin feels warm against mine as I arch up into him.

"We're definitely overachievers," he says in a voice so gravelly it's rough against my ear.

I loop my legs around his hips and pull him tighter against me.

"No one could ever fault us," I say between shallow breaths, "for not caring about what we commit to."

Vin's mouth pushes against mine, urgently but gently, like I'm sheet music and he's reading me, determining how hard or soft he wants to play each note. The man kisses me like he needs air. It's as swift and impulsive as his music, each note faster than the last. I slide my tongue against his, memorizing the way he tastes.

To counter the speed, I slow things down by kissing the corners of Vin's mouth. The one that contains smiles both charming and reluctant. I trail my mouth down Vin's neck, inhaling his subtle scent I can only detect when I'm close enough to him. A bubble of black tea, dark berries, and eucalyptus surrounds me, intoxicates me. I've carried the scent of butter and lavender with me, and our aromas fill the space.

Vin pushes up on his arms, distancing himself briefly, and I feel the loss immediately. "We're always trying to get better," he says, his voice thick with desire.

"Right. We care too much," I whisper up to him.

His face hovers inches above mine, and in the span of a few deep breaths, he just looks at me. Really looks at me.

"I care about you, Chryssy," he says, his voice shaking slightly.

Vin's nerves add weight to this moment. We're as vulnerable as we can be right now, but even though we're half-naked, it's still not as exposed as we've been before with each other.

I feel safe and comfortable with this man. Like if I really wanted to leap feetfirst, I could. And he wouldn't just catch me. He'd be right there jumping with me.

He sucks in a long breath before adding, "And I like you. A lot."

I rub my thumb along his lower lip slowly, taking advantage of the extra beat to linger in this moment. My entire body buzzes as bliss courses through my veins, my heart happily working overtime.

"I like you, too, Vin," I say, my voice coming out just as uneven. It dawns on me that it's not because I'm nervous to say it or that I don't mean it.

It's because I do.

My real feelings can no longer disguise themselves as pretend ones. They're as real as the flowers blooming in the garden.

Within seconds, the last pieces of clothing are on the floor.

Then, he looks at me the way he did when he was listening to Vivaldi's third movement—like I'm his favorite song.

The next movements happen fast then slow, before picking up speed again. It's the rhythm to all the songs I love. The ones that make me feel good.

"Is this okay?" Vin asks when a quiet noise escapes me.

"More than okay," I say. "It's just…it's been a while."

He nods. "For me too."

"I want this," I admit. "I want you."

"There's nothing I want more," Vin says, a full smile taking over. "You know how I got so good at playing?"

"Other than being a natural-born talent?" I narrow my eyes, pretending to think hard about what the answer could possibly be. "Hmmm. Practice?"

A low laugh tumbles out. "Lots of practice."

Vin presses kisses into the side of my neck that I feel all the way down to my toes. If this is what practice means, I'll practice with him any chance I get.

And that's exactly what we do.

We practice for the rest of the afternoon.

Chapter 16

VIN

We arrive at the *Sweet Dreams, Seattle* studios in downtown Seattle an hour before we go live. The producer, Nancy, leads us to the set, which looks like a real kitchen. The sage-green island has ample counter space for Chryssy to do her thing. Behind the kitchen is a staircase, windows, and a dining room off to the side to give the illusion that we're in a home. This set in particular reminds me of the comedy Leo and I made a cameo in, but in that movie I didn't have to cook.

Overhead, twenty or so lights are positioned at different angles, casting a cool blue over us. Because the show airs for late-night viewers, we're meant to look like we're cooking in the glow of moonlight. The atmosphere simultaneously feels so real and so...fake.

The ingredients for Chryssy's egg tarts are already set up, premeasured and prepoured. A crew member brings over prebaked egg tarts, per Chryssy's recipe, for her to taste-test and to ensure that they look as they should.

As we near the top of the hour, we're informed about how everything will work with timing and movements.

"We have a few viewer-submitted questions and recent, most-searched questions just for fun. See how much you really know about each other," Nancy explains, pointing to the teleprompter in front of the counter. "They're questions we think viewers are up all night thinking about. Hence the segment, *Up All Night*."

"That's not what we had prepared for today," Chryssy tells Nancy.

She looks at us curiously. "Did you need to prepare for things you would already know about each other?"

There's a too-long silence before Chryssy finally spits out a too-hard, nervous laugh. "Of course not. I'm sure we can get through a few questions about each other. Right?" she says, reaching to link her arm through mine in a display of affection. The casual touch feels anything but, especially after what happened between us two days ago.

But we're here. Might as well put any other doubts to rest.

"Vin," Chryssy whispers when Nancy leaves, "quick, what's your favorite color? Wait, I think I know. Is it black?"

"You think they're going to ask us basic questions like that? It's probably going to be the deep shit," I say, irritated. The plan was to cook and cook only. "Stuff like, what's your greatest fear in life."

"Ending up alone," she answers. "Just tell me. Favorite color. Go!"

"Hey, this will be okay," I say softly, giving her arm a squeeze. "We know things about each other, Chryssy."

"Yeah, you're probably right," she mumbles. "This won't be edited, though."

"If you need to make up something in the moment, I'll go along with it," I offer. "I had a pet hedgehog? You bet I did. Even named him Sonic. I have a tattoo of Bach on my back? Got it when I was nineteen."

Chryssy's expression softens. "Bach, really?" she asks with a smirk. "I think I'd have remembered that from..."

She tries to hide her smile by looking down at the ground, but I still catch it.

My cheeks heat at the reference to our afternoon together. I step closer to Chryssy as I answer her. "Actually, I hate needles," I admit.

She looks up at me, confused. "But the other day. The acupuncture."

"I promised you I'd try," I say. "And I couldn't say no to Rose."

Across the studio, the thud of a dropped box startles us. I become more aware of all the movement in the studio. Gaffers adjust the lighting while cameramen frame their shots. Producers fast-walk across the kitchen set. Showtime is approaching.

"Hey, if you don't want to do this or need more time, I can pretend I had a spoiled sandwich earlier," I say, throwing out a lifeline. "Do you want to smell my invisible flowers?"

My attempt to make Chryssy laugh works.

"That's a kind offer, but I'm okay," she says. "I jumped off a building attached to you. I can do this. I've visualized this moment for days, but it only now hit me that this is going to be live. There are so many people who watch this show."

Now she's rambling.

I step closer to Chryssy, hoping the proximity calms her. "Before performances, I still get nervous, too," I admit.

"You do?" she asks. "Huh. I guess I figured you'd be used to it by now after all these years. Do you have some kind of quirky preshow ritual?"

"I like to oil myself up and then roll around in glitter," I joke. "But yeah, I still get preshow jitters. The fact that people have taken the time to come see us and have paid hard-earned money to be there means a lot. I want to give them everything they expect and then some. There is something else I do that helps ground me, besides, you know, the glitter. Do you want to do it with me?"

Chryssy studies me before agreeing. "Glitter me up."

I shift my footing before revealing myself to her. "I like to peek out at the audience, find one person, and make up a name and backstory for them," I share. "At the Sydney Opera House, there was Lucas who designed theater sets, competed in amateur ice-sculpting competitions, and had a time-share in Bora-Bora. Then there was Matilda at

Carnegie Hall, who was one of five siblings. She was a data engineer by day, a jazz pianist by night, and had a soft spot for Classical Chinese poetry."

Chryssy looks surprised. "That's...not what I expected you to say."

I nod. "I know people have expectations of me, of the Chao Brothers. If I can feel connected to at least one person in the room in a city I don't know anyone in, it makes the need to impress more manageable. I need to win over Lucas and Matilda, not every single person there. Otherwise, I'm performing to a sea of faces and strangers I'll never know the names of."

"I kind of love that," Chryssy says softly.

"It helps, I promise. Want to try?" I ask. "It's better for it to be more rooted in reality than in your imagination, and we can't see viewers on the other side of the camera. We can see people in this room, though." I point to a crew member busy setting up coffee on the craft services table. "Who's that?"

Chryssy looks from the crew member back to me. "You just make something up?"

"Let's start with a name."

"That's Azalea," Chryssy says after a few seconds.

"And what does Azalea do? Besides provide food for everyone to stay energized on set," I ask.

Chryssy's breathing steadies as she thinks. "Azalea has a food-styling business on the side, has a fondness for yacht rock, and bakes angel cake every year on the first day of spring."

"You nailed it on your first try," I say, impressed.

"When we're live, I'll be teaching Azalea how to make egg tarts," Chryssy says, the worry lines between her eyebrows softening.

"Exactly."

"Thank you, Vin," she says, taking a step closer. I pull her in for a hug that she returns. "Did they put lavender cream on you?"

I clench my jaw, resisting a smirk. "No."

She looks around for the source of the scent. "Whatever it is, it's soothing." Another whiff passes under our noses and Chryssy sniffs the air. "Where is that coming—"

"It's me, okay?" I say between gritted teeth.

She gasps under her breath. "You did not."

I avoid Chryssy's eyes. "I told you I fucking love bath bombs."

"It works for you," she says. "You smell like fields of lavender baked in the sun, and not at all like dish soap."

I grin back at her. "I...like it, too."

A musical laugh escapes her, seemingly shaking loose any remaining nerves she has. I hope they fizzle away like the bath bomb I enjoyed earlier today.

Before the top of the hour, we've changed into our outfits and had hair and makeup done. Nancy begins the countdown to showtime verbally and with her fingers. "We're rolling in three..."

Next to me, Chryssy takes a deep breath in and shifts her focus to Azalea.

"Two..."

Behind the island, I place my hand on the small of her back, circling the spot with my thumb. Chryssy straightens her shoulders and looks directly into the camera.

One, Nancy mouths.

A green light blinks on. And we're live.

"Welcome to *Sweet Dreams, Seattle*. I'm Chrysanthemum Hua Williams, also known as the Heartbreak Herbalist, and I'm here with my boyfriend, Vin Chao," Chryssy says, the words rolling easily off her tongue. I wave to the camera as I lean against the island.

"Also known as the Heartbreaker of Cello Rock," I say with a little shrug.

Chryssy shares what we'll be making tonight and explains the benefits of honey, lavender, and chrysanthemums.

We start with the dough and mix flour, butter, and cold water together. Chryssy teaches me—and in turn the viewers—how to cube the butter and work it in until the dough forms coarse crumbs.

I take lead with the ingredients while Chryssy focuses on the instructions. It requires everything in me not to tuck the strand of hair that's come loose from Chryssy's low bun behind her ear as she brings the dough together.

The dough needs to rest half an hour to absorb moisture, but because we don't have that kind of time, various stages of dough have already been prepped by the show's crew.

More TV magic.

Chryssy removes the rested dough from the set's fridge behind us and shows viewers how to roll it out. There are a series of folds and more rolling to create the right amount of flakiness. As she does this, I ask the first question of the show.

"Who is Vin Chao's girlfriend?" I read from the teleprompter.

"You want to take this one?" Chryssy asks.

I face the camera. "Well, her name is Chrysanthemum, which you already know." I succinctly describe the work Chryssy and her aunties do at the inn and talk about In Full Bloom like the good brand ambassador that I am, complete with a full spelling-out of the online shop website where they can preorder.

"I didn't even have to pay him to say that," Chryssy says. The crew behind the cameras chuckle. If only they knew.

Before she can ask me a question, I hear myself adding more to my answer.

"But beyond work and labels," I say, "Chryssy is incredibly empathetic and kind. She cares a lot about people, whether you're being treated by her or not. She's inspiring as hell, and she makes the best food I've ever eaten. In fact, Chryssy loves healing ingredients so much that she once went as a piece of ginger for Halloween. And if you ever need a Billy Joel song rec, she's your go-to."

They're details that will add to the illusion of our relationship. At the thought of this, I don't know which word, in particular, to believe. Illusion or relationship?

Chryssy grins up at me as her fingers sink into the dough.

"So yeah," I say, inhaling deeply. "That's my girlfriend."

"You inspire me, too," she whispers to me.

She makes a quarter turn in the dough and continues rolling it out, this time asking me a question.

"Where's Leo?" she reads out loud. My mind pictures Leo in a red-and-white-striped shirt and hat, wearing glasses and holding a cello, like he's a musical version of Waldo. To the Chaobreakers, that's how it must feel.

I straighten. "I've had to go to the Wildflower Inn to heal my tendonitis before our world tour. I'm lucky that it affords me time to spend with Chryssy. Leo accompanied me there, but he's been heads down with new music and rehearsing. Stay tuned." I cringe at my pun.

Chryssy gives me a nod of support. That should cover it. I sigh in relief, and Chryssy moves on, explaining as she washes her hands that we're going to let the dough rest for another half hour. By now, I'm sure viewers know that we have a slab of well-rested dough waiting for us in the fridge.

"In the meantime, we'll make our filling," Chryssy says, her breath catching. I follow her gaze to the glass of hot water containing only lavender buds…because there aren't any chrysanthemums. In the whirlwind hour leading up to the show, we didn't double-check to make sure they had everything we needed.

"We'll have to uh, do a little imagining," Chryssy says. "We have lavender, but we'll need to pretend that there are also chrysanthemum flowers steeping in this hot water." She then proceeds to describe what mums look like, using her hands to depict the bloom.

"I might have something," I interject.

I disappear from the set, returning a few seconds later with one of the In Full Bloom packaged flowers Chryssy gave me. I tear it open and add the dried chrysanthemum to the hot water, watching as the stringy petals bob up and down.

"The product is great," I say. "I carry it with me everywhere I go. See how the flowers bloom?" I then, nearly word-for-word, re-explain the benefits of chrysanthemums that I learned from Chryssy.

There's a flicker of surprise on Chryssy's face, but she moves on to the next question as we give the chrysanthemum time to steep.

"How do you know when you're mad at each other?" she asks, not hesitating with her answer. "When you're mad, you clench your jaw."

I don't waver, either. "You do this wriggling thing with your nose. It scrunches. Twitches. It's quick and subtle, but it's your tell."

"What, like I'm working magic?" Her finger flies to the tip of her nose.

"Yes, but your spells are recipes," I say, catching on to her *Bewitched* reference. "And you don't think so, but I'm convinced you also make love potions."

She shakes her head as she strains the flowers and adds honey to the water. "Either way, I'm just trying to make my troubles go away," she says playfully.

I smirk. "It'll take a lot more than a nose twitch to get rid of me."

Like a preset expiration date.

"Maybe my jaw clench and your nose twitch aren't so far off from one another," I say, running my hand along my chin. "Frustrating people exacerbate it."

"Oh yeah?" She narrows her eyes at me and dramatically wriggles her nose, as though she's pretending to try to make me disappear.

An amused noise slips out of me.

I'm buzzing with excited energy and realize I should've found a person of my own to create a backstory about. Something to focus on other than Chryssy. Somewhere in the depths of my brain I've been collecting tidbits of information about her, safekeeping them for later. Surely not for a moment like this, but it doesn't hurt. And somewhere in her, too, whether she meant to or not, she's been storing pieces of me.

Per my request, I get to crack all the eggs. Chryssy whisks them together with the evaporated milk, vanilla, and honey-flower mixture to create a custard while I work on rolling out the premade dough. We're able to answer more questions as we cut out circles and line them in the molds.

"Viewer Amanda is wondering what our best date was," Chryssy says. A look of worry etches into her expression. She thinks we'll have to do some seriously heavy improv lifting here. We've never gone on a proper date.

I gently push dough circles into the molds, but my eyes are on Chryssy.

"I don't know that I can speak for Chryssy on this one, but I know for me one of our most memorable dates was this one night when we ordered room service and watched *Sleepless in Seattle*," I start, describing our Yin Night. I say this directly to her, as though the cameras and crew aren't around us. The people in headsets, in director's chairs, and all the equipment fall away. I'm just here cooking with Chryssy in the way we have almost every night this past week. What felt overly fabricated at first is now, without a doubt, more real.

"We were up way too late talking and stuffing ourselves with fries," I continue as Chryssy's mouth parts. "I think it was the closest I'd ever come to perfect."

A tight breath escapes her lips. She might think I'm embellishing my feelings to make this convincing, but as I talk about our Yin Night, it strikes me that it really was perfect. I hope we get more nights like it.

"We have one last question before we bake the egg tarts and call it a night," Chryssy says, straining the mixture. She explains the next steps about baking the egg tarts and for how long while I execute, carefully pouring the filling into each shallow mold until they reach just below the lip. "Very nice, Vin."

"Thank you, Chef," I say, moving to the next mold.

Her face beams with pride. "Here we go. Final question. Viewer Miranda wants to know if Chrysanthemum's family is cursed to never find lasting love and Vin is a heartbreaker, do two negatives cancel each other out?"

The words come out of Chryssy's mouth before she seems to process what she's said.

Chryssy stares at the camera, stunned into silence.

I'm midpour when I freeze, too. Her family's curse has been exposed. On live television.

I recover first, ignoring the overflowing mixture now dripping onto the counter. "By cursed, you probably mean, Miranda, that by dating me, she's cursed for a breakup." I set the bowl down and spread my hands over the counter. "And normally, that would be true. But not this time. So, if you're looking for the secret to lasting love, it's this: Find a woman like Chryssy. And that breakup you're all expecting? It's not gonna happen." I turn to her. "At least not on my end. I think I'd be the biggest fool in the world to ever let a woman like Chryssy go."

I steal a glance at Chryssy, who looks as surprised as I feel. For four excruciating seconds, the studio is quiet. It's dead air and live television is unforgiving, but no one says a thing. I can't take the words back now even if I try—but strangely, I don't feel the desire to take anything back.

Chryssy's lungs seem to finally remember their job, and she takes an audible breath.

She slowly turns back to the camera and says, meekly, "We— You heard it here first."

Chapter 17

CHRYSSY

I make a stop for BBQ pork buns at Pike Place before heading over to see Dad. There's a lull between lunch and dinner, so we have the place to ourselves.

Dad started his restaurant nearly fourteen years ago, right around the time I left for college. He debated calling it Empty Nester or Filling the Void as a symbolic representation of the times, but ultimately landed on Pearl. It's objectively a much more appealing name.

Tables line the perimeter of the restaurant, and the U-shaped oyster bar stands in the center. Stools surround it so customers can watch as their oysters are freshly shucked and served. On the other side of the large windows is a view of Elliott Bay. The blue water glitters as the sun hits it. It's the kind of stunning Seattle day where the entire city reminds its residents that it can still show off when it wants to.

Dad greets me with a side hug, and I hand him his bun and a present. "Happy Father's Day!" I say.

Dad rips the wrapping paper off, revealing a Velcro wallet with the words *Big Shucks* printed across it.

He chuckles. "Thank you. That's one shell of a gift." Dad eats half of the bun in one bite. "And thanks for that. I haven't had breakfast yet," he says before taking another. "A cook called out sick, so I had to step in to prep."

"You need to be eating breakfast, Dad. Make sure you're taking care of yourself," I say. "Have you had any water today?"

Dad crumples the bun wrapper in his palm. "I had coffee. That has water in it."

He pours crushed ice over the oysters to keep them cool. I lift one to examine its top. The light brown swirls into shades of white and mossy green before blurring into the dark brown of the shell's edge. "Are you busy right now? Have time to shuck a few oysters?" I ask.

"For you, I've got all day," he says, wiping up water drops on the counter with a linen towel. "Except for when dinner service starts. Then I gotta go."

I set my bag on a stool and walk around to the center of the bar.

"I got in a fresh batch of Kumamotos this morning. Already scrubbed 'em," Dad says.

Before we get started, he presses a few buttons on his phone. Billy Joel's "Only the Good Die Young" flows out of the ceiling speakers seconds later.

Dad sets a bowl of ice between us for the shucked oysters as I fold a clean kitchen towel in preparation. We get to work, silently falling into step with one another. I was always my dad's right-hand woman in the kitchen, helping him scrub clams, shuck oysters, and chop vegetables.

"You haven't come by in a while. How's In Full Bloom going?" Dad asks. "You look tired."

I balk. "Dad, no one likes to be told they look tired."

"Sorry, I'm concerned is all!"

I grab one of the small oysters and rub my thumb over the deep grooves of the shell. Ever since I first tried them, Kumamotos have been my favorite because of their mild brine and fruitiness.

"The flower farm we're in talks with can't give us their mums this year. Florists want them for weddings, which is honestly good news. Chrysanthemums are having a revival," I say. "Well, all chrysanthemums but me. The inn is booked out for the year, and preorders keep going up. The cooking show led to more interview requests and more social media followers." I shake my head.

"Those all sound like good things," Dad says, confused. "Everyone wants to talk to the Heartbreak Herbalist."

"Yeah, that added fuel," I say with a tight laugh. "I worried that the title would be limiting, but interestingly, being the Heartbreak Herbalist gives people something tangible to grasp. It's helpful when heartbreak—and for many, TCM—is more abstract." A real smile forms. "People have been open-minded to healing in a different way than they have before." I set the oyster on the towel. "But it was still too much exposure too fast, and we haven't found a new farm to partner with. We weren't ready. I wasn't ready. Then again, who knows what will happen now after..."

"After... the show?" Dad guesses.

"You saw that?" I ask, glancing up at him.

"And miss the chance to see my daughter become a big TV star?" Dad asks. "Of course I saw it. The staff and I watched it here."

I cringe. "Great, so now everyone who works for you knows your daughter is cursed."

No. Now *thousands* of people know about the curse, something that's remained mostly hidden for hundreds of years in my family.

"How'd that get out?"

"I'll give you one guess," I mutter.

"Great-Aunt Angelica?"

"Ding ding," I say with forced pep, relaying what I learned from my aunties. As soon as Auntie Violet watched this happen live, she sent out feelers to the family to figure out how word got around. "Great-Aunt Angelica talked to someone named Miranda who worked at the Chihuly Garden and Glass gift shop. At least she got a discount on glass ornaments."

Dad shivers. "I got stuck chitchatting with Angelica for an hour at a Christmas party one year. The curse was all she talked about," he recalls.

"Sounds about right," I say. "It's just…it's one thing when you believe something about yourself. It's another when thousands of people believe it about you." I take a long breath in. "If everyone believes it, does it make it…even more true?" My voice cracks at this. This must be how Vin feels.

I catch Dad's concerned expression at my admission.

I try to shrug it off, mostly so he doesn't worry. "It'll all be fine. Great, in fact. Vin handled it."

"I'd say," Dad replies, and I can tell he's trying to figure out how to navigate this topic of conversation. "Is he coming to the launch party?"

"Yes," I say, warming at the thought of him. I don't know if it'll be as my boyfriend or what, but it'll definitely be as our brand ambassador. I turn the oyster in my hand, positioning it belly side down, and tuck it between folds in the towel.

"It's been a while since you've introduced anyone to family," Dad says, swaying his shoulders to the music. "Regardless of who knows, I'm glad you're not letting the curse stop you from being happy."

I'd always wanted to be able to talk to Mom about my relationships, but it was a romantic notion to think that we would talk about boys while painting our toenails and eating ice cream. I can't remember a single moment I've ever had like that with her. Conversations in general always skewed toward the curse, or away from it.

Dad positions the oyster knife into the hinge and works it up and down until the oyster pops apart, turning the blade sideways so it can't snap back together. In one smooth, gliding motion, he slides the knife across the length of the oyster. He removes the top shell, lifting the belly cradling the oyster and its liquid to his nose.

"These are gonna be good," he says. "They're limited right now, but I wanted them, so I waited. We're in for a treat."

"You waited for these specifically? Don't you have hundreds of oysters come through here a day?" I ask, laughing.

"Thousands, actually," Dad clarifies. "But I wanted these ones. I only had to wait a few months."

"Interesting." I grab an oyster and grip it a little too hard, the ruffled shell digging into my fingers. I go quiet for a minute, retreating into my thoughts.

Dad rests his oyster knife against the towel. "Now that everyone in the Emerald City knows you're cursed, I think it's time we talked about this." His tone takes a serious turn. "You've always heard your mom's side about why we split. Maybe you should hear mine."

"What more is there?" I ask. "Cursed is cursed."

The lines in Dad's forehead deeply groove in reaction to this. "It would be too easy to blame the curse for all of our problems."

I scrunch my nose. "Then why do you? Why was that the reason I heard all the time for you two breaking up?"

Dad sighs. "I think your mom really believes the curse to be true, at least to some extent. I don't know how the story has evolved over time that the Hua women would never find lasting love, but it seems to have taken on a life of its own through the generations. But here's the thing: I never stopped loving your mom. Even after the divorce. I wish it were that easy. But emotions linger. The happy and the sad."

This makes me pause. "What, you don't think it's real?" I ask, not quite believing what I'm hearing about the curse or my dad's feelings toward Mom.

"I think the consequences are very real," Dad says. "I think the trauma that has been passed down is real. And I think the fear is real. What I don't think is real is that any of you are destined to never find lasting love. I certainly don't want that for you, Chryssy. It's why I'm glad you and Vin found each other. That you're giving love another chance."

"Sure, but—" I start. "Did you just say 'love'?"

Dad looks over at me. "What did you think I said?"

"'Glove'? 'Above'? 'Dove'? Anything but the L word." I suddenly take great interest in an oyster. "'Love' is a strong word. I mean, yeah, I like the guy."

Dad laughs. "Is that what it's being called these days?" he asks. "In my day, when two people looked at each other the way you and Vin look at each other, it was called love."

I hesitate, wondering how much I should tell Dad. He's opening up to me, so I can't lie to him. "It's not love," I say firmly, the words feeling false in my mouth. "We're helping each other. We're pretending to be together for a while."

"What's that even mean?" Dad asks, angling his head toward the oyster tucked in his towel. "That seems unusual."

"We're faking a few dates, and then we're both going to move on with our lives. It's simple. Date, break up, move on," I say, waving my arms around. The oyster knife cuts the air.

Dad gently takes hold of my flailing arm and lowers it to the counter. "That doesn't sound very simple. And that's not what Vin said. Didn't he declare that he has no intentions of breaking up with you?"

He did, and he only said it on-air to all of Seattle. To prevent myself from reading too much into his words and starting to question just how fake this fake thing is between us, I've clung to the two words prefacing his final declaration: *I think.*

"I'm sure he was just being nice," I justify. We haven't addressed it—or what it would do to his reputation—yet. All I know is that it was incredibly romantic, but romance is confusing and complicated. Even if I want what he said to be true. "Pretending to date was the worst idea, and I never should've agreed to it." I say this defiantly, as if that might make it feel and sound convincing.

"Because now you both have to move on?" Dad asks, clearly trying hard to follow along.

"No, because now I'm happy. Can't you see how bad that is?" I groan, crumpling a towel between my hands.

"Is this a millennial thing? I'm lost," he says. "So you're happy, and that's...bad?"

"Exactly!"

"I don't understand the world anymore."

"He was frustrating when I met him. There was no way I thought I'd catch feelings. He was a heartbreaker. I was the last person who was supposed to fall for him. Honestly, I'm mad at myself. All I had to do was protect my heart, and I didn't. And now I love—like— him," I say. The words ring out loud and true. I can't reverse them, can't put them back in their shell.

Dad gives me an amused smile. "Is this a revelation for you?"

"Kind of," I say. "This is not good. You know what my fate holds."

He shakes his head. "This Hua family belief system has really gotten into all your heads. It's an intergenerational game of telephone."

Here's where I'd say he doesn't get it. That he's not the one affected by the curse. But that just isn't true. He's been hurt by it, too.

"I think there's a lot more to the curse that you don't understand," he says, his words nestling into my brain. "It kills me to see you living in fear of relationships ending all the time. If you go into a relationship thinking about the end, you won't enjoy it while it's happening. That's no way to exist."

If only Dad knew how fearful I've been or about the plan I have to keep myself protected. How, if I can control love, it won't control me.

"But my relationships do all end. Every single one has, even the one I was sure wouldn't," I say. "I need someone who's just right, you know? Not too hot, not too cold. Someone who, when it ends, can't hurt me because it was just…meh."

"Sorry, but a meh love sounds pretty terrible," Dad says. "But if you love—sorry, *like*—Vin now, does that mean you want too hot now?"

"Of course I want too hot, but can I really have it?" I question. "Why would I do that to myself? Go into one extreme just for it to go away at some point."

"You think the solution is to put up a shell to protect yourself," Dad says, tapping his finger against the belly of an unopened oyster. He sets his oyster knife on the counter. "Chryssy, I fell in love with your mom the night I met her. That's probably another reason she didn't think it would last. How can something last forever when it was love at first sight?"

I blink. "Exactly. How can it?"

"I meant that sarcastically. I think it can. Hell, I know it can. That's what happened," Dad says.

My heart aches in my chest at these revelations about my parents and their broken relationship. A marriage destroyed because of a belief system, according to Dad.

"The curse is so ingrained in your mother's side of the family. When we were together, she was always so worried that the curse was going to break us up. At first we were in a bubble," Dad shares. "Then your auntie Violet's husband passed, and the curse became all your mom talked about. I had to constantly remind her that the rest of her family's fate didn't have to be ours. At some point, I couldn't convince her anymore that I wouldn't leave. It got to be too much, always being told that I was going to do something I had no intention of doing. She thought I was lying to her. Ultimately, I never felt heard. My reassurance wasn't enough. My love wasn't enough."

"I'm sorry, Dad," I say, patting his shoulder.

Dad sighs. "I don't want this to sound like I'm blaming your mom. I was old enough to know better. And I wasn't perfect, either. I could've stayed and tried other ways to convince her. There are days I wish I had," he says, shaking his head. "But no one wants to be constantly questioned about their love for you. We all have stories we tell ourselves, don't we?"

I nod distractedly. It was how I was with Chris, blaming him, blaming the curse. Blaming everyone but myself. But I have some ownership here. Maybe I've been looking at this all wrong.

I can feel the cells in my brain shifting as this information twists into a new shape. Was that how my parents started? Mom initially believing Dad when he fought for them before intrusive thoughts took hold and history was destined to repeat itself? But their history doesn't sound fated. It sounds like a narrative that was not only told repeatedly, but one that was bought into. Over and over again.

Are we telling ourselves stories? Like how Vin tells himself he needs to work nonstop to compensate for his parents' abandoned dreams. That he needs to continuously be improving. That he's a heartbreaker. That he's not going to be the one who breaks up with me. Was what he said on live television just a story to cover for me? Or was it the truth?

The squeaky wheels of a delivery man's hand truck interrupt my thoughts.

"Thanks, Jim!" Dad calls out, waving to the guy as he walks past rolling boxes with images of potatoes and onions printed on the sides. "You know, when I first opened, I had a few oysters and a dream. At first, people mostly stopped by just to ask for directions to the Gum Wall. But I knew I made the best Oysters Rockefeller on this side of Elliott Bay, and when we were featured on a fancy show one day—not unlike the one you were on—overnight we had a monthlong waiting list to get in."

"Oh, yeah," I recall. "That was incredible."

Dad smiles. "We weren't ready. Didn't have enough staff. Didn't even have enough ingredients or tables. But when the reservations came in, we made it work. I took earnings from each night, invested it in more ingredients for the next booked-out day. I learned how to negotiate." He chuckles, shucking an oyster without any effort at all. "It wasn't easy, and we didn't always make people happy. We had to say no often, and even closed for lunch some days to catch up."

"Now this place is practically a Seattle landmark. A real gem. Or a pearl." I nudge Dad when he's not in a precarious position with the knife.

"It happened because of the exposure. My version of an irritant. And it's because of that kind of irritant that pearls are made," Dad says. "You and In Full Bloom are exposed right now and have more demand than you have product. Use that, let it irritate you. Your pearl is in the making."

I nod, taking a second to think about how much the aunties and the inn have meant to me over the years. We've been able to help so many people with their heartbreak. I love the idea of it being a pearl in the greater Seattle area, too.

I wiggle the knife tip into the part of the oyster where the shells meet. It doesn't budge. I remove the knife and try again, pushing harder against the hinge. My knife slips, and the tip jabs into the layers of towel.

"I haven't done this in a while," I say, grateful it was the towel and not my hand taking the hit.

"Here," Dad says, angling a new oyster in the towel to demonstrate. "Apply just enough pressure, not too much. It can be hard to shuck oysters because they're built to keep their shells closed. It protects them from birds, fish, hungry people named Chryssy and Dan. But if you're shut so tight, you'll always be in the dark."

I bob my head up and down slowly in long nods. "Did you just tie this back to our earlier conversation? You just tried to make a metaphor for opening myself up to love, didn't you?"

"It was before I realized halfway through that oysters literally stay closed for survival reasons," Dad says. "And that's what I'm trying to tell you not to do. Because when you do open yourself up, unlike oysters, you'll survive. Hmm."

"I appreciate the effort, Dad."

"Let me try again. When your heart gets broken, it feels like it's life or death. Okay, that's not any better. I guess what I'm trying to say is, you need to slice that adductor muscle and open yourself up to love. Take the risk. That's the best you're gonna get," Dad says, scratching his chin.

"Don't play the final note before you've started playing the song?" I offer, Vin clearly on my mind.

"Yeah, that's better," he says. "If I ever try to make another mollusk metaphor, stop me. My last pearl of wisdom, or at least a question to mull over: If what Vin said is true and he doesn't want to let you go, will you let him hang on?"

It's a typical moment for me and Dad, one that we've had several times before. His open-ended questions about following in Mom's cardiology footsteps, taking the leap out of med school, joining the Wildflower Inn. Never once have I regretted heeding his advice, even if it is disguised as a rhetorical question. When I hang out with him, there's always food and food for thought.

For the rest of the afternoon until dinner service begins, we don't utter the words "oyster" or "curse" again.

Chapter 18

VIN

When it comes to artichoke hearts, Chryssy's anything but delicate.

She scoops one out a little too aggressively, and it flies across the counter and lands at Goji's feet. He sniffs the heart and hops away.

"Why are you throwing food at Goji?" I ask, stepping fully into the kitchen. I immediately notice that she's eating her comfort food.

"Oh, hey," Chryssy says, turning her phone over. "Done practicing? You've been at it all day."

I push my hand through my hair. "Did I wake you this morning?"

"I caught the last bit," she says, the corner of her lips turning up. "Way better than my phone alarm."

"I had some energy to get out," I explain, pointing toward the teapot on the counter. "I was hoping I could get some...tea."

"Is that a new type of coffee?" she asks.

I grunt. "Ha ha. I don't want to be jittery for the rest of the day."

Chryssy pours hot water into a cup for me while I select rosebuds from the wood apothecary cabinet. I drop the flowers into the water.

From behind the rim of the cup, I eye the carnage of artichoke petals and fuzz in front of Chryssy. "I know why you're avoiding me," I say before realizing it could be about the curse *and* about what I said. "You want to talk about it?"

Chryssy pierces the center of the artichoke heart with a fork. "I'm trying to avoid having to talk about it," she admits. "This comforts me, though. Want some?"

I join her, dipping the tender meat of the artichoke petal into a lemon-and-rosemary-infused olive oil. I pull the base of the petal between my teeth. "Artichokes don't make it easy, do they?" I comment, remembering the last time she prepared them. There's so much prep, trimming, and peeling. "And they're an intimidating-looking vegetable."

Chryssy pokes the now-flat petal tip. "I don't always want to work so hard for my food, but these are worth the effort. It's funny, though. The parts of artichokes we eat are actually flower buds. We harvest them before they bloom. They start out tough-skinned, but the steaming softens them," she explains. "The thick layers of petals protect its tender heart."

She's knowingly made an apt metaphor for me—for both of us, really.

"We are artichokes," I say, resigned.

I drop an artichoke petal onto the side of the plate with the rest of the discarded bits.

Chryssy reaches for my arm, touching my tricep for half a second before pulling back like she thinks she's touched something she shouldn't.

"How do you do it?" she asks, flipping her phone back over. A row of headlines in a Google search stripe the screen.

New Heartbreak for His Collection?
How Long Will This Flavor of the Week Last?

Has Vin Met His Heartbreaking Match?

Can the Heartbreak Herbalist Fix This Heartbreaker?

Chryssy: Cute or Cursed?

"The articles, the speculation," she says, glancing down at a pile of artichoke fuzz.

"Screw them," I say. "I know that's easier said than done, but they're looking for crumbs."

She peers up at me, her next bite halfway to her mouth. "I hate the way they're talking about you, about our relationship, about me. It's not right."

"No, it's not," I agree. "When Leo and I started making headlines, I read every article, watched every snippet. The good and the bad. Then I learned that no matter how great Leo and I played, and no matter how much we cared, people were going to say what they wanted. There was nothing we could do about it."

"The curse has caused so much pain for people in my family, and now it's just...clickbait," she says, her lips quivering. "You know what my dad called the curse the other day?"

"Did he say it was briny?" I guess.

A little laugh escapes Chryssy. "An intergenerational game of telephone," she says. This time her laugh is humorless. "And somehow, I don't think he's wrong. He told me his side of things, and I don't know, it's not what I expected. I went my entire life thinking he and my mom both blamed the curse for their relationship's demise. In a way it kind of was, but he never believed in it. It makes me so sad for them." She presses a hand over her heart.

I think for a moment. "Come on."

"Where are we going?"

"Just come with me," I repeat. "And don't worry, we can still avoid talking."

I guide Chryssy through the backyard to the Plotting Shed. Rose's garden sits behind the small structure.

"What are we doing back here? This is Auntie Rose's sacred space," she says, glancing around nervously.

I grab a pair of shears and snip the air a few times. "She's only a *little* intimidating," I say. "Fine, she's a *lot* intimidating, so let's make this quick."

She gives me a look. "Hilarious."

"You'll also need these," I say, tossing Chryssy a pair of gloves from the workbench.

"Vin, what is this?"

"It's my garden now," I say, putting on a sun hat and gloves. "Not Rose's."

"Is this some kind of power play, or are you being serious?" Chryssy leans closer to get a better look at my gloves. "Are those embroidered with your name? Where'd you even get them?"

"These aren't the kinds of questions we need right now," I say. "But in return for cello lessons, Rose gave me a little plot to create a garden of my own."

Chryssy gasps. "Lessons? When? I always thought you were just practicing. This is where you've been coming instead?"

I rub my gloved hands together. "More recently, yes."

"Is Auntie Rose...a Chaobreaker?" she whispers.

"She'll be tough to crack, but I'm working on it," I say. "I wanted to plant herbs for you, but I figured this was a more productive use of the land. We're going to plant chrysanthemums. They can be your next batch for In Full Bloom. I know it won't make a big dent, but it's something."

Her eyes soften. "I can't believe you got Auntie Rose to give up her garden," she says. "But then again, I also can't believe she got lessons out of you."

"It was worth it." I take a step closer. "Chryssy, you're selfless. You hold everybody's shit and don't ever complain about it. You have the biggest heart, and you fill it up with everyone else's heartbreak and pain. But you don't need to keep all those feelings inside. You can take what you can handle. Don't overwater yourself." I wrap my arms around her. "You may be named after the chrysanthemum, but you don't have to let yourself always bloom last."

Chryssy gives me a funny look, circling her arms around my waist. "I appreciate you saying that. My parents—my whole family, really—went through so much in their relationships. And when people come to the inn, they're already fraught with emotions. My aunties feel stress, too. I guess I just...feel it all."

"I wonder what it might look like for you to set some sort of guardrails," I suggest. "Kind of like these garden beds."

"You think I should put myself in a box?" she asks.

"It's more like a boundary," I say. "Because yeah, these garden beds keep the flowers in. They also keep other things out."

Her eyebrows lift in surprise.

"When hard things happen, I know you can handle it. And when you deadhead chrysanthemums, they come back stronger," I add.

Chryssy leans into me, and I plant a gentle kiss on her forehead.

She eyes me suspiciously. "When did you learn so much about flowers?"

"Rose had some wisdom to impart before she relinquished total control of her garden," I say, shrugging. "So, I'm just a guy standing here in a sun hat and lovely embroidered gloves asking you a question: Will you garden with me?"

She slides the gloves on, smiling. "I haven't touched dirt in weeks. I've become so imbalanced. My last Yin Night was in Vegas." Her grin falters. "I've been down this path before. It doesn't lead anywhere good."

"You've been busy," I say. "Maybe this can be a Yin Day. Get those fingers ready."

We venture into one of the rows, and I kneel in front of a garden bed with a few vases in hand. She takes a spot at a garden bed opposite me.

"Pretend I'm not here," I say. "I mean, I will be because there's a good amount of work to do, but this is your time."

For the next hour, we cut the flowers in Rose's former garden in silence, collecting them to donate to senior living communities. Once the beds have been cut and cleared, we propagate chrysanthemums from the existing small patch in the main garden.

Chryssy sets her shears on the grass beside her. "What you said the other night at the show...did you mean that?" she asks, finally breaking the stretched-out, afternoon-long silence.

I pat a mound of dirt before turning to face her, my forearm draped over my thigh. "Every word of it. You wiggling your nose is your tell."

Chryssy smiles as she plucks off the petal of a daisy.

I love her.

"You mentioned that a breakup wasn't going to happen on your end," she says. "But you were just saying that, right? To help cover for me?"

She plucks another daisy petal from its head.

I love her not.

I'll never forget Chryssy's face when the question about the curse came through. I wish I could've turned back time. In the moment, I reacted. I only had a few seconds to come up with something, but what I said wasn't just for show.

A ladybug lands on one of the clipped flower stems, standing very still before flying off. As it leaves, a feeling solidifies in me.

"Chryssy, I don't want to break up with you," I say. "I want to stay in this."

It's a big statement that should scare me. These aren't words I've ever said to anyone before, but for some reason, when I say them to

Chryssy, the aggressive beating of my heart doesn't feel like fear. It feels like excitement.

Her mouth parts a little, her eyes widening in parallel. "You mean..."

"The plan's off. For me, at least," I reveal. "I'm not breaking up with you. I won't do it."

Chryssy shakes her head. "You want to be with me? Don't you want perfect? Because I'm anything but—"

"I want you."

"But what about your record label?" she asks. "The tour. The tickets."

It's a fair question. The day after *Sweet Dreams, Seattle*, Jim and Greg wouldn't stop calling to discuss my "outburst" and how this might misconstrue what Heartbreak on Tour really means. The phone calls stopped when ticket sales soared.

I run my fingers over a dandelion weed. "At some point, when you're always misunderstood, you start to think people are right about you. I deserved my reputation. I know what I've done to earn it. And I'm not saying I'm the best boyfriend, either, because that would be a lie. I'm away a lot, I'm stressed often. I don't think I'm very fun to be around when I'm busy. I care deeply about my work. I have so much to live up to and goals I want to accomplish," I say. "I may not know exactly who I am, but ever since meeting you, I know it's not a heartbreaker."

"That's a lie," Chryssy says, my heart sinking as she maintains a neutral face. "You're a lot of fun to be around." She shoots me a sly smile. "And for what it's worth, I stopped thinking of you as a heartbreaker weeks ago." She pulls one more petal off the daisy before setting it down.

I love her.

A smile stretches across my face.

"You're like a bonsai tree, in a way," she adds. "You were restricted and manicured to look perfect, your branches directed to be grown in a specific, heartbreaker way. If we can transplant you, break you free from your small pot, you'll grow wild. Your roots will spread. It'll take time, but I think it's possible."

"Maybe," I say. Maybe there's still potential there. Or maybe my growth has been limited for good.

"I guess by *not* breaking up, that kind of helps your reputation, too, don't you think?" Chryssy asks. "It is a long game, though."

"With you that's what I want," I tell her. "And it has nothing to do with my reputation."

She shakily exhales, but her features soften. "I want you, too," she responds. "I-I just don't know that it's possible."

I frown. "Because of the intergenerational game of telephone?"

"That, yes," she says, her nose wrinkling. "And I was engaged once. Even that didn't work out. We both stayed together longer than we should've."

"He wasn't your love song," I say, realizing Chryssy and I might be more similar than we thought. Where she would stay in relationships despite them not working out, I'd run from them at the first sign of trouble. Both of us have been looking for something we'd never had.

Chryssy shakes her head. "The curse will always be there, like background music. It's not loud or obvious, but even if I try to ignore it, I know it's still playing."

I think for a moment. "Then let's face the music. Together," I finally say.

She dips her chin, considering this. "Who knows what we're up against?" Chryssy says. "Literally everyone has been negatively impacted by the curse. I've never seen a long-lasting, perfect—no, not even perfect...healthy—relationship like you've seen with your parents. How can I be the exception?" She pokes at the dirt. "I've been told stories and heard rumors my entire life, but what if there's been static on the line? Rust from over the years. How can I know for sure that what everyone's been saying is even true? I feel like I don't understand what the curse is or what it means anymore."

"What if we tried to understand?" I suggest. "Let's turn up the knob on this music and hear what the sounds really are. Listen to what kind of tune is playing. Let's see what we can be."

"And how are we supposed to do that…" she says, trailing off as she looks toward the moon garden.

I follow her line of sight, understanding right away.

"Some people say I'm good at breaking things," I say.

She lets out a half-note laugh and then grins. "I'll get the shovel."

Chapter 19

CHRYSSY

What is that doing here? It was supposed to be destroyed," Auntie Rose says, her mouth a hardened line. "Daisy? What happened?"

The Curse Box sits on the Plotting Shed's workbench as my aunties, Vin, and I pace around it, wondering how to best go about this.

"And demolish this beautiful, handcrafted box? It's an antique," Auntie Daisy says, wringing her hands. "They don't make pieces like this anymore. You see the mother-of-pearl inlay here—"

"I don't care if the whole thing's made of gold," Auntie Rose states. "Who knows what damage has been done by having this around."

"Some would argue there's no evidence curses are real," Auntie Daisy states, her expression unchanging.

"You don't believe that, though," Auntie Rose says.

Auntie Daisy tilts her head. "Well, no. I forgot, okay? I hid it until I could figure out what to do with the contents of the box. It's all we have left of our ancestors."

"They really left us the good stuff, huh?" Auntie Rose exhales heavily. "First the dating scheme, then the curse gets exposed to everyone in the Pacific Northwest, and now this. How did I get roped into any of it? And why us? We don't know anything."

Auntie Violet moves around the perimeter of the shed opening all the windows and doors. "Oh, please," she says. "Don't act like you don't live for drama. You were a divorce lawyer, for crying out loud."

"Our guests will know we're unwanted women!" Auntie Rose says. "We're all allowed skeletons, but I prefer them in the attic, not outside our inn."

It pains me hearing this, knowing that this is what they think of themselves.

Auntie Daisy raises her hand. "Can I get a count of how many of us are in a good headspace for this?"

Vin tentatively raises his hand.

"Is it ever a good time to deal with a curse head-on?" Auntie Rose asks while she busies herself by moving vases from one end of the shed to another.

Auntie Violet plucks out a flower as Auntie Rose passes by. "Cut flowers aren't so bad, are they, Rose?" She smirks. "Flowers inside, sacrificing your garden for the betterment of capitalism. I like this side of you."

Auntie Rose rolls her eyes. "Don't get used to it."

Auntie Daisy lowers her hand. "So...no one's in a good headspace except Vin. Great."

"I'd like to do this together," I say. "Use our collective knowledge to try to understand what this curse really is. It's grown over the years. It's taken over our lives like ivy."

"If it didn't before, it certainly has now," Auntie Rose grumbles. She starts spritzing the shed with sweet orange essential oil from a spray bottle. "Let me at least clear the negative energy from the space first. We need more Yang energy in here."

"Oh, Rose. It's not like people haven't known," Auntie Daisy says. "And I heard Aunt Angelica is working on a book about the curse."

"I thought it was a reality show. She asked me to produce it,"

Auntie Violet says, picking up on Auntie Rose's cues and grabbing the broom. "I can't say I love the idea of our pasts being dug up."

Auntie Rose flaps her hands at her sisters. "You're both wrong. It's Aunt Rosemary, and she's trying to persuade her grandchildren to write a screenplay. Or was it her daughter she was trying to convince?"

More rumors. More games of telephone. So much for collective knowledge.

"Can we focus?" I plead.

Auntie Rose sprays orange scent around the Curse Box.

"Yes, focus. If we're doing this, we're doing it as a team," Auntie Daisy says, hesitating. "Right?"

"Yes! People! This box holds all the answers," Auntie Violet says, inching around us all with her broom, sweeping dirt and other negative Curse Box associations out the door. "If we want Chryssy and Vin to have a chance at being together, it's important we try to understand what we're dealing with here. We need to see what's in the box."

"I wouldn't say it holds *all* of the secrets, but, yeah, we should probably look inside," I clarify.

"For love," Auntie Daisy adds.

At the mention of love, I glance at Vin. His gaze is already firmly planted on me. I redirect my eyes back to the box on the table.

"Or at least for the hope of it," Auntie Rose says, her bunched forehead relaxing.

A breeze sweeps through a far window and pushes the aroma of citrus around. Hopefully, this uplifts everyone a little.

"This hasn't been opened in decades. Generations have gone by and not one peek," Auntie Violet says, stopping her sweeping and looking up. "Right?"

"Mmm," I mumble. Vin and I both know what happened in the Dandelion that night he arrived, but we're taking it to the grave with us. Which, depending on what's in this box, might be a lot sooner than we both anticipated.

"It's time we take charge and get a look for ourselves at what's in here," Auntie Daisy says. "So who's gonna do it? I'm not touching that thing."

"Don't look at me," Auntie Rose says, lifting the spray bottle. "I'm spritzing."

Auntie Daisy's eyes widen. "I'm too nervous. My palms are sweaty."

I swallow. "I guess I could—"

"I'll do it," Vin says, stepping forward. "I'll open the box." We continue *not* mentioning that this wouldn't be his first time doing so.

"Good! Yes!" Auntie Violet says, toasting Vin with the broom. "Admirable on and off the stage."

We all gather around Vin as he lifts the lid on the writing box very slowly. The moment feels heavy and dramatic, which is on brand with the Hua women.

Vin removes a stack of notebooks and an empty leather binder. In one of the notebooks is transparent-looking paper with what looks like Mandarin written on it. The writing was done quickly, the Chinese characters angled on the pages.

"This must be 4G's handwriting," I say. In the lower corner is a seal pressed in red ink. "Is this his seal?"

"Could be. Seals were originally used to authenticate documents and then later art," Auntie Rose says of the red square with Chinese characters carved in the center. "But this doesn't look like art. Maybe it's a contract."

"We can confirm it against 4G's rose illustration in the kitchen," Auntie Violet says. "If the two seals match, then this has to be his handwriting."

"When I last saw this—I mean, when I imagined what would be in here—it looked like a cookbook. Or that's what I thought it would be," Vin says, tripping over his words. "Here, see. It says something about herbs." The wrinkle in Vin's brow is emphasized as he concentrates. "The ink's faded, so it's hard to fully understand."

"There's a sketch of a chrysanthemum. And a mushroom," I note, indicating the small illustrations in the margins of the page. "What if it's a recipe?"

"Can't we let things be?" Auntie Rose pushes. "This is a lost cause. Yesterday, one of the showers broke randomly in a guest's room, and now I think I know why. Look at the imbalance you've already created." She looks pointedly at Vin. "Don't try to disturb the past. What's done is done."

"If you're getting cold feet, Rose, rub them with oil and drink tea," Auntie Violet retorts. "You also don't need to be here for this."

"Well, someone needs to supervise," Auntie Rose grumbles, staying put.

Her earlier statement lingers in my ears, saddening me. "You're hurt," I say, wrapping my arm around her. She returns my gesture. "Burying this down deep might feel good right now, but you know that's not healthy. We always talk about prevention. That's how I'm trying to approach this. In the same way you all taught me. I may not be able to stop the curse or repair the damage it's already done, but I might be able to prevent it for future generations. Maybe even for me. I'm doing this, but I can't do it without you."

I must have gotten through to her because Auntie Rose gently removes more journals whose pages are marked with dried, pressed flowers as delicate placeholders. "There are a bunch of ingredients listed here. Many are scratched out. The ones I can see, though, I don't know what most of them translate to. My Chinese isn't what it used to be," she says.

Auntie Violet moves her hands back and forth a few times before finally taking the leather binder into her hands, riffling through thin pieces of cloth with characters inked on them. A gasp escapes her. "Look. A secret compartment," she says, her voice low.

"A secret compartment with a knob?" Auntie Rose asks, crossing her arms. "It's a drawer, Vi."

Auntie Violet carefully slides out a small bundle of envelopes, ignoring her sister. "Looks like letters." They look so old, as though they might disintegrate on the spot at any moment.

"Who are they from?" I ask.

My imagination runs wild as the aunties and Vin translate silently. Instead of wallowing in my uselessness and going down the mental spiral of why I haven't learned Mandarin yet, I seek out context clues. Stamps. Burned corners. Water stains...or teardrops. What if they're love letters from before the betrayal. Or maybe it's eighteenth-century China's equivalent of a divorce decree.

"Calendula," Auntie Rose says, squinting at the characters sprawled across the paper. "Our grandmother?"

"What does she say?" Auntie Daisy asks. She slides her yellow reading glasses up the bridge of her nose and peers at the paper over Auntie Rose's shoulder.

Auntie Rose holds the paper closer to both of their faces. "It says she doesn't want to meet. She's leaving the country." She blows out a frustrated breath. "There are so many smudges. The writing is too faint. There's a good amount here that's lost to time."

"It must be addressed to 4G," I say, looking through the other pockets in the binder.

"But it isn't. It's addressed to...Lily?" Auntie Violet says, her brows creasing. "Like Great-Great-Great-Grandmother Lily?"

"Èyùn? The reason we're all cursed?" Auntie Rose asks.

I glance between my aunties. "Who are the other letters from?"

"The same. Lily and Calendula. Looks like they had been writing back and forth," Auntie Violet says.

"Why did Lily want to get in touch with her great-granddaughter?"

"I thought no one had heard from Lily ever again," I say. "It's odd, isn't it? The handwriting from Lily's letters looks the same as the handwriting in these notebooks."

"Okay, here. Lily wrote that she burned it. Got rid of something?" Auntie Violet says, angling the paper differently and coming at the words from a new perspective.

Auntie Daisy hums as she thinks. "She burned the ingredients? The blends?"

"She must mean recipes. So she burned the heart herbal blend. We know that already. Why is she rehashing history?" I ask. "What else is in there?"

"*The recipes are long gone. I made sure of it. Here's what I remember,*" Auntie Rose translates. "Then she lists five ingredients."

My mouth goes slack. "Do you think she's trying to re-create *the* heart herbal blend? What are the ingredients?"

Auntie Rose squints at the smudged, slanted writing. "I can only make out three of them. The rest are a very different style."

"It can never be easy," Auntie Violet says on a sigh.

"Is that Old Chinese?" Auntie Daisy wonders.

"Why are you looking at me?" Auntie Rose appears unamused. "I'm old, but I'm not that old."

I trace the lines and curves of each character. "They look like little drawings. This had to be well before Lily's time," I guess.

"I don't know what those are, either. I learned some Traditional Chinese, but mostly Simplified," Vin says. "It's like a code, or a puzzle."

"What, like she used different variations of Chinese to add an extra level of security?" I ask, half joking. Then the realization hits that maybe this isn't a joke, and that Lily really did want to make it harder to crack this blend. But who was she protecting it from?

"The instructions are so vague," Auntie Daisy observes. "Is that an eight or a nine? I can't tell." She points to one of the complex characters that looks more traditional in style. "That sounds like too much ginseng."

"The blend should help with tonifying Qi," I say. "Why is she sharing it with Calendula?"

Vin thinks for a moment. "For posterity? In the early 1870s, a music editor named Robert Keller helped get Johannes Brahms's compositions into print. There's handwritten correspondence that still exists. Music notes are drawn out on these letters. Brahms was communicating the music to get them into the record."

"Okay. And?" Auntie Violet says, waiting eagerly.

"Maybe your great-great-great-great-grandmother was the Brahms of herbalism," Vin says.

I spin one of my earrings as my mind swirls with new information. "But she's the one who destroyed the recipes, not made them. In these letters, it sounds like she's trying to re-create the tonics that she got rid of. Why would she do that?" I ask, trying to process everything.

Auntie Rose's eyes zigzag down the letter. When she reaches the bottom, she shakes her head.

"What is it?" I ask.

"Eh, it's too hard to read. She was probably 4G's scribe and documented everything," Auntie Rose replies.

"Let me try," Auntie Daisy offers.

Auntie Rose quickly stuffs the letter back in the envelope. "No, no. There's nothing useful here." She waves her hands in front of her like *good riddance*. "Look at us! We're speculating, just like always."

"We do know something. Lily started documenting the heart herbal blend," Auntie Violet says.

"We can get these three ingredients while we figure out what the last two are," Auntie Daisy suggests.

Auntie Rose frowns, looking out the Plotting Shed's window over the main garden. "Sure. If that will give you closure."

A renewed sense of optimism surges through me. "It's time to understand what this blend was all about," I say. "Who's up for an adventure?"

Chapter 20

VIN

Turns out, everyone wanted an adventure.

Chryssy and I, her aunties, Leo, and a couple of guests find ourselves together in the late morning trampling through the forest in search of mushrooms.

"Man, this was supposed to be a relaxing forest-bathing situation," Leo says, slogging behind me. "Not a repurposed curse-breaking endeavor. Can you slow down?"

"It's not like that," I say, stepping quickly ahead of Leo by a few strides. "We're just trying to understand it."

Leo scoffs. "*Curse understanding* doesn't have the same ring to it."

"There are no spells or potions involved," I say, though I can't be sure about the latter. Pretty sure the word "tonic" was thrown around a few times.

"Can't we get lion's mane at a grocery store?" he asks. "I've seen it before at Whole Foods. Then we can walk through the woods quietly without a task and focus on being present, which was the point of this to begin with."

"I'd love it if you'd stay present. Just keep your eyes out for lion's mane while you're at it. Quiet is preferred," I retort.

We stick close to the other guests while Chryssy and her aunties go off on their own. We didn't have to go far for today's mushroom hunt. Apparently, Whidbey Island is a treasure trove of community and state parks for foraging.

"The recipe specifically called for *foraged*, wild lion's mane," I say, most of my attention dedicated to finding dead logs.

"It still could've been foraged," Leo says. "Just by someone else. Whatever, it's fine. This just seems to be amping up your anxiety when it should be doing the opposite."

"I'm trying to stay focused," I say, scanning hardwood for white, rounded mushrooms with a mane of hair. "If we're going to follow the recipe, we need to do it as accurately as possible. This way, we know for sure it really was foraged."

"Fine," Leo says, taking his phone out and searching for photos to reference. "But I'm calling it by its other name. Bearded tooth fungus. Now that'd be a great band name."

"The technology addiction's strong," I say, eyeing him. "You've been away from the inn for three hours."

"I had a feeling Mom called," Leo says. "My instincts are still intact. I called her back this morning and told her we're still coming for their anniversary. She says hi, by the way." He side-eyes me. "And she wants to know if Chryssy's coming."

"To Franklin? It's in two days. Isn't that a little soon?" I ask. Bringing Chryssy home feels like a big step, especially in the middle of trying to figure this, us, out. "I don't want to overshadow Mom and Dad's celebration."

"What are you, worried that they'll like her more than you?"

"That's exactly what I'm worried about. And that they'll think it's their anniversary gift," I say. "Chryssy and I have enough pressure as it is with this curse situation."

"You mean curse understanding," Leo says, snickering to himself.

"Could be nice to bring her. You know Mom will go all-out on making the guesthouse extra comfortable for her."

The thought of this *is* nice, Chryssy meeting my parents. Staying in the guesthouse together. Besides the inn, my parents' farmhouse has been the only other place I could relax.

"Let me know either way so I can tell Mom. Then I can shut my phone off forever. Destroy it. Throw it into these woods. It was a mistake turning it on." He faces his phone toward me. On the screen is a photo of Aubrey with snow-peaked mountains blurred in the background.

"Weren't you going to unfollow her?" I grumble.

"The question you should be asking is who's taking the photo?" he says, bringing the phone closer to his face.

"Her sister? Her mom? A friend? A tripod?" I rattle off.

"Or a new boyfriend," he says. "One who's actually around."

"This is what our life looks like," I say. "What are we supposed to do? Not tour as much? That's how we meet Chaobreakers. It's how we make most of our money."

"Given how many breakups you've had, Vin, you're not very good at talking about them," Leo says, patting me on the back.

"I'm realizing that," I mumble as I examine a tree stump.

Leo's eyebrows pinch together. "Aub—my ex—understood what our life entailed, and she supported it. It's not that she made me feel guilty about it," he explains. "She just wanted something different for her life, which is entirely fair for her to want. I guess I didn't realize the full effect the pace of our lives had on our relationship until she left."

"Did she at least communicate that to you before she broke things off?" I ask, trying to pinpoint why exactly it is I'm feeling defensive.

Leo kicks at a rock in the path. "I may have busted out the ring before we had a chance to talk in-depth about our future," he reflects. "Maybe I moved as fast in my relationship as we do in our careers."

Like Chryssy and me.

This comparison slithers in and out of my mind before I can fully grasp it, lingering just long enough to be worrying. Chryssy and I were practically strangers before we started fake-dating. And the line between fake and whatever we are now, well, that moved quickly, too. Would Chryssy coming to Franklin be too fast? Did we jump too quickly to opening the Curse Box?

To me, though, fast was never a bad thing. If anything, the faster the better. My unsettled thoughts are in direct contrast with the peaceful forest surrounding us. I must be the Yang to this forest's Yin.

"That's probably not a new boyfriend taking the picture," I say, circling back to Leo and Aubrey. "It's too soon. I bet she misses you just as much as you miss her." I've never been great at consoling, but I do hope this makes him feel better. "I thought she didn't like skiing."

"The actual skiing part she wasn't a fan of," Leo says, dragging behind. "Hot cocoa and cuddles by the fire afterward? *That* she was a fan of. Oh god." He pinches the bridge of his nose.

"Sounds like she's doing whatever she has to in order to get her mind off of you," I reason.

Leo lets out a lone, sad laugh. "I appreciate the effort."

"What happened to chilling out in the forest? We should probably instigate the no-phone rule everywhere," I say. "You've been working hard at the inn."

He makes a *pfffttt* noise. "Don't you want me to look at the contract? You've only been reminding me every time you see me."

"Well, yeah. The label's been waiting," I say, scanning tree bark up and down. "I'd think your first inclination would be to look at that instead of looking at your ex's photos on social media, but hey, to each his own."

"Reading a bunch of legalese isn't going to get us out on tour faster or make me feel any better," Leo says, sliding his phone into his pocket. "And what if I don't even want to do the tour anyway?"

I look at him, losing focus and tripping over a tree root stretched out into the trail.

"What's that supposed to mean?" I ask, catching myself.

Leo shrugs. "It means I'm tired. It means I miss my relationship. I don't know what it means." He kicks a rock farther down the path. "Rehearsals are going to be rough."

"You'll get back into the swing of things. I know it feels like you'll be starting over," I say, patting his back. "But the tour is part of our last contract, not this new one. It's not up to us."

"Why do you even want to sign this contract?" Leo questions. "We'll be trapped with terms we don't like. Is that really what you want?"

"We'll push back. That's expected in negotiations," I say, thinking of the conversation Chryssy and I had in Rose's garden. They'll need to be lenient. I'm not breaking up with Chryssy or breaking a contract.

"What I'm getting at is bigger than that, Vin," Leo says. "Is this what you hoped our life would be like?"

I've lost focus of the trees. All of them have started to look exactly the same. "What kind of question is that?" I ask. I can't believe what I'm hearing. "This is what we worked for our entire life."

"That's not what I asked."

"Our life has...elements of what I hoped it would be," I admit. "It's not like I had a specific scenario in mind. We get to play cello as our job. We have money, can buy our parents nice things, play sold-out shows. What more could you ask for?"

The knot in my stomach grows. I should've thrown his damn phone into the woods before he had a chance to see his ex on it.

"What more—" Leo stops, turning to face me. "Oh, I don't know, hmmm, love. A family. Time to travel for fun instead of work. Staying in one place for more than two weeks. Being home for dinner every night. What a concept."

I frown at a chipmunk. "Once we get this contract in place and finish the world tour—"

"And finalize the movie score and complete our next album and rehearse for *that* world tour, then we'll have time to live a life, right?" Leo says.

"Exactly."

"No! You know why? Because there will always be more to do. Always," he says. "We can always improve, always make more albums, always, always, always." He leans against a tree, burying his face in his hands. "I think what I've been feeling is stagnant. I just haven't realized it until now."

"What are you talking about?"

Leo makes a literal *ugh* sound. "Have you learned nothing at the inn!" he says, throwing his hands up. "I'm stuck. Static. Flat. Not moving."

"And you're the one who wanted to slow down," I mumble. "That's why it'll be good to start playing again. That'll get you feeling like you're going somewhere."

"Being busy makes you feel like you're moving forward," Leo says. "But you're just running in circles."

"Thanks for the life perspective," I grunt. "You know, one day we won't be able to play anymore."

I'm fully aware I'm giving him a half-assed response, but it's not like we can just quit.

"One day? One day when? When we're eighty? And then we finally have a moment to stop, only to realize we were too busy working and

YIN YANG LOVE SONG

not really living? What's the point of working so hard if we can't enjoy it?" Leo asks. "Being here, doesn't it make you want this?"

"A forest?" I ask, trying to make him laugh.

Leo does not want to laugh.

"Time to walk in the woods. Hunt for mushrooms! A home to go back to. A couch!" he says. "A life."

"Who needs a couch when we get to do what so many musicians can only dream of one day doing?" I ask him.

"You know what I mean."

"I don't know that I do."

Leo makes a face. "Then maybe you're not paying close enough attention."

"You're still healing," I say. "Let's talk about this after the trip."

"I'm tired of blaming heartbreak," Leo says. "Yeah, I'm hurting, but what I'm saying is also true. If anything, this breakup has opened my eyes. Our work will not love us the same way we love it. All those dreams, Vin, they're not going to fulfill you."

"I know the past month has been a lot," I say to Leo. I hate the urgency in my tone. It's like I'm trying to convince him of something, but of what, I don't know.

Leo balks. "The past month? Vin, our entire lives have been a lot. Our careers started so young."

I wait him out, letting his words wash over me. He's not going to hear anything I say anyway.

"Can you honestly tell me that you're not tired?" he asks. "That a little part of you isn't fed up with how things have been?"

"Honestly, Leo?" I say, releasing a frustrated breath. "Here's what's real: There's still a lot we need to accomplish. You'll realize that when you read the contract."

"I think we might be starting to want different things," Leo mumbles. "What Mom and Dad have. That's real. What my ex and I had. It was real. What you and Chryssy have, it's—"

"Beautiful!" Chryssy says on a satisfied-sounding exhale as she joins us. "Isn't it?"

It takes me a second to realize she's talking about our surroundings. A light wind blows through the trees, and against the forest floor the leaves cast shimmery shadows that play off the sunshine. It's like we're under a nature-made disco ball.

"Have you found it yet?" she asks.

"No. We're getting a little off track," I say. Leo scoffs at my loaded statement. "We'll refocus."

"Yeah, we're still looking, too, but apparently Auntie Violet has a weird knack for finding morels so we're now following that lead," Chryssy says. She looks over to where her aunties are crouched down and pointing at something in the distance. "I better get back. They look like they're onto something. Oh! Look what I found. For you."

She presents me with a dandelion from behind her back. A cut one. A cliché. For me.

I wrap my hand around her fingers, the long green stem between both of our fists, the puff on top. A feathery full moon on a stick.

"Make a wish." She smiles at it and turns, pulling her hand away so that I'm left holding the flower.

The dandelion unlocks a deep-rooted memory. One of Leo and me as kids running through park fields between hours of practice sessions, arms stretched wide. Among yellow dandelions, I'd find a rare puffy one. I didn't think about it at the time, but now it fascinates me how dandelions start as one thing and become another, reblooming after their initial flowering. They transform for survival, their starry seeds dispersing to take root on new land.

There's a squeezing sensation in the left side of my chest when Chryssy looks over her shoulder at me. Within seconds, lasting no longer than the length of a whole note, what Leo was saying isn't so off-key.

A home. A life.

Chryssy with her moon garden out back, an herb garden next to it. Patience Risotto and artichoke hearts simmering on the stove. Kissing Chryssy in the kitchen. Light music playing in the background. Sunshine streaming in through the windows of our bedroom. Sprigs of lavender and dandelions adding color and wishes into our life. Maybe even, one day, children's laughter.

A home. A life. Ours.

There's no cello, no stadium tours, no hours upon hours of daily practice.

I don't know where I fit into this vision at all.

Chryssy's back on the trail with her aunties, looking high and low for the mushrooms.

"Mm-hmm," Leo murmurs beside me, eyeing the dandelion's puff. "Whether we break—sorry, understand—this curse or not, you can't tell me that your love for that woman isn't real."

"Love doesn't happen that fast," I say quickly, though the crack in my voice says otherwise.

My love for cello came fast. My career trajectory was also fast. Love, though? It certainly doesn't happen in weeks, let alone months, but I suppose that doesn't mean it can't happen. When Mom and Dad met that day on the subway, wasn't their falling fast?

"I know, baby brother, shocking. You work fast, fall in love slow. Until now." Leo swings his arm over my shoulder. "Have you ever heard this quote by Lao Tzu?" he asks. "'Nature does not hurry, yet everything is accomplished.'"

I grunt, this time in annoyance at him.

A smile crosses Leo's face as he looks up at the tree canopies. "Nature isn't rushing or giving us all four seasons at once. We have explosive growth, harvesting, resting, and renewal. Everything that needs to happen happens, but in its own time, even if that means sometimes flowers bloom early. Let's be more like nature, Vin. We can't rush the seasons. We also can't slow them down."

When did my brother become so profound? Or at least learn about people who were?

"Don't overthink it. Let's just slow down for a second, for real," Leo says, moving away from me and taking his steps in half time. "Hurrying won't get you anywhere faster, even if it feels like it."

He's wrong. We worked hard, made moves quickly, and didn't slow down on purpose. All our efforts are what got us ahead.

Despite not being here for a stroll, I listen to Leo. Hundreds of trees and plants surround us, their bushy green leaves bathing me in a sense of calm.

My steps become heavier and slower as I gain awareness of how fresh the earth smells. How the browns and greens of the forest subtly shift hues as the sunlight leisurely streaks across the sky, casting new, shadowy shapes on the ground every few minutes. We follow the edge of the trail, our feet padding quietly over the earth. There's an occasional crunch from rocks and sticks, but for the most part it's peaceful out here.

Birds chatter with each other in distant trees, and the bushes rustle with wildlife. Around me, the forest becomes a soft symphony of music I only hear when I truly listen.

Maybe this place is noisier than I originally thought.

I refocus my eyes from Leo to the fallen trees, hoping to spot the cream-colored forest jewel. In the distance, I see a blur of white set against the dark wood of a jagged tree trunk.

I'm drawn to the stump like the lion's mane is a ringing bell calling me toward it. "There it is," I whisper. As if I could scare it away.

I'm careful making my way to it, winding around plants and

smaller logs. I hear Leo behind me, bushes shaking as they brush our pants. I reach the mushroom and stare in awe at its dangling long hairs, like icicles on a velvety snowball.

From what Chryssy told me, lion's mane is a powerful ingredient in TCM to maintain Qi. It tonifies the heart and brain and supports the liver, lungs, and kidney. And I'm about to slice it off a tree. I've come a long way from nonstop rehearsals and meetings and recordings to…this.

I tuck the dandelion into my shirt pocket, careful not to disrupt the puff. I twist the knife in my hand as I analyze how to approach the first cut, deciding to start around the edges, loosening it. The entire mushroom peels away from the bark, and a thin layer remains.

I grin, holding the shaggy orb in my hands like the treasure that it is. I gently run my hand over the long strands of the mushroom, the texture impossibly soft beneath my finger pads.

My entire body feels as light as a leaf as I inhale the smell of damp moss and wood. A sense of hopefulness washes over me. Hope that Leo will get through this, hope that we'll better understand this curse. Even hope that our record label will accept our change of heart.

From my coat pocket, I remove Chryssy's dandelion, the fluffy seed head still intact.

I breathe in, like I'm about to blow out candles, and let it out, the delicate seeds scattering in the wind.

I make a wish.

Chapter 21

CHRYSSY

Vin's parents are tending to the chickens when we arrive at their house in Franklin, Tennessee. Vin, Leo, and I deposit our luggage and their cellos in the entryway and head outside to say hello.

When Vin asked me to come home with him after our mushroom excursion, I couldn't not meet the star-crossed violinists, no matter how serious this trip felt. It took a year and a half for me to meet Chris's parents. This is a big step. Too big, I worry, and during our ingredient search. While we're gone, my aunties will collect the remaining ingredients and reach out to their contacts. In a few days, we'll hopefully have everything we need.

I take a deep breath, noting how different the air smells here than on the island. The tree leaves are practically neon green, and the sea of grass is just as bright. Vin's parents' eggshell-white farmhouse sits on thirty-three acres of mostly wooded land with a barn and guesthouse out past the pool. I like to imagine his parents sitting on their wrap-around porch watching the trees change color, shed their leaves, and grow them back.

By the sound of it, they live a much more peaceful existence now than they did when Vin was a kid. Between practice schedules and moving around the country to work with the best instructors to touring globally, they all lived nonstop lives.

"This place is incredible," I say as we cross over grass to a fenced-off area behind the barn. "I thought you grew up in the San Gabriel Valley."

"That's where I was born. We moved around a lot, and our house looked nothing like this. We mostly lived in apartments," Vin says.

"When you both played cello?" I ask. "Did your neighbors hate you?"

He huffs a laugh. "There was one grump, Mr. Mack, but the rest were nothing but encouraging."

"I like to think Mr. Mack made us better," Leo says.

Vin nods in agreement. "He was our first critic. The first of many."

"And now this," I say, waving toward the house. "It's a place you'd see in the magazines."

"We wanted to buy our parents their dream house once we had the money to," he explains. "I thought they'd go for something on the coast. A Nantucket cottage or a California beach house."

"Happy medium by landing on a farm in Tennessee?" I ask.

"Something like that. Dad wanted land and Mom wanted chickens," Vin says. "She had this vision of sipping cocktails with her hens and gossiping about neighbors."

We approach the chicken coop, which is a small replica of the main farmhouse, complete with two stories, a wraparound porch, and a small pool.

Vin's mom is crouched down talking to a hen in the screened-in outdoor area, the ends of her wavy, light brown hair peeking out from under a sun hat.

His dad notices us right away and leans his broom against the porch beam. "Bella, the kids are here!" he shouts.

There are hugs and introductions between me and Vin's parents, and me and the chickens. Vin's careful to avoid adding labels, and his mom tells me to call them Isabella and William.

I hold out a package. "This is for you and William," I say to Isabella. "Happy thirty-five years!"

Isabella tears open the packaging, revealing a needlepoint pillow I powered through as soon as Vin told me about their love story on the clamming trip. I didn't know I'd get to give it to them myself.

"Thirty-five music notes," Isabella observes, looking delighted.

"For your love song," I say, stealing a glance at Vin.

"It's wonderful. Thank you, honey," she says, as William nods to me appreciatively. A chicken with deep red feathers and a bright cherry comb and wattles nudges my calf. "That's Lucy. And over there is Ethel." A chicken with all-white plumage bob-walks toward us.

William claps Vin's and Leo's shoulders at the same time. "It's so nice to have you both here," he says. "Thanks for fitting us into your busy schedules."

"Of course we'd come," Vin says. "This is a big celebration."

"Thirty-five years is a long time," Leo says.

William looks at the ground and nods. "Sure is."

"Glad you could fit us in before the tour," Isabella says. "How long is this one?"

"Six months," Vin says, glancing over at me.

"Wow. That's a long time." I press my lips together.

"Will you be joining him on a few of the stops?" Isabella asks me.

My eyes meet Vin's. "I'd like to. I don't know. We haven't talked about it," I admit. "I've never been outside the country, but I've heard Paris is romantic."

"You must," Isabella says. "They scored the Louvre as a venue."

"Another recent win," Vin says.

"We're flying in for the Acropolis," William says, whistling. "Can you imagine playing in that venue, Bella?"

"Only in my dreams," Isabella says.

"Can't wait to live out of hotels again," Leo mumbles.

Isabella glances between her sons. "Let's get you all something to drink. Lemonade? Arnold Palmer?"

I say goodbye to my new chicken friends through the fence as my phone buzzes in my pocket.

Auntie Violet: We may have a lead. There's a rare bookstore owner who apparently knows Old Chinese. Setting up a meeting for when you're back.

I respond with a thumbs-up, and follow Vin and his family into the kitchen.

As I step into the room, I freeze in place. The kitchen is three times the size of the Wildflower Inn's, with robin's-egg-blue cabinets lining the walls. The island in the center is the size of two large dining tables and topped with black granite to serve as a clean contrast to the exposed ceiling beams and distressed brick wall.

"Is that a La Cornue?" I ask when I spot the French range. "It's in the ocean color, too."

"The boys got that for us for our wedding anniversary last year," William says. "They couldn't be here in person to celebrate, so we got a very fancy gift."

I take it all in. "Wow. You know how some people's guilty pleasures are looking at expensive homes on Zillow and fantasizing about other lives? That's me with kitchens," I admit.

Isabella and William laugh. "Then I think you'd appreciate this," Isabella says, opening a kitchen cabinet to reveal an entryway to another room.

"Pantry?" I guess.

Isabella smiles. "Cookbook library. Wait until you see the rest of the house. Vin, give her a tour while I make drinks," she instructs. "Leo, could you throw together a cheeseboard?"

"The only thing I can guarantee you is that it will look thrown together," Leo says, loading a variety of paper-wrapped cheeses into his arms. "How many guests are coming?"

"None this year," Isabella responds, lifting a shoulder in response to Vin and Leo's confusion.

"Isn't the party tomorrow?" Vin asks. "Everyone usually comes in the day before. I expected a full house and was ready to disassociate when Aunt Gina made her usual song requests like we're an instrumental jukebox."

"You can disassociate later. Your father and I decided we wanted to do something a little different this year," Isabella says, securing grapes from a basket. "Nothing big or flashy."

Vin frowns. "But you live for big and flashy. Don't you want to celebrate?"

"We'll still be celebrating, just on a smaller scale," William assures him.

Isabella plucks a grape off the vine and eats it. "Especially because I've won the lottery."

"Finally," Leo says. He cuts into a hunk of blue cheese. "You've been wanting to win for years."

"Took long enough, right?" Isabella says with a shake of her head.

I gasp. "Are you serious? Congratulations!"

Isabella laughs. "Oh, honey, sorry. Not the *lottery* lottery. The lottery for vehicle passes for the synchronous fireflies! We're driving out to the Smokies tomorrow night."

"It's a whole thing," Vin says.

Isabella waves him off. "Every summer, this rare species of

synchronous fireflies flash in unison. It's supposed to be transcendent. Life-changing, even. The only way in is by winning a spot through their lottery system. Every year we're unsuccessful."

"Until now. Congrats," Vin says.

Isabella does a little celebratory dance. "We can take a carload of people," she says. "You're all coming, right?"

I nod excitedly. "I must see this."

"Mom even had her convertible VW Beetle painted gold for good luck," Vin says. "She calls it her Firefly."

"Affectionately," Isabella says with a knowing shrug. "And you all laugh, but it worked!"

"We can't all fit in the Firefly," Leo says. "You four go. I'm happy to stay behind. It's too romantic. I can't handle that shit right now."

"If you're staying here, you want to take a look at that contract?" Vin asks.

"Dammit, Vin," Leo snaps. He tosses the rounded cheese knife down on the counter. "I'll look at it when I look at it. I don't need you hounding me every second of my life about it."

Vin's eyes become steely. "We can't talk about it until you review it. We need to get back to the label."

"They can wait," Leo says, storming out of the kitchen. "So can you."

"Don't talk to me again until you've read it," Vin calls after him.

Sudden silence falls on the room, and I'll say anything to break it. I link arms with Vin, my brows furrowed. "So tonight. It's romantic?" I ask.

Isabella offers me a small smile as she takes over the cheese plate responsibilities.

Vin tears his eyes from the door Leo slammed behind him. "If you find beetles, bug bites, and crowds romantic," he mumbles.

"Perfect. Count me in," I say.

"I'll show you around," Vin says, clearly wanting out of here.

We start on the second floor and wind our way through the upstairs halls as he points out the various rooms and their uses. There are five bedrooms and seven thousand square feet, so each room is spacious. I'm talking mostly to myself about all the herb and flower themes the rooms could be decorated in, probably overdoing my *oooh*s and *aww*s as I peer into each room.

I peek into an end room as Vin makes a U-turn and heads back down the long hallway. "Oops. Is that your parents' room? I didn't mean to look," I say.

Vin shakes his head. "They sleep downstairs," he says, retracing his steps and following me into the space. The room feels used, the bed haphazardly made, a novel with a bookmark tucked in at the halfway mark on the nightstand. Reading glasses are folded up next to the lamp. A second nightstand, which would typically be on the other side of the bed, is noticeably absent. A navy robe hangs on the back of a chair.

"Guests, probably," Vin mutters. Feeling like I've walked in on a private moment, I quickly exit the room.

I follow Vin downstairs, commenting on the beautiful furniture choices. My aunties would love it, too.

"Mom designed it," Vin says absentmindedly.

On the first floor, we breeze past the living room, the non-cookbook library, and a practice room for when Vin and Leo visit.

"What's all this?" I ask, poking my head into the practice room.

"There shouldn't be anything in there," Vin says, confused. Pushed up against the couch are boxes, sheet music overloading music stands, and cellos of varying sizes out on display. "I haven't seen all of these things together in...ever."

He looks uneasy at being unexpectedly thrown into and confronted by his past.

"It's a Chao Brothers Museum," I say, scanning the items on display. "They're bigger than I imagined you playing as a child."

"That one's from my tween years. We rented cellos as kids," Vin says, spinning slowly, looking at everything one by one. "They can be expensive instruments." He nods toward the one in front of me. "That's the one I played at thirteen. We had just come back from an event in Prague, and a wealthy benefactor who had enjoyed our performance gifted us our own cellos. First time I ever owned one."

I nod slowly. "I thought that kind of thing only happened in classic literature. At thirteen I was color-coordinating my braces to holidays, badly belting 'Uptown Girl,' and memorizing the anatomy of the heart." I playfully nudge Vin. "We're not so different, you and I."

Vin smiles, the crease between his brows softening. "What's with Billy Joel?" he asks.

I lift a bow and pretend to play. "My dad loves his music. We'd always listen to it when he'd teach me how to cook. After my parents' divorce, it was a relief to have something tangible to focus on: food and Billy. If I followed a recipe, the meal would turn out the way it was supposed to. When I listened to his songs, I could count on the same notes, the same lyrics."

"It's your comfort music."

"I'm an artichoke and Billy Joel girl, what can I say?" I set the bow down, eager to see what else there is. I continue exploring, plucking a string a little too hard. A low hum echoes across the room before I press my hand against the cello's neck and the noise cuts off. The vibration of the string tickles my palm.

My lips curve. "Oops."

"Miss, there's no touching allowed," Vin says mock-sternly, his demeanor relaxing.

I slowly run my finger down another string. "I thought this was an interactive museum. Are you going to kick me out?"

Vin draws closer. "Keep it up, and I just might have to."

I hold both arms up. "I'll keep my hands to myself then."

"That's not allowed, either." Vin pulls me closer to him. Like the instruments and sheet music around us, we're frozen in this moment, our faces inches apart. "I know I sprang this weekend on you," he says as my heart ditches its steady beat for something more sporadic. "But I'm really glad you're here."

"It's only fair. You've met most of the Hua women," I say, running my palm over his chest. "I'm happy to be here, too. I want to know all of you. And I needed to meet the people behind one of the best meet-cutes I've ever heard."

"What happened to happy endings being a lie?" he asks.

"Maybe not everything has to be tragic," I say, though there's skepticism layered into my tone.

"I think they like you already," Vin says. "My mom's very protective of her chickens."

"She's never showed any of your other girlfriends?"

Vin raises an eyebrow. "I couldn't say. I've never introduced anyone to my parents before."

A sort of dizziness takes over. The kind that feels like the flip-flopping-stomach type of excitement of something…new? Nerve-racking? Real?

"These instruments have been more places than I have," I say, focusing on a more solid topic of conversation. "You know, for someone who never takes vacations, you've really been around the world."

"I've seen the inside of many concert halls in the world, yes," he corrects.

"What's it like when you're on tour?" I ask, my voice filled with more concern than I expect. "Will we see each other at all?"

Vin takes a deep breath in. "If I'm honest, it'll be new territory for me. I've never had a—never had someone while on tour."

"We'll figure it out," I say. The future is looking more and more like a big question mark.

Vin nods. "It'll take some getting used to." He runs his long fingers across the strings of a taller cello. He cringes when the untuned notes come out all wrong. "I played this one from fifteen on after an unexpected growth spurt."

I study Vin's face as his eyes follow the notes on sheet music.

"What?" he asks.

The cellos of varying sizes suddenly look like measuring sticks of Vin's life, capturing the accomplishments and the growing pains. "Is it hard for you to see all this?" I ask.

"Everything in this room is a reminder of the hours of practice, the years of sacrifice," he says. "These weren't just instruments to me. They were one-way tickets to somewhere."

I hear what he doesn't say: the loss of a childhood, but the gaining of a bright future.

"It's like nothing, and everything, has changed," he whispers.

I give him a curious look. "What's changed?"

Vin lets out a one-syllable laugh. "I used to love playing. Not that I don't now. I just had the most fun doing it. The idea of it ever being a job never crossed my mind. Those dreams formed when I started getting paid to perform. I could play cello and make money for it? It sounded too good to be true."

I reflect on this as I take in the cellos that hold the memories of Vin's youth. In the span of seconds, I imagine what they must look like: the cello from the footage of him playing for the president. The cello he broke a string on midcompetition, also captured on camera. The one that broke his nose. I don't know which cello it is, but I'm sure it's in here somewhere. It's a garden of cellos, the instruments telling the story of Vin's life in a visual way.

The crease between Vin's brows is back. "But where are the other things? Where are the horribly drawn paintings? The baseballs? The snot-covered stuffed animals?" he asks.

My shoulders drop, feeling the weight of what Vin is saying.

He sits down on a trunk I imagine is filled with stacks of sheet music. Maybe old bows. Perhaps more black button-ups.

"Even though it took everything, it also gave everything." He sounds like he's trying to convince himself. Vin takes a loaded pause before asking, "What if my best years are behind me, but they're lost to time?" His eyes lock with mine, and I see more than just the worry that coats his voice. There's also panic.

I rest my hand on his shoulder. "You could not want to change a thing about your past but also want parts to be different. Both can be true."

His gaze falls on enough cellos for a small music shop behind me. "What I can say is at least the gains were worth it," he says, pushing his hand through his hair before standing. "Gains allow you to buy fancy stoves for your parents."

"It is a nice stove," I agree softly, stepping back a little too far. I bump into a stand and send sheet music flying. The sound of metal clanging brings us back to the moment, and the tension floats down to the ground along with the pages.

"Hope you didn't need those," I joke.

A flicker of a smile breaks through Vin's stormy expression, lighting up the entire room.

"Nope," he says, wrapping his arms around me. "Just this."

I stand on my tiptoes to reach all the way around his shoulders as I return his hug.

We're surrounded by Vin's past, and I don't know where I fit into this picture on a grander scale, but I safekeep this moment just for me. Store it away like my own version of a one-way ticket, but with an unknown destination. Wherever it takes us, I can't help but disagree with Vin.

I think it only gets better from here.

Chapter 22

VIN

The next day, I drive Chryssy around to show her the town after a morning of us responding to emails and phone calls. The rest of it is spent practicing while Chryssy teaches my mom how to make almond pear jelly.

Leo and I stay out of each other's way, only crossing paths when we're both in the kitchen at the same time for snacks.

An hour before we're set to leave, a summer storm rolls in fast, as though Vivaldi himself composed the weather patterns of Franklin. Sideways rain beats against the windows, the doors, the roof. It's practically the third movement come to life.

But today, Mom's motto is that of the postal service. A little lightning in the sky isn't coming between her and the lightning bugs.

The fireflies are still on.

Thankfully, by the time we begin our drive out to the Smokies, the weather clears just enough.

It takes just under four hours for us to make the drive east. Highways cross sprawling green fields and, soon enough, tree-covered mountains. With the top down, Chryssy and I can barely squeeze into the back with my cello lying across both our laps. We look ridiculous, but Mom insists on taking the Firefly to the fireflies.

The threat of more rain puts everyone on edge, but we make it, arriving to an almost-full parking lot. Apparently, no storm will deter anyone from cashing in on their lottery winnings.

"This was a terrible idea," I say to Dad, who's helping maneuver my instrument out of the backseat. "It's damp, and this cello cannot get wet."

The fading light overhead exaggerates the lines in Dad's face. The deep crow's-feet, his prominent forehead wrinkles, his hair grayer than it is brown. It's not lost on me how much older my parents look, and when the time between visits increases, there are new details to add to my memory of them.

"The tree canopy will catch any rain, but to be extra safe, your cello can have my raincoat," Chryssy says beside me. "It's going to sound incredible out here."

Maybe. Even though we play in outdoor landmarks around the world, those environments are more controlled. Out here in the woods, the dropping temperature and humidity will impact the pitch. The lower ranges may be harder to hear. I won't have acoustic feedback. Nothing good can come from this.

"The storm's over and done with. This is all your mom wants. She doesn't care what you play," Dad says, lowering his voice. "She played the anniversary card to get the rangers to allow you to do this. When else will people get to listen to a world-famous musician play while watching synchronized fireflies? It's a once-in-a-lifetime experience. And one of them is a Chaobreaker!" He grins proudly.

Just one? Those odds don't sound good.

Clearly Mom's not the only one excited about this, so I let it go. We're here. I'll play one song, and then we can forget it ever happened. Forget that it doesn't feel right that I'm playing solo publicly for the first time since Leo and I teamed up. We should be playing together.

We follow my parents across the parking lot. Chryssy and I fall back behind families and couples making their way to a wooded area.

My mind flashes to yesterday and the upstairs bedroom. The glasses. My dad's robe slung across the back of a chair. His slippers at the side of the bed. No trace of Mom anywhere.

"Vin?" Chryssy says softly.

"Sorry," I say, squeezing my fist. I flex to evaluate the pain, which hasn't been as intense since I've started daily acupuncture sessions with Rose.

We walk deeper into the woods, following the still-damp, tree-lined trail. Petrichor and wet earth scent the air, as excited chatter surrounds us. I want to be fully in this moment with Chryssy, but Leo's words scratch at the edge of my mind. He may not have committed to saying the actual words, but enough context is there for me to feel uncertainty in our future.

"I think Leo's done," I blurt out. "Or changing. I don't know."

Chryssy breaks her gaze away from the sepia-tinted crescent moon and looks directly at me. "Done with...the inn?"

"He's reached his limit with performing. With our life." I huff out a laugh severely lacking in humor. "He's tired. And he asked me if I was tired."

Leo's pulling away, I can feel it. He's going through a lot. Maybe this is part of the process. Doubt everything before coming back to what's important. He'll come around. We're always drawn back to the music. To playing together.

Chryssy's eyes lock onto me, 100 percent of her attention dedicated to this moment. "And are you?"

If eyes are windows into the soul and all that crap, I need to pull the shades down. I tear my eyes from hers and follow a tree's straight line up to the sky, where a few stars are already visible. I do the same to the tree next to it, and the one next to that. We're so small and inconsequential next to these plants that live for hundreds of years. Trees purify our air, protect against floods, are homes to wildlife, and no doubt more than I can even think of. Are trees tired?

A patch of white on a trunk catches my eye. "Of course when we're not looking, we find more than we'd know what to do with," I say, nodding toward the lion's mane.

Chryssy coughs out an unexpected laugh. "Should we take some back just in case?" she jokes. "I might have room in my suitcase."

I grin and take a moment before answering her. "I don't have time to be tired," I finally reply.

"But are you?" she asks again.

I stop trying to dodge her straightforward questions. I nod twice. "I'm so tired. I hate to even say that out loud."

"You're allowed to be tired, Vin."

"Fine. Then I'll take a nap." I watch Chryssy's reaction. She's steady, listening, waiting. "What we have doesn't happen for most people. My parents sacrificed everything for us. Their money, time, focus, it all went to us. To help us succeed. We had good reasons for pushing."

"Your reasons then might not be your reasons now."

"We can't just give it up," I press. "Not when we're doing better than we ever have. This is what we've worked for."

She considers this. "At what cost? Is it worth not seeing family that often? Not traveling for yourself? A tense relationship with your brother?" she asks, the expression on her face matching her empathetic tone. "Is it worth pushing yourself to the edge of burnout?"

"I'm not burned out," I say quickly. "I love what I do, and I know music can be healing, but it's not like I'm out there personally saving lives. For the most part, it's fun."

"I'm sure there are fun parts to it, definitely. But your job is still high-pressure. You can love what you do and still be exhausted from it," Chryssy says. "I'm not saying you're there yet, and being burned out is in no way any indication that you shouldn't be doing what you're doing."

If anyone was burned out, it was my parents, who worked multiple jobs to pay for our instruments and lessons and travel fees. And that was on top of the mortgage and loans and bills and getting food on the table. I get to live out my dreams. I have no right to be burned out.

"And Vin," Chryssy says, cutting my thoughts off, "you may not think you're burned out, but your body might. Insomnia is a common symptom of burnout. Your body isn't a machine that can operate nonstop. Machines break down, you know. Even instruments need tuning and restringing. Your body is an ecosystem that needs taking care of." She draws a long breath in. "It sounds like the boundaries between your work and personal life have become blurred a little. I know this well."

"From med school?"

Chryssy nods. "'Rest' was not a word in my vocabulary. I prided myself on wearing the busy badge. But it was more than just the overworked type of burnout. It was also existential. When I spent more time at the inn, it was then that I realized my values no longer aligned with what I was working toward in my career." She links her arm with mine. "My life didn't have meaning anymore. I needed a fundamental shift. It was hard to let those original dreams and my accomplishments go, but I'm better off for it. I felt like I had something to prove, too."

"What, you think I have something to prove?" I ask.

She throws it back to me. "Don't you?"

I grunt. "Maybe. Yes. Of course there's something to prove. We want to be the best at what we do. And I may have been born naturally good, but there's always room to improve. I guess I didn't realize how quickly we'd reach our goals, and how often those goalposts would keep moving. How much we'd need to keep up. I have to be better than the next concert, the next album, the next performance, just to stay relevant. To stay on top. Just to stay in the game."

Chryssy exhales. "That's a tiring game to play. And who says you have to keep getting better?"

"I was born with this innate talent," I say. "It's all I've done, all I've worked toward, for my entire life. I have to make it work. What else can I do?"

"So you feel stuck. Like you have to do this forever?" she asks.

There's that word again. Stuck. Stagnant.

"I guess yeah, I feel a bit stuck," I admit. "In my reputation, with the music genre, with the direction of our career. If we keep going down this path, I'm not sure we'll ever be able to get off before it's too late. Or at least take a right turn every now and then and experience new things. What else am I even good at? I've never had a chance to find out." I frown.

"Maybe you need a chance to figure that out," she says. "You've been a little busy. I wonder if you need a fermata."

My head swivels in her direction. "Did you just say *fermata*?"

She smiles. "A musical notation symbol that represents a pause or a rest. Exactly how long is up to you."

"On a rest, or on a *note*," I add. "Why do you know that?"

She gives me a look. "My point was to emphasize the *rest* piece. And I may have been listening to more of your music."

This draws a surprised laugh out of me. "And why are you doing that?"

"It wouldn't at all be to feel a little bit closer to you," she says, her face and tone serious enough for me to believe it. "I want to understand more about your world. You've been learning a lot about mine. You need a fermata. A pause."

"There are no pauses in life, Chryssy," I say.

Chryssy narrows her eyes at me. "Fine. In our world, they're called breaks. It's more than that, though. If you think about what Leo's saying, it sounds like your lifestyle itself is unsustainable. Are there things that can change to help support a more balanced life?"

"I get what you're saying, but I just don't see how it's possible. It takes a lot of work to stay at this level, to keep getting better," I say.

Chryssy waits a few seconds before responding. "Vin, without water, flowers can't grow. Water is your rest. You might be off the stage for a bit, figuring out what you want from your career. From your life," she says. "Figuring out what balance means to you. It isn't fifty-fifty, and there's no one right way to do it. Maybe it means that sometimes you'll have busy periods, but you need to also make sure you have time off from being so go-go-go."

"I guess."

She stops me and faces my direction. "You've been in the spotlight your entire life, practically. You've thrived under some harsh conditions. But there's a part of you that you still get to discover. When you do, I think it's going to be beautiful. And maybe it's only me who sees it, and not a sold-out crowd." She wraps her hand around mine. "Flowers bloom even when no one is watching."

I nod. I hear her, I do. But I'm not entirely sure what to say, or where I would even start. Our type of life is not built for balance. Chryssy's eyes dart down to her phone when it buzzes in her palm. She taps into an email and immediately types out a response.

"And you're telling *me* to be balanced," I say. "You just responded to an email in the woods. How are you getting service out here?"

"Another store is interested in stocking In Full Bloom," she says, sliding her phone into her rain jacket's pocket.

For all the rest Chryssy's been telling me to get, along the way she, too, forgot to take her own advice. Between helping me, Leo, her aunties, and managing In Full Bloom, she's as overworked as it sounds like she was in med school.

"I appreciate what you're saying. It's just…at first I didn't want to let my parents down, but now there's so many more people we'd be disappointing if we're not good enough," I admit. "Our fans have high expectations for us. *I* have high expectations for us."

"You can still play incredibly without being perfect," she says. "Be good at what you do and have high standards for yourself, but what if you also did it for the experience of it? Because you love it, and that's it? What if people's approval of you and their high expectations didn't matter? You can't control what awards you're given or where you land on the charts. You can't even control what people think about you, whether they believe you're a heartbreaker or not."

"Isn't that what we were trying to do by pretending to be together?" I ask. "Control the narrative?"

"We can only control it so much. Us breaking up," she starts, the corners of her lips turning down, "that might not have immediately changed how some people saw you." She taps her chin with her pointer finger. "Between your childhood and skirting burnout and wanting to be perfect, I think I've identified where your heart might be a little broken."

I frown. "You think I'm heartbroken?"

"I believe everyone is, just a little," she says, sidestepping a puddle. "Let me preface with this: Being heartbroken doesn't mean *you're* broken. I'm pretty sure your unaddressed heartbreak has to do with time. You didn't get to build many relationships as a kid, and your busy schedule prevents deep bonds now, too. I think that lost time—and the idea of more time sacrificed with those you love—hurts."

I don't feel broken, but I think Chryssy could hold me together if I let her. I want to let her.

We tuck into a dry opening under thick foliage and venture a little deeper into the woods. "Life has always felt like a race. Like I'm running out of time," I tell her.

"When you play in a few minutes, what if you didn't concentrate on playing perfectly or worry about what everyone will think afterward? What if you played for the pure enjoyment of it?" she asks.

"I don't know. This is my job," I reactively say. "I take it seriously."

"Actually, *this* isn't," she says, gesturing around us. "Tonight is not your job. In fact, tonight's about your parents. I think it'd be the perfect time to let loose a little. Who knows what you'll discover about yourself."

"I generally try to keep the self-discovery sessions to when I'm not in the middle of a performance," I say, though it's further from the truth than I intend. Music has always helped me see things clearly. Playing a song is when I do my best thinking. Why would that be any different, even in the middle of this muggy forest?

We make it to the designated spot, where Dad sets up camping chairs for each of us, giving Chryssy and me some distance from him and Mom.

"Would you try something? For me?" Chryssy asks as she reaches for my bicep to steady herself on the uneven ground.

"For you?" I repeat. If only Chryssy knew how much I would do for her. "I'll do anything you want."

A small smile appears. One that I put there. I will do whatever it is I need to in order to keep her smiling.

"In the middle of the song, I want you to switch to a new one. After, let's see how you feel," she proposes while I set up my cello.

My heartbeat quickens. "I haven't practiced the third movement that way." I exhale. "It's not a good idea, but if that's what you want, then...okay."

I assess the families and couples and individuals making themselves at home for the next couple of hours. It's a more intimate venue, and all I see right now are people I can't let down. People I can't mess up in front of. I don't make mistakes. It's not what people expect of me or deserve from me. I'm not trying to hurt my reputation more. I need to be excellent.

"You see that guy right there?" Chryssy asks, nodding toward an older gentleman sitting in a fold-out chair reading a book. "That's Frank. He has a beagle named Biscuit and has been to every continent, including Antarctica. He's seen the wonders of the world, and all he wants in life is to have a good time. Think you can give him that?"

I dig my heel into the earth to create an indent for my cello's endpin. "I think I can," I say, smiling. "Thank you."

"Just stating the facts," Chryssy says, nudging me.

We're out in nature about to watch beetles light up. The weather shifted our plans for the day. There aren't good acoustics, no microphone for everyone to hear me play, and at any moment it might rain again. Leo's tired. I'm tired. I don't know how to define what Chryssy and I are, what we're even doing at this point by trying to understand the curse. And yet here I am, with my cello, about to play for unsuspecting strangers and a man named Frank in the Smoky Mountains.

Against the darkness that came quicker than I anticipated, a thin sliver of the moon peeks through the trees. I stretch, tune, warm up, and wait for the ranger's signal, which is set to happen after her introductory speech. I'll set the mood and build anticipation just before the fireflies are expected to light up.

There's chatter all around us; the human voices are a stark contrast against the quiet of the forest. Despite my initial worry of the third movement being too energetic for this calm setting, it's surprisingly perfect. This environment is anything but serene. We're the lucky hundred and forty who won the car lottery and have weathered the storm to be here. The mood is electric with the energy rivaling that of a concert about to begin. The fireflies are the rock stars on the verge of changing everyone's lives. And me? I'm the warm-up band to the real show.

I take a slow, deep breath and position my bow over the strings. When the ranger points to me, I'm off.

Vivaldi's Summer, third movement, starts off quick. After five seconds, I hold the strings down, nailing the sudden silent moment after the fast-paced beginning. Two seconds later, I pick up where I left off, keeping the notes crisp, sharp.

Mentally, I'm tentative, not sure how to approach playing alone. My hands, though, are confident, knowing, and they guide me through the motions.

As I hit each note at the right time and on the right pitch, my confidence grows. My fingers fly across the strings, moving up and down my cello's neck.

There's no time for hesitation.

I don't have sheet music. I don't need it. I feel this one in my bones, have each note etched into my memory.

I feel alive and connected to myself in an entirely new way playing the classical music that formed me. Playing the music that made me first fall in love with the cello.

And then, in an early transition, I'm two seconds too fast. When I tilt my chin up and glimpse a look at people's faces, no one's even noticed that I've rushed the middle. Frank's tapping his foot, his book closed on his lap. Everyone's caught up in the music and moment.

I can feel my shoulders loosen, mirroring the sloped branches weighed down with raindrops on the trees surrounding us.

My fingers don't stop, my bow is a blur, but time becomes thicker, slower. I'm breathless, the unrelenting pace of the song demanding my energy, focus, precision. I think of the heartache, the heartbreak, the precarious future with Leo. Being at the top of our game, on top of the charts. The fame, the fortune, living the dream. The imminence of a storm, the darkness, the rain.

And then I think of Chryssy, of sunshine, of hope. I think of that fine, delicate line right on the edge of broken and healed. The fine, delicate line between fake and real.

Halfway through, as I make the notes climb, somewhere between the thin layers of my short-term memory, I remember Chryssy's request to switch songs.

What song, what song, what song?

I shuffle through my mental repertoire of music I've played live that would merge well with the vivacity of this one.

Then it comes to me.

It happens so fast I don't have time to overthink it. At the high note halfway through the song, I start the descent and slow everything down gradually, so it sounds natural.

I draw my eyes up to Chryssy's, not focusing on anyone else's reactions or faces around us. I just need to see hers.

The notes don't form enough of an identifiable song yet, but Chryssy immediately knows. Her eyes go wide and glossy, her lips slightly parted. She doesn't look away from me once.

Something inside me twists like a tuning peg tightening a string. My love life has always been an out-of-tune, offbeat song. One that I couldn't hear in its entirety or even imagine the subsequent notes for. But when Chryssy entered the picture, she filled in the empty lines with music. Brought me closer to hearing something worth listening to.

Vivaldi's composition melds into a Billy Joel classic. I don't slow down all the way to the typical pace of the song but back off my momentum just enough to try to make the two pieces sound cohesive. It's kind of working.

I've never played "Vienna" before, but I'm able to play it by ear, recalling the tune in my head from when Chryssy shared it with me. She was trying to get me to listen to the lyrics, but what I heard was the tune. The way it made me feel. That's what I try to recall now.

Turns out, fragmented lyrics wedged their way into my memory. And maybe it's true. What is the hurry about? Cool it off, I recall, before burning out. It's a song about slowing down, not rushing, truly living. It's about appreciating what matters.

I become distracted, as Chryssy's words circle my brain, while my hands continue to play. The soft spot in my chest aches, but it doesn't hurt. It's the way she talked to me without judgment, how she doesn't need me to be perfect like I think everyone else does.

Right now, I play for her, but there's a realization settling inside me that I want to play for her always.

The notes dance around us, and together we're in the center of the storm, in the eye of a hurricane, in the middle of a forest, surrounded suddenly by the sparkling of fireflies. Dots of gold flash and vanish almost immediately. They're noiseless, but I can hear their song, their pulse, their beat. I was very wrong: This is romantic as hell.

The way Chryssy beams in the glow of the fireflies, I can tell she thinks so, too. She doesn't seem to mind. I take a deep breath to slow the twist, fearing that whatever is changing inside of me will break.

At first, the lightning bugs twinkle on and off and out of rhythm with each other. I move between the two songs, merging the classical sensibilities with the rock rawness. In all my years of playing, I've stuck to the script, stayed between the five-line staff.

But being here, out of my comfort zone in so many ways, weaving musical genres together and creating new meaning from existing meaning is so liberating. It's by no means perfect; the songs have opposing energies, but somehow it still works. In a way, they balance each other out. Like Yin and Yang.

I end my performance with a few more notes of Vivaldi's Summer, bringing the two songs back together. I slide my bow across the strings, the final, low note slicing through the night air.

But for me, the song isn't over yet. Let loose, Chryssy had said.

I lean my cello against the chair, grab Chryssy by the waist, and lift her into a kiss. The string running through my core tightens before snapping loose.

All I hear is the sound of my heartbeat thumping and the soft moan as Chryssy presses her lips harder into mine.

Everything goes quiet, and for once, I don't mind the silence.

Around us, the fireflies blink slowly into one steady heartbeat of a glow.

Together, they begin to flash in sync.

Chapter 23

CHRYSSY

On our last day in Tennessee before heading back to Washington, we're tasked with helping Vin's parents clean out the chicken pen and coop. It's a late spring cleaning I'm a little too excited to partake in.

Vin and I meet his family at the coop, and they give me a skeptical once-over. I'm dressed in the most casual clothing I brought: flower-patterned jeans and an embroidered white top with sleeves that puff out from the shoulders. At least I know Lucy and Ethel will appreciate my outfit.

I cover a yawn, a consequence of a later-than-usual night out. After watching the fireflies, Vin's dad had enough energy to drive the four hours back. All I remember is drifting to sleep in the crook of Vin's shoulder as his playing echoed in my mind. I'll never forget watching Vin play live for the first time.

We all greet each other with various enthusiasm, Leo's and Vin's being the lowest. I'm sandwiched between two moody brothers, and their tension creates a new energy I haven't felt from them before.

Isabella, William, and Leo have already guided the chickens to a temporary enclosure. It's all hands on deck as we clear out what I learn are called feeders, nesting box trays, perches, and drinkers from the coop.

"Everyone good?" Isabella asks, clearly also sensing the mood.

"Great," Leo says, clapping his hands together. "We better get started. Lots to accomplish today!"

It's lost on no one that this is a jab at Vin.

Vin returns Leo's snipe with a glare.

"How about we don't ruin Mom and Dad's weekend?" Vin says, grabbing a shovel. "Unless you really don't care anymore."

"Someone please tell Vin that maybe I'd care more if the gas wasn't always pressed down to the floor," he says.

"Tell him yourself," Isabella says.

"I would but he said not to talk to him until I've read the contract, and I haven't done it yet," Leo says.

"You're being a child," Vin says.

"Yeah, *I'm* the child," Leo says, making a face.

Vin scoffs triumphantly. "You said it."

"Thirtysomethings and you're both being children. What did your mother just say?" William says, looking visibly uncomfortable with having to be the bad guy. "Get moving. This coop won't clean itself."

"This is not how you act in front of guests," Isabella says, eyeing her sons.

I brace myself for a fallout. For blame. For someone to fly the coop. To go for a drive. To guess whether they'd come back. I've heard enough family stories, seen enough with my own eyes. The end is imminent.

"It's just Chryssy," Leo says.

"*Just* Chryssy?" Vin asks. He drops his shovel as though, of all the things Leo has said, this is what's made him mad. I shouldn't be flattered, but I am.

"You know what I mean," Leo says. "We love Chryssy. Well, *I* don't love her in that way. I can't speak for Vin, though."

Vin picks up his shovel, thrusting the cutting edge under the chicken coop bedding. "Are you still talking?"

"Yeah, but not to you," Leo says. "Someone tell Vin that I don't love Chryssy like that."

They hold each other's stares for another beat before breaking.

They cover their mouths, holding back muffled sounds.

Is that...are they...laughing?

"Stop using 'love' and 'Chryssy' in the same sentence, man," Vin says, shoveling the bedding into a composting bin. "Read the contract when you want. We'll sort out the details later."

"Thank you," Leo says. "And to set the record straight, I'm not a child."

Vin grunts. "Thanks for clarifying."

And just like that, the fight's over. No one else looks surprised by this sudden turn of events.

"Speaking of setting records straight," Vin says, sticking the shovel into a mound of dirt. He faces his parents. "Do you two have something to tell us?"

Leo furrows his brows, looking confused. "What would they have to tell us? Is there something to tell us?"

Isabella and William eyeball each other. "We do have something to share," Isabella says slowly. "We wanted to wait until after your visit so we could focus on having a nice time together."

Leo and Vin both stop what they're doing.

"What is it?" Leo asks, as Vin's fingers tighten around his shovel's handle. "Oh god, did someone die? Was it Uncle Wilbur? It was Uncle Wilbur, wasn't it?"

"No one died," Isabella says, reaching for William's hand. "Your father and I are..."

Suddenly, I'm ten years old and sitting on the couch in my parents' living room. They're breaking the news that things are going to look different from now on. That while they won't be living at the same house anymore, I'll still see them both. That they love me and that this has nothing to do with me. That this has everything to do with the curse. We were doomed from the start. When Mom said *we*, it was no question that she wasn't talking about her and my father. She meant me and her.

The rest of that night is such a blur I only remember it in flashes. Dad's hand covering his mouth, like he's covering up the words he wanted to say. Instead, he lets Mom speak for them both. Mom's sigh of resignation. The wave of her arm like a white flag in surrender to our family's curse.

When she said she was tired of fighting, I took that to mean against the inevitable. That night was the last fight between my parents. Mom left midargument. Went for a drive to cool off, Dad had said, his eyes puffy from crying. I spent the rest of the evening under the covers reading my mom's medical textbooks about the heart, thinking one day I could fix them. That one day I could make the pain my family felt go away.

I close my eyes, my heart breaking in anticipation for Vin. My stomach clenches, bracing myself for the destruction of the perfect marriage he witnessed growing up. The perfect love he's looking for and wants to feel.

"...selling the house," Isabella finishes, her voice cracking.

My eyes fly open. I touch my fingers to my cheek, my gloves coming back wet with tears. I blink the rest away, looking over at the chickens, over to their miniature pool. Doing anything I can to make my tears evaporate without drawing attention to myself.

Leo reacts first. "Which house? This house?" he says. "Surely you don't mean this one."

"This was your dream house," Vin finally says.

Isabella looks between her sons with a face so sad I can't help but mirror it. "Dreams change," she says.

"Is that why you have all of our instruments out?" Vin asks. "Those should really be in cases."

YIN YANG LOVE SONG

"We need you to go through your stuff," William says. "While you're here."

Isabella and William glance nervously at each other, pulling their hands away. "There's more," Isabella says, clearing her throat. "We've separated."

And there it is.

Without thinking, I move over to Vin's side and take his hand in mine, giving it two squeezes.

"Who? You and Dad?" Vin's jaw flexes. "From each other?" He follows his own question up with another one. "You said 'separated,' not 'separating.' Past tense? When did this happen?" he asks.

"Oh, does it really matter?" Isabella asks.

"It does," Vin says. "I want to understand what was happening that you felt you couldn't tell us."

"It was six months ago," she answers.

"*Six* months? And you just, what? Pretended to be together?" Vin asks, cringing at his phrasing.

"We weren't pretending to do anything," William says. "We just didn't tell you."

Vin exhales sharply. "That's not any better."

"You two have so much on your plate, and then you and Aubrey," she says to Leo, who flinches at the sound of her name. "We didn't want you to worry. Not involving you two was the right choice. Our problems aren't your problems."

"Oh my god, is this why we're cleaning the coop?" Leo asks. "Is this the last spring cleaning ever?"

"What the hell was this visit even for?" Vin asks. "Is it for show? Is this all just part of an act?"

"Of course not. And sue me for wanting to see my sons. When's the last time we've all been together like this?" Isabella asks, shaking her head firmly. "Your father and I still have so much love for each other. What we share deserves to be celebrated. Thirty-five years is a beautiful milestone."

Hearing this stuns me. Like, actually shocks me, and not because I didn't once get a read on their heartbreak. It occurs to me that maybe this is because... there isn't any. Or at least there isn't anymore.

If a relationship can't even last for a couple who separates but still loves each other, how could it for someone who's cursed? I came here looking for proof, for inspiration. Instead, we're just witnessing another breakup. It strikes me now that when Vin talked about his parents and their perfect relationship, I needed to know that it was true. That it was possible.

I try to hold the shock in, to keep it compressed inside of me. This is not the moment to explode with feelings like I'm some kind of emotionally unhinged firework.

The backs of my eyes prick with tears again, and my vision blurs. I envision guardrails. A garden bed around my heart. I do not need to hold this pain. I'm thinking the words but clearly don't feel them because I'm suddenly vibrating choppy, gasping wheezes, drawing attention to myself.

"How?" I hear myself asking.

The way everyone's heads turn in my direction confirms that they, too, have heard this.

"I'm so sorry," I say, pressing my hand over my chest. "Ignore me, please."

"You might as well ask, honey," Isabella says. "We put you in this situation."

This time, it's Vin who squeezes my hand.

"I just... you're separated but live together *and* are celebrating your love?" A frown settles on my face. Vin and Leo know about my family's curse, but his parents don't. "My parents divorced when I was young. They don't talk. We don't do joint events. They sure aren't celebrating their love for each other. I don't understand…but I want to." Pressing my palms into my eyes to block my ducts doesn't help. The tears are back, and it's so embarrassing.

"How do you do it?" I ask, noting that they're both still wearing their wedding rings.

Isabella kneels down to pet Lucy. "In relationships, sometimes there's an expectation that you must be in sync all the time. I admit I expected that. When William and I first started dating, we didn't miss a beat. But that's impossible to maintain, especially over three decades," she says, looking between all of us. "Somewhere along the way, we not only fell out of sync, but we started playing different songs completely. We stopped growing together. We haven't quite gotten back into rhythm yet."

"There's a lot of great aspects to staying on the beat with someone," William says. "But there's beauty in asynchronicity, too. Let's not downplay thirty-five years. To make it this far requires communication, a willingness to be vulnerable. Not thinking you have all the answers. Remembering intentions. Not being afraid when your partner changes and evolves." He looks over at Isabella, and all I see in his eyes are admiration, affection, and care.

Isabella takes a deep breath in and links arms with William. "Sometimes that means you change together. Sometimes it means changing apart," she says. "We decided to take time to find ourselves again. Independently."

"What does that even mean?" Vin asks. "You're still living in the same house, aren't you?"

"There was no need for anyone to move out right away while we worked through our next steps," William says. "Your mother wants to travel and see the world outside of concert halls. There are a few hobbies I have my eye on. Maybe I'll even live abroad."

"Who knows what else? That's kind of the point," Isabella says.

There's nothing and no one to blame. In front of us are just two people who have nothing but love and respect for each other.

Conceptually, this makes sense. But not just being amicable but *loving* toward each other? This is the stuff of heart-wrenching movies, not real life. Isabella and William's relationship was the song I hoped Vin and I could cover. And now... it's static on the record player.

"I'm sorry... I just... I need some air," I say, dropping Vin's hand. I leave the pen and round the corner toward the field. My sneakers crunch over sticks and dirt, every step taking me farther from Vin.

Amicable split or not, this whole thing feels like another reminder of what I've known my entire life. Nothing. Will. Last. I am not the exception.

Hua women get left. We accept it. It's only a matter of time.

The shout of my name makes me turn around. I see Vin running through the field. Running after me. The chase leaves him breathless.

Hua women also don't get followed.

Vin stops two feet from me, running a hand through his already unkempt, windblown hair.

"I'm so sorry, Vin, about your parents, this whole weekend, everything," I start.

He turns his light brown eyes on me, and it doesn't take much to see the sadness behind them. "Sorry?" he asks. "Chryssy, you have nothing to be sorry about."

I do, though. I feel guilty and filled with regret. I made that about me. I *cried*.

Vin paces a small patch of grass, burning off his excess energy.

"I can't believe this," he mumbles. "I... I've been so busy I didn't even know my own parents were having relationship trouble. No. Growing apart."

"It's what happens," I say, wanting the strength to help him but feeling too tired to be anything but sad. "Sometimes it's one thing, other times it's a culmination of a bunch of little things."

He dips his chin to his chest. "Or it's one big thing that leads to the rest of the little things," he counters. "Why bother if it all ends?"

I cross my arms. "Some people say it's about the journey. That it's better to have loved and lost and all that."

Vin's mouth is a hard underscore. "And is it?"

I shake my head. "It's silly nonsense we tell ourselves to feel better temporarily. They're happy-ever-after movie endings in the form of pithy sayings."

"My parents' life was so focused on us," he says. "All their sacrifice during our childhood, just for it to lead to this. At least we were successful and made everything they gave up—what they're giving up—worth it." He furrows his brows. "And I was just going to throw it away…"

Doubt, hopelessness, fear, panic—all the emotions that have typically accompanied my previous breakups—surge through every square inch of my body.

"Maybe we should continue on with our original plan," I spit out preemptively, drawing a metaphorical line between us in the grass. "A relationship with me won't last, and I made you a promise. Are you sure you don't want to break up with me? June's nearly over. We'd be right on target for when this was all supposed to end anyway."

This would be for the best, for both of us. To prevent the heartache we'll both feel in the future. If we call it off now, we can spare ourselves. Do Future Chryssy and Future Vin big favors. I can still help him.

"I guess we made it this far," Vin says.

I look anywhere but at him. "We should follow through," I add before the back of my throat constricts. "We're nothing if not committed, and we still don't know enough about the curse."

After a long stretch of silence, Vin sighs through his nose and folds his arms over his chest.

Tears stream down my face. "So, break up with me. Now, tomorrow, at the end of the month like we planned, whenever, just do it. Rip the flower head off," I say.

Maybe if enough breakups happen, one day I really will come back stronger.

His eyes pierce through me when I say all this. He doesn't object.

My conviction strengthens. "Or I'll break up with you, how about? It's never been done before, but with everything we learned, I don't know what to believe anymore. We can put a stop to your heartbreaker reputation if that's what you want."

My chest pinches, like my heart is actively shrinking. A flower closing in on itself. I've accepted so much when it comes to love and my family and the stories that have been passed down. Even if I didn't want to anymore, what am I supposed to do?

"Let's get back to the inn, and we can figure it out then," Vin says, looking past my shoulder.

"You can get everything you ever wanted," I whisper, offering him another opportunity to put the deal back on the table and run.

Vin looks at me for a few heartbeats. "Us breaking up with each other isn't going to get me anything I want," he says. "But I don't know what I'm supposed to say here."

We stand opposite each other, facing off and playing another unspoken game of chicken. Fitting, given the coop half a field away. This time, though, it's Vin who breaks first. He takes a step back, turning to go.

I ready myself to watch him leave. *This is for the best*, I repeat to myself.

But then, in the slightest of surprising movements, Vin turns his hand out, extending it toward me. I look at it sadly before eventually placing my hand in his.

We leave the conversation where it is—a question without answers—and walk back in silence toward the soon-to-be-sold farmhouse.

Chapter 24

CHRYSSY

I'm not waiting in a back alley alone. I don't care what time of day it is or how cheery it looks." Mom casts a glance at the colorful lanterns dangling overhead. "Why is this place accessible only through a sketchy back door?" she asks.

"This place isn't for the public," I say, having noticed the locked front door and its lack of signage. "The store owner prefers it that way. She doesn't want to attract tourists, I guess."

When Vin, Leo, and I returned from Nashville a few days ago, the Plotting Shed looked as though my aunties had been busy solving a murder case. String led from one printed-out photo of a person to another. The zigzagging of the points of contact was dizzying.

The aunties did have success, though, when one introduction became a solid lead. Through their vast connections from their former lives, they learned of Melody Chan. She's an East Asian Studies instructor at the University of Washington and the owner of a rare bookstore in the heart of Seattle's Chinatown-International District.

At that point, Vin and I wanted a break from this so-called adventure to give ourselves some time to think and process everything that had just happened. But once you get a Hua woman started, there's no stopping her. We're seeing our mission through.

Or, at the very least, Auntie Violet, Auntie Rose, and I are meeting with Melody Chan and making a game plan based on what we learn. If she can't help translate the remaining ingredients, then maybe this is the end of the road. We'll never know what the heart herbal blend's full recipe is.

Unfortunately for us, the store hours are even rarer than Ms. Chan's books, and they seem to be determined by her whims and her teaching schedule. This is the second time we've attempted to catch her in the store.

When Mom learned we were visiting the Chinatown-International District, she insisted on coming with. Apparently, Auntie Violet had promised to treat her to bubble tea and lunch months ago. After pulling a twelve-hour shift at the hospital, Mom wants her boba and Peking duck.

"I'm tired and don't have my wits about me," Mom says. "Why can't I come in with you?"

My gaze bounces from a parked car to a dumpster to the high stacks of cardboard boxes filled with leafy greens and bags of rice, and finally lands on the door Auntie Violet and Auntie Rose just walked through, leaving me behind to make excuses to Mom.

"We're . . . working on something," I tell her. "For your birthday."

Mom eyes me suspiciously as she sips her matcha bubble tea. "I can't imagine what you'd be getting me from somewhere that makes customers enter through a back door." She furrows her eyebrows. "And it's June. My birthday isn't until December."

"We're very proactive?"

Mom straightens. "You're lying to me."

I swirl my jasmine milk tea around before taking a drink, pulling up boba through the wide straw. "I'm not." *I'm protecting you.* I huff out a breath. "We'll be fast. Do you want to go hang out at the bakery across the street? You can stock up on bolo buns and milk bread."

What happens inside the rare bookstore needs to stay between Auntie Rose, Auntie Violet, me, and Melody Chan. And Auntie Daisy, who's taking over today's sessions at the inn, once we catch her up.

"I don't have enough freezer space," Mom says, though she considers this. She eyes me up and down. "What's with you today? You seem...distracted. Is it because of whatever all of this is?" Mom waves her hand toward the alley. "We shouldn't even be back here."

I look at the ground, my chest tightening at being observed. I thought I was doing a pretty good job of hiding my irritability. I don't know what I was thinking bringing the Curse Box to my aunties and asking them for help. It was too dangerous unearthing what belongs buried deep down.

When I look back up at Mom, all I find is a brick wall. She's headed toward the door, clearly deciding to take matters into her own hands.

Her general pace is set to power walking, a skill she developed working in hospitals to get from Point A to Point B as swiftly as possible. Here, too, she wastes no time.

Before I can catch up and stop her, we're in Ms. Chan's bookstore. We lift our shoulders to make ourselves as narrow as possible so we can get through the back storage area, which is stuffed with stacks of boxes.

The front of the store is more organized and presentable to potential customers willing to spend hundreds, if not thousands, on old books. Curtains are drawn, covering the storefront's windows and shrouding the entire place in mystery. Floor-to-ceiling shelves line every wall, each one filled with leather-bound books protected behind glass. Though rugs cover every square inch of floor and mute our footsteps, the creaky wood underneath announces our presence.

Auntie Rose and Auntie Violet, who are at the front of the shop, turn to us. They're all set up with the letters and journals spread across the counter.

"What are you doing—" Auntie Rose starts before a third voice cuts her off.

"Here we go," says a woman around my aunties' age. She has a serious, angular face and forceful yet kind eyes. She sets down a large bound book.

This must be Ms. Chan. She's slightly shorter than Auntie Violet and way more intimidating than Auntie Rose. Her long hair is darkened by the low light from the Art Deco lamps, which simultaneously create ominous shadows and a cozy glow in the windowless space.

"I've pulled a reference for the two characters you're inquiring about," she continues. "I believe this will solve your mystery." Ms. Chan looks up at me and Mom and, without missing a beat says, "Your tea can go here." She taps a tray already holding Auntie Violet's and Auntie Rose's bubble teas.

To keep her as far back as I can, I grab Mom's drink and set both next to the others. I too-sharply angle my body in front of Mom to block her view, and bump into a wood table covered in a leather desk pad and a magnifying glass. The Curse Box is sitting on top, my movement making it rattle.

Mom covers her gasp. "Is that what I think it is?" she asks.

I watch her regard the box. "I don't know…what do you think it is?" I carefully ask.

Mom turns from me, knowing how stingy I've been with information. I may feel out of it, but at least I'm still a vault. "Wasn't Daisy supposed to destroy this? What's going on?" she asks her sisters.

To Auntie Violet, Auntie Rose gives a little shrug. "We're trying to understand the curse," she says as casually as she would tell someone what was for dinner. Auntie Rose directs her attention back to Ms. Chan. "What did you find out?"

Ms. Chan runs her fingers down the page. "This one was trickier because half of it has been smeared off. I was able to piece it back together, and it looks too close to this character to be anything else," she says, pointing to a character that looks like a little drawing. "Oolong black tea. There used to be different words for the meaning of 'tea.' See how this character was modified to become 'cha'? This is the version of 'tea' we use today."

Auntie Violet nods. "Thank goodness we found you," she says, writing these nuggets of information down in her purple notebook. "What's the other one?"

Ms. Chan flips to a different part of the book. "This one was much simpler. You see how this component turns into this and the line comes down underneath?" She drags her finger over to the drawing next to it. "Your final ingredient translates to 'flower.'"

"'Flower'?" Auntie Violet repeats. "This is how our last name used to be spelled." She smiles. "That's fun."

"Yes, very fun. Now what's the flower?" Auntie Rose asks. "I can see it being rose, though honeysuckle will help clear toxins and move stagnant Qi. Safflower wouldn't surprise me, either." She leans forward on the counter. "So?"

Ms. Chan adjusts her blouse. "That's all it says. Just... 'flower.'"

"That can't be—" Auntie Violet starts.

"It has to be something," Auntie Rose says at the same time. She reaches for the book but is stopped by Ms. Chan placing her hand on Auntie Rose's. They both pull their arms back quickly.

Auntie Rose clears her throat. "I thought you could read Old Chinese."

"And I thought this was going to be a peaceful afternoon in the store," Ms. Chan tells Auntie Rose with a smirk.

Auntie Rose and Auntie Violet once again talk over each other, trying to squeeze more information out of Ms. Chan. While they're distracted, Mom takes me by the elbow and drags me to a quieter corner of the bookshop.

YIN YANG LOVE SONG 275

"Is this for real?" Mom asks. "You've all been trying to break the curse?"

"Understand the curse," I correct, avoiding Mom's eye contact by zeroing in on a framed Chinese wood-block print hanging over her head.

"Were those letters and journals? With a recipe?" Mom asks, rubbing her temples. "Wait." She puts one hand up. "Don't tell me."

"That's what I was trying to do in the first place," I say, starting to turn away.

Mom reaches for my arm. "You really think opening the box and doing this," she says, gesturing back toward Ms. Chan, "will help?"

I don't have a great answer for this. But after everything that happened with Vin's parents, what I learned from Dad, and how hopeless it all feels, I might as well be honest.

"Last week, yes, I held out hope," I admit. "Now? I feel a bit silly chasing down ingredients and translations for a long-lost blend. You must think we're—I'm—ridiculous."

The groove between Mom's furrowed brows deepens. "Tell me about it."

I pretzel my arms across my chest in defense. "Wow, thanks."

"No," Mom corrects, her voice softening. "Tell me about what you found. I want to understand, too."

I should ask if she means it. If she's sure she really wants to know. I should warn her that there's no going back. You can't stuff knowledge back into a box of any size.

Instead, this moment feels like something I've wanted—no, longed for—for years. Mom's listening, waiting for information. When it comes down to it, I want her to hear me for a change. And in this rare bookshop with Auntie Rose, Auntie Violet, and Ms. Chan standing twenty feet away, I have evidence. And backup.

And so, I spill my guts, sharing every detail about the letters, the journals, and how we still don't have answers but we're trying. I'm breathless when I finish talking. This time, Mom avoids eye contact with me.

Behind us, Ms. Chan flips through more pages as Auntie Violet and Auntie Rose insist that there must be a specific flower referenced somewhere in the notebooks or letters or in one of the character's components.

"No one's leaving here without answers," Auntie Rose demands, the firm yet desperate tone of her voice finding its way over to us from across the room.

Mom looks over my shoulder at her sisters, maybe realizing how this affects more than just me. "If you're running around forests and getting Old Chinese characters deciphered, then Vin must really mean a lot to you," she says, nodding a little.

On instinct, I brace myself. "I know, he'll never like me enough to stay," I echo her words from decades ago. "We were doomed from the start."

"What?" Mom asks, her head snapping back to refocus on me.

"It's what you said," I clarify. "When I liked any guy. When you and Dad split up."

Mom pulls out the chair in front of a desk featuring a textured globe. "I said those things?" she asks as she takes a seat.

I blink, confused. "Well, yeah. Anytime I liked someone."

Mom's eyebrows rise in what I hope is recollection so that I can stop feeling like I'm making it all up in my head. "Oh." She rubs her forehead with the back of her hand. "It's been a while. Even longer since you've told me about any of your crushes."

I resist the urge to make a sarcastic comment about the curse. There's already been too much hurt. Normally, I'd absorb the feelings rising in me and contain them in garden beds, like Vin had pointed out.

I drop my pointer finger on Antarctica and give the globe a spin, as though I might be able to redirect the attention. As the continents morph into one and then slowly separate as the planet slows down, I'm reminded of a flower time lapse. I don't always have to bloom last.

"I wish I could've," I finally admit, no longer holding back. "The constant curse reminders... they affected me. I felt—feel—so lost."

Mom's mouth drops open in silent protest. "I didn't know you felt that way."

I spin the globe again, giving myself somewhere else to focus.

Mom clears her throat. "I'm sorry, Chryssy. Maybe I was trying to warn you, or... I didn't know how to deal with my own pain around heartbreak. Either way, it was wrong." She remains in her seat, giving me space. Mom watches, mesmerized, as the countries whirl into a blur of colors. "The fish was cold," she says suddenly.

"What?" I ask, looking over at her.

"The night I met your father," Mom says. "The fish was cold. He had to apologize to me about it."

"No... Dad thinks he had sent out an undercooked fish," I say, replaying the story I've been told. "It wasn't raw?"

"It was cooked, all right. But then it must've sat too long until it got to me." The frown pulling Mom's face down reverses, and she lets out a quiet laugh. "Either way, trout brought your father and me together. You might think you're lost, but the fact that you're hunting down answers also tells me that you feel strongly about this guy." The globe slows to a standstill as Mom's words hang between us. "Whether it's strong like or something even stronger than that, I hope you hang on to it."

Something flickers through me. Hope? Surprise? Shock?

"Seriously?" I ask.

Mom pulls her cardigan tighter around herself and crosses her arms. "A while back, a patient came in with severe chest pain and shortness of breath. He was convinced he had takotsubo cardiomyopathy."

"Broken-heart syndrome," I state.

She nods. "It's rare and sometimes overlooked, and females are more likely to have it. I was skeptical, but this patient believed it enough that it felt true. He went so far as to print out research and bring medical textbooks in." Mom inhales and sits up straight. "He was persistent. I did an exam, analyzed his health history, and ran all the tests and then some."

"Was he right?"

Mom shakes her head. "No, he'd had a silent heart attack. After all the tests came back, he told me that he had recently gone through a painful breakup. It might as well have been broken-heart syndrome," she says. "Our hearts go through so much. Stress, heartbreak, love." She sighs deeply. "And still, they keep us alive."

"It breaks. It heals. It perseveres," I say. "No wonder it's where our spirit lives."

"Sometimes I wonder if I was like this patient to your father, wearing him down with the curse. I was so convinced. I didn't see it at the time, but looking back, I must've exhausted him." The corners of her eyes have taken on a glossy sheen. She wipes at them, preemptively blocking any tears from falling. "Sorry. This is too much."

"It's okay, Mom," I reassure her, kneeling in front of her. It dawns on me that Mom's pain has always been masked with blame. It's easier to explain something away when it's happening *to* you. "I think, more than anything, Dad saw the curse as exhausting. Not you."

Mom holds a hand against my cheek. "I want you to have a better life than I did. I want things to be different for you."

I hold my hand against hers, the pressure smushing my cheek up. "A few days ago, I might've believed that. Like things could've been different for me, for real this time," I say, hearing the words and how they sound exactly like what I said about Chris. "With the discovery of the blend, I thought maybe things could've been different for all of us."

"Oh, Chryssy."

"Somehow I'm always proven right, even when I want to be wrong," I say, my voice cracking. "I really want to be wrong."

Mom grabs my hands and stands, lifting me up with her. I anticipate her telling me that this is just the way things are for us and that it's time to come to terms with it. That there's no use pretending we'll ever break the cycle. That there's no point in hoping that our fate could be anything other than what it has been.

But then she holds her arms out. They hang there, suspended, until I step into them and return her hug.

"I'm sorry," she whispers against my hair.

I don't know what she's sorry for, exactly. I wonder if it's for scaring me off from middle school crushes, or for the reminders that I'm doomed. Perhaps it's rhetorical, and she's sorry that we're all cursed to begin with, against our own wills. Maybe it's for all of it.

I squeeze her back, sniffling into her shoulder. I haven't denied my feelings for Vin, and she hasn't spoken her words of warning. Maybe there is hope, after all.

"So you do think I'm ridiculous," I say, cough-laughing through my tears. "You haven't said otherwise."

Mom smiles. "Maybe you're ridiculous. But you know what you also are?" she asks, shaking my upper arms. "Brave."

The word lands squarely in my chest, like a soft arrow that doesn't pierce. Vin's use of the same word surfaces in my mind.

"I don't think of myself like that," I say. "I have a lot of fears. I'm scared of more heartbreak."

"And yet here you are in a back-alley bookstore trying to translate an old recipe to understand a generational curse so you can be with someone you love," Mom states. "Who can say what will last and what won't? If you ask Auntie Rose, she'll tell you nothing lasts forever, and to never sign a contract that binds you to it. You have fears, Chryssy, and you're still giving love another chance."

"That's the thing with chances. They don't always have the best odds," I say.

"But it is something you can calculate," Mom says. "I think about this for my patients. What are the desired outcomes? Is the risk worth it? Sometimes the odds aren't great, but we have to try anyway."

"Maybe you're braver than you think, too," I tell her.

"At work, yes," Mom says with a humorless laugh. "In life, not even close."

The thwack of a book closing behind us draws our focus.

"All of this has worn me down," Ms. Chan says. "I'm closing for the day. Everyone out."

Auntie Violet sighs dramatically.

"You didn't give us the name of the flower," Auntie Rose says, standing firm.

"There isn't one," Ms. Chan says, holding up the tray of bubble tea for us to claim. "I've done all I can."

Auntie Rose's shoulders slump.

I can feel her defeat from across the shop. "We'll figure it out," I say loudly. After my conversation with Mom, I'm surprised to find that I sound hopeful again.

"Did someone spin this?" Ms. Chan asks, walking up to the globe and twisting it just so. "I had China facing that shelf." She angles a stiff hand toward the far wall and rotates it a touch more.

Mom and I shrug, playing innocent and keeping this harmless secret between us.

We exit Ms. Chan's shop. The Curse Box is nestled inside Auntie Rose's oversize cloth bag.

"That woman. She frustrates me," Auntie Rose says, shaking her head. "Now what?"

Mom straightens her sweater and squints up at the bright, cloud-less sky. "We now know the word means 'flower.' If this is the last ingredient standing between us and this blend, then we have to figure out which flower it is."

Auntie Rose and Auntie Daisy stare at Mom as though she's just offered them a fake prescription.

"'We'?" Auntie Rose asks Mom with enough suspicion for three detectives. "You work with beta-blockers and blood thinners, not bee balm. Do you know anything about flowers?"

Mom levels her sister with one glare. "I know that roses are prickly," she retorts.

"It's a natural defense," Auntie Rose grumbles.

Auntie Violet waves Auntie Rose off. "This is great news! We could use a fresh mind on this. Peony was always the best in her classes. She might spot something in the letters."

Auntie Rose shrugs—in agreement or disagreement, who's to say—and walks past us toward the street. Auntie Violet fast-walks behind her, sharing more ways Mom could help.

Mom and I watch on, amused.

"Dad really sent out cold fish?" I ask. Mom's story clearly caught on one of the corners of my brain.

"Lukewarm, at best," Mom says.

I drain the rest of my bubble tea, giving up on the remaining tapi-oca lodged between ice cubes. "Good thing he opened a raw oyster bar then," I joke.

Mom wraps her arm around me. "Let's go. I was promised Peking duck."

Chapter 25

VIN

The heart-shaped seats are comfier than they look. I'm sitting between Daisy and a guest named Ruth, who I met the first time I was in this circle. I'm sitting directly across from Chryssy, who's holding a sleepy Goji in her lap. Three other guests occupy chairs. The only thing we have in common is our awkwardness. And apparently heartbreak.

Just when I was starting to appreciate the quiet, it became quieter than it's ever been between me and Chryssy. *That* kind of silence I can't stand. We made it back to the inn a few days ago, but the only time I've seen Chryssy was when she left to go to Seattle with her aunties for an appointment. Anytime I was frustrated as a kid, I'd escape into music. So that's exactly what I've been doing.

That is, until Leo told me to meet him here this morning. Of course, I showed but he never did, and I didn't expect to see Chryssy here.

I tap my foot on the grass, jiggling my leg as if it could pound a tunnel through the ground for me to escape through, even though no one's forcing me to be here.

"Thank you for joining us today in the Heartbreak Circle," Daisy says in a calming tone. "This is a safe space. You don't have to talk, and you can share as much or as little as you'd like."

I exhale slowly, cursing under my breath. I remind myself that I can walk away just as easily as I did last time.

Daisy crosses her hands in her lap. "Studies show that pain from heartbreak appears in the brain the same way as pain from a physical injury. In the same way that everybody's heartbreak is unique to them, the healing process is, too. For some, talking helps. Who'd like to share? Our hearts are open."

A guest named Penny is the first to speak. "I think for me, it's that I don't know where to put my sadness. When my fiancé left me the night before our wedding, it was like he just stabbed a knife right here," she says, pointing to the spot below her heart. "The hurt, the humiliation...it all lingers. I don't know that it'll ever go away until I know why. Why did he leave?"

"A little closure would be nice," Ruth says. "There are already so many unknowns in the world. Why must the end of relationships be, too?"

"Thank you," Penny says, wiping her eyes. "What about for you? Did you get closure?"

Ruth purses her lips. "No, but I gave it. After my diagnosis, things changed in my relationship. I needed a radical shift in my life, and I wanted to do it with my girlfriend. But radical shifts weren't her thing. I was the one who initiated the breakup, but it hurt like hell."

Everyone nods with her, validates her. I find that I'm nodding, too.

"Breakup," the fourth guest, wearing a hot pink sweater, grumbles. Her voice is tinged with a tone opposite of the cheery vibes her clothing gives off. "That word is too basic. Too simple to capture the entirety of what happened. A part of me has died! And everyone else just goes about their days like everything's fine. How can the world look so gray while everyone else's has color? It's bullshit."

"Not everyone's worlds," Daisy says, tipping her head toward the circle. To all of us. "If you leave this circle with anything, I hope it's that you know none of you have to suffer in silence. You are not alone in this."

"When Belinda died, I thought I'd follow shortly after," an older man named Garen starts. His voice is quiet, requiring us to lean in to hear him better. "I still expect to roll over in the morning and see her there. And I can still feel her hand in mine." He pauses to collect himself. "I still have all those damn throw pillows on the bed. I used to hate them, and now I can't fall asleep without them."

"Losing someone can be one of the most painful experiences we have," Daisy says.

"It's as though a part of me is missing," Garen says, scratching his white beard. "The worst part is that when I think of our memories, I only find the ones I regret. The ones where I let my bad moods spoil what should've been joyous occasions. I think about our fights, as rare as they were."

The silence after this is excruciating. I don't know how to sit in this particular breed of discomfort.

"Recollecting memories has a funny way of doing that," Chryssy says. I sit up straighter at her words, eager for more of them after the drought. "Your brain might be remembering the not-so-happy moments, but there were happy ones, too, right?"

The man stares at the empty seat in the circle. "Oh, sure. Many. For our first Christmas together, Belinda wanted a tree that wouldn't die, but it couldn't be plastic because that'd just end up in the landfill. So I brought home a cactus. Every Christmas, we'd decorate our outdoor cactus tree. I still have the scars from the annual light-stringing." The man looks at his arms. "I donated the lights the year after she..." He shakes his head. "But one bulb covering had rolled behind a few boxes. It's like Belinda was telling me, *not so fast*."

The group mutters acknowledgments, like they have similar stories of their own about the ghosts that haunt them.

"As soon as I saw that bulb, the first thought that came to mind wasn't how special our tradition was," Garen says. "I thought about the one year the lights went out and I didn't bother replacing them. Probably ruined Christmas."

"That's just a thought, though, isn't it?" Daisy gently presses.

"Did Belinda tell you Christmas was ruined?" Chryssy asks while she pets Goji.

Garen looks down at his hands. "Well, no. We did everything else the same that year. It was...wonderful."

"Our inner voice has a lot to say, but it isn't always right. And just because it has a lot to say, that doesn't mean it's who we are," someone says.

Everyone's eyes turn on me, and it's then I realize I'm that someone.

Chryssy watches me, waiting to see if I'll say anything else.

I don't. What else is there to say?

After a prolonged silence, Chryssy speaks.

"My inner voice does a lot of talking, too," she says. "In relationships, I'm always the one being left. That's how I viewed myself for a long time. I never felt in control." She keeps her gaze fixed on Goji. "But then I was reminded that I have done the leaving before. I left cardiology. I left med school. I even left love behind. I did these things, even when I was scared. When I did the leaving, that was me taking the situation into my own hands. When circumstances weren't right, *I* made the change."

"You didn't let your inner voice win," Ruth tells her.

Chryssy sits back, her imploring eyes locking with mine.

It's a strange thing, being in this Heartbreak Circle. While I've always done the breaking, I've never done the listening. I may have had my reasons for ending relationships, but I also caused pain, annoyance, and confusion for many of my exes. All in the search for something perfect. For something my parents have—*had*.

The truth reverberates through me like a low note. Playing cello may have come easier for me, but I still had to work at it. Why did I think perfect love would come without effort?

"I thought I knew what perfect was. Turns out, I don't have a clue," I say, encouraged by Chryssy's vulnerability. "The only thing that's ever been flawless to me, I guess, is music. Notes I read, notes I play, notes I hear and feel."

"And you do play them perfectly," Penny interjects, holding her hands up like she's not willing to hear otherwise.

I nod at her in thanks. "It's just...I've always had somewhere to put my emotions. I translate whatever it is I'm feeling into music. It's like an extension of me that lets the ache out." I dig my heel deeper into the grass, grounding myself. "But now I'm wondering if all that was a distraction preventing me from learning how to sit with the discomfort."

Is that what I'm doing now? Sitting with the uneasiness of my parents and trying to avoid it? Keeping my frustrations surface level and letting the pain out in the form of sad musical notes? Even if I were, is that so wrong?

But if I always had somewhere to redirect my emotions, then I've never had to live with them. I could avoid the uneasiness and consequences of the lack of relationships, rest, or recovery. The slipping away of time. Busy, busy, busy. Sacrifice from everyone in my life, including myself. What would it be like to exist with that? Address it, even?

Everything Chryssy's been saying is true. My heart has been out of balance, and there's some breakage there.

"I always thought my achievements would make my parents happy," I add. "But their relationship had nothing to do with whether or not my brother and I were a success. Now they're splitting up. My parents kept their separation from us for so long. I'm disappointed."

I pause, replaying my words. "Not in them, though. I mean, yes, it's disappointing that they broke up. Sorry, I'm not good at talking about this stuff."

I want to stop there, having said too much already, but Daisy urges me to go on.

"What I'm trying to say is, I'm disappointed in myself," I say, closing my eyes as my cheeks burn at this reveal. I want to dissolve on the spot. Perish into a puddle on this heart-shaped chair. Evaporate and take everything I've just overshared with me.

And then...nothing.

I squint one eye open. I'm met with compassionate faces around the Heartbreak Circle, and it almost feels like the nights I cooked with Chryssy. Safe, patient, comforting. There's room for me to sit with this.

Right away, I know deep down I'm not leaving this circle without sharing the rest of it.

"As much as my parents' love story was—and frankly, still is—beautiful, I don't know that a love like theirs is what I want at all." I press on. "Not because they broke up, but because love can't be replicated." It's like I told Chryssy in Las Vegas: Even if you play the same song over and over, it'll always have its own subtle variations. "I need to play my own love song."

My eyes float over the group's faces until they find Chryssy. She's frozen in place, like she's been holding her breath this entire time. The tension in her seems to melt away a little when we look at each other. After days of silence, this moment of quiet connection is so loud.

Chryssy breaks eye contact first when Garen responds to what I've said.

"The music you make with someone you love is the sweetest sound you'll ever hear," he says. "You can count on that."

"I believe it, Garen," I say before turning in my seat to the woman next to him. "Penny, I appreciate your compliment. I didn't always play flawlessly, though. Still don't. When I first started playing cello, I spent all day in my room. There wasn't enough time in the day for me to get as much playing in as I wanted. Then, in my middle school years, there was a stretch of time where playing became tedious. A chore, in a way. Fifteen minutes felt like a lifetime, when it had originally felt like a few seconds. Luckily, that didn't last long."

"What changed?" Penny asks.

"I started taking it note by note," I share. "One note turned to two, three, four. Then I'd tell myself to play one piece. That was all I had to do for the day. Of course, once I got started, I played a lot more."

"What if you started tackling each emotion note by note?" Garen muses.

I nod in agreement. "Emotions. But also relationships. Love. Flowers grow inch by inch, don't they?" I ask, turning my focus solely on Chryssy. "Over time, maybe even after a long time, you get a garden. And the flowers, herbs, plants, they all die. But then they come back. And even if not all of them do, you've still got a garden, and probably a damn pretty one at that. Sometimes the garden is full, other years it won't be. But the garden still exists."

The world becomes blurry, a drop from above hitting my cheek. I look up expecting rain, but the sky is bright blue. I press my fingers against my eyes, feeling...tears?

"I've lost things in my life before," I say directly to Chryssy, pushing on. "I refuse to lose you."

"I can't guarantee a lifetime together," Chryssy says, moving closer to the edge of her seat and stirring Goji awake. "My heart's handled it before. But with you? Not a chance." She draws in a quick breath. "Vin, with our track records, we wouldn't make it thirty-five months, let alone thirty-five years."

The guests look intrigued—and slightly confused—but they don't interrupt. Daisy doesn't even try to redirect the conversation.

"I've chased perfection my entire life. In love, in my career. I practiced until my fingers bled to be flawless," I say. "I've worked until I've gotten it right in everything but my relationships. But you know how we'll at least try to get it right?"

A small gasp escapes Chryssy's lips. "Practice," she says, blushing as she laughs.

"Lots of practice," I affirm. "It's like you said. I wanted to be in love in a song. But it wasn't until I met you that I realized that the songs I considered perfect were just illusions. And illusions leave you unsatisfied and alone. I want our love song to be better than perfect. I want it to be real."

"Even if real doesn't last forever?" Chryssy asks.

"Every song has a beginning and an ending. The very fact that nothing lasts forever is what makes something real and why it's so important to appreciate it when you have it," I say. "Anytime we put our hearts on the line, we're all risking heartbreak. Chryssy, I want to find a rhythm of our own. I want to put my heart on the line. Show me where the hell that line is."

"Are you just gonna sit there?" Garen asks me.

"Don't let us get in your way," Penny encourages.

I cross the circle and kneel in front of Chryssy. Goji looks back and forth between us, his nose twitching.

"Show me the line," I whisper.

Chryssy's cheeks fill with pink as she slowly holds out her hand to me. "Is this the line?"

I kiss the top of her hand.

"What about this?" she asks, pointing to her cheek.

I kiss that, too.

Chryssy points to her forehead. "Or maybe it's here?"

I plant a kiss on her head.

"I think it's here," I say, brushing my thumb against her bottom lip.

"Put your heart on it," she whispers.

I tip Chryssy's chin back and kiss her squarely on the lips.

Everyone in the circle cheers.

Chryssy breaks into a smile that's in direct competition with the sunshine, the stars, every beautiful symphony in existence. The laugh that follows is a song I want to hear for the rest of my life.

Then Chryssy strokes my cheek and says, "Let's plant a garden."

Chapter 26

VIN

I don't feel the prick, but I feel the heat. It spreads across my skin, a light tingling creeping down my forehead.

"That okay?" Rose asks.

"I think? It's not painful," I say as she wipes an alcohol pad across my temples.

"Good," Rose says. "I have a few more left."

I'm lying on my back on the warm bed, trying to remain as still as possible. There's slight pressure next to my eyebrow.

"I want to add a few more to your arm. I'm glad that's been working."

"Uh-huh," I say.

"Make sure you're breathing," Rose reminds me.

I slowly take in a stream of air through my nose.

"You're very tense," Rose says. "Can you unfist your hand, please?"

"I was just getting used to doing this in my arm. Not sure how I feel about the needles in my face. Leo admitted to me that he was terrified of this at first." I stare at the white ceiling while Rose moves around me. "That surprised me."

"Did it? Why?" she asks.

"He's always been the one not terrified of anything," I explain.

"Not of reviews or shows, or about not getting enough practice in. When we started playing as the Chao Brothers, he never had any doubts."

"And you did?"

"When we first started, I guess I wasn't sure what people expected from us or if we would be a one-hit wonder. Would people want to keep hearing us play rock songs? When we had toured earlier, audiences wanted to hear classical music. That I could do. I didn't realize that there would be such a big audience for the kind of music we play now. I worried it wouldn't be sustainable."

"I take it you think Leo had no worries?" Rose says.

"When something scares him, he actively runs toward it. I prefer knowing what I'm getting into."

"It's what makes you both great musicians in your own way. And for what it's worth, onstage you're both fearless. Or so it seems." She focuses on my forearm. There's more pressure as she places another needle into a specific spot.

I nod against the small pillow. "I appreciate that. Sorry, I'll be quiet now. I feel like I should be meditating or something."

"This is your time," Rose says. "There's no wrong or right way to do this. If you'd like to keep talking, please continue."

I tap a slow rhythm out on the sheet. "Oh, okay. Uh. Yeah, I don't know. Leo would be so relaxed before shows. I envied that. He'd be incredible, and he didn't have to go through all the excess stress over nothing," I tell her. "There's no guarantee for how long this will last for us. We still need to go through the contract. Honestly, I don't think he wants to keep going. After the breakup and being here, he's different. Not in a bad way. I guess for the first time he's... I think he's scared. If that's even the right word."

"What would he be scared of?" Rose asks.

I clench my jaw. In my heightened state of awareness, I feel each muscle tighten. "Working so much that he never actually lives." I wait a beat to see if Rose will respond, but she doesn't. I fill the silence and add, "I never thought *I'd* be fearful of that, but I'm starting to think that maybe I am."

Rose takes in a sharp breath. "I didn't have this realization until it was too late," she says. "When my wife left, the first feeling I experienced wasn't sadness. It was anger."

"At the curse?" I venture a guess.

"At myself. Toward the curse I felt annoyance, I suppose. I knew we wouldn't have our entire lives, of course," she says, "but it wasn't until she was gone that it struck me that I wasn't fully there for the time we did have."

"Even though you knew you and your wife wouldn't be together forever, can I ask why you still married her?" I ask. "Weren't you afraid of being heartbroken?"

Rose uncaps a bottle of essential oil. "Every day," she admits. "Which is why I practically married my work. I spent more time at the firm than I did at home, and I was great at what I did. I convinced a lot of people to get prenups." She squeezes a dropper, and oil rises up the tube. "To others, the curse probably sounds dramatic. Extreme. At points in my life, I thought it was, too, even though I had grown up with it. We talked about it as easily as a parent might check in about how school was that day. You hear stories, you're part of this group." A look of disappointment appears on Rose's face. "Then things happen, and, well, sometimes it's easier to believe in something than to think something's wrong with you."

"I know that well." I turn my head to follow Rose as she circles the acupuncture bed. She drops oil onto a smooth rock, and the room fills with the scent of lavender. I never thought this scent would calm me.

"I didn't want to admit it to myself, but I loved my wife more than anything, and that terrified me," Rose shares. "When she left, for reasons not unlike Leo and his ex-girlfriend, it felt like I had been proven right. I went straight back to work, and my first thought was, 'Good. Work will never leave me.'" She gives her head a firm shake. "I hated myself for thinking that. Ultimately, I felt so badly about all that time I lost with her that I quit the job that took me away from her. My sisters and I started the inn a few years later so that we could give our heartbreak purpose. At first it felt like punishment, and then it felt like the thing that saved me."

"I'm sorry, Rose," I say. "It sounds like you were trying to protect yourself. Just like Chryssy has been trying to do. It really is an inter-generational game of telephone."

Rose's eyes slide over to me, her eyebrows furrowed.

"Is protecting ourselves really so bad if we're sparing ourselves from pain?" Rose asks. "A box held the so-called truth to our history, but the truth feels more subjective these days. Why add more stories into the mix and confuse things further?" Her eyes go distant as she says this.

"Do you feel any relief at all about what we've learned?" I ask.

Rose straightens her shoulders. "It doesn't matter what I feel. Change is hard for people."

"It is," I agree, shrugging against the bed. "Yet here I am, letting you poke me with needles. And who knows what else will happen with Leo?"

"You think we should tell my family about the Curse Box," Rose says, watching me.

"They'll all be here for the product launch tomorrow, right?"

Rose nods.

I think on this. "Honestly, I don't know. Keeping secrets is exhausting, but you also can't rush people when they're not ready," I say. "The truth is probably always better." I contemplate my own situation. "If Leo is done with the Chao Brothers, I'd rather know and deal with the pain than keep him from living the life he wants or having a choice in what he does."

"Why tell them when they can't do anything about it?" she poses. "The Hua women aren't used to having choices."

"Aren't they? It's like the inn was your second ending," I say. "You played through the first ending, but now you're living your second with different notes. One that you chose."

"Mister Wise Guy," Rose mumbles.

I grin. "What did you put in these needles? Does acupuncture always make people this insightful? Leo was quoting Lao Tzu the other day."

Rose lifts her eyebrows. Her version of smiling. "My technique gets the best results," she says. "Maybe Leo's about to find his second ending, too. As are you."

"I don't want to stop playing music," I say for the first time out loud. Maybe, in the back of my mind, the question was outstanding, saved for later. But later is now. It's a relief to think it, in the middle of being vulnerable and exposed. It's not just who I am, but who I want to be.

I want the music. I don't want the strings attached.

Rose taps a needle into my ankle, warmth zinging in the area. "Who says you have to?"

"For a while, I questioned whether I could do this without Leo," I reveal. "The reality is I probably could do it, but I wouldn't *want* to. It's always been the two of us, and that's what I've enjoyed about it."

If Leo no longer wants to play, it would be a huge shift. We'd get past it, but I don't know what that would look like for me.

I sink deeper into the bed, my restricted thoughts starting to flow through me. It would take time to figure out, but what's the hurry?

"You've played solo before," Rose says as I look up at her. "What would it mean if you did it again?"

I turn my head back to face the ceiling. I'd keep going, but I'm on a path I don't want to be on. I don't want my brand.

"I don't have a good answer for that," I tell her.

"Then what's a bad answer?"

I rub the calluses of my fingertips with my thumbs. "I guess the bad answer is that I'd stop playing completely."

"I'd agree with that," Rose says. "I speak as a newly inducted Chaobreaker, but please don't stop. Though if you started playing without Leo, I guess we'd become…Vinheads."

I huff out a laugh at this. "I'm not sure I could handle my own fan club."

"I think you can handle a lot more than you think," Rose says. "What are the songs you hear in your heart? Play those." She spritzes the air with lavender essential oil. "I'm going to let you rest for half an hour. Try to relax. Breathe. And don't even think about running out like last time. I don't want to stand guard, but I will if I must."

"So, I'm trapped in here. That's a comforting thought," I mumble.

She clears her throat, and I promise her I won't leave.

The door clicks shut as she quietly exits the room.

I look around for something to distract me. I read each and every book title that lines the shelves. My glance darts over to the row of essential oils, and I read those labels, too. Citrus, more lavender, bergamot. Linen curtains graze the leaves of a thriving money tree sitting in the windowsill.

I slowly move my neck back to see what I can find in the room behind me. A small shelf with boxes of acupuncture needles. Alcohol wipes. An infrared heat lamp.

Soft spa music trickles out of a purple boom box that looks like it was made in the eighties. I tap my fingers along the bed and puff out my cheeks in an exhale.

Somewhere behind me, a clock ticks, ticks, ticks. Has it been thirty minutes yet?

I stare at the white ceiling until I'm so restless that I attempt to close my eyes, shifting in the bed to find the most comfortable position.

At first, my mind wanders, skipping around from thought to thought.

Leo makes an appearance as the outcome of the Chao Brothers looms. Then come my parents and their new lives without each other. A nagging guilt of potentially turning down gobs of money comes creeping in. I wonder if, in the end, my heartbreaker reputation will continue to precede me.

My thoughts turn to Chryssy. We're out in the Plotting Shed, and she's a miniature version of herself, trapped inside the Curse Box. She slides her hands along the sides, trying to find a way out but can't.

In the silence of the room, I can both feel and hear my heartbeat quicken. This is the opposite of what Rose instructed me to do. I'm definitely not breathing through this.

I think that's the end of it. That I'll be stuck here for twenty-seven more minutes trying to keep my body and mind still and to not fight every urge to get up and move and do anything but this. But then the thoughts come back in full force, morphing into something else completely. Something more peaceful.

It happens the way I hear a song just by looking at the notes. The way I can hear it before I play so I know how I want to approach it. I'm back with Chryssy, and we're hand in hand walking along the beach, trudging through mud. We're not clamming, just being. It's a Yin Night, and she's showing me her favorite movies. They're not so tragic anymore. I'm playing my favorite music for her. She tells me her preferred Billy Joel songs, and I play those for her, too. I hear her musical laugh so vividly that, for a second, I think she's inside the room.

Years pass in seconds. Glimpses of an entire lifetime where we don't once break up. We never end. I wish she could see what I do. It's not perfect, but it is real.

I'm warmer than before, my body lightly buzzing with energetics or heat or whatever it is that these needles are doing to me. The corners of my mouth tug upward, just a little. My fingers unfurl, the back of my knuckles brushing the cotton sheets. My feet turn outward. The bed under me is so soft I could melt into it.

And then I do what I haven't been able to in years.

I relax.

The door clicks open, startling me awake.

"It's been thirty minutes already?" I ask groggily.

"Not quite," the voice says, but it doesn't belong to Rose.

It's Leo's.

"How'd you get past the guard?" I ask, watching him cross the small room.

Leo sits in a floral-patterned chair in the corner, facing me. I tilt my head to see him from where I lay.

"I wanted to talk to you and figured this was the best way," he says. "You can't run away."

"Didn't you hear what happened last time? You can't trap me." I shrug as best I can. "You here to talk about Mom and Dad?"

I may have shared how I feel with the group, but I haven't with Leo. Somehow, we've managed to avoid talking about it since we got back.

Leo sighs. "Two breakups in one year. I imagined them growing old together, being grandparents together. But they seem okay, don't they?"

"Mom will travel. Dad might take up curling, learn a new language, pick up a violin again. Sounds like they want to go to their own auditions. Metaphorically, of course," I say. "And after being apart for a while, who knows?"

Leo smirks. "Always the romantic," he says. "After Aubrey, holding out hope like that felt impossible. But maybe you're right."

I grunt. "You said her name."

"Huh. Yeah," Leo says, rubbing his chin. "I guess I did. I never thought I'd get to this point." He leans forward on his knees, clasping his hands together. "I read the contract."

I let a long silence pass. "And?"

"And I think it warrants a bigger discussion," he says, his tone serious.

Where I'm typically the serious one, I find myself trying to lighten my own mood for what I think is coming. To delay the inevitable.

"You want to have that conversation *now*?" I ask, gesturing toward myself.

"I found that during acupuncture, my mind was clearest," Leo says. "I was totally relaxed, and I couldn't do anything else. My mind was present. That's where I need you for this conversation. Feeling good and present."

"This is an intervention," I mumble, holding a hand up. "Before you say anything, I want you to know that I support you. If you want to leave, not play music anymore, live your life, I care first and foremost about your happiness. And your health. I know I said all those things about the contract, but you were right. There's more to life than achieving. We'll contractually still need to do the tour, but after that you're on your own. I know I can be a lot."

A warm buzz zips through me. Getting all that out feels like a release.

"You've always been like that," Leo says. "For as long as I can recall, you've always been so mature. Much more mature than me, your older brother. I remember one time after you locked yourself away practicing all day, I had to kick open your door and insist you come outside to take a break."

I groan at the memory. "Mom was not happy about your theatrics. I didn't have a door for the rest of the year."

"Technically it was my room, too. I did learn something that day, though," Leo says.

"Silver fringe door curtains make for horrible acoustics?" I ask.

"Okay, I learned two things." Leo shifts in his seat. "I also learned something from you, Vin. I didn't go back outside. I stayed in and practiced with you. That was the first time we played together. I thought, well shit, if you, a prodigy, needed to practice that much, then what did it mean for me? You taught me diligence and the value of hard work, just by observing you. I carry that lesson with me every day."

This is a nice moment. Too bad it's going to be followed up with what Leo's here to do.

"Thanks, man," I say, gritting my teeth. "Now get it over with. Break up the band."

Leo laughs. "I didn't come here to break up with you, Vin. I needed rest, not retirement."

"Hold on," I say, frowning. "You still want to be a Chao Brother?"

"I'll always be a Chao Brother. It's literally my name."

"But you want to...keep playing?" I ask.

"There were a few moments when I wanted to throw it all away," Leo admits. "But, with a few modifications, I think what we do can be fun again. And despite everything I'm about to say, I'm excited for this tour and to reconnect with Chaobreakers. To hang out with you for a bit."

"That'll be nice," I affirm.

"But now, let me be your older brother for a change," he says. "We need to take care of ourselves. The way we were living is unsustainable. I have different desires now than I did when we first started. So yes, I want to keep playing, but our lifestyle and schedule can't go on the way they have. I need balance. I want there to be time to enjoy what we've accomplished, as well as what we're working on. I haven't felt that in a long time, even before the breakup."

I agree with him. "I want that, too. There's time to work toward our goals. It's not all going to happen immediately," I say. "But also... I want to start incorporating more of the music we fell in love with."

"Classical?"

"More of a mash-up style," I say. "Vivaldi meets Billy Joel."

Leo's forehead crinkles in surprise. "I think we can have a lot of fun with that. One day maybe we can even tour with a classical orchestra."

I point at him. "Exactly."

"This is going to be better for both of us," he says, leaning back against the seat.

I return my gaze to the ceiling. A sigh escapes me, yet I'm still not fully relieved.

"There's something else," I say, feeling more clearheaded than ever. "You may not be breaking up with me, but I think—I think we need to break up with our label."

I wait for Leo to say something. I envision the different paths, readying my defense. We could negotiate, try to get even more money for having to put up with a calculated brand. We could threaten to walk away and let them counter against themselves. Or we could walk away for real and start new. Rebuild our reputation and redefine what we play.

It's a big move, but our label hasn't grown with us. We can end on good terms, with respect, even. Over the years, we've all benefited. But now, they're the only ones who will benefit while we lose touch with who we are. While we lose balance. It's not a true partnership if we don't feel like we're being accurately represented.

Doing this won't mean our reputation will be automatically restored. It does mean we're one step closer to reclaiming it, though. And I won't just have Leo in this with me. I'll also have Chryssy.

I can be labeled, but it doesn't have to define me.

"It's time to move on," I say. "And musicians evolve all the time. They pivot and try on new lives, sometimes from album to album. It keeps things interesting. Yo-Yo did a bluegrass album. No more being heartbreakers. No more secret relationships." I recall what Chryssy said about me being like a bonsai tree. "People can't put us in small pots anymore."

"Okay" is all Leo says.

I sit up. "That's it? Okay?"

"No more small pots," Leo says, giving me a satisfied smile.

He takes out his phone, and we make the call.

Chapter 27

CHRYSSY

My family arrives to our product launch at the inn with an excitement that rivals placing fourth in the Dragon Boat Race. To the Hua women, today is all about free food, a chance to gossip, and having a front-row seat to world-class musicians.

"Spectacular. So glad I could make it to the show," Auntie Primrose says, fanning herself as she watches Vin and Leo play together in the main garden. There's no set list, just an exploration of various classical and rock pieces mashed together.

"Actually, it's a tea party to celebrate In Full Bloom," I correct, adjusting our limited offering of teas on the table. "I recommend the rosebuds. It'll help cool you down."

Auntie Primrose's maroon-painted lips spread into a smile. "Right! Of course!" She lifts a box of our limited-edition chamomile, roses, and chrysanthemum trio pack and shakes her wallet. "Do you take credit?"

There weren't as many customer complaints as I anticipated for the limited-edition strategy we implemented. Dad was right. If anything, the exclusivity—and transparency about our situation—created a longer waiting list. Turns out, sometimes people don't mind waiting, especially when you offer them a discount for the inconvenience on their next order.

We liked Salty Stems so much that we're going to partner with them, even though they committed their chrysanthemums to wedding florists this upcoming fall. That's where the chrysanthemums Vin and I propagated will come in handy when they bloom in the next few months, even if it is another limited-edition run for now. Salty Stems, did, however, have marigolds and plenty of them. We included that in the launch while we figure out a fifth flower.

Along the edges of the gardens, long tables are topped with wildflowers, herbs, and candle votives. Every single one of the inn's teapots and teacups have been set out on lavender tablecloths while dozens of platters present miniature scones, sandwiches, egg tarts, and fruit for guests to grab.

Dad swings by after Auntie Primrose leaves. "Load me up! I want one of each," he says as I bag up his order. "Looks like you used your irritant for good."

"I figured if people are willing to wait for oysters, maybe they wouldn't mind waiting a few months for flowers," I say, nudging him. "People can sign up to be alerted when we restock. Everything still feels...incomplete, though." It's unsettling, this feeling I have.

"Even though we try our hardest to get the answers we think we need, rarely is anything in life wrapped up in a pretty bow," Dad says between bites of a flower-pressed almond cookie. "Whether it's work or life."

Dad grabs another cookie and tells me he's going to go find my mom to say hello, surprising me.

Vin takes his place, his hands stuffed into his dark jean pockets, a black T-shirt hugging his lean muscles in all the right places. The grin he wears makes my heart swell like a dried flower in water.

He holds his hand out. "We're taking a break. The aunties told me to come get you for a quick meeting."

I turn away at his use of "aunties" to hide the smile playing at the corners of my lips.

Vin's mouth jerks as he explains himself. "There are so many of them," he says. "It's easier this way."

"You're both sounding good," I tell him, placing my hand in his. "It doesn't seem like Leo's missed a beat."

"He insisted on practicing all night for today. We eventually got there," Vin says.

I laugh. "I think you could play every song purposefully out of tune, and no one here would care."

We cross the yard to the Plotting Shed, where my aunties are already waiting.

"What's with the secret meeting?" I ask, closing the door behind me. I spot on the workbench four of the five ingredients we were able to find in the past couple of weeks.

Auntie Rose nods toward the garden. "It hasn't gotten rowdy yet, has it?"

"They might start rioting if Vin doesn't get back out there soon," Auntie Violet says, leaning against the wall of the shed, arms crossed.

"Leo's out there to hold them over until I'm back," Vin reassures her.

"Practically the entire family tree showed up for us today, and now they're left unattended," I say, looking around to each person. "There's bound to be a few broken branches."

"What's this all about, Rose?" Auntie Daisy asks.

"Maybe we should wait for everyone," Auntie Rose says. "Where's Peony?"

As if summoned by her name being spoken, Mom pokes her head into the shed. Ever since Ms. Chan's a couple of days ago, Mom's been cautiously curious to read the letters and flip through the journals. She even took a stab at translating, identifying a few faded characters, the most notable being that Lily wrote how apologetic—or regretful—she was.

"You all look shady. You know that, right?" Mom asks, joining us. "What's so urgent?"

"Good. You're here. Now we can start." Hesitation flickers across Auntie Rose's face. "Okay, well, this is a big day for us with the product launch. And it's been a big two weeks." She rubs her hands together. "Now that certain truths have come to light, I need to also be truthful. I haven't exactly shared everything I know."

Auntie Daisy looks at Auntie Violet and Mom with concern. "What is it that you know, Rose?" she asks.

Auntie Rose grimaces. "I know the point of finding these ingredients was to understand, and we couldn't even do that. But maybe what I learned will help you find a bit of closure," she says. "You all know I love you more than anything else in this world, right? And that anything I do is to protect this family."

"Rose, what's going on?" Mom asks. "You're scaring us."

Auntie Rose crosses the shed and lifts the Curse Box off the shelf. From the "secret" drawer, she reveals an envelope. She expels a tight breath before removing the letter.

"Lily made sure the recipes were long gone, not so that no one else could re-create it," Auntie Rose starts, "but so that 4G couldn't re-create it. She goes on to explain that she needed to protect herself and her kids. She wrote that she was sending Calendula this box— probably this Curse Box—with their correspondence. To take it with her to Měiguó."

"America," I translate. "What are you saying?"

"I'm saying I don't think Lily was the one doing the betraying. At least not in the way we've all thought. In the way we've all...been told," Auntie Rose says, looking down at the letter and avoiding our eyes. "The handwriting from the letters is the same as the notebooks. These aren't the letters of someone vindictive, but someone who wanted to help."

"You're saying it was Lily who actually helped people. That *she* was the one who made the tonic that was going to help a lot of people and not 4G?" I ask.

"Is that even possible?" Auntie Daisy asks. "Women didn't have the kind of freedom men had. She wouldn't have had the resources to run her own herbal shop or meet with customers."

"Lily could've used his equipment, his ingredients. She wanted to help a lot of people and give the blend away for free," Auntie Rose says. "I think she came up with the recipes while 4G took the credit. He took his wife's work as his own."

We all gasp and exchange unsettled glances.

"That would explain why the seal is the same on the art and in the notebooks. It's 4G's name in the stamp," I think out loud. "But it's Lily's letters—and her handwriting—that give him away."

"The letters were the missing link," Auntie Violet says in amazement.

"The recipes, the illustrations...everything. They're all hers?" I shake my head in disbelief, but somewhere deep inside me, what I'm hearing feels true. "This is...Are we sure about this?" I ask.

"In those days, women wouldn't have been able to divorce their husbands," Auntie Rose explains. "Something about the fact that she went through the effort of tracking down her children, even after all those years, tells me she didn't want to be away from them. She wanted to meet Calendula in person."

"To tell her the truth?" Mom asks.

"To clear her name. Who knows what 4G told his children about their mother. When I read between the lines of this letter, there's no doubt in my mind that it was Lily who had been left," Auntie Rose says, setting the letter down. "And her kids were taken from her."

Vin's eyebrows furrow as he makes a move to riffle through the letters in the box. "There was something in this one—the one with the tea stain—where Lily calls her husband something with money or profit. Like 'profit-minded,' maybe?" His finger hovers over a specific line. "Maybe he wanted to sell it for a lot of money to people?"

"It doesn't sound like the townspeople cursed her. She's blaming 4G for her loneliness," Auntie Daisy reasons. "And 4G would've been pretty mad if that was going to make him rich. Mad enough to curse her."

"If they had different ideas about what to do with the blend, his grounds for divorce could've been anything. Unfaithfulness, jealousy... at one point in time, men could divorce their wives for talkativeness," Auntie Rose adds.

"So she's left and banished," I say. "Lily destroyed the recipes, the blend. That's all true."

"But she destroyed it to prevent her husband from getting his hands on it and profiting," Auntie Daisy tells us. "From taking advantage of people."

"She spent the rest of her life trying to get the record straight," I say. "To still try to help."

"I think I was able to piece some of the blurry characters together," Auntie Rose says, reading a section of the letter out loud. "'*I have been shamed. Discarded. Threatened. Because of what I've done, I will be alone for the rest of time.*'"

"'For the rest of time'?" Auntie Daisy asks, peering over Auntie Rose's shoulder. "Are you sure that doesn't translate to '*for the rest of my days*'?"

"What's the difference? That sounds the same to me," Auntie Violet says.

"That's an important distinction," Auntie Daisy says, reading the letter to give her own analysis. She slides her reading glasses up the bridge of her nose. "'Yǒngyuǎn gūdú.' Forever alone."

"But who? Her only?" I ask, looking at the letter myself. I surprisingly recognize a few characters. "Is that 'wǒ' or 'wǒmen'? That's important if she's saying 'I' or 'we.'"

"She seems to mostly talk about herself, so I'm sure it's 'I,'" Auntie Rose states.

"But she does use 'we' at some points, doesn't she?" I ask.

Auntie Rose sighs. "Yes. She does," she says. "Maybe Calendula interpreted this as 'we.'"

I gasp. "That must've been when the curse started."

They're words lost to time and to future generations who don't share the same language. Words open to interpretation and how we each label things. We should've gotten Ms. Chan's personal number so she could clarify this now.

"If Calendula received this box with their letters and took it to America," Vin recounts, bringing us back to the bigger picture, "she must not have believed Lily enough to meet with her. But how did she interpret this translation?"

"We'll never know," Auntie Rose says. "The correspondence ends there."

Auntie Daisy takes a seat on the stool, resting her forehead in her palm.

Auntie Rose glances around to each of us. "I'm sorry for not telling you sooner. It's my duty to protect you all. We've lived with this curse our entire lives. We can't go back in time and change—or break—anything. I thought this information would just hurt more, but now I realize that would've been taking a choice away." Her voice is filled with a combination of sadness and guilt. "A woman was blamed, and we were so quick to believe it. We've been honoring a man who ruined a woman's life. And her work."

"You shouldn't have kept this from us, Rose," Auntie Violet says.

Auntie Rose nods quickly. "I'm so ashamed. I was trying—"

"I mean you shouldn't have had to live with this on your own." Auntie Violet wraps an arm around her. "You've always worked so hard to protect the family. But what if, instead, we all protect each other?"

Auntie Rose returns her hug. Auntie Daisy abandons her stool to hug them both as Mom curves around all of them. I can't resist joining in.

"This information isn't easy to hear," Auntie Daisy says, lifting her head. "But when has any of it been easy?"

"I guess the question now is, how do we interpret any of it?" I ask, as the group hug dissembles.

"I don't know, but then how do you explain it all coming true? Every Hua woman," Mom says, trailing off.

We're all silent for a moment in our own thoughts, each of us processing what this means. If it means anything at all.

Lily's legacy, her history—they've been misunderstood for generations. Maybe we've been thinking about the curse, ourselves, *her* all wrong. Maybe we labeled her incorrectly, and she was never Èyùn, and the only misfortune was that we believed the rumors.

"We've heard so many versions," I say. "I don't know what's true, but there is something we can do: Honor Lily. We pick up where she left off. Finish the work she never got to."

Vin nods. "Honor her legacy and the blend she burned so that profit wouldn't prevail."

"We owe it to her," Auntie Daisy says. "Our entire lives don't have to be a lie."

"Imagine all the women who took this belief to their graves," Auntie Rose reflects. "Poor Mother never got to know the truth."

"This isn't something we can just break," Auntie Violet says. "Our lives have been impacted. What's done is done. What are we supposed to do with all this?" She gestures toward the workbench, waving off the ingredients as though they've personally insulted her.

Auntie Daisy lifts the lion's mane. "We could just use what we have," she suggests. "I'm sure we can figure out the recipe if we go through enough items." She rattles off various ingredients that might work.

"If it's not accurate, what's the point?" Auntie Violet says, visibly frustrated. "We got this far just to not be able to finish it."

As some of my most favorite people in the world gather around in the Plotting Shed, my mind whirs. In my childhood and through med school, I always felt like I was on my own. But not only in an independent way. I felt alone. I tried to understand where I fit in and how to navigate life, but also my own family's politics around the curse.

When the aunties took me in, it felt like I finally had my place in the world. For the first time, I belonged. But it wasn't just because I had a new sense of purpose or a place to live. The realization hits me like a ton of tea. The bond my aunties and I share hasn't ever been about the curse but about heartbreak and helping people instead. The Hua women can have a relationship like that, free of rumors and false ideas about ourselves. My aunties and I have proved it. We protect each other.

There's more to our story.

"I think it's time we tell everyone what we know," Auntie Rose says first, the words coming out shaky. "So that they can make a choice of their own."

I nod in agreement. So does Vin.

"I do hate the idea of everyone living life under the illusion of a lie, especially my daughter," Auntie Daisy says.

Eventually, Mom nods. "Even in the short time since I've learned about this, there's a small part of me that's relieved," she says softly.

"We can't tell them!" Auntie Violet exclaims. "What would we even say? Oh hey, thanks for coming. By the way, everything you believe to be true about yourself and your family lineage? Wrong!"

"Do we not have an obligation?" Auntie Daisy presses. "We have cold, hard facts and letters. If we get to be free from this curse, the rest of our family should be, too."

I scan the page of the notebook with the chrysanthemum and mushroom illustrations and ingredients. "It doesn't matter what this says," I say, tapping the pages gently. "What if this is just another belief?"

Vin and my aunties look at me expectantly.

"Do we think this blend holds the answers to why we've all been hurt and guarded our entire lives? Why we're all supposedly not going to find lasting love?" I ask, glancing at Vin. "It's not going to have magical powers and turn back time." I close the notebook for added effect. "And I wonder if maybe some blends—and beliefs—are better when they're lost to time."

"It's easier said than done to just stop believing something," Auntie Rose says. "This history, this curse, this belief…they've been so deeply ingrained in everyone's identities."

"You're right. But you know how, in TCM, one disease can have many treatments, and that there can be one treatment for many diseases?" I ask. "This curse has been a disease. One treatment is the truth, which half of them won't believe, even with letters and journals as proof." I hold up a second finger. "Another is by someone having a relationship that doesn't end badly, but that will take a long time to prove anything to anyone. But there's a third treatment."

"Well, it can't be the blend," Auntie Violet says. "We don't even know which flower Lily meant."

"We don't need to. Instead of mixing and matching and waiting for a sign, what if, instead, the flower ingredient was us—the Hua women—putting all our broken hearts into it?" I propose. "The final ingredient is a little bit of each of us."

A long silence follows.

"What I'm proposing means we won't ever know what Lily created," I say, my tone tinged with sadness. "I wish we could. I want to honor her, and right the wrong. But I still think we can. I never knew her, and I only thought of her one way for my entire life, but I think she'd like this instead."

Auntie Rose takes a seat on a stool. "And how do you propose we do this?"

"Is this where we all have to sacrifice our most beloved item or offer up a drop of blood? Because I've got a rare blood type and need every last drop," Auntie Daisy says.

"It's nothing like that...yet," I say. "The entire family tree is here. Let's all do something together. We have angelica and poppies in the main garden, right?"

It's Vin who catches on to the spark of my idea first. He adds fuel. "And primrose, rosemary, and jasmine," he says, recalling what Auntie Rose has taught him.

"It'll be hard for the Huas to let go of this belief," I say, "but maybe it'll be easier to give them something new to believe in."

Auntie Daisy nods. "It would be something new for them to attach to."

"The curse is what has bonded us. But what if it's this blend instead? This new belief?" I pose. "I want this to bind us together for who we really are, apart from the curse."

My aunties look between one another, contemplating what I've said.

"Is this lying?" Auntie Rose asks. "This isn't the actual blend."

"We'll tell them everything we know," I say. "As for the blend, we did find it, didn't we? We're simply following our interpretation of 'flower,' a word that really does exist in Lily's blend. We're covering all our bases."

Auntie Daisy hums as she considers this. "Is it possible to change the past? No. But can we change our story? Yes. Is it possible to change how we think about that story?" She sighs. "I hope so."

While Lily might've believed 4G had condemned her to a life alone, she also attempted to do good and find her way back to her family. Why is it that the bad reputation gets passed down instead of the courage part? Maybe our strength lies in the ability to rewrite the stories we tell about ourselves. I want to regain that strength, find it somewhere deep down in myself from my ancestors.

"I've rewritten the story of my life before. I can do it again," I say.

"Let's stop chasing ghosts," Auntie Violet says, agreeing. "Let's do something for Chryssy and Vin. For future generations."

"For all of us," I add.

Mom taps the workbench. "Ladies, let's go wrangle the Huas."

"Get Aunt Angelica in here, and word will spread in a matter of minutes," Auntie Rose mumbles as she stands.

While the aunties do that and collect the remaining ingredients from the garden and kitchen, Vin and I gather pots and heat water for the tea. The Plotting Shed won't hold everyone, so we set up everything in the Heartbreak Circle.

"Where's this coming from?" Vin asks when we're left alone for a few minutes.

If Vin's willing to try to shed his label as a heartbreaker, why can't I try to shed my belief in the family curse?

"I just want them to be okay. We don't need to hang on so tight to our beliefs. For you and your work, for me and the curse," I say, twisting the stud in my ear and fixing my gaze on his.

The Hua women were cursed to never find lasting love. That doesn't mean we won't find love ever. I was so focused on the end that

I failed to see the good in the beginning, or in anything after. It's a blessing—not a curse—to get to experience love at all.

Someone in the family broke up, got divorced, or lost their partner. A story was formed around that occurrence. A story that fed the curse, the ultimate belief that we've shaped our lives around. The one that defines us and gives us a reason for the shitty things that happen. I'm tired of being defined by something like that.

"The curse...I want to leave it in the past," I admit. "I want to start over without it."

Vin grins and holds my hand against his heart. "We'll write our new song together."

I pull Vin in for a kiss, and something that feels a lot like hope surges through me.

The noise level increases as the Hua women shout out questions about what's going on. The group files past potted plants, filling in the circle.

When all the ingredients are gathered, we get started.

"Thanks for coming today, everyone," I say to my family. In the crowd, I see my own face reflected in the faces of Mom and Dad, who are standing together—a sight I haven't witnessed in years. Magnolia is back from her travels abroad, and her mom, Chamomile, is by her side. I notice my younger cousins, the next generation—my second cousins Clove, Poppy, Jasmine, and Rue. It's a full, beautiful garden of women across the generations who have weathered every kind of storm. And here they are, still standing. Still returning every season to face what life gives them. Still blooming.

"We wanted to bring you here to celebrate the launch of In Full Bloom, but we also thought it might be nice to do a tea blending ceremony together," I say, fancying up my language. There are some *oohs* from the group. "I wouldn't be who I am without any of you. And we wouldn't be who we are without each other."

My aunties join me, bringing with them the ingredients listed in my great-great-great-great-grandmother's notebook and letters, as well as the remaining ingredients. Auntie Violet passes out each flower, herb, and root to the woman named after it.

"What's all this about?" Great-Aunt Angelica asks, holding her flower up to the sun.

"We've dug up some information recently," I say. "Metaphorically and literally."

I tell everyone about what we found in the Curse Box, the letters, and the journals. The misunderstanding and how Lily isn't to blame. How we were never cursed to begin with, but that a translation mix-up led us to believe we were.

"Hold on," Great-Aunt Rosemary, who's sitting closest to me, says. "You're telling us this curse isn't real?"

"How do you explain all the heartbreak? Everything that's happened?" Auntie Cami calls out.

"What, we just picked bad partners and now need to accept it?" Magnolia asks, pouting.

"Where'd you say you got these letters?" Auntie Primrose asks.

"I'd rather blame the curse!" someone else shouts, silencing everyone.

The air is as still as the Hua women as they process what we've shared.

"What does this mean for us?" Great-Aunt Angelica asks, quieter this time.

"I don't know," I confess. "But this blend is meant to represent the bond we have with each other, the bond we have with our ancestors, and the possibility of new beginnings. Just because things have been one way doesn't mean they can't ever be another. We have the blend's ingredients, and now we have all the flowers."

"You may have proof, but we're all living proof," Great-Aunt Angelica says skeptically.

As expected, there are a range of emotions and mixed feelings, but the collective weight starts to lift like a dense fog as more people warm up to the idea.

I'm filled with more hope. There are constants in our life—the sun rising, the moon glowing, flowers blossoming, dying, regrowing—but our outlook on life can change.

I move to the side so Auntie Rose can share a story.

"One year, due to a combination of colds and a full guest list, we didn't do any weeding," she says, sweeping her hand out toward the main garden. "Didn't deadhead a single flower. We worried everything would die, but still, we just let it be. And yet, everything still bloomed." She pauses for a heartbeat. "What sorts itself out when we get out of the way? What happens to us when we get out of our own way?"

"Sometimes it's okay to just let things be," I say, looking at the loving gazes of Auntie Rose, Auntie Daisy, and Auntie Violet. "But this is something we can finish. We're all in this together. We always have been."

Auntie Daisy explains the plan to everyone as Auntie Violet adds the prepped ingredients to the hot water. It's executed perfectly, even for a bunch of wildflowers who are used to doing their own thing.

Then, one by one, my family walks up to the pot and drops in their ingredients.

Great-Aunt Angelica walks up, her brows creased. As she drops her Chinese angelica root into the pot, she says shakily, "To fresh starts."

Poppy's next, bringing with her a handful of wild poppies. "I've been streaming this, and everyone's loving it!" she squeals.

"We also honor our ancestors who couldn't be here with us today. Juniper for Mother," Auntie Violet says, dropping a few juniper berries into the pot. We do this for all my great-, great-great-, and great-great-great-grandmothers, and the women branched off from them.

And finally, we honor the one who was there from the very beginning: Lily, my great-great-great-great-grandmother.

Auntie Rose does the honors, bringing forth a handful of dried lily bulbs. Her hands are trembling as she carries the weight of history—and the truth—in them. Though Auntie Rose's expression is stoic and as hard to read as ever, an unexpected tear rolls down her cheek as she sets the bulbs in the pot on top of all the other ingredients.

Nature swirls together in the hot water, the colors draining from the petals and bulbs.

There we are. All in one pot, together. The act is met with smiles, even if a few of them are directed at Vin and Leo.

I catch Vin watching me with a smile on his face from behind the group. I give him a smile right back.

I pour cups of tea for everyone after the blend steeps. This isn't for the curse. This is for us, right now, right here.

We toast to new beginnings.

Chapter 28

CHRYSSY

One and a half months later

"Where are you taking me?" I ask as Vin leads me by the hand.

"Keep your eyes closed," he commands. "One more step."

I tap the ground in front of me, trusting Vin as he guides me to who knows where.

"Okay. Open them," he says.

It takes me a few seconds to process that we're in an antique shop, filled to the corners with a mishmash of clothing, books, furniture, lamps, and art. I don't know where to look first.

"You took me antiquing for our first official date?" I ask.

Vin's been in New York City rehearsing with Leo for all of July while I've been working on In Full Bloom and expanding our flower offerings. The chrysanthemums we planted in Auntie Rose's garden are growing like wild, and they look like they'll bloom in the next month or so. At this point, every flower counts. To keep up with the steady growth and repeat customers, we're in talks with flower farms outside of Washington.

Despite the early success, though, my aunties and I can't say yes to every opportunity if we want to maintain some semblance of balance in our lives. We do what we can with what we have. We are a small family business, after all. And when there's time between my work at the inn and In Full Bloom, I recipe-test and record my podcast, now as the Heartbreak Herbalist.

Tomorrow, Vin leaves for the first stop on his tour, but until then, we have right now.

"I'm getting a couch," he says.

I tear my eyes from a shell-shaped pewter soap dish. "You. You're getting a couch," I say. "Today?"

He nods. "I'm not leaving this store without one. Is this okay?"

I laugh. "It's so romantic. In other words, it's perfect." In my periphery, a neon-green couch trimmed in pink bullion fringe draws my focus. "Is something like that close to what you had in mind?"

Vin clocks the nearly glowing piece of furniture. "Let's do a loop before committing to anything right away," he says quickly.

We round a corner, passing by stacks of baskets and a table with a bicycle base.

"The fact that you have an eighteenth-century cello tells me you appreciate well-loved items with a story. We're bound to find something like that here," I say.

"This cowhide chair is calling my name," Vin says, sitting down in it. "What's this one's story?"

I laugh. "It's faux, so there's not much of one, but it suits you."

"Pass. It's not as comfortable as I'd prefer, and we'd need enough room for you," he says.

I pull him from the chair, and we continue roaming, picking up small items along the way.

"Do you think this terra-cotta frog would look good at the inn?" I ask. "It feels like a need." I lift it, turning it over to assess its drainage capabilities. "Let's circle, and if it's still here on the second round, we'll get it."

We pause in front of a fun house mirror that makes our heads look twice the size.

"I'm proud of you," I say, lifting my chin to make it extra long in the mirror's reflection. "First you drop your label. Now you're buying a couch."

We move on, passing by an art wall covered in oil paintings.

"I'm glad we called them mid–acupuncture session," Vin says. "When they offered more money on the spot and promised to think up a new narrative, I was too relaxed to allow the urgency of their tones to sway me. Still, leaving our label of ten years feels a little like being onstage with a cello that has a broken string and being forced to perform."

The Chao Brothers are free agents, but they'll undoubtedly land on their feet when they're ready. After Vin and Leo complete their contract, they'll get to think about what they want to do next and what they want their lives to look like. There will be time to rest, time to dream. Time to be.

"You're better at improv than you think," I say. "And you clearly didn't need a breakup to sell out a world tour. Maybe the Chaobreakers want to see you happy."

"It's a new era. Who knew even heartbreakers can experience love?" Vin says playfully. "I'm happy, Chryssy. For the first time in a long time, I'm excited about what's to come."

When the Chao Brothers' tour wraps, instead of jumping right into their next album or getting started on the sequel to the film they recently scored, Vin and I will be sneaking away for a real vacation to southern Italy where the only cello Vin will be touching is a limoncello.

"We get to watch each other bloom," I say, beaming at him.

"It's going to be damn beautiful." He clears his throat. "Here's something else I haven't fully figured out how to say," Vin starts. "I want this couch to fit its future home properly. Should I be thinking about what couch best fits the style of my place in the city or… somewhere else?"

My pulse picks up speed. "Well, you'll be on tour, and it would cost way too much to send a couch from Seattle to New York City. I think it only makes sense for the couch to be delivered to the Dandelion," I say, my cheeks warming. "Then when you're back, you'll have somewhere to, you know, sit…"

"Mmm, good call," he says, nodding. "I do need somewhere to sit."

"And to practice!" I add. "We don't want the couch to be lonely at your empty apartment."

Vin reaches for my hand. "No, we definitely wouldn't want that."

I give his hand a squeeze as we stroll, the little extensions of ourselves connected to each other. "And when you're back, and after finally getting the vacation you've earned, we could turn my bedroom into *our* bedroom."

"I'd like that," Vin says. "Especially because I've lost my bedroom to your podcast."

"But only until we find a place of our own?" I ask.

His face brightens. "You took the words right out of my mouth."

A place of our own. I've never had one of those until the Dandelion. Until now.

A mustard midcentury piece catches my eye. "What about this beauty?" I ask, sprawling back on it. I hook my elbow on the back of the couch, cross my legs, and pose dramatically.

It takes him hardly a second to say, "It's perfect."

My eyes flit to a rose-colored, argyle-patterned love seat. I launch myself toward it as I drop my bag on the ground. I wriggle around on it. "Comfy!"

"Even better," he says.

I gasp and speed-walk to an armless couch in the shape of purple lips. "I'm sorry, but how can you say no to this?" I run my hand back and forth on the couch's cupid's bow, my fingers dipping with the curves.

Vin nods. "You're right, I can't. I love it."

I stop midrub along the lips' velvet fabric. "Why was this so hard for you before? I anticipated a good amount of pushback."

He joins me on the couch. "Before, none of the couches had you on them," he says.

My breath catches in my chest.

He cringes. "Too romantic?"

I place my hand on his cheek. "I think I'm starting to not mind romantic so much," I whisper.

"And to think, if I hadn't unplugged you," Vin mumbles.

"It all started with a little electricity. Or lack thereof," I say, stroking my thumb across his skin. "Do you still have to leave tomorrow?"

"To kick off our sold-out tour?" he asks, pretending to think. "Nah."

I laugh. "Good." I reach into my purse and pull out a freezer bag. "I have something for you."

Vin takes the bag from me and lets out a low, rough laugh. I soak up every square inch of his lit-up face and commit it to memory.

"Think they'll let me take bath bombs on the plane?" he asks.

"I know the hotels you'll be staying in will have bathtubs," I say.

"No in-room hot tubs, though," he says, mock-disappointed.

I lean in closer. "A regular bath works just fine for what I have in mind."

Vin's eyes darken a shade as he swallows. "What scent?"

"Your favorite," I say. "Lavender-mint."

He opens the bag and inhales deeply. "Delightful."

"Save me one for Paris," I say. "I can't wait to see you do your thing onstage. And now in every venue you play in, you'll know me."

"Maybe I'll make up new names and backstories for you at all the shows you come to," Vin says.

"I've always wanted to be Ivy for a day," I joke. "Short and sweet."

"You got it," Vin says. "And the first stop after the show: the Eiffel Tower. Time for you to see the sparkly lights for real." He lingers in this moment, like he's holding a music note just to make it last a little longer. "I'm going to miss you."

We just did a month apart, but now a week away from Vin feels too long. I'll join him when I can, and he'll fly back between shows. My aunties will be joining, too, for the historic venues. And on this girls' trip, Auntie Violet will get to go backstage after the show.

During one of the Chao Brothers' extended breaks, we'll also be attending Magnolia's winter wedding in Scotland. After creating the Hua Family Blend, a couple of family members refused to believe anything we told them, but the others have been remarkably open-minded. Magnolia being one of them. When she reached out to her ex for closure about why he ended things, they both realized their love story wasn't over.

But honestly? That was the least shocking development. I'm not sure what surprised me more: Mom going to dinner at Dad's restaurant or Auntie Rose getting Ms. Chan's phone number, and not for the purposes of understanding the curse.

"I actually have something for you, too," Vin says. He pulls out his phone and taps the screen a few times. A tune streams out from the speakers. There's a combination of high and low notes, alternating in pace throughout. It's an upbeat and passionate sound with a few unexpected notes sprinkled in. It's catchy, whimsical, unique. It reminds me of the exact moment a flower blossoms.

"What do you think?" he asks.

"I want to hear it again," I say. "It makes me feel…hopeful."

"It's for your podcast," he says. "But if you hate it, I can delete it right now and come up with something new."

The threat of tears comes immediately. "You wrote me a jingle?"

He smirks. "Honestly, it's more for me. That royalty-free tune you use really needs to—"

I interrupt him with a kiss. "I love it," I say. "You captured the exact energy of the podcast. It's clear you did your homework. Which episode inspired you?"

"All of them," he says. "But that's not what I was trying to capture. I got to know the incredible woman behind each episode. That's what inspired the tune."

"Thank you," I say, pressing a hand over my heart. "Want to know something else I'd love?"

Vin eyes me suspiciously.

"Can I see your tongue?"

Vin smirks. "I think you've seen it plenty," he says, sticking the tip of his tongue out quickly and pulling it back even faster.

I laugh as he gazes past my shoulder at a Victorian-style sofa pushed up against the wall. I desert the lip couch—with only slight hesitation—to examine it with Vin. The fabric is teal, the ornate wood framing around it lightly scuffed. The silhouette reminds me of a crown.

I lift the tag around the couch's foot. "This was hand-carved in the 1800s. Is this your new cello-playing couch?"

He grins. "It's pretty great, though it's not a very cozy movie-watching type of couch."

"No, but it's an excellent 'reading in a long dress and looking out onto a field' couch," I say. "Try it!"

"Am I even allowed to? I feel like I should be wearing a long button-down coat to sit on this thing." He lowers himself gently onto the seat.

"It suits you," I admit, observing it from different angles. "I had a feeling you were a nineteenth-century-furniture guy."

Vin gives the couch a little shake. Its wood frame is sturdy despite its timeworn edges. "Solid. If this one lasted a few hundred years, I think it can last a few more," he says, looking up at me.

"Add a few pillows and blankets, and I think it'll hold up on Yin Nights," I assess.

After In Full Bloom's growth spurt and being thrown out of balance, I've had to also put metaphorical garden beds around my Yin Nights, which were the first to go when life got busy. Since our night in Vegas, I've added more romantic comedies into the rotation. Nowadays, the happy endings don't bother me so much.

Vin nods. "Sold."

"Congrats!"

"Thanks. Yeah. Cool." Vin exhales. "I'll just…hang out and rest on this," he says, sliding the tag off.

"That's one of the best features of couches. Good hang-out-ability," I say.

Vin smirks. "And then some, I'm sure." He pauses. "Think of everything this couch has seen. Everything it's been through. I want this couch to witness us growing old together. And not just this." He stands and glances around the store. "I want a dining room set. I want a drawer to put my clothes in. I'll even take that fun house mirror. We might as well throw in the terra-cotta frog while we're at it. Chryssy, you make me want the whole damn house."

I beam at him under the fluorescent lights. "I've always thought I lived up to my namesake. Short roots and all. I never imagined I'd find a place to settle down and plant them," I share. "And then I met you, and I learned that roots can be some*where*, but they can also be with some*one*."

Vin leans his forehead against mine. "I love you, Chryssy," he says.

I pull back just far enough to see his eyes. "I love you, too, Vin."

I press my lips against his softly, taking my time with it. Because what's the rush?

It takes less than two seconds to break a person's heart.

But it takes even less time than that to fall in love. While the lead-up might be millions of heartbeats, in that moment of falling, all it takes is one.

To say the words "I love you."

"I want you."

"I need you."

"Be mine."

And then there was Vin, the one who there was *supposed* to be a breakup with. The one who wasn't Just Right. The one who said, "Show me the line."

A single heartbeat.

To which I respond, "Yes."

And the heart beats on.

ACKNOWLEDGMENTS

Books are a lot like flowers in that they take time to grow, require nourishment and encouragement, and have a lot going on inside of them while looking very pretty on the outside. I'm so lucky to have a fantastic team who has green thumbs to help me grow and advocate for my "flowers."

To all the healers out there, thank you for everything you do.

To my editor, Alex Logan, I am so grateful to you for your insightful feedback that helps me make every book the best it can be. I've grown as a writer because of your honesty when something's not working, and your validation when something is. I love working together!

Estelle Hallick, thank you for being the best! Your empathy, excitement, and creativity never go unappreciated.

If publishing is a garden, I feel so lucky to be in Forever's. Thank you to the rock star team at Grand Central / Forever working so hard behind the scenes: Beth deGuzman, Leah Hultenschmidt, Dana Cuadrado, Caroline Green, Carolina Martin, Daniela Medina, Grace Fischetti, Jeff Holt, Mark Steven Long, Marie Mundaca, Emily Baker, and Xian Lee, Sara Schaller and the production team, the sales reps, Mary Urban and the digital sales team, Melanie Schmidt and the audiobook team, Francesca Begos, Joelle Dieu, and the subrights team.

Sanny Chiu, thanks for another beautiful, eye-popping cover. You perfectly captured Chryssy's essence. Will it ever get old seeing mixed-race characters on book covers? No. It will not.

To my agent, Ann Leslie Tuttle, thanks for always having my back and for your guidance. What a journey this has been, and I'm excited for what's to come. Thank you also to my film agent, Mary Pender, and the team.

To the booksellers, librarians, Bookstagrammers, BookTokers, book bloggers, reviewers, journalists, book clubs, festival and event organizers, and podcasters, you have my deepest gratitude.

I've never had a community like the one in Nashville, and so much of that has to do with my incredible local indie bookstores. A special shout-out to Katie Garaby (who is the ultimate champion for all romance authors), RJ Witherow, Tara Leimkuehler, and Elyse Adler, and to the amazing folks at Parnassus Books. You've championed me and my books from the start but have also been a safe and happy place for me to return to, and for that I'm eternally grateful. I know I take far too long to sign and stamp and doodle in my books, but secretly it's because I'm just trying to hang out with you all for as long as I can.

Also, thanks, EO, for teaching me how to breathe through stressful moments.

Mom and Dad, you fostered my love of reading ever since I learned how. Thank you for never saying no to books. To my sister, thanks for swinging by the romance shelves in every bookstore you go into to say hi to Olivia and Rooney. Add Chryssy to the list! Auntie Rae, thanks for responding to my very random texts to fill in my gaps of knowledge—and for the tips on all the best places to eat in Taiwan.

Patrick, you are my best friend forever. Thank you for, well, everything. You fill my life with so much laughter and love. Without you, I would always have cold extremities and be wildly out of balance. There's no love song I love more than ours.

To my wonderful readers, whether we've connected in real life or online, I hope you know how much you mean to me. I love seeing your DMs, social media posts, emails, reviews, and words of kindness and support. From the bottom of my heart, thank you.

ABOUT THE AUTHOR

Lauren Kung Jessen is a mixed-race Chinese American writer with a fondness for witty, flirtatious dialogue and making meals with too many steps but lots of flavor. She is fascinated by myths and superstitions and how ideas, beliefs, traditions, and stories evolve over time.

From attending culinary school to working in the world of Big Tech to writing love stories, Lauren cares about creating experiences that make people feel something. She also has a food and film blog, *A Dash of Cinema*, where she makes food inspired by movies and TV shows. She lives in Nashville with her husband (who she met thanks to fate—read: the algorithms of online dating), two cats, and a dog.

You can learn more at:
Website: LaurenKungJessen.com
X: @LaurenKJessen
Instagram: @LaurenKJessen

YIN YANG LOVE SONG
READING GROUP GUIDE

Dear Reader,

Like Chryssy, I discovered the world of Traditional Chinese Medicine (TCM) later in life. Acupuncture was how I first made my way into this world just a few years ago. I was asked a lot of questions about my lifestyle and health so that my acupuncturist could determine the best approach in her treatments. I'd go back week after week, and the heat and zings of the acupuncture needles would jump-start my Qi. After each session, I practically vibrated with energy flowing through me. Yet I felt calmer.

Like Vin, I have a busy mind and life, and find it difficult to rest. I've flirted with—or really been in a full-on love affair?—with burnout. The scene where Vin is in the acupuncture room looking around for anything to distract him, well, that wouldn't be a totally far-off representation of what it's like for me when I'm supposed to be relaxing. His striving for perfection? *Totally* don't relate… (Okay, fine, I can relate.)

Writing this book was more healing than I could've imagined when I first set out to write it. I am not 100 percent of any of the characters I write, but I saw a lot of myself in both Chryssy and Vin. Eerily enough, I even experienced a health struggle similar to Chryssy's during the writing of this book, which forced me to completely rethink how I care for myself and how I rest. Strangely, this also meant that the hard—but true—advice that Chryssy had for Vin about taking care of himself almost, in a way, felt like Chryssy was talking directly to me.

TCM wasn't a huge part of my childhood, but it's become a bigger part of my adulthood. Now I cook with herbs and roots, make Qi broth, drink flowers, use products with TCM ingredients, benefit from acupuncture, check in with myself on how I might be Yin or Yang deficient (which includes analyzing my tongue), and think more critically about food as medicine. Balance is something I'm more conscious of, and I'm trying to get better at gaining awareness of my body and listening to what it needs. When I do push myself too hard, it's Chryssy's voice I hear reminding me to slow down. (I've even started implementing her Yin Nights into my life.)

Thank you for coming along on this journey with me by reading *Yin Yang Love Song*. In addition to making you laugh and swoon, I hope this story can be a reminder, if you need it, that you are allowed rest, you can change your life or your mind any time you want, achieving perfection is impossible, and that you can bloom even when no one is watching.

Take care of yourself,

Lauren

Discussion Questions

1. Traditional Chinese Medicine plays a large role in this book, as does Yin and Yang. In our bodies, and in the natural world, we have Qi, or life force. What is your perspective on this approach to health and well-being?

2. Chryssy and Vin agree to fake-date to benefit their careers. Would you ever fake-date someone? What would you need to gain from it, if anything?

3. Chryssy thinks she is cursed in love. Do you believe that families—or people—can be cursed?

4. If you could be naturally talented at anything, what would it be and why?

5. If you were a prodigy, what types of pressures do you think you'd feel? How would being a prodigy impact you as an adult?

6. At first, Chryssy and Vin each have a preformed idea of who the other is, which impacts how they interact. Have you ever had a negative opinion about someone that turned out to be totally wrong? How can we best get past our biases?

7. Heartbreak comes in all shapes and sizes, and everyone's healing journey varies. Would you ever go somewhere like the Wildflower Inn to heal from heartbreak?

8. After experiencing burnout in a past career, Chryssy has Yin Nights to make sure she rests. How do you rest or recharge?

9. If you were known for something—negative or positive—and found great success in it the way Vin and Leo have for being heartbreakers, do you think it would be challenging to leave that reputation behind? Is it hard to see past people's reputations?

10. Chryssy's aunties love Sheryl Crow so much that they name a dragon boat after one of her songs, and Vin's right when he guesses that singing "Soak Up the Sun" would gain them an advantage during the race. What song or songs get you excited or inspired before or during an important event?

11. Chryssy and Vin make Patience Risotto to slow down after big news. Are there any recipes that you make when you want to relax or feel comforted?

12. Do you think what Chryssy and her aunties discovered in the Curse Box is a blessing or a curse?

13. The writing in the letters and notebooks that Chryssy and her aunties find is fading and smudged. Have there ever been family stories that you've misinterpreted or lost due to time? How has that impacted the present?

14. Chryssy and her aunties decide to tell her family about what they discovered in the Curse Box. Do you agree with how they handled it? How would you approach delivering news like that?

15. What does your love song sound like, or what do you want it to sound like?

16. What type of couch would you pick for yourself?

The Wildflower Inn's Lavender-Mint Heart-Shaped Bath Bombs

Bath bombs are like little luxuries—a spa in your very own bathtub. Homemade bath bombs are even more fun, though, because you can choose your own scents, shapes, and colors. Of course, at the Wildflower Inn, our main scent is lavender mixed with a little mint, but you can pick anything you'd like for your own. To avoid soaking in food coloring, I opted for something more natural (purple sweet potato powder), but this is completely optional. Enjoy your homemade bath bombs in a hot bath with an even hotter cup of tea (with the Chao Brothers' music playing in the background)!

—Auntie Violet

Materials

Gloves (optional)
Measuring cups
Large mixing bowl
Whisk

Metal spoon
Heart ornament mold (or silicone molds)

Ingredients

¾ cup baking soda
⅓ cup citric acid
⅓ cup cornstarch
⅓ cup Epsom salt

2 teaspoons of purple sweet potato powder (for natural purple coloring) (optional)
40 drops of essential oil (24 lavender and 16 mint)
2 tablespoons coconut oil

Method

In a bowl, combine the baking soda, citric acid, cornstarch, Epsom salt, and the purple sweet potato powder. Whisk together.

Add the essential oils and coconut oil. Whisk until combined. You want the mixture to be as fine a powder as possible and free of clumps.

Fill both halves of your bath bomb molds with the mixture, gently tapping down, until they are filled. Don't press the mixture in too hard to the mold (it might result in cracking once it's dry).

Bring the halves together, pressing gently. Carefully remove one side of the mold, leaving the exposed heart-shaped mixture facing upward.

Repeat the previous two steps for your remaining molds, and leave the exposed tops on a sheet tray to dry for 1–1½ hours.

Carefully remove the other sides of the bath bombs from their molds. Remove the mold from the top. If anything cracks while you're removing it, no worries! You can press the mixture back into the molds to reshape it (and let it dry again).

Once all the bath bombs are out of their molds, leave them out to dry for 6–8 hours, or overnight.

Once the bath bombs are completely dry, wrap them in plastic and store somewhere dry. Enjoy in a bath or foot soak!

Chryssy's Chrysanthemum-Lavender Egg Tarts

Recipe makes 10–12 egg tarts

I wasn't an egg tart person until I ate this one. Everything about this egg tart is delicious and delicate, from the dough to the soft filling, yet it's jam-packed with flavor. In Traditional Chinese Medicine, honey, chrysanthemum, and lavender all have benefits. Honey is Yin nourishing, tonifying, and hydrating, and it helps clear toxins. Chrysanthemums also regulate Qi, clear heat, restore balance, reduce inflammation and blood pressure, and are a powerful antioxidant. Lavender is calming, helps clear toxins, and has heartwarming effects. In these egg tarts, the honey and lavender are more prominent. Chrysanthemums have a light flavor, but the antioxidants are still in there from the steeping. If you're bringing treats to a gathering and want to impress, this is a fun one to make. It was a big hit on *Sweet Dreams, Seattle*!   —*Chryssy*

Please note that while these ingredients can offer various potential health benefits, individual experiences may vary. Before you make any significant changes to your diet or lifestyle, consult with a trusted health care professional, especially if you have any underlying health conditions, are pregnant, or are breastfeeding.

Materials

Large measuring cup

Measuring spoons and cups

Mixing bowls

Spatula

Plastic wrap

Rolling pin

Fine-mesh strainer

Whisk

Round or fluted cookie cutter
that matches the size of your
egg tart mold

Sheet tray

Egg tart molds

Ingredients

2 cups + 2 tablespoons all-
purpose flour (lightly
packed)

¼ teaspoon salt

12 tablespoons unsalted butter,
cubed (cold)

3 tablespoons + 1 teaspoon
cold water

1 whole chrysanthemum flower

1 tablespoon lavender buds

1 cup hot water

¼ cup honey

½ cup evaporated milk

3 eggs

1½ teaspoons vanilla
extract

Method

Dough

In a large bowl, mix the flour and the salt.

Add the cubed butter into the flour mixture, and with your fingers, work it all together. Pinch and smear the butter until the dough looks like big crumbs. Chunks of butter will still be in the mixture—that's what you want.

Add the cold water and mix with your fingers. The dough will still be crumb-like. Wrap the dough in plastic wrap, and let it rest in the fridge for 30 minutes.

Once the dough has rested, roll it out on a floured surface into a large rectangle. It's best to work quickly so the butter doesn't get too soft and sticky.

Fold the sides of the rectangle toward the center, turn it, and roll the dough out again. Repeat this a few times. Wrap the dough in plastic wrap, and let it rest in the fridge for another 30 minutes.

Filling

While the dough is resting, make the egg tart filling.

Steep the chrysanthemum flower and lavender buds in the hot water for 10 minutes.

Strain the flowers and buds out of the water and stir in the honey. Let this mixture cool.

In a separate bowl, whisk the evaporated milk, eggs, and the vanilla extract together. Add to the honey-flower water and whisk until incorporated.

Strain the mixture through a fine-mesh strainer into a large measuring cup or bowl with a spout for easy pouring.

Putting the egg tarts together

Preheat the oven to 350°F and position the oven rack so it's in the middle.

Position the egg tart molds evenly across a sheet tray. If you aren't using a nonstick mold, lightly butter the inside of the mold so the dough doesn't stick.

Roll out the dough until it's ¼ inch thick. Aim for a rectangle, but the point here is to get the dough as large as you can to get as many circles out of it as possible.

Using the cookie cutter, cut out circles in the dough.

Lay the cut-out dough circles in each of the egg tart molds and gently press to fit. Extra dough may come off the top as you make the circle fit into the mold. Save this.

Bring the excess dough together and roll it out again. Cut out more circles. Repeat the previous two steps until you don't have enough dough left.

Pour the filling into the molds until it reaches just below the lip, about ¾ full.

Carefully slide the sheet tray into the oven. Bake for 25–30 minutes, until the filling sets and does not jiggle. You can test this by gently tapping the tray.

Remove the egg tarts from the oven and move them to a cooling rack. Let them cool for 8–10 minutes before enjoying.